RAYSTAR OF TERRA
ALIEN ALLEGIANCE

Kurt Johnson and Bruce E. Mitchell

Cover Artwork
Diogo Lando, Infinity Book Design

Cover Design
Morgan Krehbiel (www.morgankrehbiel.com) and Infinity Book Design

Editorial Work and Interior Design
Perrin Davis, Three Muses Creative, www.threemusescreative.com

Printed in the United States of America.

For Kiran and Barb

Foreword

A lot has been written about the impact teachers have had on their students (*thank you, Kurt*), but little has been said about the reverse: the timeless existence of so many in the hearts of a few. I was an English teacher at Evanston Township High School for thirty-two years. I *still* remember many of my students and, more importantly, I bless the unheralded thousands who shared their lives and thoughts with me. I have come to believe that we are all composites: hybrids of our history, amalgams of our interactions, no matter how peripheral, how long forgotten…the unfathomable essences of who we are.

In this communal vein, *Raystar of Terra: Alien Allegiance* is a combination of young and old imaginations working together (and by emotional extension, those of our daughters) to channel our main character, Raystar.

Long ago, in one of my junior English classes, one of my female students raised her hand and said, "Mr. Mitchell, do you know that when a boy and a girl raise their hands at the same time, you always call on the guy first." This may sound trite, but I was shocked to learn of this—and a bit humiliated. No, I didn't know "what I didn't know." That one girl not only changed the way I managed my classes but also the way I looked at equality, acceptance, and perspective.

Equality is a major theme in Raystar. All the creatures on the planet Nem' are equal in their potential for good *and* bad, with no judgment given until their actions reveal their true character. Raystar is young in years, only thirteen, but old in soul, given her capacity to comprehend and connect with others without making them *feel* like "others."

For all of us during these last few years, it has been dangerously easy to separate from friends because there have been so few opportunities to make relationships meaningful through the affirmation of physical and emotional contact. In Toni Morrison's *Beloved,* one of the characters says, "Love is or it ain't. Thin love ain't love at all." *Amen.* A "thinning" of relationships has been one of the major consequences of the COVID-19 pandemic.

Love is thick! Raystar, like all of us, must learn the complex navigation of her feelings.

Acceptance of the world "as given" is another of Raystar's strengths. She sees the big picture, the enormity of the universe, its vastness dwarfing the modest speck of her own existence. Stephen Crane wrote, "A man said to the universe, 'Sir, I exist!' 'However,' replied the universe, 'The fact has not created in me a sense of obligation.'" In other words, nothing personal, but the universe doesn't care. It is a vast system of exchange…without favorites.

In her extraordinary journey, Raystar must forge her own meaning—her own small exclamation, "I exist!"—in a dangerous and challenging world thousands of years and billions of kilometers away from her people on Earth. Her struggle for survival as the only Human on the planet Nem' is daunting, but Raystar offers hope through her example of resilience, guts, and determination. She could easily be subsumed into her lonely uniqueness, but Raystar chooses instead to engage, to fight for her own identity, to live among others.

The imbalance of one's perspective can be an experiential cave you rarely explore without a reassuring walking stick to guide your steps. Just as I found out when questioned about my own prejudices, what we *think* we know is the biggest bat in our brain's belfry, echolocating with misconceptions! Raystar, a Human, is just as vulnerable as any other human…flying blindly into her heart's cave, overwhelmed by emotions and events she cannot control.

One of the challenges for you, our reader (and by the way, thank you for your interest!), is to travel with Raystar in a strange world where very little is familiar or known. As authors, we hope that Ray-

star's quest to find allegiances as an alien among aliens will challenge and expand your own horizons. Bon voyage!

On a personal note, this novel is the consequence of a relationship that goes back to 1986, when Kurt was a student of mine at Evanston Township High School. We published *Raystar of Terra: Peace, Love, Family, and War* five years ago and have now cowritten the next chapter of her story, *Raystar of Terra: Alien Allegiance,* which we feel arrives at a particularly crucial juncture in our country's, and even the world's, evolution. Like Raystar, we are making decisions in the intense "now" of a tipping point: open vs. closed, community vs. self, sacrifice vs. pleasure, democracy vs. dictatorship, technology vs. spirit, Renaissance vs. Middle Ages, science vs. myth, human vs. inhuman, light vs. dark...the list is as endless and multifaceted as the choices we now make for ourselves and for our planet.

Raystar of Terra: Alien Allegiance is a humble attempt to find universal truths among these opposites and to connect them in the exploration of what is possible in the blending of different realities. As with all journeys, there are losses, but there are also the "founds" that accompany the realization that there are no separate paths, just as there are no separate creatures to take those paths. No one walks alone.

—*Bruce E. Mitchell*

I wanted to cry. Sleep. Drink water. Be held. I had neither the strength nor the energy to do any of that. I'd left everything on the field. I was empty.

My parents' assault tank shuddered as plasma bolts hammered its shields. In the shelter of the massive tank's armor, I couldn't see the incoming fire. But my mind's eye recreated a panorama: orange comets streaking down from thousands, quite literally, of invading ships, all silhouetted against a sky blackened with smoke.

It wasn't difficult to conjure the image. Just twelve minutes before I'd witnessed that fiery storm *from the outside.*

I sucked in the cabin's processed air and pulled my knees to my chest. This trembling self-hug wasn't meant just to reassure myself—I did it more to contain my power. A craxy, molten, and omnipresent righteous rage pushed against my throat, my heart, my chest. My anger boiled over as I sifted through mental images of what had been done to me, to my friends.

No. No. No. Self-control.

If I lost it, Mom, Dad, my sister, my friends…could meet a death *at my own hands* much more horrible than what they'd suffer from incoming fire. At least a plasma bolt from an invading ship would be quick. The death that I could unleash wouldn't be.

Nannites, you see, were an integral component of my blood, right down to my genetic structure, thanks to advanced biotechnology not understood by modern science. This Human "control" DNA was my birthright from a war that had ended 1,800 years before—a weapon that was the Homo-sapien "solution" to an epic conflict between Humanity, its many Allies, and the Convergence.

Back then, the Convergence was comprised of 800 different worlds and thousands of different races and creatures. Its outward expansion along the Orion-Cygnus arm put Humanity squarely in its way. Yep. Humanity lost that war, and with the addition of the worlds controlled by Humanity, the size of the Convergence grew to 1,300 worlds, while my people all but disappeared.

But the nanotech inside of me, my ancestors' legacy, remained after Humanity's fall. The various DNA- and cell-sized technologies that flowed in my veins alongside my "regular" blood had become insanely powerful weapons. I could access and control the coveted remnants of Human tech that were scattered across the Convergence. I could destroy *and* create, but this power came at a price.

The "tech" implemented within me needed vast amounts of energy to operate. *Organic* material, preferably—any organic material. I shuddered at the thought of what I'd done.

I'd fed on another being.

I had literally consumed a sentient being to fuel my power. Sure, I'd done it out of self-defense, and I'd do it again, but that didn't change the fact that I'd taken another life. I told myself that it was the only way to be free.

I had been inside Nurse Pheelios's mind, intimately aware of her matter as it joined mine, her consciousness as it eroded, her fear and confusion as her self-awareness faded into nothingness.

Nova and gravity wells. I clearly couldn't fully control my power, and I didn't trust the tenuous control I had exercised over it at all.

My parents used to joke that I hadn't come with a *Care and Feeding of a Human Child* instruction manual when they adopted me. That was *before* my powers manifested. I needed that instruction manual now more than ever.

My nannites were killing me. I had three days to live.

"Inbound Convergence transmission," Dad's voice boomed through the command center via our tank's audio systems. "Our security is compromised. I cannot block the message!"

It could only be…*HIM.*

Jurisdictor Godwill's skeletal grey face—the face of the leader of the coup and now the dictator of the planet Nem'—surged toward me through the blue wall of 3D vid screens that illuminated the assault tank's command room. Hologram or not, I shrieked and grabbed my knees tight to my chest at the sight of him.

The things he'd done to me. Just yesterday.

The memories flashed through my mind: his rotten-caramel breath as he pressed his face close to my mouth; the pressure of his leathery, cool fingers as they slid down from my breasts to my stomach, probing for just the right spot to inject me with liquid death; the sharp pinch of the surgery chair's straps against my chest, across my hips, my feet; the ties that bound my wrists, my ankles, my neck. *And that needle*—feeling his hands slither over my body while the restraints held back my struggle accentuated the terror held in that gleaming needle, as I envisioned how and where it would pierce me.

I remembered watching his hand rise and then pause above me, his grey, claw-like fist clutching the injector. The needle reflected the flickering yellow light of his makeshift underground lab. His black eyes glistened high above me, strapped helplessly into the surgery chair; his gummy smile stretched into a manic grin. Finally, his hand began its inevitable meteor-fast descent. The blow crushed into my chest, and with it came pain sharper than I ever before could have imagined as the needle pierced my sternum, penetrated my heart.

That had been the *first* injection.

As a preemptive move as Humans faced total defeat in the War, they'd locked down their weapons, bases, mines, and resources so they could not be accessed without the right DNA, the right code. Godwill's Human reclamation solvent was designed to convert my Human nannites into a version safe for consumption by Lethians that would give them access to Human tech.

Though I was the only Human on planet Nem', small populations of us remained scattered throughout the Convergence, like weeds in a garden. Godwill's mission was to hunt down the "weeds" that possessed this Human nanotech, technology that almost two millennia later was still beyond the understanding of the scientists of the Convergence. Godwill had found a way to convert our nanotech into a form transferrable to Lethians, who essentially ruled the Convergence—despite their denials.

Hunting enhanced Humans like me was easy. My DNA powers manifested themselves when I reached puberty, permanently turning my hair and eyes purple. And collecting the nano was even easier than spotting my purple hair: all he had to do was inject me with his evil nanosolvent. It dissolved its subject into a primordial soup that could be stored and re-injected into Lethians, and his plan had been to distribute it to the soldiers belonging to his covert branch of the Lethian military.

Three times I'd been injected. *Three times!* It normally only required one shot to "convert" a Human, but my nannites were different. They were a command set, apparently unique and incredibly powerful.

Not powerful enough, though. In roughly three days, once Godwill's Human reclamation solvent finally overwhelmed my own nannites, I'd be dead. Or rather, I'd be Raystar soup. My weaponized Human nano would be all that remained. That seemed to be what this Void-cursed hunt for Humans was all about.

Godwill's image on the holovid solidified. His black, pupil-less eyes shone with an impossibly dark light that blazed from his even darker soul—the blackness of blackness. *Where were my friends? My parents? I was alone in the assault tank's command center.*

His glare was personal. Everyone always says, "It's not personal." *It is always personal.*

When I escaped from his lab and destroyed the Convergence's only supply of purified Human DNA collected over thousands of years....

Heh. That definitely made it personal.

His sickly grey skin looked like a too-small wrapper for his skull, tugging at his lips so much that they never really touched; the result was a perpetual, gummy, broad-toothed grimace of evil. Loose patches of flesh underneath his singed, spiky black hair formed an angry purple seam that extended from his right eye down to his chin. I wondered whether I was responsible for those wounds during our recent fight. Or maybe they were from shrapnel that erupted forth after the titanic plasma blasts from the cannon mounted on our family's tank. Or maybe the *OTHER* thing that had hunted me—Godwill's first Human victim, his first experiment with the Human reclamation solvent, a boy named Artem—maybe *he* had inflicted those injuries. Artem was now *something* else, an unknown.

I hoped Godwill felt great suffering. He deserved to suffer.

Nevertheless, I shrank further into the command chair, fighting off panicked memories of plasma fire. The acrid scent of my own burnt hair made me recall the feel of the sandy soil mixed with clumps of dying green under my knees and in my hands as I squeezed the dirt, struggling for air. Concussive waves had thumped in my gut as plasma bolts streamed down from the heavens, sending geysers of dirt upward. Pillars of fire and smoke were everywhere. Thousands of invasion ships screamed past, tearing apart the atmosphere as they raced to their various missions. An overwhelming monsoon of energy projectiles blew the nova out of everything with a cacophony of sound, light, and force.

Yet I also remembered what I'd done to him—the furious, insatiable hunger as my nannites activated, the giant claws of lightning that manifested into meter-long energy blades extending from my fists. They pierced THROUGH his energy barrier and sank into his ribs, his stomach. He SHOULD have perished. But no. Some creatures just will not DIE!

After, Godwill had been thrown into an inferno of a building hit by a volley from my parents' massive assault tank. Wounded as he was, he *should* have died!

I heard the crackle of static electricity and caught a spark as it sizzled down from my hair into the chair's fabric. *Control, Raystar.* If I lost control of my nannites, I risked hastening my own death. Any energy I took away from holding off the Human reclamation solvent would only speed death along.

Suddenly, a puff of smoke and a hair-thin crack of microlightning appeared. A small hole formed in the command chair's armrest.

No. The Universe may be going down the gravity well, but I will MAINTAIN control.

"Raystar of Terra," he rasped, leaning toward me, attempting to tear his way through the 3D image through sheer will. "You have taken away my life's work. I *will* find your friends and family. You should kill them before I get to them. Their continued suffering is my path to you. Or do not kill them."

"In the end, it does not matter." Godwill's face contorted into an insanely wide grin. His lips pulled back his corpse-like skin, revealing even more of his raw, purple gums. "I am your FATE…. I am coming. For YOU."

I didn't deserve this insane persecution. I was thirteen, probably smaller than most every other Galactic out there, and for all I knew, I might be the only Human still alive. I had done nothing except be born. Anger like lava, hot, red, and glowing in my darkness, flared up deep inside me, granting me a stubborn, willful strength. *I alone had destroyed his life's work. I could defy him again. Forever, if need be.*

I gripped the arms of the command chair and propelled myself forward, rising to meet Godwill's black-hole gaze. I grimaced, eyes burning and pulse pounding, as I felt the familiar tickle of a nosebleed and tasted the iron tang of blood on my lips. *Ah, there it is, the activation*

of my nannites. Air crackled as a nimbus of static sparks grew around me. I was *done* being afraid.

Godwill's craxy grin turned scornful. "Little Human, rebellious as always."

The bad guys had done horrible things to me, my friends, my family. I would be the payback.

"…I will take them all from you. Your parents, your sist-." The transmission was broken, and Godwill's image faded.

My parents' assault tank catapulted sideways as it took a direct hit from the Convergence Dreadnought above us. I pressed deep into the embrace of the chair's protective gel. *This isn't over.*

"Commander," Mom's silken, imperative tone floated to my ears through the tank's speakers as I began to hyperventilate, still staring at the empty space left behind by Godwill's departed image. "Would *now* be a convenient time to direct our attention to the generously provided targets above us?"

I pictured her in my mind: sitting there in the cockpit, the scar running from her eye to her chin flushed purple with an intensity that her voice didn't reveal. I imagined her black hair, which normally cascaded over her shoulders, was now probably braided and lying over her chest, and her golden, almond-shaped eyes contrasted against her blood-red Glean skin. She was beautiful. And a deadly efficient pilot.

The tank's inertial dampeners had protected us from all but the most violent shocks, but it shuddered nonetheless as she sent the tank spiraling through the ruins of the ancient Human city to dodge the rain of plasma fire.

"I am not eating pastries," Dad boomed gruffly. "Or thinking about how my cape looks against my battle armor."

I blinked. Godwill's threats were temporarily displaced by my parents'…uh…conversation.

"Yet, despite your manly *inattention* to feeling great with style," Mom paused, and the vid in my head imagined her dramatically pointing all four of her graceful, manicured hands toward the heavens while raising an eyebrow, "there remains an intact armada above our city."

"Nova and gravity wells, Sathralea, it is *not* an 'armada.' It is a Void-cursed Battlegroup."

"And?"

"And?" Dad's voice cracked, "And that, that *ship* above us, is a *Dreadnought!*"

"Adversity. Character building." Their banter was unconscious, the product of trust and teamwork, I thought. "This is why I love you."

"*Character building?*"

"Less talk, Nent, my love. KILL THEM." And then, "Muuuahh!"

If I ever fell in love, I'd want that. I blinked again, inhaled the chemical air, and shook my head. *Love? What the nova was I thinking about?*

Dad stooped as he burst through the doorway from the cockpit into the command center muttering something about "character" and "females" and gave me the once-over like he was checking out a piece of equipment. With a grunt, Dad placed himself, with a grace that belied his size, into the gunner's chair. He was the largest Glean I'd ever seen. The combat chair groaned loudly and his armor creaked as the restraints flowed over him, creating an "X" running from each shoulder to the opposite hip.

Our chairs were the same size. While I could have stretched out in mine, Dad had to pack himself into his. Glean males were usually nearly three meters tall and weighed around three hundred kilos. His skin was the color of my blood; his eyes were a deep, deep gold; his hair was as black as space. As his four arms blurred across various consoles, his Glean Ascendancy Commander stars glinted light off his combat suit's upper shoulders. The sight of him flooded my thirteen-year-old heart with respect and daughterly love.

Holovid screens flickered to life, and the tank's armaments focused on the cloud of enemy ships. We weren't going to win, but we could make sure they kept their distance.

Dad scowled at one readout on the screen. "Sathra," he said through the audio system to Mom, "we do not have full power in the primary cannons. AI is connected to the reactors. We cannot disconnect him."

"So, we...*run?*" Mom spat out the word like a bad taste.

The landscape blurred like dripping green paint as we raced away from Godwill's destroyed prison camp. We flew low to the ground, moving too fast to see the details of the dark, leafy 'natch fields. Kilometer-high skeletons of buildings in the ancient Human Ruins slumped over each other like bleached trees in a lifeless forest. Behind the Ruins, and towering above the land, loomed the shadow-dark Mesas. The three enormous plateaus dwarfed the lifeless Human city that ringed their bases.

The Convergence Dreadnought floated above the 'natch fields, the Human Ruins, and the Mesas as still as could be, like a planet hanging in the sky. In the darkness of the morning—or rather, in the shadow that fell from the kilometers-wide bulk of the Dreadnought—I could make out thousands of blue pinpoints streaming from its underbelly. It took me a moment, but then I understood: as lovely as schools of fish swimming in the deep blue sea, planetary assault ships were pouring out of the Dreadnought, and some of those thousands were moving toward Blue River, our city.

And...*you know*. The rest pursued us.

Orange plasma bolts pounded our tank's shields, and the shots that missed tossed clods of dirt tens of meters into the air or exploded in flowery blasts against the brittle, greying Human Ruins. Ancient buildings collapsed on themselves or sagged into other buildings, which in turn imploded into clouds of dust and fire.

The hits our tank's shields absorbed sounded like the patter of steel raindrops. The shields were holding...which was very, very good.

"Nent?" Mom called.

"*Ah*," he grunted, at last finding a firing solution. Our tank broke its silence, and Dad's command chair creaked as he leaned back to take in his work. "Shove *that* up your gravity well!"

Twin forward and rear autocannons screamed into the sky with white and blue plasma lances. As they took the hits, the attacking ships exploded and careened into buildings and the 'natch around us. Our Glean assault tank was roughly forty meters long and thirty meters wide. Four autocannons were mounted to the top, and four more were positioned below. Intended to take and hold a position

even against enemies in orbit, a battalion of these heavy tanks could stand off an invasion force.

As the assault ships and fighters exploded in the maelstrom, Mom said softly over the speakers, "*More.*"

"Sathra, we risk overloading the generat–."

"FIRE. THE. CANNON."

Dad grimaced. Leaning forward again, his two nearest arms became a blur as they moved over the console in front of me. *Aha!* He was activating the tank's primary autocannons. As the generators stirred to life, I felt their vibrations in the pit of my stomach.

Dad's uppermost right arm reached up to flip switches above our heads. If he got it wrong, our shields would fail. Our engines would fail. The power would be out. We'd be dead.

For an infinitely long and terrifying moment after he'd completed his firing sequence, Commander Nent Ceridian held his breath, widened his eyes, and stilled his hands. Then he whispered, as much to Mom as to the tank's synth, "*Fire.*"

The lights flickered off, and the air circulation fans audibly spun to a stop. Our breathing was the only sound, our sweat the only smell. And then the enormous cannons swiveled, and with impossible, delicate grace, stars as big as houses danced from the tank's twin muzzles.

VROOM! VROOM! VROOM! The stars streaked toward their targets. Each mini-nova hit and destroyed a Convergence ship, and it all happened in a breath's time. The pattern repeated several more times in quick succession, pausing only to reacquire targets.

"Oh, my," Mom whispered clearly through the speakers. A building-sized destroyer blossomed into a spectacular orange blaze and somersaulted into the Human Ruins in a titanic explosion. Other ships simply vanished into flames, never making it to the ground.

As our tank wobbled and lost altitude, presumably due to whatever Dad had done to divert power to his firing solution, my stomach jumped into my chest. But then the fans whirred back to life, and while the tank tipped again, it soon stabilized.

Tell them not to do that! I need power.

It was AI, in my head once again! I was ecstatic to hear his voice.

AI. My best friend. He'd been with me since I'd been adopted—or given; the truth was unclear. Every Galactic owns some sort of artificial-intelligence attendant, referred to as either "Synth" or "Attendant." I'd named mine *AI.* AI was indeed some form of artificial intelligence, packaged in a fist-sized, slightly rusty, diamond-shaped pendant. He was all I had left from my organic parents, and beyond the unique place he had in my life, he was clearly different from other attendants.

The Human reclamation solvent Godwill had injected me with was fighting with my own nano. And now, this made sense: AI was my key to keeping it at bay. The battle AI was waging against the solvent was an enormous energy drain that threatened to reduce him to an inactive state—an unplugged machine.

Please ALSO remind your explosion-junkie parents that I am keeping you alive.

AI, they know, I retorted.

Yeah. Well. We should have seen this coming. This whole thing is a big clusterf–."

Where are you? I blustered into his rant with my own thoughts. I'd been unconscious when my parents rescued us from Godwill's prison camp. Dad and AI didn't get along so well, so I assumed Dad had taken AI from his usual station around my neck, just above my heart.

I'm connected to the tank's power core through leads in the storage bay. Nonch, Mieant, and Cri are here, and they seem okay.

I breathed a sigh of relief. AI had saved me time and again, and in return, I hadn't exactly been nice to him.

Thank you.

Milliseconds of silence stretched into full seconds.

AI?

Ray, you're going to die a horrible death.

I blinked. *I mean, I know—*

If I LOSE POWER, you will die. If you use your nannites, you will die. And I stand by what I said earlier: if we don't find a cure quickly,

you're going to end up as a puddle of recycled nanotech for Godwill. And that's just what's happening inside of you. Look around you!

Why are you telling me this? I know.

You've been acting like a child, Raystar. This is deadly serious. Other lives than your own are at stake. You must watch everything you do, and everyone around you, if you want to make it through this.

I balled a fist. With such a brutal bedside manner, he'd make a great doctor.

I think I can help you, Ray, but I'm only minimally functional while I'm keeping the solvent from converting you. I'm not able to babysit you. So, if you want to live, you need to follow my directions. Mine alone. Do you understand?

The tank swayed as the incoming ships' weapons continued to pound us. I looked down at my hands, swallowed hard, and nodded.

And none of this is your fault, Raystar. Mostly... Finally, his stern tone relented. My cheeks grew hot as I remembered flushing him down the waste recycler.

Before I could respond, the tank was suddenly hammered, as if by a giant fist, and sloughed down into the dirt. Thrown from the chair, I landed face-first on the ceiling as the cabin sank into blackness. Stars blanketed my vision.

Quickly, emergency lights brightened on the tank's floor, casting red light high *above* me. Dad grimaced, his eyes glowing, as he scrambled with the controls. He was hanging upside-down from the command chair—because, of course, he had wisely strapped himself in. Ozone-filled smoke wafted through the air momentarily until the circulation fans reactivated and the cabin lights flickered back on.

"THAT is a Dreadnought," Dad muttered through his microphone to Mom. As he hung upside down, his hands flying over the console, he grumbled to himself, through clenched teeth, something that sounded like it had an "I" and a "told you so" in it.

A *single* blast from that Goliath above us had knocked our shields offline and had slammed us, upside-down, into the dirt. Glean assault tanks were designed to hit targets in space, but Convergence Dreadnoughts were designed to take those hits and to then take the planet.

Under Godwill's command, the 98th Battlegroup had arrived with an armada (sorry, Dad) of 6,000 ships. At least a thousand of them were Dreadnoughts identical to the ship parked above our little part of Nem'. Battlegroups were the hammers of the Convergence, and a part of me wondered how my ancestors had stood up to the combined might of more than 500 Battlegroups during the Lethian–Human War.

From the cockpit, Mom righted the tank, and I tumbled right-side up, managing to guide myself onto the soft command chair instead of the very not-soft floor. While the tank's gravity compensators ensured that its passengers didn't get completely squished, *if there is a next time,* I'm wearing my seatbelts. As I stuffed myself into the chair, I strapped in.

"Synth, covering fire!" Mom commanded as the view screens flickered back to life, revealing our home in the distance. Our compound glowed in the darkness, not three kilometers away!

The fifty-meter-high energy dome encircling our compound was awash with splashes of inbound fire. Spaced every ten meters or so, on blood-red pillars a meter thick, were our autocannons and sensor arrays. The arrays were responsible for projecting the shield over the compound, and viewed at night, with the orange fire of the autocannons' plasma distorting the air, they seemed to peer into the darkness like robotic monsters (which of course, they were).

It wasn't exactly the innocent little farmhouse I'd thought it was for most of my life. *Nothing is what it seems. Nothing.*

Following Mom's command to the synth, streams of golden plasma lanced up toward the approaching assault ships from our "gargoyles." Their gold barrage washed harmlessly over some ships and utterly obliterated others. I blinked as the immense firepower was unleashed into the heavens.

Mom raced the tank forward like a huge rat caught in headlights, hurtling toward the shelter of our compound. *This rat had legs.*

"Synth. Broadcast the Ascendancy distress signal on all Convergence military channels, following this message: 'Convergence ships,

cease fire immediately. I am Lady Sathralea Ceridian, Ascendant. I am with my husband, Commander Nent Ceridian of the Glean Gathering Special Operations Division. Identification is attached. You are in violation of the Lethian–Human War Treaty Protocols. Cease fire. I repeat, *cease fire.*"

She finished speaking just as we reached our compound's massive energy shield.

Safety, at last. Right?

The tank shuddered as its nose sank and plowed into the dirt. A moment later, its antigrav thrusters and power core failed, and the back end of the hulking war-machine thundered to the ground. Screens flickered, several emitting sparks and smoke before simply turning dark. Pitch black was everywhere for a nanosecond, until red emergency lights softly chased it away with their urgent glow.

Dad removed his safety harness, leapt to his feet, and loomed over me. "Nova and gravity wells, Daughter!" he exclaimed as he simultaneously brushed me off with his lower hands and turned my bruised face this way and that with his upper hands. He said, "What have I told you about combat missions?"

"I…" I stared through my purple bangs into his worried face. *Uh.* "Take a deep breath before you shoot?" I peered up at him, wincing at his expression. "Plan, plan, plan? Know your enemy? Eat 'natch?" As he glowered at me, I poofed purple hair off my face. "Use the bathroom because you never know…"

"Gnnngh," he huffed as he stomped into the storage bay, presumably to check on Cri and our friends. The doors hissed open and then hissed shut behind him.

It wasn't a fair question.

The doors hissed open again, and Dad leaned into the room, his two sets of hands pointing at me and his golden eyes blazing in the red of the emergency lights. *"Wear your seatbelt!"* The doors hissed again as he turned and entered the storage bay.

In synchronicity, just as he left the command center, Mom entered the room from the forward cockpit. I closed my mouth and, just like déjà vu, blew my purple bangs out of my eyes as she approached. *Uh oh. What would I get from THIS parental unit?*

Mom had never told me how she'd gotten her scar. Normally it stood out as a pink line scuttling down her cheek from above her right eye to her chin, but in moments of great emotion, it changed dramatically. At this moment, her cheeks were wet, the scar was a deep purple against her vermilion skin, and her long, black-as-the-Void curtains of hair were plastered to her head and face in a beautiful combination of sweat, tears, and grime. She was breathtaking, even after mortal combat.

Clad in a white battle suit with black straps across her thighs and waist to holster her four blasters, Mom rushed toward me. In the red light, the Glean seal and creed—"Peace, Love, Family, War"—shone on the breastplate of her armor, and her white cape billowed behind her like a giant flying creature coming in for a landing.

"My Raystar!" Her lower hands gently grasped my shoulders into an embrace while her upper hands squeezed my face into fish lips. She kissed my forehead and then moved to lift me out of the chair and fully take in the sight of me. My face was illuminated by the sunshine that streamed from her golden eyes.

"My brave, foolish child! You are..." A frown suddenly clouded her lovely face. "...You are *not strapped in?*"

With that, she pulled me against her chest into a four-armed hug. She held me, my feet dangling, for multiple breaths. I didn't mind. At all. I was about to be fourteen. And the world was ending.

With perfect timing, the cargo bay door hissed open once again, and a smaller and younger but nearly identical version of Mom, albeit with a dirt-stained face and disheveled hair, stepped through the hatch. My sister, her tattered clothes revealing amounts of skin that I'm sure Dad didn't approve of, froze as she took us in.

Mom set me down and rushed over to my older sister. Still weak from the battle with Godwill, I stumbled, grasping for the support of the chair.

In two strides, Mom pulled my sister close into an even bigger hug. "Baby!"

Her lower hands lifted my sister around the waist and used one upper hand to crush her into an embrace. The other cradled Cri's head against her chest. Cri was certainly much taller than I, but still nowhere near as tall as Mom.

Neither Mom's passion, nor her embraces, were resistible. We were still her babies.

"Stop!" Cri managed to gasp, smushed as she was. I noted that she wasn't struggling too hard, though.

Mom pulled back a bit, and they looked at each other for a heartbeat. Mom's joy fractured against Cri's glare.

"At least *she's* okay, right?" my sister said, pointing at me.

"That's not…," Mom started.

"I'm your REAL daughter. Maybe one day you'll get that!" My sister dodged past our mom, gave me a wide berth, and exited the tank. "Before it's too late!" she shouted, as the doors closed behind her.

Dad had stepped through the cargo bay in time to catch the tail end of Cri's outburst. Mom lowered her face to her hands. As she shook with sobs, her black hair poured around her shoulders in stark contrast to her cape.

Dad gently pulled Mom's hands to his mouth. Sadness passed between their glowing eyes as he gently kissed her fingers. He then sighed and followed after Cri. As he walked past me, one giant hand gently brushed my cheek, while another pressed AI's pendant into my hands—an unexpected baton of hope in the chaos of my emotions.

"Children," Mom urged into the cargo bay, "come. Quickly!"

Mieant's grey hands grasped the doorway as he awkwardly pulled himself through. He had been the coolest kid in school. At school, he'd been my bully. Now? He was somewhere between my ally…and my sister's boyfriend. Lethians were nearly as tall as Gleans but had only two arms. Mieant's grey skin, pupil-less black eyes, black hair, wiry frame, and distinctive lips—a soft, red, and sensuous upper lip

underpinned by a cobalt-blue lower lip, both of which were down-turned—lent him a haughty, disengaged, yet appealing aura. Mieant looked every bit the son of aristocrats.

If the Convergence was a democracy, the Lethians ruled that democracy. In fact, Mieant's parents were the Co-Governors of our Solium4 Quadrant. I'll get into *that* in a bit.

"Where's Cri?" he asked, his questioning eyes darting from me to Mom and then back to me. I pointed to the door. He nodded, his face carefully neutral, and then hurried after my sister.

A pair of orange orbs, each double the size of my fist, wove and snaked in the red-tinged darkness beyond the doorway, getting larger as they approached.… But that was not the first thing to come into the cabin light. Mandibles, the size of my forearms, preceded a midnight-blue head as large as my chest. The orbs were, in fact, iridescent orange eyes that crowned that weaponized head. Just behind the orbs, a pair of feathery sensor stalks waved ahead, considering everything in their path. Just below them, six smaller eyes reflected light like polished onyx.

"Shells!" I cried, arms open, stumbling toward my best friend, Nonch. Mom's eyes grew wide as she stepped aside. Nonch reared up and embraced me with what should have been six claw arms—sword-like appendages that ended in orange insectoid hands. I saw blood-soaked bandages in the spaces where his other two claw arms had once been; they were ripped off during our battle with Godwill.

"Raystar-Friend.…" Nonch's three-meter-long, vaguely centipede-like form chugged toward me. He held perfectly still as I wrapped my arms around my second-longest friend, after AI, on this Void-forsaken, 'natch-covered planet. Nonch's armor was razor-sharp and edgy. but his carapace was smooth. Warm.

Crynits were the natural shock troops of the Convergence. They could withstand the vacuum of space, take a direct hit from a plasma rifle, and with six claw arms, were weapons in and of themselves. As he lowered to my height, his two giant, matte-black top eye-orbs regarded me. His sensor stalks waved briefly, as if taking me in, and then gently bopped me on the head. They had the weight and feel of giant pillows.

"Nonch," Mom said, with a nod in his direction, "of Broodmother Krig."

He disengaged from our embrace and bowed to her. "Lady Ceridian."

"So formal," she said, resting one hand on his head while gesturing urgently toward the tank's exit ramp with the other three. "Come. We must get to the shelter of the house."

He thrummed by on a hundred legs. As he passed, he leaned toward me so only I could hear him utter, "Raystar-Friend mine. This is the time of choosing. Remember your promise. Broodmother will not take kindly to my defiance."

Mom's hands warmed my shoulders as she guided me out of the tank after him.

You are so cragged, Ray. AI said in my mind. I didn't disagree. *No way can he come with us.*

We don't even know where we're going, I replied. AI responded with silence.

But a cold chill wriggled its way up my spine. Nonch, days before we'd been captured by Godwill in our school library, had made me *promise* to take him with us, no matter what. He wanted to escape off planet with us—escape his mother's plans, whatever *they* were. Live a different life. Run away with us.

And so it was the time of choosing, of me choosing to honor the promise I'd made that day in the library. My commitment to honor our friendship.

The doors eased open, and Mom firmly guided me outside into a cacophony of sound, light, and destruction.

High above us, our compound's force field was a pond of golden ripples as a rain of incoming fire and flaming meteors of debris from exploding ships. As they impacted the force field, the air filled with crackles of ear-splitting noise. *VZZZSHOOMS!*

Nonch's words haunted me as the streaks of light above reflected in my eyes. Isn't each moment, each second, of a life a time of choosing?

I sprinted away from our deceased assault tank to the farmhouse with one hand over my head. I kept my other hand (*I only had two!*) imperfectly clenched over my mouth, stifling a scream at the back of my throat. Incoming fire from ships above streaked, thundered, and exploded against the force field fifty meters above us.

I'd nearly made the porch stairs when the Dreadnought fired its *second* blast of the morning. While our tank could fire house-sized projectiles that reached into space and pierced the bellies of armored ships unlucky enough to find themselves in our sights, a blast from the titan above whitewashed over our entire dome shield and ignited an inferno of 'natch that blazed for hundreds of meters in all directions. A pyre of sparks scattered skyward.

Mom and Dad had planned for nearly every eventuality. Legger packs? *No problem.* We could have stood off the Nem' Planetary Defense (planetary police) cruisers all year. But a Dreadnought siege ship had thousands of cannons like the one that had just hit us, which could fire over 100 rapid pulses per second. From space.

And it had hit us only once?

Primal instinct threw me to the ground. Just as quickly, I got my feet and hands under me and scrambled upright. I windmilled my arms as I darted the remaining meters to our kitchen door. Dad held it wide, motioning me to hurry.

Home. I was almost there.

The sound that stopped me a meter from safety was a plea for help from a distant ally—a fellow descendant of Terra. Kin from my past, from our now-dead planet.

The piercing "squeas" from the gratcher pen rose above the noise of incoming fire and plasma cannons.

Oh…no.

There was a time when I wouldn't have started a day without a hearty eggs-and-fried-gratcher breakfast. Gratchers had evolved from Terran pigs. I'd seen vids of ancient pigs, but gratchers were nothing like them. They had mottled brown skin and saber-like teeth. A small gratcher could easily weigh 800 kilos. Herd leaders, on the other hand, weighed in around 5,000 kilos and left craters wherever they stomped. Our own herd leader, who we lovingly named "Chunks," was easily that large. It was Chunks, my Terran blood-brother, who had saved us before.

Earlier in the week, before the—uh, well, the planetary blockade—Jurisdictor Godwill had shown up at our compound with a squad of Nem' Planetary Defense officers, the start of a conflict I hadn't known even existed. He had come to take me away from Mom and Dad. AI opened the gratcher pen's confinement shields just as the NPD were *about* to attempt to take me, just as Mom and Dad were *about* to shoot them, and…well, I digress.

Chunks was fiercely territorial. He'd changed the game that day, nearly destroying the NPD's cruiser with his giant tusks. On that day, I stopped having gratcher for breakfast. It seemed like bad form to eat your savior. I started giving the big guy my dessert on my way to school. I wasn't completely sure we were friends, but I had no doubt that we had a connection. Maybe we are all connected to everything else? I don't know. Maybe we just don't recognize all those connections until they rise up and declare their existence, their linkages.

Regardless, I owed him my life. Mom had told me that we don't leave anyone behind. Chunks and his herd, like me, were Terrans. My, uh, people.

I looked back across the courtyard and made eye contact with Chunks. He stood as still as a boulder while his herd ran helter-skel-

ter, wide-eyed and panic stricken. Acknowledging me with a massive stomp, he shook his head at the barrier. Swinging his massive jowls back toward me, he fixed me with a reproachful glare with one eye high up on one side of his giant, tusked head.

I swallowed hard and looked up at Dad and then back to Chunks.

"What?" Dad pulled me into the kitchen. I pulled back, surprising him.

"The…." I stuttered, pointing. "What about our—what about the gratchers?"

"The WHAT?" Dad looked at me like a third eyeball had opened on my forehead.

"We can't leave them with…." I waved at everything around us.

"RAYSTAR CERIDIAN!" Mom's cool cracked as she glared at me from where she stood behind Dad. "COME INSIDE! RIGHT. NOW."

What is your major malfunction? AI yelled in my brain. *Get in the house!*

Another Dreadnought blast smashed the shield. The compound's lights darkened and the ground shook. Sparks sprinkled from our reactors off to the side of the yard. The golden shield I'd called home burned like a fire lit in the middle of a sheet of paper. Actual sky could be seen clearly through parts of it before the glowing shield reformed over the gap. The lights came back on.

Ray. You promised me you'd listen.

I balled my fists. This whole thing wasn't right. I made a last, fleeting moment of eye contact with Chunks. He blinked, turned away, and lowered his hulk to the ground. He rested his head on his front legs. His planetary sister had let him down.

Fine. I thought back to AI. *But I need something from you.* I told him what I wanted as Dad nabbed me, pulling me inside. He slammed the door shut. Like *that* would end the matter?

"Children, away from the windows. Sit," Dad said, pointing to the part of the kitchen closest to the basement stairs. Nonch was coiled, snake-like, with a meter of his midnight-blue body rising up. Iridescent eyes regarded us like suns over his arcing mandibles. Mieant's arm encircled Cri, and his black hair blended together with hers as he dipped his head toward her—so much so that the torrent of hair shielded her face from me as she let him lead her. Together, they leaned against a wall by the basement door, and as a couple, sank to the ground.

I took in our ordinary kitchen: tile floors, a central table, cabinets, a sink, and a food-processing station. Stairs leading up to the second floor and our bedrooms. Three oversized chairs, and one Human-sized, high-top chair. It was nothing special, but it was my home. Familiar smells of pancakes and spices had been replaced by the stench of ozone and fire.

Dad rose to open a cabinet I don't remember ever being opened before and grabbed multiple tins from inside. He brought them over and handed one to each of us. Field rations.

Warily, I opened the container. It smelled disgusting, but it activated my hunger. I was mildly allergic to Galactic food—maybe it was a conspiracy that Galactic food never was 100 percent compatible with Humanity. But my nannites demanded energy. The war inside of me required fuel. Perhaps all wars—both internal and external—require fuel. Hunger was a now my constant companion.

Cri defiantly scrunched her nose and with a lower hand, pushed her tin away from her, across the floor. Without asking, I grabbed it and used my fingers to scoop the pink clay inside into my mouth. Cheeks bulging, I emptied the can in three scoops. Cri eyed me, frowning as she realized she'd inadvertently done something nice for me.

I really don't know what I ever did to deserve her consistent ire.

"Lady Sathra," the house synth said soothingly. "I have detected an Ascendancy signal." I glanced around for another tin of food.

"It is about time, Sathra," Dad muttered. The Ascendancy were the good guys. *Us.* The Glean Convergence, of which Mom was apparently royalty. Ascendant. As in, "in line to the throne."

"Darling," she replied, placing an elegant hand on his cheek. Mom activated the screens over our central-kitchen-table-turned-command-console and demanded of the synth, "Identify who it is. Broadcast our status."

"Signal has been broadcast, and receipt is confirmed, Lady Sathra." The synth paused, baffled somehow deep down in its emotionless, synthetic-intelligence core. "It is your younger brother, the Heir."

Mom looked at Dad with worry creasing her wide-eyed expression. Her scar deepened to a dark purple against the red of her skin.

"Void take us," Dad swore. "What is that…he…*doing?*"

Something nasty is about to happen, AI whispered. I clutched him tightly, his weight a comfort over my heart. He warmed in response to my grip.

A fourth Dreadnought blast hit the compound. The house shook and the dishes rattled in the cupboards. Something upstairs crashed. White dust that drifted from the ceiling blanketed our hair like an early frost.

"WARNING. MASSIVE CRITICAL SYSTEM FAILURES," our house synth monotoned. Its core was apparently back online. "There is a 100 percent shield failure. Generators offline. Atmosphere cannon offline. Autocannons offline. Force field offline. Household power and appliances offline. Hangar power offline. Water to 'natch field contro–."

"Okay!" Dad boomed. "Everything is offline! Great novas." Then to himself, as he tinkered with his wrist console, he added, "Tell us something we do NOT know."

"Affirmative, Commander Nent. I am enacting automated defense and distress protocols." White light flashed through the kitchen windows, followed by a "WHUMP" that rattled the dishes again. More dust drifted down from the ceiling. Dad's eyes grew wide.

The synth continued: "Ascendancy hyper-space distress beacon launched. Base self-destruct armed. Awaiting base commander instructions. Commander Nent Ceridian authorized to initiate self-destruct sequence."

Wait. What?

Cri flipped her hair back, eyes glowing gold, and our gazes met in shock. In that terrifying moment, we were sisters again. *Self-destruct?*

We had only recently discovered that our parents were, in fact, nobility. Mom was in line to lead the Glean Convergence. Dad was a hero. They'd come to Nem' to hide me. The façade of my life was shattered, leaving me raw, open, and afraid.

Lady Sathralea Ceridian, Ascendant, and Commander Nent Ceridian exchanged a dark glance. In that second, Mom's cape flowed lazily behind her, and she looked every bit the noblewoman she was: dignified, self-assured, powerful. And as Dad straightened, hands unconsciously going to the giant blasters at his thighs and across his chest, I had a vision of legions of troops behind him.

"We must meet him," Mom said, her four hands alighting gently on Dad's forearms and shoulders as she looked up into his eyes.

"I hate this," he said, not breaking the intensity of their connecting gaze. "The compromise we made to stay out of everyone's way. And *he*," Dad spat the word and clenched his fists, "pursues *us*."

Mom nodded. "Yes."

Dad slumped. "I'll take them to the basement," he continued, turning toward us. "AI can guide them to our contact in Blue River."

The fear I was gripped with made me fall quiet and still. *Guide us? Where were they going? Why were we going?*

6

In the youth of our youth, Cri and I loved to play hide-and-seek in our basement. It was our playground, with stacks of crates and dark labyrinths of tunnels providing endless places to hide, and the darkness wasn't so dark that it was scary. We had lots of secret nooks that we stuffed with blankets and pillows for clandestine meetings.

It didn't look like a playground now, with its industrial concrete walls, Galactic-alloy steps that clanked with each foot fall, and swirling red emergency lights. *No. It wasn't a playground at all.* It was a bunker. It had always been a bunker. We'd played in it mindlessly, never realizing its true purpose.

My mind raced and my heart pounded as yet another illusion was shattered. I struggled to keep my breathing even as I followed my sister and my friends down into my past. Memories, unbidden, flashed through my mind.

"I don't know," I replied to my six-year-old sister, afraid that my not-knowing would make her laugh.

"You don't know where you came from?" Her golden eyes glowed at me, and she frowned prettily at the impossibility of my response. Mom had put her jet-black hair in pigtails, and they bobbed around her chubby cheeks as she shook her head at me. We sat cross-legged on a blanket, our backs against the yellow- and black-striped door we'd been warned not to touch. Cri was breaking cookies in half, putting some on my plate and others on hers, as we struggled to understand the big questions.

I looked down at our cookie party. At my two brown hands, so different from her four red ones. I don't know how or why I didn't know where I came from; I just didn't. I looked back at her and poofed purple hair out of my eyes. When we're very young, we don't prejudge anyone. We don't recognize differences. We just experience our own emotions; it's later that the rest of the Universe gets involved and changes the way we see things. Four hands, two hands, it didn't matter. What does?

She smiled. "Well, we're…you're family now," she said, putting an extra cookie on my plate. "Do you remember your mommy or daddy?"

My face grew hot as I met her gaze. I didn't. I remembered a woman and a man who maybe could have been my parents, but I couldn't see their faces. I remembered their warmth, their strong hugs, but mostly their smells. Ozone. Cookies. Laundered clothes. Hey, it wasn't roses or anything, but it's what I remembered from their embraces.

I remembered them hugging me. A lot.

"No," I looked down at my fingernails. At our plates. She'd given me more cookie halves than she'd given herself.

Cri shrugged. "Well, we can share my mommy and daddy." She nudged me as she split another cookie and paused before she put it on my plate. I looked from my hands to her eyes. She took in an exaggerated breath, and then, before taking a bite of the cookie, added, "As long as you don't take them from me."

"Why would I do that?" I frowned at her, horrified. I knew how important they were.

My sister looked at her broken-cookie half and frowned.

I blinked the memory away.

Before today, I would have said we kept supplies and stored some of our harvest down here. Now, I'm wondering what we needed all

this space for. The bunker extended beneath our entire compound. The hide-and-seek tunnels were large enough to fly my two-seater dart through.

Shrink-wrapped blasters, batteries, armor, and generators were everywhere. Not at all *just* last year's harvest. How could I have missed this? Weapons, grenades, missiles, Glean uniforms…this was a fully stocked supply depot.

My parents hadn't lied to me. They just hadn't told me everything. Or *anything*. I clenched my fists as I considered what I actually knew.

I didn't know my biological parents; my memories were blurry and out of my mind's reach. And as for why I was here, how I got here, and why Glean royalty would need to be my adoptive parents? I had no clue.

And I felt even more clueless as I thought about the rooms of the bunker. Most were furnished with sinks and cots. We could have fed, clothed, armed, and housed hundreds of Gleans down there.

"Make haste, children," Dad urged us along from behind.

In front of me, Nonch flowed smoothly from the stairs onto the concrete floor. His sensor stalks were laid against his back like hair. I could read my friend's body language. Fear was a strange emotion to see on a Crynit. They, of all of the Galactics, shouldn't be afraid of anything. But maybe, there was a lot to be afraid of.

I shivered. My shoes clanked on the last stair and then thudded dully as I stepped onto the cold, concrete floor of the bunker.

"Children," Dad said. We stood in a semicircle in what Dad called the "staging area," which used to be called "the big space at the bottom of the stairs." "Your survival will depend on your following my directions." He paused, considering each one of us in turn. "We have a tunnel that will take you toward Blue River. Our allies there will be on alert for you."

Nonch's sensor stalks raised in full alert mode. We all blinked.

"The Elions. You met the youngest of them in school. They will know what to do next."

Alar? The green-eyed, ridiculously cute, fluffy guy we'd saved at school?

"There is one more thing. The self-destruct sequence is active, but you MUST destroy this base when you leave. It cannot fall into Godwill's hands."

Cri gasped. She glanced at me, her eyes aglow, then flashed her gaze back to him. He reached one massive lower hand into a pouch on his body armor. An upper hand caressed her head and the other two gently grasped her shoulders. Dad wasn't an expressive guy, and Cri's eyes flared and then tightened slightly as she searched his expression for meaning, for why this moment was so different than any other.

He took a small device from the pouch and eyed it. "Destroy this base once you're far enough away to ensure that Godwill's forces cannot follow you. While they may guess, they must not know you are

going to Blue River. You must get to the Elions before they make the connection."

Blowing out a breath, he handed it to her. I recognized it immediately. Blood pounded against my skull.

Cri's mouth froze in a panicked 'O.' Mieant frowned, his glance traveling from Dad to Cri and then to the device. Nonch, who had coiled half of his body, considered us, his sensor stalks extended. His black and midnight-blue coloration seemed to disappear into the red strobes of the emergency lights.

That is so cragged, AI muttered to me. He was my constant, my only reassurance of reality. And he wasn't being very reassuring.

"Dad?" Cri gazed up into our father's eyes, the small grey rectangle carefully balanced on her trembling palm.

He took her face gently in his hands. His eyes glistened. Something wet fell from his great height and landed on the floor with a soft pat.

"I'm so proud of you, Cri."

"*Dad?*" she whispered.

"Remember your training," he said, tapping her lightly on her neck, where her tattoo shone. "Eyes and ears. Your tattoos will be of use to you in the future."

That was the military grade nano-ink he'd applied to her before we'd been captured. It recorded everything. Mom had been so nova'd about it.

He sucked in a breath and turned to me, motioning me to come closer.

I approached, and once I was in arm's reach, Dad swept me into a hug and simultaneously pulled Cri in as well. He squished our heads on either side of his face and took a deep breath, as if he were smelling us. As if it was for the last time.

"You both are my lights, my stars in this darkness." Dad's frame shook like a quake under a mountain. He exhaled deeply.

"I'm sorry to ask this of you," he said to me as he placed the second encrypted detonator into my palm. Composing himself, he whispered to us, to our terrified, communal hearts, "It will take both of you to activate the self-destruct order. Godwill will come after you through this passage. We will delay him as long as we can. *Be very far away.*"

Dad had put us both through self-destruct drills several times a year since I was strong enough to press the detonator button. Never in my wildest dreams did I ever think I'd have to go through with it.

And what was going to happen to them? My heart pounded as I realized that *he hadn't said anything about meeting us in Blue River.*

I looked at Cri, and she looked away. Dad noticed the exchange and said, "More than ever, daughters, you must be sisters. Together, you will be safe." And then to Cri, he added, "This is not Raystar's fault, my Cri."

"I..." stuttered out my sister's reply.

"Your mother and I chose. We knew the risks, and you two are paying for our gamble. I hope one day you will see that we did what we thought was best for you. For both of you. I hope that in the coming turmoil, you two can learn to rely on each other." After a kiss, he released us and rose to his feet.

Turning to Mieant, he wrapped the Lethian in a giant hug, and Mieant didn't resist. Dad paused, suddenly stern. "Young man, know that *I* know you have intentions toward my daughter."

His eyes glowed, illuminating Mieant's wide-eyed, mouth-half-opened, red-blue expression of shock. If you'd dropped a pin in the farthest reaches of the bunker, you'd have heard it in the epic silence that followed.

"Treat her well. I would be...*unhappy* to learn that you did otherwise." Mieant's shock turned to panic, and his expression froze as Dad patted his head. Cri's shock registered on her face as her gaze darted between Dad and her boyfriend.

Then, Dad bowed to Nonch and then wrapped him in a Glean hug that dwarfed Nonch's nearly three-meter length. Gleans were huge, and they hugged with hugeness. Stepping back, he regarded us.

"In this place, you are all our children. Thank you for being my daughters' friends. My wife and I will protect you to our last breath. I fear...." His last two words chilled me: Dad had never said "I" and

"fear" in the same sentence. "I fear that we have limited options."

He pointed to Cri's tattoos, the ones he'd put there. They weren't permanent, of course, or Mom would have killed him. He'd used military nano-ink, which recorded and broadcast a body-camera vid of everything Cri saw and even served as a locator. It was how Mom and Dad had found us when we'd been held in Godwill's prison camp.

"Remember, those record everything. Remember that you beat Godwill once before. WHEN you worked together. Remember that together, you are strong."

Dad turned to go but froze at the base of the stairs. He spun around and in two quick strides moved toward Cri and scooped her up.

"My first child. My first love. I am so proud of you. Everything you've done. Who you are. My Cri." He pulled her close and inhaled her, and she let out a small sound, a sigh.

He blinked up at the ceiling, then he caught me up with his other two arms. I smelled dirt and his hair and felt his heart thundering in his chest. "Raystar. You are *our child*. Anything else is a lie. I love you. Sathra and I are infinitely better for having you both in our lives." He squeezed us hard, placing his huge head between ours.

Then he set us down and marched upstairs to the kitchen. The door slid shut behind him.

I turned to Cri. Her eyes were wet and huge. She brushed a strand of hair behind her ear, and I sucked in a ragged, halting breath.

The door opened and Mom glided down the stairs, her combat boots clanking rhythmically on each step. Without pause, she grabbed me.

"Little Raystar!" she exclaimed, pulling me close and planting a kiss on my forehead. Dropping to one knee, she grabbed Cri. My sister was shaking.

"Cri!" Mom sobbed. "You. Raystar. You two." She squeezed Cri harder, and I heard the breath escape from Cri's mouth. We stayed there for a minute, an hour, I couldn't tell, before Mom released us. She wiped her eyes and removed items from the weapons belt that encircled her hips.

"Here," she gasped, handing me a blaster of non-standard design. "Take this," she continued, "it is from your organic parents." She paused and then added, "It was to be a gift for when you were older." I stared blankly at the weapon in my hands without really seeing it.

"You're older now," she finished, pressing the blaster into my hands.

Mom turned to Cri and gave her two blasters and matching swords. I recognized the set as her own weapons, each bearing the Ascendancy crest.

"Mom? *Please?* What's happening?" Cri said in a small voice as she gripped Mom's shoulders with her upper two hands. "Don't go away. *Don't leave us.*"

Mom looked intently into my sister's pleading gaze. Her golden eyes glowed like stars and cast long shadows of us on the bunker's walls.

"Each moment we have is precious. Those people out there are threatening you, Cri. Threatening Raystar. Threatening my husband. *My* family. What would you have me do?" More softly, she added, "What would *you* do?"

Cri blinked and peered into Mom's eyes. Mom hugged her again, smiled sadly, and turned to face Mieant.

"Young Asrigard." His black eyes were huge, his face expressionless. Mom took a step toward him and pulled him into an embrace. "I'm sorry, Mieant. For this moment, you are my child. You are not alone." She kissed his forehead and, after a moment, released him.

She turned then to Nonch. "Dear Nonch, you are perhaps the most capable and the least prepared for the galaxy's betrayals." With that, she pulled down Nonch's mandibles so the crown of his head faced her chest and hugged his head. "On our soil, you are our responsibility, part of our brood. I am proud to call you my own." Her tear dropped soundlessly onto his black chitin, and she kissed his head. Nonch flowed back a step, his sensor stalks touching where the tear had landed. He was used to friendship between us kids, but I don't think he'd ever experienced a grownup's sincere affection—other than from his Broodmother.

Mom then faced AI, lifting him from where he hung around my neck. She set him loose, and he simply floated in space.

"Machine. All those years ago I did not realize how much your stewardship and friendship would come to mean to me, to my family. I am lucky in this life to know you." Mom bowed deeply to AI, and he glowed with deep warmth, a fire from within.

As she rose to her full height, she resignedly wiped her wet and matted hair away from where it clung to her red cheek. Her facial scar, already an angry purple line, turned almost black as she sucked in a breath and regarded us.

"Remember what you have gone through. Circumstances forced you together, but your courage and respect for each other transformed you into a family. It matters not that you are Human, Glean, Lethian, Crynit, and Machine. You have trusted each other, protected each other, nurtured each other's strengths. In these moments and beyond, continue to trust. Strengthen it. Trust is your salvation."

"Peace. Love. Family," she said, and then paused. Slowly, she clenched her four hands into upraised fists.

"WAR."

Mom walked up the stairs and exited into the light. Shadows swept in behind her as the door whooshed to a close. Air circulators hidden away in the darkened corridors of our basement—uh, bunker—gossiped quiet whispers we could feel on our faces like a soft breeze.

Mom's last word echoed once through the corridors. "WAR."

Cri gasped and sagged to the grey cement floor. Her knees were splayed and her shoulders shook under her hair as she sucked in difficult, ragged breaths. Mieant knelt beside her, placed an arm around her, and whispered comfort into her ear. I wanted to turn away. His words were not for me. I didn't want them, but…I couldn't look away. I imagined the feeling of a warm arm around me, the solace of touch.

I turned my gaze to the blank wall and focused on the immediate future. A comforting arm was not a part of that future.

My eyes burned. I wiped away the wetness clouding my vision as AI glowed a soft yellow and slid through the space between us.

Everything is completely nova'd, I said to AI. Somehow, this was all my fault. Mom and Dad had come here to hide *me.* From whom? What? Why?

Ray, except for maybe not flushing me, there's nothing we could have done differently. Nothing you could have done differently, he replied. *This is* not *your fault.*

My fingernails dug into my palms as I balled my hands into sweaty fists. If that was true, then we were just destined, fated to be up the Galactic gravity well. There didn't seem to be any point in thinking or doing anything if destiny just chose what we were going to do.

"You are communicating with AI?" Nonch interrupted. In the red strobes of the emergency lights, he looked like a horror show. I blinked at him.

"What?"

"You are silently communicating?"

I shrugged. I wanted to get back to my self-pity and anger.

"It is good that you can do that. It is like Crynit pheromone talk."

I put my hand on Nonch's mandible, unconsciously welcoming the touch. Leaning on his strength, I looked up into my friend's matte-black orbs.

AI might be right, but I felt that I wasn't good enough to save the ones I loved. How else do you measure goodness except in your capacity to help others?

"Did you say something?" I asked Nonch.

Nonch paused, considering me. Then he gently removed my hand from his scythe-like mouth with a blade arm. "Your parents are pawns. Just like his," he said, pointing at Mieant.

Mieant raised his head from Cri's shoulder and frowned at us. "What do you mea–."

"The Crynit has it right," AI interrupted, still hovering in the air where Mom had placed him.

"Sir?" Mieant started, taking his arm from around Cri's waist and looking hard at AI. My sister grabbed at his hand with one of hers, and then another, as he rose. He momentarily resisted but found himself out-handed, so he leaned back down and helped Cri get to her feet. We formed a semicircle around AI.

Nonch stretched to his full length, his iridescent eyes reflecting the red emergency lights that cast wild shadows against the ceiling and walls. Mieant looked at him and demanded, "Explain!" His unblinking eyes were like two Void-black chasms in an already darkened room.

"We are all pawns," Nonch replied, his sensor stalks whipping forward to punctuate each word. "The four of us being here, at this moment, is no coincidence. Jurisdictor Godwill does not need two Battlegroups to crush Nem' under his boot." He turned to me, his razor-sharp mandibles crackling through the air with the sound of metal on metal. "The single Dreadnought above us could have annihilated us, your parents, Blue River…all of us…without a second thought. But to have two full Battlegroups, over 12,000 ships here? The force being applied to this tiny farming world is much greater than any threat we…." Nonch paused and then adult-voiced the rest of his thought: "*We children could ever hope to create.*"

"My parents are still alive," Mieant retorted, his grey face scrunched into a scowl. "As Solium4 Quadrant Co-Governors, they have the entire Quadrant's fleets under their command. If we could find them, we could get help. Godwill's ships would not stand a chance."

"Dad told us to go to Blue River," Cri chimed in, brushing strands of black hair from her face. Her almond-shaped eyes glowed slightly as she added, "and find the Elions."

We all looked at her. "We have to go there, regardless," I said, glancing at AI for affirmation. "They can help me with my nanoinfection, right?"

AI flashed green, signaling his agreement. For a Machine, his emotions were easy to read.

Cri glowered at me. "There you go again. It's always all about you. Our parents just abandon us for Architect-knows-what reason, and all you can think about is you!"

"About me? Like me *dying* in three days? You're such a *spike*! I haven't done *anything* to you!" I yelled back at her. Ozone filled my nostrils. My purple bangs obscured my vision and microsparks glittered at the ends of my hair, sparkling from strand to strand. *Control, Ray.* I couldn't lose control.

"You're the spike! All this," she gestured with her four arms at the Universe, "is because of you and your stupid freakiness! You're a self-centered Human freak!"

We both took a step toward each other. With great swiftness, Nonch caught me with the dull side of his blade arms and pulled me back.

"Cri, stop it!" Mieant implored, wedging himself between us and directing his gaze to his girlfriend. "Your parents, my parents…that nanocreature pursuing Raystar, Godwill. It is too convenient, too easy, to only blame one individual." He shifted his gaze to me. "Nonch is right. This is much larger and broader than just us." After a moment's pause, he continued, "Blue River. The Elions. I believe they are not only where we need to go, but our only option for where we *could* go."

Nonch nodded. "We must flee now. On our way, we will pass through the Crynit…" He hesitated uncharacteristically. "…city. I will get Broodmother to help us, to send warriors with us through our underground tunnels."

"And let us not forget," Nonch continued, "there are *two* Battle-groups converging on Nem'. The 301st has not yet arrived. We must find safety and plan, or we will be forever reacting to circumstance. Children of chaos."

"What about Raystar?" Mieant asked Nonch. "I thought Brood-mother did not like Humans?" I blinked and swallowed.

"It will be fine," Nonch replied, raising his sensor stalks.

"But…," Mieant persisted.

"It will be fine."

Cri continued to glare at me, but her anger was now spread among all of us: me, her boyfriend, Nonch, and common sense. She said, "Do we even *know* where Dad's escape route is?"

"This bunker," AI replied, "connects to a tunnel that leads to Blue River."

"Underground is safe. We will also have shelter from the Storm Wall," Nonch added.

Architect. I totally forgot about the Storm Wall. It was due any day now. The giant, kilometers-wide storm literally rolled from one side of the planet to the other every three weeks or so. Some thought it was an ancient Human Terra-forming project gone awry, especially because it started at the Mesas, plateaued mountains only a few kilometers away from our compound, and scraped around the planet to an identical set of Mesas on the other side.

There were many theories about the Storm Wall, but none had been proven. Galactic tech strangely began to malfunction as it moved closer to the Mesas, preventing any scientific study of them and thus of the Storm Wall. One thing was sure: we did not want to be caught in that storm. I wondered if even the Dreadnought could survive its wrath.

"We need to leave. *Now*." AI flashed a holovid image of what was going on outside in the middle of our semicircle. "I'm tapped into the farm's external cameras."

On the holovid, Mom and Dad were standing just outside the kitchen door. Mom's white cape drifted behind her, slowly revealing the two blasters strapped to her thighs. I knew her others were at her chest. Dad's sizable muscles were exaggerated by the battle armor, and his enormous blasters were proportional to his size. Mom and Dad's eyes glowed as they traded gazes, the light illuminating the contrast between their jet-black hair and blood-red skin. Mom's scar was a livid purple line down the right side of her face. Things were not good.

In the close-up image, Dad sighed and pulled his wife close with all four arms. They stood on our kitchen porch, underneath a sky darkened by the Dreadnought yet lit by thousands of blue-white stars— the invasion fleet's ships.

A minute passed. Mom tilted her face up to his. Her upper two hands on his cheeks, she gently pulled him closer for a kiss.

Another minute, a hiatus, passed while their lips touched. I felt like an intruder in their private sanctuary. But seeing their love for each other…gave me resolve. And tore at me.

This was all my fault. My stupid purple hair, my stupid purple eyes. The stupid DNA in my body.

Their choices made, hand in hand, Mom and Dad turned, walked off the porch, across our courtyard, and toward our compound's exit. Dust swirled up with each footfall as they strode away from our home.

The view panned back as a different vid feed activated in order to closely track my parents. The new angle revealed Chunks, our herd leader. He was nudging his much smaller herd mates into a rough cluster. While the rest of the compound's shields were tied to the farm's main power plant, the gratcher enclosure had its own smaller power generator. The faint yellow glow shimmered and then disappeared. I blinked. Chunks immediately whirled to face the perimeter leading out into 'natch fields. He tentatively placed his nose where the field used to be, expecting a shock.

"SQUEAAAA!" Chunks' deep rumble nearly blew out the speakers. With a shake of his massive head, he thundered toward the leafy shelter of the endless green field. As the last of his herd vanished into the dense foliage, Chunks stopped, spun around, and faced our house. In my heart, he was facing me. He dipped his giant head, pawed the ground, and then turned to follow his tribe into the greenery of our history together.

Thanks, I thought to AI. He'd done what I'd asked earlier, when we were in the kitchen: he'd set our gratcher herd free. I couldn't bear to see our gratchers trapped, especially after Chunks had saved us—and had somehow become a friend to me. Who knows how the invading Convergence force might have entertained themselves with our innocent beasts?

AI flashed green, acknowledging my gratitude.

As the gratchers escaped, a smaller ship, perhaps a kilometer long, was landing lengthwise approximately half a kilometer from the farm's entrance. It wasn't as large as many of the landing ships, but it easily dwarfed our compound.

I realized that my sense of scale was off on an epic level. *About everything.* Dad once told me, "There is no absolute standard of magnitude." Everything is dwarfed by something LARGER. The Convergence, the galaxy, you name it. "IT," the universal "IT," kept revealing itself to me as WAY bigger than *anything* I could imagine.

Then a new image flashed from the ship, one of Godwill striding down a landing ramp. His black robes billowed, showing their red interior as wind curled them in his wake. AI zoomed in, and we watched as Godwill marched within two hundred and fifty meters of our farm. He stopped, widened his stance, and folded his hands behind his back. His head was tilted back slightly, and he seemed to look directly into the camera—which meant he was looking directly at us. His lips peeled back first into a gummy grimace and then a wicked smile. Or perhaps he was practicing opening his mouth wide enough to consume us.

And then he waved. Toyed with us. Mocked our vain attempts to escape or anticipate him.

"Let's go!" AI shouted.

"We don't," I snapped at AI, "leave anyone behind. ESPECIALLY OUR PARENTS!" My eyes locked with Cri's as I recalled Mom's lesson to me. *Leave?* That was not an option.

"Ooops," AI said as he shut down the image.

"Turn it back on!" Cri shouted, pulling free of Mieant.

"I have a bad connection," he said blandly, pivoting in the air toward my sister. His glow shifted from yellow to red.

"You ingot!" Cri screamed. "I'll…."

"You'll do *exactly* what I say." AI's tone was Galactic steel. He glowed red, and I could feel the heat emanating from him warping the air. "Your parents are about to give themselves up so you can escape. Do not squander their trade and waste their lives."

Control your sister! AI said to me. *We're nova'd if we don't leave now.*

I'm not leaving them either!

"Nonch! Mieant!" AI shouted, lighting up the basement with pulses of red. He was furious. Mieant blinked and grabbed Cri. Nonch snaked toward me, wrapped his claw arms around my body, and lifted me off the ground. We both struggled against our captors' grips.

"Follow me," AI commanded my friends as he dimmed to yellow. "I'll turn the feed on. You two need to chill." Cri struggled in Mieant's grasp, her black hair a mop that cascaded around her face, framing golden eyes that blazed between the strands. I was completely incapacitated by Nonch's grip.

"We have to hit the armory before we leave." AI then projected the vid feed in front of us as he led us deeper into the labyrinth of our underground bunker.

He flew down a corridor, turning on the holo in midflight. My sister and I watched, each of us immobilized by our friends as they stumbled to catch up with AI.

The scene outside had changed. Mom and Dad now stood at the edge of our compound.

"Why are they standing there?" Nonch asked.

"The end of your compound is the end of Glean territory, I think," Mieant gasped, struggling under Cri's weight. "The War Treaty says that the Convergence cannot come on Glean soil. Your mother is Ascendant, and she has claimed this compound's land as part of the Glean Gathering's sovereign territory."

"Focus! Kids, grab what you need," AI boomed to Mieant and Nonch as we reached the armory. He signaled to my sister and me and, with intensity, warned, "Behave yourselves. I will get the restraints, and I will drag you both to Blue River if I have to. And after we kick everyone else's butt, I will shove you both into the galaxy's great gravity well for being a pain in my virtual butt. Now…MOVE!"

I mean. Sure. Uh, arming myself for the journey seemed pretty okay. Or like, it sucked not so much, at least. Right? I grabbed some weapons enthusiastically.

Nonch hadn't wasted a moment following AI's invitation. He'd thrummed to the shelves and started attaching blades, weapons, and various odd devices to their respective places on his body armor. Mieant found a suit of combat armor and then occupied himself with collecting all the things that fit on it, as well as larger, deadlier weapons whose weight he seemed perfectly capable of carrying.

Six plasma grenades seemed about right for my combat load. I was still a little shaken by AI's motivational speech, but I dimly remembered that two grenades of my set were fatter than the other four. Were they painted with a different symbol? AI projected a new scene from the surface, a panorama of the Dreadnought and the thousands of ships in the invasion fleet swarming like firefly wasps. Completely distracted, I anchored the odd-sized grenades to my armor. *Focus!* I fastened three more on the other side of my armor.

Balance. Dad had taught me its importance in combat, especially when you're in a running battle. Because you know, in a running battle one has to always consider...*what?* Running battles happen more than one might expect. Well, they happen to me.

I shoved a first-aid kit into a pocket of the armor and then searched for extra ammo for the blaster Mom had given me. *Huh. My blaster doesn't use ammo?* It was smaller and uniquely designed to fit a Human hand. I looked it over carefully: "Full Charge," it said. *Um. So, it uses energy? A battery?* I hunted around for batteries that seemed to fit it and came up with nothing. There was no time to figure it out.

AI's projection of images of the invasion fleet continued, and suddenly Mom and Dad appeared. And Godwill! They glared at each other with deep hatred.

Mom? Dad? What the nova are you waiting for? SHOOT HIM.

In my mind, in my alternate multiverse, I imagined the scene unfolding as such:

> Mom and Dad pulled out their combined eight plasma blasters and...BLAM! BLAM, BLAM, BLAM, BLAM, BLAM, BLAM! KABLAAM!! Godwill was obliterated.
>
> Dad grabbed Mom and smashed his mouth against hers. She wrapped her arms around him (and probably a leg as well) and crushed him to her. With their combined eight arms, they were like an octopus of affection. I barfed. Cri also barfed. It was how they were—crushing enemies made Mom and Dad *goofy.* That was the word for it, right?
>
> Post-octopus, they simultaneously but cinematically turned their gaze to Mom's big jerkhead of a brother, the Heir. In this multiverse, he was jealous of their love, and furious that no one cared enough

to engage in over-the-top PDA with him. Embarrassed by his voyeurism, jealousy, and feelings of complete inadequacy, he drew his four plasma pistols with deathly intent.

Sathra, the true Heir to the Glean Gathering, and Nent, the Glean war hero, the Commander, were always faster than evil. More BLAMMING! ensued, and then more octopus-ing.

The four of us proceeded home afterward, a family once again. Mom, her hair disheveled from all of their whatever, whipped up some dinner. It tasted good, but we had to pick chunks of charred bad guy out of it as we ate. And then? After a full belly, I finally got back to the real injustice: how spiked and nova-awful my summer vacation had been! All I'd done was work on the farm. The 'natch farm.

I HATE 'NATCH!

None of that really happened. Way above the three of them, above our compound, in the sky above Godwill's stupid ship, floated the nova-cursed Dreadnought. *Thousands* of ships, intent on the subjugation of Nem', swarmed between where we stood and the Dreadnought. Most of the ships were heading toward Blue River. More than enough were landing around Godwill's ship.

"Time's up!" AI yelled, and he flashed out of the armory and down the corridor. Since he was projecting vids of what was happening outside, we all hurried along to follow him. We finally caught up to him at the entrance to the waste recycler.

The vid showed a second figure striding down the ramp to stand beside Godwill.

"Oh!" Cri gasped. I looked at her and then back at the image. It was a Glean, easily half a meter taller than Godwill. Half a meter taller than Dad, even. His white cape flowed in the soft breeze. *Who was that?*

"Spike me!" AI said, shutting the image down. "We go now!" The door to the waste recycler opened. The smell that wafted out was horrible, a bouquet of waste, of decay. "In! In! In! Go straight to the back and push at the wall. The metal will give! Gogogogogo!"

Nonch raced through the waste, holding his sensor stalks high to avoid contact with, uh…everything…and shoved the back of the metal container wall open with his four remaining blade arms. Mieant, followed by Cri, covered his face against the stench and ran after him.

Go! AI urged me.

Put the picture back on. I want to see.

Ray. You saw what you saw. We need to go.

What did I see? Who was that?

Move! I started forward, toward where Nonch was holding the walls apart.

Tell me, now! What's going to happen to Mom and Dad? Who was that?

I pushed my way through the metal as Nonch held it apart. He snaked his body through and then released the same Galactic alloy AI had ripped through six days before.

Ray, that was your uncle. The Heir.

We poured out into a tunnel that smelled of old paper and honey. And poo. Lots of poo. Our olfactory senses were being overwhelmed, over SMELLED. Because, you know. We'd just walked through poo. My parents' dilemma was shoved aside in my frontal lobe by the stench.

Dad must have recently cleaned out the recycler. Even so, brown sludge was most definitely coating our shoes. Cri gagged and doubled over. Mieant, good boyfriend that he was, held back her hair as she emptied her stomach on the dusty floor. Only a second later, he doubled over, too. I didn't have anyone to hold my hair back. Their discomfort wasn't altogether that bad to watch.

What? Is that petty?

I turned to Nonch to ask him what he smelled. These were Crynit tunnels, and Crynits communicated via pheromones. His experience had to be much more intense than what my senses were feeding me. My mouth was just about to open as he decided to shake the "stuff" off his feet. He vibrated all along his three-meter length, flicking poo everywhere. I spun away, but too late—droplets of it spattered across my face and neck.

"NONCH!" I shouted, my hands spread in the air. We all shouted, except for Cri and Mieant. They were still retching, but now dry heaving their revulsion. "NONCH...Nonch...Nonch...." my cries echoed into the pitch black of the tunnel's abyss.

"Quiet!" AI hissed as he hovered a little beyond us in the tunnel. He spun his diamond shape so the longest point aimed forward, into the darkness. I listened, stared hard into the wall of darkness. I didn't hear anything.

He flashed yellow once and then illuminated our tunnel in a clear white light. I raised my shoulders and wiped my cheek on my shirt.

"Yeccch!" Cri gagged, shaking her feet and flinging clumps of the mixture stuck in her boots' treads.

"Cri!" Mieant said, hopping away from her, scowling as he shook off droplets she'd inadvertently flicked on his pants.

She looked at him and then back at her boots. "It smells disgusting."

"It's all over my shoes, too," he replied.

"So, *you* want to walk around with it on your boots?"

He looked at her, his matte-black eyes wide, and said, "We are fleeing an invasion force?"

She huffed, more to herself than anyone else, a response: "Well, I don't want to smell while I flee." Her words created more echoes. "Flee…flee…."

AI's glow made it easy to see our surroundings for about eight meters in each direction before the distance succumbed to utter blackness. *Nova.* This tunnel was clearly not made by Gleans or Lethians. And it was huge. *What was this place?*

We had emerged from the recycler through a door that had to have been around for countless years. The tunnel we now found ourselves in was at least ten meters wide where we had entered and vaulted above us another ten meters high. I ran my finger along the closest wall by the door we'd entered. *Huh.* My fingertips came away dry but with a residue. I poked the wall. It was firm but gave slightly, kind of like wax.

Mysteries continued to pile up. I could buy that there was a network of underground tunnels. It was rumored that Nem's ancient Human cities were actually underground. But to think that I'd lived above these tunnels for my whole life…and to think that there was even an actual DOOR leading to them from our basement? *I mean, bunker.*

Nothing was as it seemed. What did I know that was actually true? I reconsidered the yellow-brown tunnel. Every three or so meters, the walls appeared to be ribbed, as if the substance that lined it had been secreted. *This couldn't have been made by Humans,* I thought. It looked like we were inside a giant snake. Something alive, organic, sentient had made—*secreted*—these walls.

"This tunnel is from before Broodmother," Nonch whispered to himself. His armored head peered down the length of the corridor and then followed the waxy ribs up to the points where they joined at the top.

"Do you know where we are?" AI asked Nonch, as if he expected Nonch to know. Nonch didn't reply, as he was otherwise occupied: he had curved his armored midnight-blue body against the wall and was licking the waxy material! He moved his mandibles as if he was savoring a flavor and then slouched down toward us. His claw arms left grooves in the dirt.

"So old," he muttered, "I can taste the years."

"Well, bowls of 'natch for you," Cri replied. Standing up, she wiped her mouth with her sleeve. Her hair was a tangle around her face. She turned from Nonch to AI. "Put on the feed. I want to see my parents."

"Hush," AI whispered.

"Put it on!" She lunged at him, shouting, "I want to see Mom and Dad!" AI zigged out of her reach; Mieant grabbed two of her arms and pulled her back to him.

"Cri!" Mieant said, "Stop!"

"*Everyone!* Shut up," AI implored. He'd pivoted toward Nonch and eased himself between the Crynit and me.

Cri shrugged Mieant off, raised her four hands, and dipped her head at an angle—the universal "I'm cool, get the nova off me" sign.

AI ignored us all as he tentatively floated through the air toward Nonch, who was still chewing the wax. He had, however, turned his head toward me. I took a reflexive step backward, away from my friend.

AI spun around to face Cri, Mieant, and me. "Seriously, you kids need to whisper."

"Hatred," Nonch said firmly, his voice echoing through the black tunnels. "Pain. Death. Cries for help."

AI rotated to face Nonch squarely at eye level. We'd all gone silent as we considered our nearly three-meter-long armored friend, who was, after all, an apex predator. My eyes were glued to him. I heard a faint giggle: I couldn't be sure, but it sounded like Cri. The furrow in my brow deepened. Did Cri think this was funny?

Focus. "Shells? What do you mean?" I said, taking a step toward him. AI moved between us, his glow shifting to yellow.

Nonch's feather stalks rose. A shiver ran through his body, and perhaps it was my imagination, but it seemed like he had spread out his four arm blades, just as Sarla had done during our recent battle. I froze.

"There are messages in these tunnels," he continued, as if in a trance. "Reinforcements never came. They killed my fellow Crynits by the millions." His body rippled with a shiver. "Without mercy, they slaughtered us."

Mieant stepped toward Nonch. Mieant's black eyes carefully studied Nonch's luminescent ones. "These are Crynit tunnels," he whispered to himself, thinking furiously. "They are from before…the War? *Nonch?*"

But Nonch was focused on me. I took a reflexive step backward.

"Nonch," Mieant said again, placing a hand on our friend's mandibles. "How old are these tunnels?" Cri had crept up beside her boyfriend and had placed two of her hands on his shoulder. She paused there, eyes wide, as she forgot everything, even our parents, in the strangeness of Nonch's words.

"That's not the right question," AI interrupted, again moving to separate Nonch and me. He pointed at Nonch and continued, "A better question is: *Who slaughtered the Crynits?*"

My friend drew his body up, his blade arms opening for combat. His multifaceted orange eyes reflected AI's glow. I heard him suck in a breath.

Slowly, Nonch breathed out a response: "Humans."

10

Nonch rose until he loomed meters above me. He seemed poised to attack...*me*. Cri giggled.

Completely inappropriate, Cri. Has everyone gone insane? I thought.

As Nonch loomed over me, a part of my brain distractedly wondered how the great gravity well unlucky I had to be. I'd held off death by nanoinjection (well, I hadn't escaped that yet), Godwill's prison camp, and a Convergence Dreadnought, just to enter an ancient Crynit tunnel filled with hate memories from the Lethian–Human War that were now compelling my best friend to attack me.

I was hungry and exhausted. The main consequence of the nanosolvent flooding my veins was the fatigue—bone-deep fatigue—that had depleted my capacity for willpower and perseverance. In addition to not having showered for at least three days, I smelled, quite literally, like crap. Frankly, it was a challenge to distinguish any smells in this stinky mélange. *Heh.*

"Nonch," I raised my hands with the palms out. Adrenaline pulsed through me. Mieant wrapped his arms around Cri and pulled her away as AI's light changed from yellow to orange. The air around him heated as he hovered between me and my other best friend.

"Crynit," AI said, so loudly his voice echoed into the depths of the tunnels. I felt exposed as "Crynit, Crynit, Crynit" repeated and faded into the distance of the tunnel.

"These times are not those times," AI continued, "and thousands of years have passed. *THINK!* Those deaths are far away in your history. Your kind and the Humans have *never* been natural enemies!"

Nonch trembled. His self-control was a live wire that tugged his muscles one way and then another.

What's happening, AI? Thank the Architect I could communicate with him silently.

These tunnels are made of a wax-like secretion Crynits use to build their hives. They build and bore, just like Terran insects. But they embed their thoughts, history, and messages in the material using traces of chemicals. These ancient tunnels have a pheromone history, a patchwork of memories. Humans and Crynits were enemies at the time these tunnels were built. Think about it, Ray. These tunnels were built during a time of death and pain. Crynits were part of the Nem' invasion force. Humans killed millions and millions of them. Right. Here.

Nova and gravity wells. Why couldn't we have escaped into tunnels that had been created for a garden walk or a birthday party?

AI continued: *What is happening, right now, is that Nonch is trying hard to NOT kill you. So calm down.*

Unbidden, my hand hovered over my blaster. "Calm" was not happening.

Nonch flared his sword arms and leaned slowly, minutely in my direction. I had no doubt, as I stood within range of his arms, that his reflexes were faster than mine.

Was I really going to shoot him? After all we'd been through? I couldn't change the behavior of others, but I was certainly responsible for my own actions. I would live the way I wanted, regardless of anyone else. I did not want this. Everything is easy to say, to think, in moments of calm. It's a lot harder when you're facing the tip of the spear.

Sighing, I lowered my hands to my sides. I wasn't going to pull a blaster on Shells.

"Hey," I said. "It's me. Raystar," I sucked in a breath and continued, "your best friend."

Cri giggled again, louder than before. I ground my teeth.

What is wrong with that girl?

Nonch opened his mandibles and leaned toward me, his sensor stalks bridging the distance between us and touching either side of my head. I smelled rain; I smelled his salt; I smelled his tears.

"Raystar-Friend," Nonch said, turning his head downward. "THESE. ARE. NOT. Those. Times," he continued, struggling to articulate his message as much to us as to himself. "The anger of the ancients is overwhelming."

Nonch sucked in a deep breath. I squinted at him. *How much do I really know about him? About Crynits in general?*

AI sighed, clearly relieved by something different in Nonch's tone. His light changed back to white. Nonch's sensor stalks surrounded my head.

"Apologies for my not-control, Raystar. Friend-Mine." He moved his sensor stalks away from my head and turned in the direction of Mieant and Cri. "Ally," he said to Mieant, and then looked at Cri. "Sister-of-Raystar, I apologize. I am now in full control of me. I think."

"Yeah, okay," AI sighed. "So, Nonch," he casually questioned, "where the nova are we?"

Cri giggled again. I frowned and looked at her. She looked at me, her expression a silent, annoyed, *What?*

Nonch looked around and then back to us. "I do not know. Broodmother's Rangers have not explored these tunnels. They are new."

"Oy," AI breathed. "I must have been a complete idiot in my last life to end up here in this life."

"Sir," Mieant said, deferentially, "being, ah, digital, are you able to identify which way Blue River is?"

AI spun like a needle, his longest tip pointing in one direction—the very, very dark direction.

Mieant continued, "So we go that way?" He looked at each of us.

"Pretty sure," AI said.

What?? "Pretty sure?" I exclaimed.

"I recommend that we proceed with our weapons out," Nonch added, pulling various devices from his combat armor.

AI started drifting down the chosen direction of deeper darkness. We slowly followed, if only to stay in his light.

"Are you okay?" I heard Mieant whisper to Cri.

"Fine," Cri said, peering into the blackness and shivering as she reached a lower arm around his waist to pull him closer. She paused and added, "No. Actually, I'm not okay at all."

Their weapons and armor bumped against each other as they hugged. Cri pulled Mom's blaster from its holster. Mieant disengaged from the embrace and reached over his back to pull a long, slender blade from its scabbard along his back. He drew a pistol from his thigh holster as well. The energy weapons whined as they powered up, like dangerous toys.

I heard another giggle, a child's laugh, rolling, bubbly, cherubic. The type that you get when a little kid gurgles and smiles with an illegally cute grin. I was about to get even annoyed with Cri when I suddenly realized that the rolling giggles were coming from behind me, rather than where she advanced in front of me. We all exchanged heavy glances.

The childish burbles shifted into ululating screams that echoed through the tunnels. Another "child" laughed in front of us and then behind us. We backed into one another, searching the darkness for the sources.

AI's light projected only so far before fading into blackness none of our eyes could penetrate. It occurred to me how very visible we must be.

The laughter of children now chorused from everywhere: some were high-pitched and others were *basso profundo*. AI, our sole light source, floated a half-meter above our heads in the circle we created with our bodies, protecting ourselves, back-to-back.

"What the nova?" Mieant whispered.

"Yeah. Totally yeah," AI whispered loudly back. "I, uh, think these tunnels are filled with leggers. They can imitate the noises of their

last kill." AI had never been timid or unsure before. "I AM sure that no one on the surface understands how many there are down here."

AI's words chilled me. *They imitate their prey?* I gulped. My blaster had small leather straps that wrapped around my wrist. I rewrapped the straps around my wrists and thumbed what I figured had to be the on switch. The blaster hummed to life, and a red sighting dot danced on the ground in front of the barrel.

"So, my friends," AI announced. We looked up at him. "It may be a bad time for this, but I have a confession."

In the deepening black hole to our right, another something giggled hysterically. Much closer.

"I've never been here before."

11

"WHAT?"

"Children" giggled from all directions in response to my shout. I'd never seen a legger up close, and now I was trapped with them in a flipping ancient Crynit tunnel literally built out of hate memories that had filled my best friend with the urge to kill me. No way did I think my life would ever take an ugly detour like this.

"Um," AI explained, "I initiated contact with the house synth after Raystar flushed me. I found this exit, but…I didn't use it." My jaw fell. Dad had made us dig through mounds of horrible biological waste to find him.

"But. You…you'd dug your way through the tunnels to get to us?"

"So… about that," dark laughter echoed from the ceiling. AI's light morphed from clear white to a sickly green. "I didn't come this way."

"Oh, for Architect's sake," Mieant muttered. He would have rolled his eyes if only they'd had pupils. Something just out of sight scraped against the walls

"Allies Mine. This direction," Nonch said, pointing at the darkness where most of the giggles had originated, "should intersect with the underground Human roadways, which should in turn lead us to the living part of Broodmother's nest."

"Don't you dare leave me, Mieant," I heard Cri whisper to Mieant.

"My gravity, never," he whispered back.

She pulled him close and pressed her lips against his. No one was *my* gravity. I wanted to throw up. Aside from Mom and Dad, I had never been anyone else's gravity. Okay, maybe I'd been AI's, but he was a piece of code. His arms couldn't envelop me. There was nothing warm about him except the heat he emitted when he was mad.

What the nova am I thinking about? AI was software first and friend second. Could something written with zeroes and ones even *be* a friend? My chest filled with pressure, anger, and feelings of abandonment, all threatening to burst through my wall of self-control.

My now-very-empty stomach growled. Blaster in hand, I scratched a tickle under my nose with my sleeve and to my surprise, the mudsullied material came away red. A nosebleed...a precursor to yet another "uncontrolled" episode. Back on the farm, when these happened, they were caused either by the Storm Wall or something really stressing me out. The blood on my sleeve popped and sparkled.

NO. Control, Ray! Even if I didn't kill everyone around me, given how hungry I was, I'd probably consume myself in the process. I clenched my jaw and looked ahead into the darkness. *I'm up the gravity well, alone. Nothing new there: welcome to the future.*

You're not alone, Ray. Not even close. You have no idea how many others care about you—starting with me. We will get through this, AI reassured me. My best friend was floating half a meter away, at my eye level. He'd been with me through my victories and my losses. He knew everything about me. I thought I knew a lot about him, but lately, I'd become painfully aware of just how little I knew at all, particularly about AI. Whether he was software or not, when I was with him, I felt less alone.

I shook my head against my own bitterness, my purple bangs reorienting themselves across my forehead. *You can feel sorry for yourself later,* I admonished myself, *right now, let's focus on where we are instead of what I don't have.*

The giggles had stopped, and the silence was oppressive. *What lives in that darkness?* My blaster felt reassuring in my right hand while my left stroked the plasma grenades on my belt. Their guarantee of mayhem was initially comforting, but then I realized that I was carrying all the grenades. *In a fight, that won't do at all.* I waved Mieant over and plucked one of the orbs from my belt.

"When you need to use this, hold this bar and pull the pin," I said, presenting the oval device to him. "You have five seconds to throw it after the pin comes out. Attach it to your belt like so," I gestured vaguely at the remaining grenades studding my own belt.

"Is it safe?" he looked at me and then at the grenade.

Nonplussed, I shot him a flat gaze and cocked my hip. "Dude, it's a bomb."

"I mean," he said before pausing and changing his grasp on the grenade like it had suddenly become scorching hot. "Um, Ray...."

"Mieant," I interrupted, carefully curling his fingers around the device and shoving his hand against his chest armor, "when you need it, pull the pin, count, and throw. If you are too close to the detonation, you die. It's easy, 'Gravity Boy.'" I smiled and patted his cheek. "And if you're going to be a mushy idiot and ignore the darkness around us, do it where something can get you first so I at least have a chance to run. It. Is. A. Bomb. No, definitely *not* safe."

Right? I was proud that I'd set my bitterness aside like a champ.

I tossed a second grenade from my belt to Cri and casually pulled a third from my belt. Mom and Dad had given Cri and me the same training, so instructions weren't needed. With familiar confidence born of our training, she snatched it in mid arc with a lower hand.

"Don't talk to him like that," she said, grabbing my shoulder between the thumb and forefinger of her upper-right hand as I passed.

"Spike you, Cri!"

I twisted against her pinch to get clear, but her other upper hand wrapped around the back of my neck. Gently, but unrelenting, she pulled her face close to mine, her golden eyes flashing against her red skin.

I sucked in a breath, blinking against the intense glow. Given the nanosolvent inside me, working to destroy me, and my last meal be-

ing the rations Dad had given us, I was physically weak. At the same time, my sanity was fraying, and I could feel blood drip onto my upper lip as resentment threatened to overflow its emotional cauldron.

"This is your fault. All. Your. Fault." She released me with a shove. I stumbled a few steps back and looked back at her, my eyes burning. I loved Cri, my big sister. *Why are we fighting?* I thought. *How was she jealous of me? And how could I have missed that?* I was Human—weaker, smaller. I didn't have four arms...*how could anyone be jealous of me, much less Cri?*

"Friend," Nonch said, interrupting my reverie, "I have studied grenades. In hindsight, I regret not taking many more so we would have a larger supply than only what you carry." I blinked and used my bloody sleeve to smear away the wetness from my eyes.

That'd be a great mascara brand: Blood and Tears, I thought. *Who would the model be? Probably a Glean—they had craxy long lashes.*

Nova. I turned to face my friend. Nonch was reshuffling various weapons and their positions on his armor. His blade arms all moved independently, each a blur. Crynits, with their multiple blade arms and several different mini-brains—neural clusters that controlled different parts of their body—were the galaxy's best multitaskers. His arms all occupied, he leaned down and plucked up the grenade I'd been holding with his mouth. *Show off.*

"You don't hold it like *that*," I admonished, rolling my eyes. Despite his fearsome looks, he was a goof.

Nonch pulled the grenade from his mouth with a newly freed blade arm and affixed it to his armor in a single fluid motion. Then he dipped his mandible-armed head slightly, as a performer would at the end of an act. I had to smile.

The small band around the center of the grenade's middle suddenly began to flash yellow, then red, freezing my grin in terror. I frantically looked first at the flashing grenade and then back at Nonch's face, where I spotted a small piece of metal hanging by one of his fangs. The. Pin.

NOVA!

I snatched the grenade from his armor, sprinted ten steps in the opposite direction, to the edge of AI's light, all within three heart-beats. The grenade's flashing band strobed so quickly as to be almost continuous. Death was milliseconds away. I spun to gain momentum, jumped, and hurled the flashing orb into the blackness.

My running jump landed me in a pool of darker blackness. In the near distance, the grenade impacted on something—a fleshy thump—before falling to the ground with a clink. The cacophony of giggles erupted and then transformed into high-pitched screams and deep roars. The shuffling that followed was similar to the noise Chunks and the herd made as they were packed into our corral— hide-to-hide, their tough sides scraping against each other like rough cloth or sandpaper. This sound was the same, but thicker, raspier. The goosebumps that crawled all over my body were silent. I clamped my hands over my mouth to stifle the scream I knew was coming.

Shuffling sounds rose to a crescendo around me. The giggling was in-my-ear loud, but now in three dimensions, including *right above me.*

I realized I'd never seen a legger up close. The plasma grenade changed that.

12

A single second passed, in what seemed like an eternity. The grenade flashed, right in front of me, revealing brown and green bristles, tightly packed on jointed poles covered in carpet. Each pole was thicker than my two legs pressed together, and together, the poles formed a hairy wall. But they weren't poles, and that was no wall. They were massive legs crammed together in the confines of the tunnel.

My gaze followed the legs upward. Mouths, concentric circles lined with hundreds of teeth, led into pink, wet gullets. Each mouth vibrated like jelly with each scream. Mucus spurted from their mouths with every phlegm-filled exhalation. Multi-meter-long tentacles, two on each side of every mouth, thrashed maniacally toward me. Six pus-yellow eyes in each cluster sat above the flailing tentacles and leech-like mouths.

"Leggers!" I screamed, without any restraint or hope for salvation.

The eternity passed, and the second ended. Somehow in my panic I'd managed (for once) to end up facing the right direction. I sprinted closer to where my friends stood. The blast of light came first, casting long shadows that made the leggers AND my friends look like figures in a black-and-white cartoon. A grotesque and conflicting collage of fear and blood lust held in my mind before the superheated plasma ball incinerated the leggers from ground zero. Bristly fur curled and charred as an inferno flared outward from the grenade blast and caught up with the leggers chasing me.

61

Then the shockwave hit.

Chunks of legger flew everywhere around us. A flaming leg, easily as long as I was tall, hit the ceiling and then bounced off Nonch's armor. Something hot and moist stuck to the back of my head. I frantically batted it away like a spider had just landed on me—I didn't want to know what the sticky thing was. Squishy legger parts slapped wetly against the tunnel floor and our bodies as they rained down from the walls and ceiling.

The shockwave tossed everyone, even Nonch, several meters down the tunnel. And then there was silence.

You okay? AI queried.

I wiggled my fingers, then my toes.

Yeah, I thought back to my friend once I was finished retching. *Extremities are all present and accounted for!* Grateful, I sucked in a breath of vomitous, burnt-meat-and-fur air.

Too close, Ray.

I heard Cri groan. The blast had dazed me, but my slowly returning awareness flicked on the switches in my brain. A feeling of warmth against my cheek grew increasingly intense, and then it wasn't just warmth I felt. I felt the weight of something bristly, like a scrubbing brush, leaning against my face.

Confused, I dared to open my eyes. Horrible yellow legger eyes greeted my gaze, spasming independently of each other. Ropy mouth tentacles draped across my chest, and a flabby tongue from the pink, toothy mouth rolled over my waist and legs. *Screaming Galactic apocalypse!* I bucked and tried to squirm out from under it, tangling myself in the mucus-covered tentacles.

"Yeeeee! SPIKE ME!" I twisted around and finally got my feet under me. The legger's head thumped and slurped after me as I hopped and flailed around in hopes of disentangling myself from its tentacles. Mucus strands stretched from my hand as I plucked away the last sticky rope encircling my arm. The severed head didn't enjoy the ride any better than I did; once freed, it rolled across the floor and finally came to rest in an oozing pile some meters away.

Well, your lungs work, at least, AI said with a chuckle. The laughter sounded good. This apocalypse of carnage could only be handled in the release of insanity by laughing at it, by defying it.

I glared at him without true malice. I was okay. *We'd just detonated a nova-cursed plasma grenade, but I was okay!* If I had to choose between immolation or getting covered in slime, I figured, bring on the mucus! My perspective solidly shifted, and my glare turned into a grin. Because great gravity wells—we'd not only survived, but we'd also blown the nova out of our attackers!

I flicked slime from my hand and turned my palm upward. AI landed on it gently, and a small chain slid out of a compartment at one of the points on his diamond. I wiped my other hand on my combat armor and lifted the chain over my head so he could return to his usual place, resting over my heart. It's where I'd always had him, my whole life. He flashed green and flooded me with familiar warmth.

AI, I began, *you feel....*

"*Ruined!*" my sister shouted, stomping her booted foot for emphasis, as she stood and faced off against Mieant.

"No!" Mieant replied, resting his hands on her shoulders, "My moon, do not ..."

"I *hate* this! This whole nova-cursed, stupid..." she yelled, clenching all four fists, "...everything! Our situation is so spiking unstarred and nova'd beyond the worst of the worst!"

"Cri!" he implored, moving toward her, but her eyes glowed as she shoved him away. Gleans are strong: Mieant stumbled and windmilled away before regaining his balance. She pulled a long knife from its scabbard at her waist. She was a sight to behold: glowing eyes, red skin, jet black hair, tattoos, combat armor, and now a drawn knife. Confused, he took a step back.

"Cri?" I took a step toward her with my hands out, in a placating maneuver.

"YOU!" she screamed, focusing her blazing ire on me. Our parents' training included considerable hand-to-hand weapon training for reasons that were only now becoming clear to me, and Cri had always been a quick study. In a single fluid movement, like water over rocks, she whirled the long blade around in her hand and placed it at the back of her neck.

"CRI!" Mieant shouted, stepping toward her once again. She warned him back with a single raised hand, her fingers spread wide. With another hand, she wrapped her nearly meter-long hair into a thick, black rope. I heard the blade cut through it with an audible "snick."

"Your fault, Raystar!" She whirled the wet hair-rope around and flung it at me. Her aim was good, and it thwacked into my chest. I blinked at my sister's hair, now stuck to my armor by legger mucus; the stench was gut-wrenching. A wet, sucking sound later, it slid off my armor and down my leg, ending up in a tangle on my boot.

"Why?" I said, looking at her, holding my arms out, palms up. "What the nova?"

She stomped to the other side of the tunnel and, with her back to the wall, slid into to a ball with her arms around her knees.

Cri's lost it, AI said. She most definitely had. I released the breath I'd been holding in and looked to Mieant for an explanation.

He shrugged. "Legger blood and gunk. No way to take a shower. All this," he waved his hands around as he spoke, "and the smell was driving her craxy. It was too much." He walked over to Cri and took a seat beside her. He leaned his head sideways, setting it onto her shoulder.

Right. Well, they were physically okay, at least.

Which just left Nonch. I blinked and began to hunt for him. If he had been knocked unconscious, Cri's yelling should have awakened him. The smell of the legger viscera should have done the same, but given how sharp his senses were, maybe *that* had knocked him out.

Figuring Nonch wouldn't have been thrown as far as we had, I walked toward the blast zone, which was illuminated by AI. Giant legger bodies lay strewn around like boulders. The carnage was so thick in some areas that I had to climb over several bristly, squishy carcasses.

I heard an intermittent scratching sound and began to follow it. As I cleared a particularly massive legger abdomen, I saw Nonch, hidden away in the shadows. He was curled into a ball, but not as tightly as he

normally would when sleeping. He looked, well, larger than normal. If I didn't know better....

"Nonch?" I called. I jumped down from the small legger mountain, my heart thumping.

Nonch uncurled slightly and raised his head, his feathery sensor stalks extending outward. I paused at his sudden movement. We'd had a few odd moments peppered with some aggression, and I wanted to make sure I was moving toward "Nonch-my-best-friend" versus "Nonch-the-apex-predator."

"I will join you in a moment, Raystar-Friend," he said. "First...I...must rest."

I frowned. "Are you okay?"

"I am well, Raystar. I have not been this good in many days. Few things compare to a full stomach."

I frowned.

Ray, uh, I may have forgotten to tell you, AI said.

What? Tell me what, for Architect's sake?!

Crynits eat leggers. Leggers are their prey.

Oh. *Ohhhh.*

I was about to throw up. I saw that, indeed, some of the legger bodies had been, well, *chewed on.* And of course, Crynits were huge. What did I *think* they ate? Well, predatory 900-kilo leggers, apparently.

"Uh, okay, Nonch," I said, backing away, "Yeah. Uh, I'll call you when we're ready to go. We should meet in ten minutes."

I looked down, noticed another half-devoured carcass, and amended my offer: "How about twenty?"

"That is fine, Raystar. I shall join you in twenty minutes," Nonch said, and with that, he curled into an engorged ball and went to sleep.

With haste, I navigated the pile of legger carcasses back to the clearing where Cri had chucked her hair at me. I then walked a meter further to where the ancient tunnel dust remained undisturbed and sat down with my back to the waxy wall. I pulled a tin of food out and, despite the stench of scorched legger, tucked into it.

Inside me, Godwill's nanoinjection and my own nano were waging a battle, and I was losing. I could feel it; my energy was draining, bit by bit, as every moment went by. Since we'd escaped from Godwill's camp, I'd had no time to really think about the fact that I was going to die in three days. Shouldn't that be consuming my every thought? I didn't know. It seemed like I was always dealing with something more important that my own death. When would *that* become important? Three days: it was nothing in the grand scheme of things, but to me, it was everything.

AI glowed warm against my chest. His heat spread through my body, easing some of my aches. I held him to my heart, curled around his warmth, and lay down for a few minutes of sleep.

I had AI. I had a friend. That was enough, for the moment.

I didn't want to offend my friend, but I HAD to say something.

"Uh, you have something on your mouth," I said in a monotone.

Nonch's…meal…was visible to me. I sat right next to his curled form and opposite Mieant, with Cri across from me, so I was the only one who could see it. I flinched. It was a brown, hairy, moist globule—a leftover of his legger feast. He picked at it with a claw hand. He located it and flicked it to the far wall, where it stuck with a barely audible "pthit."

Nonch looked at me. "Is it no longer there?"

My eyes grew to the size of saucers at the unique grossness of what he had just done. I wasn't alone in witnessing him flick raw legger from his mandibles. Cri scuttled backward on her butt and averted her head.

"What?" Nonch asked us. He then pivoted to Mieant and added in a plaintive tone, "Lethian?"

Mieant scowled, "YES! For nova's sake, just…I don't know…just stay where you are."

Against my chest, AI was all warmth and mirth, but at Mieant's remark, Nonch's sensor stalks wilted, and the air filled with the smell of rain.

"I am offensive," Nonch said sadly. His sensor stalks dropped back behind his iridescent orange eyes, and he lowered his head. "Because of what I eat?"

Days ago in the school library, when Nonch had helped me research Godwill and the Foundationalist Movement to capture Humans with control DNA, he'd confided in me that he hated being a Crynit. He said that everyone thought his kind were killers, destroyers—*things* to be feared.

Nova and gravity wells. I knew what that was like. I knew what it felt like to be the alien, to be mocked for what made me different. Even now, I could feel the Galactic food I'd eaten sitting poorly with me, but there was no Human-friendly food anywhere to be found.

I sighed, rose to my feet, and walked over to a large and newly dead legger. I withdrew a small blade from my belt and thwacked off a tip of one of its ropy tentacles. I pulled out my blaster, turned it to the lowest setting, and gripped the trigger. *I could always use some practice,* I figured, *so why not try it on something that's already dead?*

The Human gun made a noise, and then I felt a surge go straight through me. *It was connecting with my nannites!* I quickly released the trigger, but not before blue light flared from the business end of the weapon, and the tentacle began to bubble and char.

The blaster's link to me remained—I could tell—but once I released the trigger, it became inactive. *Is it drawing power from me?* I holstered the Human weapon and considered my work. The legger meat resembled gratcher steak but smelled worse than 'natch. Shrugging, I walked over to Nonch, sat down, and took a bite.

"OH! FOR THE LOVE OF ALL THAT IS SACRED IN THIS STUPID GALAXY!" Cri shouted and then gagged. Mieant stopped scowling and simply stared at me. His matte-black eyes were almost the size of platters on his grey face.

Will I die? I asked AI while chewing the tentacle, which was somehow simultaneously burnt, stringy, and gelatinous. A yellow beam flickered out of AI as he scanned the crispy tentacle.

Hmm. AI paused a moment before continuing. *Craxy as this is, legger is good for you. It's right up there with 'natch, and unlike with Galactic food, you're not allergic to it. Who knew?*

That is just... My compatriots (other than Nonch, of course) stared at me with various degrees of revulsion.

I glanced down at the crisped tentacle and scowled. All this bickering was distracting. This wasn't school, where we had time to criticize each other and pay attention to whatever everyone else was doing. This was real life, a struggle for survival. School rules didn't apply anymore.

My scowl deepened. When *wasn't* life always full of life?

"You think strange food is the problem here?" I asked the others. My purple bangs dropped in front of my eyes, so I poofed them out of the way of my glare. I paused and then launched into a diatribe. "I mean, the known galaxy is falling apart as, what—a civil war in the Convergence is being unleashed. Leggers are coming after us. I'm going to die within days. Time doesn't care. It keeps moving. What, exactly, are we doing wasting the precious time we have bickering?"

Mieant blinked, Cri frowned, and Nonch raised his sensor stalks.

"None of us expected any of this," I said, tearing off a rubbery mouthful and waving the remaining tentacle vaguely at the Universe, the tunnel, and the others. I tried to meet their gazes, but their heads bobbled as they watched me shake the rubbery tentacle back and forth in my hand. I rolled my eyes and stuck the tentacle behind my back.

"Our parents," I moaned, "are they even alive? Are they prisoners? Our planet has been invaded. We have been lied to, kidnapped, tortured. And you know what? We. Survived. And not just that: we just blew the nova out of a legger pack."

"Look around you!" I swiped the tentacle in front of me, gesturing toward the havoc we'd wreaked only minutes before. "We are strong *together.*"

Our breaths filled the silence. Mieant shifted away from Cri just a little, and his expression turned thoughtful as he took it all in. *Was I getting through to them?*

"We have to agree on a plan, or we'll *literally* die." I said. "Cri, if your anger at me makes you take action, then get angrier. We need your power, not your pettiness." She eyed me darkly.

"Look. I want you to be my big sis.' I want you to not be mad at me. But clearly, I can't change your mind," I paused. "So instead, consider the fact that you're an Ascendant, in line for the Glean Gathering throne. What you do will define *your* place in the Recorders' history, not mine. Make your actions *count*."

Cri's mouth twisted as she planned a retort, but I took a quick step toward her boyfriend and continued.

"Mieant," I said, raising my voice. "You hated me when we first met. You were uprooted from your home on Solium4 because of your parents' desire to meet me—because they thought something was coming and that maybe I was part of the solution. It was craxy back then, but what about now? Can you deny that they were onto something? Because now? Your. Parents. Are. Gone."

I paused for a moment but then kept rolling. "Where are they now? Captured? Think about it. You are the son, the scion, of the Co-Governors! Until they are found, *you* are the key to rallying Solium4 Quadrant forces, to proving our shared innocence."

"Nonch!" I exclaimed, stepping toward my friend before Mieant could reply. It was important that I get this all out before I was interrupted. "Nonch, of Broodmother Krig. You're the most peaceful and introspective of us all. You don't like how the Convergence views Crynits. *You* can change that. Your actions now will redefine how Crynits are perceived."

Nonch uncoiled himself and raised up to face me. His sensor stalks stood high, and his orange eyes burned with iridescent sparkles. Mieant was on his feet as well; his hands were curled into fists as he stared intently at me. Cri glared but sidled a step closer to Mieant.

"Plans and events have been swirling around since before any of us we were born. I'm just a Human, weaker, smaller than each of you. I'll probably be dead from whatever Godwill injected me with before," I paused a moment and inhaled, "we can fix anything. But while I started out confused and filled with self-pity, I now accept that I'm a part of this, of you. I can have an impact."

With that, I pointed at each of them. "And you. Can. Too."

Cri's expression shifted to something unpleasant as she considered what I'd said.

"I have to go to Blue River. To the Elions. I don't know what they have, or what they can tell me, but everything we've learned so far points to them as having the solution. If you come with me, I promise you that we'll do our best to find out what has happened to our parents. If we can get them back, we will."

I stopped for a moment to let everyone consider my plan.

"Find the Elions first? Are we in agreement?" All heads nodded.

I formed a craxy smile born of all the frustration, anger, and fear that had come to a rolling boil with me. "And along the way," I shouted, "let's have the bad guys feel OUR grief for a change!"

"We will SPIKE them!" Mieant snarled. Cri spared a calculated glance at her boyfriend.

"Unite!" bellowed Nonch.

It was enough.

"Let's go." I said and turned toward the darkness filling the space between us and our goal. *So much of what we seek to achieve,* I thought, *requires us to pass through the unknown to reach the known.*

AI settled his necklace over my head and rested on my shoulder as he lit the way forward with a beam of light.

Well said, kid. My heart, buoyed by his words of support, began to beat a little faster. Sometimes, that's all we need to go on—a few kind words.

14

History swirled around our boots as we disturbed 1,800-year-old dust and put ten minutes of distance between us and the sewer-like aroma of plasma-cooked legger. The stench we left behind was replaced by that pungent, musty aroma of paper and honey.

Inside my body, my nannites continued their war with Godwill's nanoinjection. My stomach was full, and I felt a surge of organic energy. A full stomach is a wonderful state of contentment and security—the fact that I'd gotten it by gorging on legger was beside the point.

In short, I felt *great*.

The ribbed, yellow-brown walls illuminated by AI's beam began to narrow as we appeared to approach a door—a portal, perhaps! AI's light was interrupted only by occasional motes of dust, but beyond the narrow hole in front of us was utter blackness, the unknown.

"I can't *believe* she ate legger," Cri whispered to Mieant, and I shot her a sidelong glance. The legger viscera had dried up, forming her newly minted bob into a spiky helmet. Mieant held her hand. I'm not sure if love is blind, but it must definitely mess with the olfactory sense—maybe with ALL the senses.

"We do what we must," Mieant responded. "You said yourself that she cannot eat Galactic food."

She looked at him, a half-frown and half-smirk on her face, and replied, "You're taking her side?"

"I'm saying I understand desperation better than I ever have before," he replied, pulling her close.

"You act like you like her," my sister said with one eyebrow raised. Mieant frowned at her. "Just kidding," she continued, leaning her head on his shoulder as they walked. "But you do act like it."

Barf.

The familiar stink of 'natch suddenly wafted around me. *'Natch??? Here???* My eyes narrowed as I looked around for my food archenemy. Nonch thrummed at my side, his body snaking as he kept pace. A sensor stalk touched my shoulders—Nonch's version of a hug, a handshake, or just saying, 'I'm here.'"

Crynits were able to use a chemical language that was fully separate from verbal communication—even Convergence universal translators couldn't decode it. Its complexity boggled the mind. The fragrances of sugar and soil, I'd learned, meant imminent Crynit violence. The particular chemical thought Nonch was currently having smelled like 'natch. In Godwill's prison camp, we'd used that smell as code for "yes" when verbal communication wasn't possible.

"Raystar-Friend, I did not ask you how the legger tasted. On a five-point scale, with 'natch at number five, the worst, and number one being the best, how did you like it?" Apparently, Nonch was emitting the fragrance of 'natch in this case because he was thinking of 'natch.

I eyed him. Crynit humor was an acquired taste. *Forget leggers.*

"You're really funny, Shells," I gently pushed his armored carapace, intending it as a friendly shove, but in doing so just managed to stumble away from him. "It was about as good as 'natch, but much chewier."

He clacked his armor, which was his version of laughter. "It is good for you, no?"

"Pfft."

"Raystar, you ate the wrong part of the legger. You must eat the leg muscles close their body or their abdomen. That is where you will find the flavor AND the nourishment."

Yuck. I imagined carving slabs of bristly, jiggly legger belly. A shiver wormed its way up my spine. "Can we talk about something else?"

Nonch's armor rattled without mirth. "I do not think anyone knows how many leggers live in these tunnels."

"A lot fewer after that grenade," I boasted with a laugh.

"In truth," he continued, "my brood has no idea. We hunt them, and they are endlessly plentiful. It is good we Crynits have armor and technology."

I turned toward him slowly as my smile dropped.

"They would most certainly overwhelm us otherwise," he continued.

AI, what is he talking about?

AI flashed orange as he responded. *Pretty sure there are a ton of leggers down here. Human tunnels. Crynit tunnels. Tons of tunnels. Nem' has an underground labyrinth.*

"Um," I said, mostly to myself. "So, uh, should we be extra quiet?" I asked Nonch. I tilted my head in the direction of Mieant and Cri, the love-starred couple, who were holding hands, chatting, and being all, well, couple-like.

"The leggers know that we are here," Nonch replied. "They are all around us. The smell of a Crynit in their area probably has them enraged."

"What?"

"They hate Crynits. After all, we feed on them." The single plasma grenade had to have eliminated hundreds of leggers. What Nonch was saying was that there were a lot more than hundreds down here. How many was that? *Nova.*

"Hey," I whispered to Mieant and Cri, "you guys still have your grenades?" Cri frowned at me, checked her vest, and nodded. Mieant confirmed that he had his as well. I felt for mine. I had one of the fat ones and two others.

I looked at Nonch. "You don't get a grenade. Those who hold grenades in their mouth don't get grenades."

"Since the fight with Sarla, I've had to adapt." Nonch mumbled, dipping his head. "I am not used to having only four arms, so I used my mouth."

"Pfft. It's just not done, Shells."

"What are you thinking, Raystar?" Mieant asked, moving closer and pulling Cri with him. They were walking on the other side of Nonch.

"Shells says there are a lot of Crynits down here. Like, thousands of them."

"I did not provide a number. If I did, it would not be thousands."

Mieant snorted. "What number then, Crynit?"

"Millions."

Mieant scowled. Cri finally got serious and asked, "Do we know how far away Blue River is? How much longer is it, AI?"

"Over land," he replied, "we're twenty kilometers away, a half-day's hike in a straight line. Down here? Not really sure."

Blue River, the Elions, and the optimism I'd had only fifteen minutes ago seemed so far away. I imagined I heard a giggle from the darkness behind us.

"SSHHH!" I whispered. "Did you hear that?"

The others all shook their heads no.

"Nonch? What about your brood? Are we close to them?" Cri said in a tiny voice. Her face, illuminated by AI's light, was streaked with mud and salty rivers.

"I can detect no scent or physical trace of my brood. Broodmother has tunnels and scouts all throughout the area—except, apparently, here. I don't know why."

We were alone with the dust and tunnels built from the Crynits' hatred—and millions of leggers? I sighed. It wasn't like the odds hadn't been stacked before.

I mean, leggers could kill us first, but an entire Battlegroup could destroy us and *the leggers, just by being too close to us.*

Ha. The Universe had no preference. Somehow, that gave me some measure of comfort. Harsh reality was at least honest.

"All of you: a little positive mental attitude, okay? We stick together. We're armed. We kicked butt last time," I said, and then paused as a horrible thought seeped into my consciousness. I looked at Nonch and then continued, "Hey, uh, Nonch? Why were all those leggers crammed in one section of the tunnel if there are so many down here?"

Nonch stopped and turned. All of his eyes—matte-black lower ones and luminescent orange upper ones—focused on me. He'd risen to about a head taller than I was.

"Is it not obvious?"

"Shells, what's obvious is that I don't know anything about leggers. I don't chase them. Or eat them. Well, now I do. But still. No. It's not at all obvious."

He gently prodded my shoulders with a sensor stalk. I thought about it some more.

Oh. *They were herding us.* We were being hunted.

A child's laugh echoed far in the distance.

15

Our blasters hummed to life as we all drew them simultaneously. The pistol barrels filled with molten light, casting orange circles on the ceiling and walls of the tunnel. For a moment, we looked deadly. Yet if the leggers were able to see our color spectrum, their light also made us targets.

Cri had two blasters and two swords. Mieant had opted for a sword and a blaster. As for me, the runt, there was no way I was getting within a tentacle's reach. I kept my sword at my side, prepared for whatever, and drew my Human blaster. Nonch carried a combat rifle and kept his three other blade arms and his mandibles at the ready as natural weapons.

Ray, you can't use your nanotech. If you do, you'll accelerate the conversion. AI, always diplomatic, just had to remind me. My nannites, the ancient Human tech in my blood, could make me immensely powerful, but using them was an enormous drain on my body. I needed to feed them before and during their use in order to stay active—and when I did use them, I became capable of "consuming" living things. The thing was, I wasn't sure I could control *what* I consumed.

Godwill's nanoinjection presented a second problem: it was actively blocking the energy I could derive from what my nannites consumed, like a protein inhibitor. Every time my power activated, I was starving—no, consuming—myself. I grunted in frustration. Blue River could not get here fast enough.

On top of all that, I wasn't sure how to use my Human blaster. It was clearly "on," whatever that meant. The blaster had connected with my thoughts when I'd roasted the legger tentacle using it; I knew because of the tingle I felt in my palm when I made contact with it. That tingle then wiggled its way into my belly, like a circuit.

If I used the blaster, its link to my nanotech might accelerate my demise. But it probably didn't use *that* much power. Maybe? It could kill me by draining my energy if I used it, but on the other hand, being dinner for a legger would do the trick, too. Understanding how the blaster might drain my energy, as well as how it used my nannites, was critical. I couldn't use it in a fight otherwise.

I pointed the blaster at the wall and pulled the trigger. The wax of the tunnel wall melted. Which was great if I was making, say, a candle or a wax sculpture in school. But not super useful at this moment in time.

"Stop playing with it," AI vocalized from his vantage point above us.

I frowned at him and then turned my ire to the blaster. I dialed it up to what I figured must be maximum power. As I pulled the trigger, I felt power pulse through my belly, and the blaster thrummed. Yet nothing deadly emerged from the barrel.

Maybe it shoots invisible rays only at enemies.

"Raystar," AI snapped, "stay close. And knock it off."

Stupid ancient Humans didn't believe in user manuals, apparently. I shoved the blaster roughly into the holster on my hip.

Twenty meters ahead, AI's light revealed a portal of sorts. As we approached, its shape became clearer. An archway as wide as the tunnel had been at the point where we'd originally entered it led to what appeared to be a bridge. The bridge appeared to be the same width as the tunnel, but it was shaped like a U—the floor curved upward, and the sides formed railings. It extended into darkness, of course, which also surrounded it completely: above, below, and on either side.

High-pitched laughter suddenly echoed behind us. I've read countless stories in which the heroine is told not to look behind her during an escape.

I looked. Our footprints in the dust disappeared into the darkness. AI's light only stretched so far, turning the yellow-brown color of the tunnel into grey shadows and then…nothingness.

Another laugh. This time, the giggle turned laughter into a scream. And then, the blade of yet another sound pierced our sanity…the sound of legs on the move. Lots of them. The dust at the edge of AI's light stirred as a breeze—first faint but constantly increasing in intensity—blew it our way. The strengthening breeze carried that familiar musky-sewer smell as well as the sounds of heavy spider legs thrumming, then rumbling, and finally thundering toward us.

My heart pounded against my small ribcage. I fought to steady my breathing. Cri looked through the portal to the bridge and then back into the tunnel behind us. Mieant planted his hands on her shoulders and turned her toward the bridge.

"Go," he said, with a shove. He looked at me and shouted, "Go with her!"

Then, Mieant turned to face what was coming. Nonch U-turned and stood at his side.

"Cri! Raystar! Get on the bridge," AI said. "I'll be above you. I have limited armaments. Once we're through, someone must blow up the archway using a grenade."

Cri was already through. It was a good plan, but I was rooted in place beside Mieant and Nonch. Out of bravery? No, out of deep-seated loyalty. I would stand with my brothers.

The giggles and piercing screams turned into a roar. From the blackness emerged a horde of leggers, each weighing at least 900 kilos, thrashing against each other and shaking the ground underfoot. Bristles scratched against bristles and scraped the waxy tunnel walls like sandpaper. Their mass created a pressure wave in front of them that blew back my hair.

A moving wall of legs was churning, clamoring, for us. I screamed. *Nova. We're just kids. Stand and fight!??* It was time to turn and *run*.

I was instantly reminded of my Humanity. There was nothing "super" about me—I was just plain old Human, one of a species, no longer extant. Cri, who had already been on the walkway, was in the lead, her arms pumping with swords and blasters. Mieant's lithe, powerful legs propelled him from zero-to-a-lot as he caught up with Cri. Nonch thrummed past me, too, his sensor stalks flat against his head. I could smell lemons. *Is that fear?*

Fast for me was slow for the rest of them. Everyone else was well onto the bridge, and I hadn't even made it out of the tunnel! AI's circle of light was slowly pulling away, leaving me behind.

Nova! AI's instructions! One of us was supposed to blow the entrance to the tunnel.

"Hey!" I said, losing sight of them as I stayed frozen in place. "HEY!"

My shout was drowned out by a cacophony of shrieks and the thunder of the leggers' oncoming bodies. The hair on the back of my neck stood on end as I imagined their tentacles reaching out for me.

I spun toward the rushing horde and pulled my blaster. I crouched into a shooter's stance, took a breath, aimed, and fired. The Human blaster thrummed and the trigger clicked. NOTHING. I pulled the trigger again and again. Click. Click. Click. Click!

"AAAAAUGH!"

I holstered the blaster with one hand and fumbled for a grenade with the other. There was NO time. *Throw the grenade. Run.*

I started to run backward, but fortunately, I first shot a glance over my shoulder to gauge the distance.

Nonch!

I skidded to a stop before I ended up impaled on his mandibles.

Nonch came back for me! This was craxy, heart-stoppingly craxy!

His three-foot mandibles circled my waist and perched me on his back. He spun and ran for the bridge. Holding me tight, Nonch zoomed away from the oncoming horde.

"Throw the grenade!" he urged.

The leggers surged ahead into the dim light. Their forwardmost

legs were like a wall of mottled bristle—thankfully, their blind rush for prey ended up impeding their progress. One enterprising legger crawled along the ceiling, its tentacles whipping like ropes in a hurricane. Hundreds of pus-yellow eyes glinted at me like blazing suns.

As I thumbed the firing mechanism on the grenade, it emitted a curious, high-pitched whine. In my haste, I'd grabbed the fat, oddly shaped grenade. Vaguely familiar symbols along its side began to blink with increasing frequency. *Oh.* I'd seen those symbols before. On the bomb Sarla used to destroy Godwill's nanocontainer!

"YEE!" I screamed as I bobbled the *tactical nuke* and sent it flying with my best underhand throw.

Innocent of its potential, it tinkled and skipped its way away down the waxy corridor. One legger reflexively caught the grenade in a tentacle and shoved it into its toothy maw. I imagined its hard teeth scraping against the cold metal, its wet tongue probing the grenade's profile for anything edible.

"What?" Nonch gasped. We were out of the tunnel, through the archway, and on the bridge. I could tell that he couldn't run that fast much longer.

"Go-go-go!" I yelled, drumming my hands on Nonch's back. The leggers had been closing in, but the one that gobbled the nuke stumbled, tripping up most of the rest of them. They were suddenly a tangle of legs, fangs, tentacles, and fat abdomens.

Three...two.... I closed my eyes.

ZWOOOSH!

The tunnel might have stood the test of time—nearly two thousand years—but I'd just detonated a mini-nuke. Behind us, the ceiling rippled like a snake; the floor and walls separated and plummeted into a dark chasm.

"Faster!" I shouted, shaking Nonch's blade arms as he ran. The bridge trembled.

We caught up to AI, Mieant, and Cri, still running.

"What did you do?" AI vocalized above the din.

"Tact–" I shouted, sending him a picture of it with my mind, "–ical NUKE…."

"IDIOT! That will …" AI yelled. The thunder behind us drowned out his words.

Nonch stumbled, and I slammed my face against his black chiton. Pain rippled across my face and tears clouded my vision. I held on to his segmented carapace as the world turned.

Dimly, I realized that Nonch hadn't stumbled. The bridge had collapsed.

We twisted, spiraled, and screamed into the darkness below.

Our free fall was a play in three acts:

ACT ONE.

Confusion. Nonch was underneath me. I was flying, floundering, floating. I reached out to secure myself to him; he was a disorienting arm's swipe away. My fingers clawed air as I rolled head-over-boots and reflexively kicked my legs out in a panicked attempt to right myself. My stomach lurched as I glimpsed AI's distant light above us before spinning further, deeper, into the darkness below.

ACT TWO.

Panic. My thoughts interpreted my senses. I was FALLING. Gravity is a pervasive and an intimate part of our lives. Our hands on a table. Our butts in a chair. Our feet on the ground. Even hugs have an element of gravity. Remove that constant pressure, and our minds are lost.

I hurtled…downward?

ACT THREE.

Self-preservation. I'd never experienced a free fall before.

How long did I have before I smashed to the ground? Where the nova was the ground?

My imagination conjured a series of needle-sharp stalagmites waiting at the bottom of my gravity-powered plunge, or perhaps a rushing river that would suck me kilometers below the surface, gasping and clawing for air, until I drowned. Extremes pushed into the extremes of my situation.

I tucked myself into a ball as I tumbled. I'd been falling for seemingly forever and ever, with AI a diminishing pinpoint of light far above me. I reached an arm to my right and stretched a leg to the left in a vague attempt to stabilize my fall. I was sure the ground was rushing up to kill me, but in a pre-death epiphany, I realized that there is nothing personal about death. I—

AND IMPACT.

Dust, sound, and pain exploded in and around me. Blackness.

And then….

I arched my back and rolled off the mound I'd landed on. Every movement was pain. My chest expanded, but no air filled it.

After a few—or a million—incoherent moments, I began to gulp dusty, chemical-smelling, tunnel atmosphere. The return of gravity, and the resulting pressure of my body on the hard yet smooth ground, was a treasure. Grateful, I lay there…. Through my eyelids, I saw light.

Ray! Talk to me. Ray?

AI was close by. Groaning, I lifted myself up with one hand onto my hip and peered up at my friend. AI floated about two meters above me, casting his white light across the wreckage we'd fallen into.

Ow.

I breathed as deeply as I could against knives of random pain and noticed that soft fingers of warm wind were caressing my face and lifting my purple hair into little flutters. Now, the air wasn't filled with

motes of Crynit tunnel dust. The air smelled, well, recycled. Everything else smelled of viscera, with the iron tinge of blood. But the air? Oddly enough, it smelled like civilization.

I rubbed my eyes and scanned my surroundings. It appeared that my tactical nuke had blown through to yet another tunnel that lay below the one we'd been in before. The wreckage, dust, and we were strewn about in uneven mounds that stretched, I figured, ten to fifteen meters in every direction. Some of the mounds were short and others were meters tall; the taller piles obstructed my view of what lay beyond. Slabs of ceiling— concrete? maybe?—that were wider and taller than even Nonch lay either on top of black dirt or pieces of brown Crynit tunnel. Here and there, a crushed legger oozed a foul-smelling fluid from underneath all the detritus.

The crushed legger was a wince-worthy testament to my luck. I wasn't broken and mangled from landing on a rock or hunk of concrete, nor was I smashed *under* a rock or concrete. Instead, I lay on something firm, yet yielding, at the base of one of the smaller mounds.

Ray! AI's mental shout broke me out of a dream-like confusion. He had moved closer and was glowing a soft purple. His yellow sensor beams rippled over my disheveled, dirt-covered clothes as he scanned me.

I squinted at him through the aches and his yellow beams. *Ow.*

A tactical nuke? AI asked, incredulous. *What the nova?*

I flinched at his tone. *How was I supposed to know?* I replied.

"How was I supposed to know?" he replied mockingly. *The flipping nuclear symbol painted on every square centimeter of the thing wasn't a hint?*

I....

AI lapsed into a frustrated silence before speaking up again. *Nonch is hurt. You landed on him. Cri and Mieant are over by that rubble. I'll check on them. You see to Nonch.*

I had to take a moment to register what he'd said. My disoriented brain slowly took it in like the morning sun, rising slowly. I looked down.

"Nonch," I whispered in AI's dim light. Nonch was the reason I wasn't pancaked all over the tunnel's, cement-hard floor. *I landed on him? What are the chances?*

I scooted off his back and onto the ground and dropped to my knees, facing him. I ran my hands across his carapace, searching for wounds that weren't hard to find. Fragments of his armor, like shattered roofing tiles, were pressed into his soft body at jagged angles. My hands came away warm and wet.

Blood.

"Shells!" I whispered, clutching him close and pressing my face to his warm armor. The musky and iron-saturated aroma of his wounds became stronger.

Half of his nearly three-meter segmented length was covered with dirt. I tried to push it off his back, but as I did, it clumped around my blood-soaked hands. My beloved friend twitched and uttered a muted sound of distress. I gasped, realizing I must have caused him great pain.

Oh. But his wound smelled *good* to me. My belly rumbled, and a tingle crawled up my back. Hungry. Always hungry. Is this how the ancient Humans were?

Two golden sparks crackled down from my hair, bounced off Nonch's shell, and disappeared into his blood. *Nova. No. I would not consume him.*

"Stay with us, Shells," I whispered. I couldn't be trusted to control my need for energy, so I scuffled back to what felt like a safe distance.

Each breath Nonch took made a rasping noise, and his body convulsed with shivers. He'd saved me in the tunnels from the leggers. He'd inadvertently saved my life when we fell. I pushed down my nannite-driven hunger and focused myself on how I could help him, how I could help *us. Where were we, anyway?*

The dirt mounds flickered with light and shadow as AI wove through them searching for Cri and Mieant. As he moved away, darkness closed in around me. Only a moment later, we were shrouded in pitch black.

Suddenly Nonch's serpentine form and the mounds of dirt became visible again. I frowned and then noticed a pale luminescence that poured from the walls and ceiling, steadily becoming brighter. None of it made any sense.

"Over here! Ray! Help me with these two!" shouted AI. As I stood and turned in the direction of AI's voice, the space around us became fully illuminated.

Walls descended from a ceiling more than fifty meters above us to the perfectly flat concrete surface we were standing on. The concrete floor extended for at least two hundred meters, going from wall to wall. In front of us, and behind us, the tunnel vanished into a well-lit distance, a vanishing point of diminishing lines.

We'd fallen into some sort of transportation tunnel. A highway? A paved road? Except for the significant debris my nuke had created, the tunnel was spotless. The concrete glinted in a metallic way—it had a faint sheen, like it was wet. The side of the road we were on was separated from the other side by some sort of translucent wall or railing that suddenly glowed to life in red, green, yellow and blue shapes.

A second later, a green arrow streaked toward me on our side of the tunnel. It was racing in my direction, growing larger and larger. I whirled to follow it as it flashed past and disappeared around a bend I hadn't noticed before. A few moments later, another one flashed by, and then another, until they were appearing every second or so.

What was the direction of traffic? I'd never seen anything like this. This wasn't Galactic construction. Were we in Broodmother's tunnels, her highways? That flicker of hope was quashed when I realized my Convergence nanotranslators couldn't make out the meaning of the symbols.

Great gravity wells! We were in a Human part of Nem'—an undiscovered Human part of Nem' that was still functional!

Perhaps this was the reawakening that my friends had discussed at school. According to Nonch, long-dead or dormant Human sections of Nem' were activating—coming alive—and beginning to conduct some mysterious activity.

I looked into the tunnel's distance, suddenly apprehensive. Where did this road lead? What if I met more of my kind? Could there be Humans down here? Would I find skeletons? What was....

"RAY!"

AI's shout shook me from my meandering reverie. I scrambled over and around the dirt mounds toward his voice and ultimately found him hovering above Cri and Mieant.

"Raystar!" Mieant exclaimed as I rounded the dirt pile. He lay with his back against a piece of concrete and had drawn Cri against him, his arm encircling her shoulder and her face on his chest. Her four arms were drawn against her chest like a mummy or a child in deep sleep, as she fit into the curve of his arm and against his side.

"Is she hurt?" I asked, rushing toward them.

"*I am fine, thanks,*" Mieant replied tersely, his black eyebrows converging into a frown over his black eyes, "and Cri is fine too." He stroked her hair and pressed his face next to hers as he slowly rocked her back and forth.

"This doesn't look like a Crynit tunnel," he continued.

"We're on some kind of underground road. It has to be ancient Human, and it's functional, I think." I worked my fingers over Cri's arms, legs, her ribs, and then probed her face and head for injuries. She appeared to be still functional, too, to my great relief.

"Yes, Raystar," Mieant said, his tone reverent, "this is why my parents came here. Human tech. Do the symbols make sense to you?" Mieant said, finally meeting my eyes. His parents, Co-Governors of an entire Convergence Quadrant, had moved from Solium4 to Nem'—to meet me, but also to find Human tech. *Look where it had gotten them. They were either dead or in Godwill's cruel hands.*

I glanced at Cri, who was snoring softly, before replying. "No, I have no clue what they mean. But I do have a feeling we don't want to be here anymore than we want to be up in those Crynit tunnels."

Mieant gulped, turning his gaze toward the black hole in the ceiling. "I miss school," he whispered.

"Yeah," I whispered back. It was funny how suddenly our school's routine—the bells, classes, desks, students—was the most wonderful thing we could imagine.

AI interrupted us as he flashed green beams at three different piles. "Hey, this is no time to get emotional. Dig out your backpacks. We need to see to Nonch and then Cri. Raystar, yours is just to the left of Nonch's bod—er—over there. Cri's is there, not too far under the dirt. Mieant, yours is farther away. At the edge of that rock pile." AI's beam flashed over a space about fifteen meters away in the curved part of the tunnel.

Relief flooded through me: each backpack contained a medkit, food, and ammo.

"Mieant, can you grab mine? I'll dig out the pack by Nonch." He replied with a nod.

For the next five minutes, with the exception of our breathing, our hands pushing through the rubble, and the scuffling of our shoes, the roadway was perfectly silent.

Deathly silent.

17

Exhausted and covered in a thin layer of mud made of sweat and dust, Mieant and I flopped down against our favorite piles of dirt. We emptied our backpacks and inventoried our ammo, food, and medical supplies. We had to save Nonch.

The tunnel was now brighter than day. A visual metronome of green arrows pulsed by, guiding long-gone travelers toward some mysterious, ancient Human destination.

At least we could see.

Mieant used our medical kits—medkits—on Nonch. A medkit is an organic nanotech paste that is keyed to work with every Galactic species' DNA. If it is smeared on an open wound, it identifies the species and modifies itself according to the needs of the tissue of that species. The gel contains both healing nano and stock material that nannites can convert into the patient's tissue—exactly the same process as the feeder cubes my dad and I had used when we tried to repair our farm's controllers.

If we'd had more medkits, we could have healed Nonch completely. They contained only enough paste to perform a field dressing; basically, they were designed to patch up a wounded soldier long enough to get him or her to help. So after wiping our fingers "clean" on our muddy combat gear, under AI's watchful eye, we applied the nanogel lightly over Nonch's wounds, at minimum, to slow or stop the bleeding. His wounds were deep.

I could have healed Nonch with my own nannites, but Godwill's nanoinjections had crippled me. The slightest use of my nanotech *could* kill me. Or it *was* killing me. I dunno. I could feel the nanoinfection inside me, warring for control, and slowly winning. *What good am I? Can I help anybody?* I stared at Nonch, riddled with guilt for my unwillingness to sacrifice myself for a dear friend.

Nonch's sides lifted and fell as the medkits went to work, his labored breathing a series of long, phlegmy coughs. Unfortunately, medkit treatments were the best we could do.

Mieant pulled two ration containers from his bag and then rolled two more across the concrete floor to me. *Food!* I nodded my thanks, wiped my hands on my armor, and popped open a canister, nearly spilling its contents in my haste. I would have gladly eaten it off the concrete, for the record.

My stomach contracted in anticipation, all of its rumbling bile pushed aside. I scooped out the pinkish clay and hungrily shoved it in my mouth. The thick nutrient- and protein-rich paste went down like a happy slug escaping sunlight. On the other hand, as Mieant forced down his second can, I could swear his grey skin turned green as he tried not to vomit.

"Void take me!" Mieant gasped as he finally gained control of his gut.

"Better than 'natch," I muttered as I cracked open the second can.

Or legger, I thought.

Silence filled the short moment as we contemplated our situation.

Mieant spoke first. "I never thought we'd end up here."

"Do you mean, like, that on the seventh day of school we'd end up in a...." I replied, waving a hand at the roadway around us.

Mieant, my now-friend and ex-antagonist, snorted an affirmation. While we had become allies, he was still wary around me—because of Cri. But it was clear that he respected me. He'd even stuck up for me.

"Do you mind that I like Cri?" he said sharply.

"That's what you're thinking about?"

"What would you have me think about?"

"I dunno, Mieant," I said. "Maybe, like, how the *nova* to get out of here?

"What is there to think about?" he replied testily. "We can either go that way," he said, gesturing in the direction in which the arrows on the road were pointed, "or that way," he continued, sweeping his hand in the opposite direction.

"Or I suppose we could go up," he called up to the darkness above us. Mieant leaned toward me, his eyes wide with incredulity at my ignorance.

"Pfft. Totally not helpful," I retorted.

"Human, you think that detonating a nuke was *helpful?*"

"We were going to be eaten," I reminded him.

He looked away. I was right—sort of. We were about to be overrun. Perhaps I'd chosen the wrong grenade for the task. But really, how could we know we'd be better off if we'd reached the other side of the bridge? *No.* I wasn't going to second guess myself. I'd made the best decision I could in the moment.

"Raystar," he said, more gently, "are you jealous of Cri and me?"

"You're such a spike," I mumbled, pulling my knees up to my chest.

After a moment of silence, he said, "Is love convenient?"

Mieant's face was an emotionless and opaque grey mask. I thought about the contrast between him and me, with my purple hair and eyes and tanned, tear-stained, and Human face.

"Lethians mate for purposes of reproduction," he continued, "but we do not act upon those—urges—until we find the one we want to spend our lives with. Some of us spend our lives looking for that love. Those that are unable to find their mate die alone and childless."

I blinked, not wanting to contemplate something I didn't, or couldn't, have.

"When we find it, we hold on to it," he finished.

"So. What does that mean? You're in love with my sister? Are you two going to become Mr. Lethian and Mrs. Glean?"

"Shut up," he barked. Cri was sacred territory.

"What the nova, Mieant?"

"Cri is unlike anyone I have met."

I sighed. This was stupid. I was dying—and now my head was full of thoughts about how I wanted a *boyfriend*? I turned my back to him and contemplated the bend in the road up ahead.

After a moment, I said, "We can't just sit here."

"I will remain here…to protect her. And Nonch," he added as an afterthought.

I looked up at the high, smooth ceiling.

"Raystar?" he asked when I didn't reply.

Silence slipped between us again.

Emotions overwhelmed me. I shouted, "Mieant, you do realize that I'm dying, right? Like, in three flipping *days*! You and Cri…I'm not jealous. Well. I am. But I need friends *now*."

I stopped, only because I'd started to hyperventilate. After a moment, I continued: "If we can't get to Blue River, I will die! How are we going to get there now?"

He opened his mouth to respond and then closed it. Silence ensued.

Then after a moment, he said, "I am…sorry, Raystar. You have always been honest with us, and you have suffered the most through all this. I realize how little I have internalized that fact."

I blinked and narrowed my eyes. I struggled to think of something petty to say that would sting him as much as their relationship hurt me. Jealousy is mean-spirited, and I hated myself for feeling it.

Great gravity wells, you and your friends are complicated.

Shut up, AI.

Mieant spoke again. "Raystar, I…."

"No," I said, whirling around to face him. I covered his lips and most of his grey Lethian face with my hands before adding, "It's my bad. I'm glad you and Cri are together."

I stepped back and looked at my feet. "I'm sorry. It's just…."

"Take this," Mieant said, gently taking my hand and placing a grenade in my palm. "You are my friend, Raystar."

"No, no, no, Mieant." I said, warmed by the care in his voice and his actions. "You may need it," I pushed the grenade back into his long-fingered hand and smiled faintly. "I have another nuke…."

Architect, AI muttered. *How sweet. I like you, too: here's a grenade. No wonder your generation is spiked! I don't know whether to be terrified or vomit into my virtual mouth.*

I coughed, wiped away the moisture in my eyes, and waved a hand at the curve ahead in the road. "I'm going to see what's around that corner."

Mieant nodded and laid his blaster beside him, within quick reach. "I will stand guard. When Cri wakes, there will be two of us to help move Nonch. Find us a way out, Raystar—a way to Blue River. We can do it. We will."

Giggles echoed from the gaping hole high above us. I straightened up and filled my lungs with the cool, chemical air.

I wish I knew what these symbols meant, I thought to AI as I watched the symbols flicker by on the translucent wall dividing the road. I didn't say it out loud, because we needed silence. We had walked a good distance from the others (well, AI was floating along at eye level, and I was walking). As we moved along, I stayed near the divider, and AI kept about a meter of distance between us.

We were approaching the curve in the tunnel. Behind us, the wreckage from the collapse loomed as a massive black mound in the whiteness of the tunnel. How much noise had that collapse made?

Perhaps a better question was, "What *else* heard it?"

A yellow light flickered from AI to the road divider as he scanned it.

You're not missing much, AI thought back, snapping me out of my reverie. *The symbols are signposts, directions, and speed limits.*

I stopped and slowly turned to face my hovering friend. My eye twitched.

You can understand the symbols?

He floated to a halt, glowed yellow, and slowly—guiltily, it seemed— pivoted the longest part of his diamond shape to face me.

Uhhhh, he replied.

You can read Human?

Um. Do I? I mean, yeah, I DO! Aren't I supposed to?

You. Can. Read. Human?

Ray, calm yourself, you're going to spark! It's a big language. How would I know if could read it? And I, well…. I forgot.

I eyed my friend.

You forgot?

AI was quiet for a heartbeat and then continued. *I didn't want to tell you. I didn't think things were going to get any easier, and I thought I could manage it.*

Manage WHAT? I demanded, making a mental note that death by suspense was a new and novel way of dying. *How can you forget ANY-THING? You're a…a flipping neural network! And how could you being able to read Ancient Human not be something I SHOULD KNOW ABOUT? Forget the symbols in this passageway! You could help me translate the symbols on the heads-up display that appears when I use my nanotech. Nova! Understanding that would be….*

No, Raystar. I'm not talking about that. I'm talking about my memory disappearing. In order to fight Godwill's infection on a cellular level, I have to track your cells and your nannites as well as the billions of the infection's nannites inside of you as well. As yours are destroyed, I'm using up storage and energy to direct your nannites' fight against the infection. I'm expending massive amounts of resources to keep the infection at bay.

Blood pounded against my temples. I felt a planet-sized headache coming on and started walking. To my left, stupid illegible Human symbols kept flickering past, making the barrier look like a streaming vid screen. We were so up the great gravity well. Nonch was at death's door. Cri, well…Cri was asleep.

How could she sleep through all this?

Mieant was, for all intents and purposes, by himself. And for all I knew, there were millions of hairy, pus-eyed leggers waiting to pour through the hole above my friends. *And eat us.* Everything wanted to eat us or kill us. Spike it, even *I* wanted to eat us to fuel my nannites.

Wait, what did he say?

"AI," I vocalized, "what resources?"

"Me," he sighed. "I converted aspects of my life and personality

cores. It was the only substance I had available with enough power to stop Godwill's Void-cursed nano. Now there are aspects of me that are gone." Consumed by me.

I stared at him, wide eyed with horror. "And some of the parts you had to convert contained memories?"

He was silent for about thirty steps before responding aloud, "Life cores, too. Yeah." His voice had a bass resonance.

"You did that for me?" I whispered to myself before adding to AI, "What does that mean?"

Rather sharply, but quietly, AI responded, "It means what I've been telling you all along: don't use your power! I'm the only thing around here with enough energy and know-how to replenish what you consume. Well, there's also Godwill, but I'm pretty sure you're not going to go to him for help. So don't use your power. At all. Because I can't sustain you, or consume my own resources, for much longer. We have to find the Elions and the control DNA so you can stabilize and fight off Godwill's nano."

I heard him, loud and clear, but I was stunned by the fact that he was literally consuming himself, burning his life and memory cores, to protect me. And when he used them up…then what?

We walked and floated in silence, reaching the road's bend in a few short moments. Red-light rings activated on the floor, walls, and ceiling, presumably marking exactly where the road curved. The lights stretched out from behind us, in the direction we'd come, and grew brighter as they neared the bend in the road. *Ancient Humans must have been able to travel quite fast to need so much warning.*

"AI," I said, turning toward him.

"Save it, Raystar. I don't want to hear you say you're sorry. I did it for me. Pfft. You're a teen. I know enough to expect absolutely zero planning, foresight, smart…."

"I wasn't apologizing."

My heart dropped closer to darkness. AI, my infinitely smart friend, my mentor, my only link to my Human parents…. "Thank you," I said.

I could swear that I heard him virtually blink.

I snatched him from the air beside me and smushed him against my heart. "No more of this converting yourself to save me. Please. If this last week is any indication of our *next* week, I *will* use my power again. And I don't want you replenishing me, or whatever, when I do use my power. We're going to find the cure. We're going to get out of these Void-cursed tunnels. No more killing yourself to save me. Okay?"

"Mngmufgufumph," he replied.

I held him away from my chest.

"Aahhh!" he gasped. "Great nova!"

Moron. My chest wasn't keeping him from talking or breathing. I was only thirteen; I hardly *had* a chest. And he *could* have responded telepathically, after all.

He glowed green, bathing me in his warm light.

"Raystar," he said, suddenly serious, "you've been the most important thing in my life since day one. I don't want you to go away. So I will make you no promises, Ray. I'll do what I must to keep you in this world."

My heart thumped and my shoulders shook. Suddenly, AI was blurry to me because of the water in my eyes. I wiped the moisture away with the back of my hand, sniffed, and said, "Let's go."

Light, like the "meteor" explosions I'd seen in the 'natch fields with my dad, suddenly flashed past me, leaving after-effects in my vision. The air screamed as it was ripped asunder by hypersonic ammunition.

An enormous black shape more than eight meters long hurtled from around the corner and slammed into the opposite wall. It crashed with such force that the glowing tunnel cracked and then dimmed. The WHUMP had enough bass to feel like a punch in the gut.

Stunned, I surveyed the damage. A spiderweb radiated out from where a giant Crynit had impacted and then slid to the ground—like a multi-hundred-kilogram black noodle.

Just then, plasma bolts screamed past me.

"Void and gravity wells! Raystar, *run!*" AI shouted. He blazed yellow, turned, and flew back toward Cri, Mieant, and Nonch.

Right. I took off toward the source of the sound and light. For reassurance, I squeezed the handle of my blaster as I ran.

NOT TOWARD *THE EXPLOSIONS, RAYSTAR!*

I winced as AI's concert-level volume shattered through my brain. My hands reflexively slammed into my ears—as if that would help. I was holding my blaster, so that smashed against one side of my head. *Yeah, that hurt.* I was learning all over again how stress makes you do stupid things.

I stumbled.

Raystar! AI yelled again.

Great nova, he was loud.

OH. He wanted me to run *away.*

But the way I saw it, the tunnel only offered two directions: toward the danger or away from the danger. My wounded friends couldn't run away from the danger, and even if they could, a panicked run down an infinitely long tunnel with leggers on our heels wasn't appealing.

No. We needed to understand this new threat. So I continued running, crouching for some degree of safety, *toward* the sound. I had just rounded the curve when....

A shadow suddenly flickered above me as YET ANOTHER eight-meter-long Crynit crashed into the ceiling. I dropped and rolled to the side, adrenaline searing through my nerves. Its huge body smashed down right where I'd been standing moments before. The impact was so hard that drops of wet, warm Crynit blood, metallic

and delicious—*spike me, what was I thinking?*—sprayed everything around it, including me.

I looked around me. Apparently, as the blast hit me, I'd lost my balance and slammed sideways into the glowing, symbol-covered divider. "Eeuuufff," I moaned. I slid down the divider and onto the road.

More detonations ensued. To call them explosions would be a massive understatement. They had staggering concussive force. And yet...a twisted part of me gleefully recognized that they weren't as large as the tactical nuke I'd inadvertently thrown at the leggers. *Heh. In an explosion competition, I'd win.*

Dust and silence fell in a vacuum left by chaos. Was the Crynit fight over? I'd seen Nonch fight back in school. I'd been terrified of Sarla at Godwill's prison camp. I eyed the dead Crynit. Whatever had done *that*, if it had indeed won, wasn't something I wanted to meet.

Metal screeched. I could hear something immeasurably heavy being dragged across concrete just around the bend. There were clanks, the tortured moan of bending metal, and then a series of snaps as whatever had just lost the fight was pulled apart.

AI?

Yah, came the tired reply. *I'm here. Wishing I wasn't.*

Quietly as I could manage, I picked myself up. He was about three meters away. The blast had flung him to the ground. Glowing blue, he floated up to my eye level, wobbling slowly.

The EMP from that blast knocked me out, he explained. *I'm hardened against it, but it was a doozy.*

I eyed him and whispered, "A *doozy*?" There he went using unknown words again. He'd always seemed age-appropriate weird to me, but I had no idea what he was talking about now.

Several of those explosions were electromagnetic pulses—EMPs. They're designed to fry electronics, he explained in response to my skeptical frown.

Oh. That's not what you're wondering about. Hovering about a meter away from me, he projected a gentle green glow across our surroundings. *I told you, some of my memory and life cores are...gone.*

My frown deepened with concern, but with that, the dragging sounds stopped. I glanced toward the now-silent bend in the tunnel. I felt warmth at my back—it was AI, I realized with relief, covering me with his yellow scan beams.

It's okay, Ray. It was my choice to use my life cores as energy. You need to focus on us getting out of here. I'll make sure you stay yourself, so you can focus on saving us all. Whatever it takes, Ray.

He paused. *Hey, did you hear that?*

If he was referring to a low thrumming sound not unlike the thunder of a massive gratcher herd, then *yes*. He could also have been referring to the crackling buzz of antigrav engines, which I heard as well. Both sounds were familiar, and both were drawing closer every second. *Everything* was drawing closer!

I frantically searched for any type of cover. The divider was too tall to climb over, and it was translucent, anyway. Gulping down panic, my eyes glued to the curve in the tunnel, I thumbed the safety on my blaster to make sure it was ready to fire. We had no place to run. No place to hide. So we just waited.

A drone rounded the corner first. Imagine a legger at least twice as large as usual, with a thick central body and six legs attached symmetrically around its middle. Now, turn it on its side so its belly is pointed at you. Subtract the legger's thick hair but add smooth black armor, an array of red sensors, and attach missiles, along with Void-knows-what other armaments, to each of its appendages. THAT's what drifted around the corner.

Its deadly presence was only somewhat diminished as it lurched toward us. Red beams as thin as my purple hair strands flickered over the two massive and very dead Crynit bodies. The drone's antigrav thrusters sputtered and rained blue-green sparks down on the glowing road, leading it to topple before stabilizing and rising again. Several of its weapon arms were missing, leaving jagged, wire- and metal-filled gashes in its armor. *What,* I wondered, *could have inflicted that damage on this beast of a machine?*

Spike me! An Eviscerator! We are so head-and-shoulders up the gravity well, AI whispered into my mind.

A WHAT-A-VATOR? I questioned.

A heavy combat drone used for boarding ships. I haven't seen one in…well, forever. He drifted off, eliciting a side glance from me.

Elite Crynit forces use them, he continued. *Huh. Isn't it strange that this one is uncloaked?*

Spidery shivers pricked down my neck and spine. As AI's words echoed through my mind, I now knew *precisely* how a geckomouse felt when a starbat swooped down and snatched it up—a flash of terrified helplessness as rapidly descending darkness hallmarked its last moment, the flicker of mortality.

Four Eviscerators suddenly appeared just meters from where we stood. A fifth—the closest to us—uncloaked itself almost directly over us, slowly blotting out the light from above the roadway as its metallic weapon arms spread out around us like talons.

Eeeee, AI whimpered.

We were surrounded by a jagged fence of weapons designed to breach armored starship hulls. Red beams flickered over AI and me. I smelled oil, and something else, coming from their metallic bodies. Titanium? Cobalt? While they were cloaked, they had been able to encircle us easily and mask their antigrav wakes from AI's very excellent sensors. And that first drone? It was nothing but a distraction.

I gulped as another thought stepped on my heart's accelerator. With as much sanity as I could muster, I slowly and gingerly, so as to not alarm any of the black-as-Void war machines, holstered my blaster. Their red sensor eyes silently followed my movements.

Remember the thrumming? I thought to AI.

Spike me, he replied as the Eviscerators in front of us glided apart in opposite directions.

"YOU." The deep, feminine voice seemed to come from all around us, and the anger and malice it contained was unmistakable. The fragrances of sugar and soil filled my nose like a fresh spring breeze. I recalled what Nonch had told me about Crynit pheromone-talk and knew this wasn't a scent of rebirth and butterflies. It was the scent of death: sugar, dirt, and decay. Wild eyed, I looked around to locate the source.

Just like that, six of the largest Crynits I had ever seen, who had simply not been there before, appeared in a circle around us with no more fanfare than the blink of an eye. Two arched themselves over the road divider. They all wore armor nearly identical to what Sarla had worn when she and Godwill marched into my school. Battery and shield packs jutted out in square bricks along their sides. Mobile miniturrets bulging along the humps of their segmented body armor scanned the area for threats, and missile racks extended from the centers of their backs, like wings on a dragon.

The drone above us moved back as a seventh Crynit, far larger than the others, uncloaked itself. It wasn't wearing any armor. *Do forces of nature even need engineered protection?* I thought.

Her black carapace was covered in random blue and red spots each the size of my head. They extended down her colossal, segmented form, which stretched down the tunnel. Her six sword arms, each literally one and a half times the length of my body, glittered with silver nannites. I was betting those nannites were able to turn her sword arms into monomolecular blades.

With blades like that, I thought to AI, *she'd be able to cut through a hunk of cobalt ten meters thick.*

Each sword arm ended in a bright orange claw hand large enough to encircle one of my thighs. But her head was what riveted me. Her sensor stalks were deep blue and blood red, feathery sails that cast colorful shadows as the tunnel's white glow filtered through them. Her two large primary eyes were iridescent jewels crowning her head, every color represented and shimmering with each slight movement she or I made. Below them were six gunmetal-black secondary eyes. Her mandibles were covered in the same sparkly nanoplate that coated her sword arms.

She was beautiful—and horrifying.

As she opened her mouth—I assumed to either consume me or speak—I saw the spikes glistening with Crynit venom. A fist-sized

drop of death collected and splashed to the tunnel floor. When a flying speck of her vitriol landed on my boot, it sputtered and hissed, leaving behind a small burn hole.

I turned my terrified but fascinated eyes toward the primary eyes of the gorgeous, massive, deadly Crynit, who returned my gaze with predatory focus. Her red-blue sensor stalks drifted toward me, fanning out the scents of sugar and soil, as she lowered her head slightly and spoke:

"You have stolen my child, Raystar of Terra."

20

After Broodmother Krig spoke, everything—even the small insects that inhabit every life-supporting planet—fell silent. Granted, there probably weren't any insects in this ancient and sterile Human roadway, but had there been any, I'm sure that in that particular moment they would have kept their 'cricking' to themselves.

I stared upward into Broodmother Krig's prismatic eyes. My purple hair blew back slightly as she exhaled. The only sound in the ancient place was the beat of my throbbing heart.

Faster than I could lift my arms to flinch, she grabbed me. Two claw hands reached around my waist, lifting me in front of her longer-than-me mandibles.

"*Nonch!*" she hissed, shaking me and bringing me closer.

"Broodmother Krig?" I squeaked.

"Where. Is. *My. Son?*" she raged, shaking me.

"I...."

"To think! *You* are supposed to be Humanity's key," Broodmother thundered. She turned her head in disgust, exhaling massively. My heart's efforts to push blood back into my brain was finally starting to loosen up my thoughts and improving my ability to speak.

Did you hear what she said? "Humanity's key," AI whispered in my head.

"Broodmother Krig," I said in a small, timid voice, "we have been on the run…."—I paused and gulped a breath—"ever since we left school! Jurisdictor Godwill hunte—"

Her head spun back to me with the precision of a plasma turret.

"Repeat what you said," Broodmother said, her voice lower now—dangerously, melodiously so.

"I…. The Jurisdictor hunted us. Captured…." I stammered.

"His name," she interrupted. "Say his Void-cursed name!"

I blinked, confused. She shook me again.

"Godwill?" I blurted out, as my brain finally regained the capacity to do threatened-brain things. "Jurisdictor Godwill?"

Broodmother fell silent, her long, colorful body undulating as she breathed. My feet dangled in the air.

"Venom and blades," she seethed. Her grip tightened as her ire hunted for a perch and found me. "Where is my broodling?"

At last! You'd think that while I was being dangled two meters above the ground in front of mouth blades large enough to bisect me, hope would be the last thing on my mind. Fear, panic—those would be more appropriate emotions. But I felt hope, just a glimmer of it. We finally had a grown-up on our side who had power, who seemed to know what was going on and could arguably be of help to us. Protect us. Or eat me. *Choices, choices.* Life was all about choices, or perhaps the illusion of "free" will?

I would take my chances, for Nonch.

"Shells—er—Nonch," I stammered, "is wounded. Badly. I came this way to find a way out, a way—uh, to get to Blue River, to get help." In her eyes, I saw my reflection as a kaleidoscope with a million colors and facets.

Broodmother's claws still had my hands pinned to my sides. I frowned, jerked my head in the direction of Nonch, Cri, and Mieant, and continued, "He's that way, with our friends."

"Broodmother Krig," AI said loudly and crisply, as she squeezed me, "I request that you not harm the Human."

As if they were a single entity, the five Eviscerators and all six Crynits turned to face my floating, diamond-shaped friend. AI had been hovering, unnoticed, slightly off to one side. He glowed an angry red—surprising, given our mutual vulnerability. Broodmother cocked her head, her massive sensor stalks swishing slightly.

"I *know* you," she said, as much to herself as to her entourage and, I suppose, to us as well.

"And I, you, Honored Broodmother."

"So, you are her guardian, *ancient thing*," Broodmother said before turning her gaze back to me. With a final glance at AI, she nodded and placed me carefully atop her neck, just behind her weaponized giant head.

"Grasp me tightly," she commanded.

I obediently clinched my legs around the seam between Broodmother's head and her first body segment, firmly but carefully, and held on tightly to the central part of her sensor stalks. She smelled like vanilla, and her sensor stalks were warm and dry.

"Two kilometers down the tunnel," I said. "There are guards posted: my sister, Cri, and the Co-Governors' son, Mieant Asriga...."

"I know who they are, child," she replied in a deeply resonant and feminine voice.

With that, Broodmother Krig, Ruler of the Crynits on Nem', launched into a sprint to save her fallen son. *You know*—the one I'd fallen on and almost killed. The wind generated by Broodmother's speed turned the soft fronds of her sensor stalks into thin whips that stung my face. The five Eviscerators flew several meters above us, their legs tucked behind them so they resembled squids. The six Crynit guards flanked us, with three on each side. The combined thrumming of their hundreds of legs sounded like war drums I could feel deep within my belly, the resonance of power unchecked.

I felt AI close by me, but I had no idea where he was. I was too busy holding on.

Nova and gravity wells, Ray. You're riding a Crynit queen! No one—especially a Human—does that.

I grimaced into the wind, sputtering as one of her feather-like fronds flew into my mouth.

She'll probably eat you after she gets Nonch back, he added with a dose of snark.

Shut up!

Broodmother suddenly jerked her head; my irritation with AI must have made me grip her stalks too tightly.

"Human child! Don't pinch your destiny too tightly!"

"Sorry!" I yelled over her thrumming.

To AI, I added, *Seriously, shut up. We're helping Nonch!*

I'm just saying. Getting eaten would be bad. The infection in you would then be inside her. Nobody wants to see a Crynit queen infected with it.

Nova me! What a horrible thought! Was that a productive thing for AI to tell me now?

I gritted my teeth and bent down low against the queen's body, holding on more carefully than ever. The antiseptic tunnel air had taken on a musty, papery smell.

Oh, no.

Brown dust clouded the air, and a hair as long as my hand that definitely neither smelled nor tasted like vanilla fluttered into my mouth. I quickly spat it out. Up ahead, I could see that what should have been a handful of low mounds of dirt was instead a writhing brown pile that nearly reached the ceiling. *Nova and gravity wells!* It was a seething mass of leggers. As we approached, hundreds more poured out of the hole in the ceiling and tumbled down onto the churning bodies. Hisses, giggles, and screeches emanated from the twisting pile of hair.

Suddenly, a light flickered on the far side of the legger mountain. I heard a massive WHUMP, and for a moment, the entire pyramid of leggers was lifted up and then dropped back down to the ground. Some were on fire. One of my friends must have thrown a grenade into the pile. Burnt flesh of legger wafted toward us, carried by the tunnel's constant breeze.

"I cannot do this with you on my head," Broodmother said. Without stopping, she gently lifted me up and then set me down. Her timing was so perfect that I barely stumbled as my feet touched the ground.

Broodmother had been running plenty fast before, but without me slowing her pace, she and her vanguard accelerated into a blur before cloaking themselves. The swirling brown dust parted before them — the only sign of their approach.

The Crynits hit the twenty-meter-high tangle of leggers with a resounding SMACK: the slap of armor on flesh and the crack of bone and chitin. The leggers farthest from the impact zone ended up tossed in all directions. Leggers crashed against the walls and ceiling; their hairy, bony bodies cracked apart loudly. Those that were hit directly by the queen and her vanguard simply liquefied; their red and green viscera splashed against the walls and road. The stench that resulted could have been a weapon in itself.

The Eviscerators floated about eight meters from the ground, their red beams piercing abdomens and severing legs. One drone dipped down into the fray and used its squid arms to rip a legger to pieces, while its four death-black comrades covered the pile with a chaotic mix of beams and missiles. Meanwhile, Broodmother and her six Crynit warriors transformed themselves into organic blenders. Their blade arms sliced through leggers effortlessly; a giant pool of liquid spread out from the semicircle they had formed.

In moments, hundreds of leggers became nothing more than a river of sticky fluid peppered with vile-smelling body parts. But quantity has a quality all of its own: while Broodmother and her vanguard were laying waste to what was already in the tunnel, leggers kept pouring from the hole in the ceiling. *Spike us all.* I was beginning to believe Nonch was right about there being millions of leggers down there; the queen and her vanguard would soon be overwhelmed.

One large legger flung itself from the top of the mound onto a Crynit warrior, its legs spread wide like a net, its fat bulging abdomen quivering, and its pink tentacles waving frantically to gain a grip. With the uniquely intense energy of desperation, the creature slammed onto the Crynit's back and used its tentacles to suction the

warrior's armored helmet off its head. One of its tentacles latched itself into the Crynit's lower eyes, pulled them out, and, Void take me, shoved several of the wet orbs into its maw! I watched in shock as the creature secured itself on the thrashing Crynit's back to rip out more eyes. The Crynit brayed a guttural staccato of agony.

Instantly, an Eviscerator appeared at its side. It wrapped the legger in its armored, segmented arms and pulled hard. The legger flew into the air, but another jumped onto the machine as it retreated, dragging it to the ground. Wounded and able leggers alike saw a chance to take out a nemesis on the ground and piled on the Eviscerator as it struggled to rise. Its motors whining and its antigrav engines roaring, the Eviscerator was pulled apart like a toy, just as the blinded Crynit warrior disappeared under a hairy, bulbous mass.

Broodmother's formation had been broken. The leggers screamed and giggled in victory, and suddenly all confusion in the legger pile vanished. Hundreds and hundreds of six-legged, yellow-eyed monsters oriented themselves to face the queen, her warriors, and the remaining Eviscerators. They raged forward, their fury focused on their compromised prey.

I saw three leggers simultaneously launch themselves at one of the Crynit warriors. As the warrior tried to engage with them, three more leggers piled on as well, leaving the Crynit no room to swing its deadly blade arms. Flattened under a mound of hair, tentacles, and screams, the Crynit flailed helplessly. Chunks of armor and the Crynit's black carapace were thrown into the air at random as the leggers *peeled* it alive.

Driven craxy by the smell of a skinned enemy, the leggers dove in and began to feast. Their child-like laughs morphed into sounds exactly like the braying gasps of the dying Crynit. Leggers really do imitate their prey, I thought. The horrible mocking was almost too awful to bear.

A contrail from a nearby Crynit warrior streaked over to its fallen comrade. The micro-missile impacted the soldier's head and exploded, shredding the attacking leggers and the mortally wounded Crynit. A mercy killing.

I shuddered at the thought of being pulled apart—while conscious—by leggers. I shuddered again, remembering how Nurse Pheelios had pleaded with me as I'd done *exactly the same thing to her. Did being alive mean killing others to survive, a universal pattern of might makes right?*

The Eviscerators managed to disengage and rise out of the reach of the leggers. As they dealt out death from where they hovered above the fray, the queen and her vanguard reformed and stood against the onslaught. Any legger that attempted to jump on a warrior's back was either blown apart or ripped limb-from-limb before it could land on a target. Over time, however, relentless numbers forced the queen and her soldiers back, despite the fact that Crynits were far superior killing machines.

Broodmother turned and thundered back to me, "We will hold them back! Human! See to my broodling!"

Nova me, Ray, AI said. *This is beyond spiked.*

Can you scan for Nonch? Do you see Cri and Mieant?

He pointed a beam. *They're on the other side of the pile.*

"TERRAN!" the giant Crynit queen roared, this time so loud that even some battle-enraged leggers flinched. Subsumed by leggers, she again turned her massive head to me, her rainbow orb-like eyes meeting my tiny, horrified, purple ones and demanding them to obey.

Nine leggers landed on her face and upper back. Broodmother Krig, the ruler of the Crynits on Nem, went down under a mass of hairy, tentacled, spidery, and massive predators.

AI? I blinked and looked at him. He hovered at eye level, surveying the battle.

They're all dying. His voice was bleak.

Time slowed. My eyes were riveted to the spot where Broodmother had gone down. The mound of leggers rose and then fell as they crushed her down.

We have to help them, I said, shaking.

Yes, he replied.

Fear, panic, hopelessness, and anger reached down inside me to tap my latent power. Like a lightning bolt, it connected and surged. My mind burned. Tingles ran down my spine and expanded as they raced through my arms and legs, to my fingers and toes, to the top of my head. Sparks crackled down from my hair.

Stay back, AI. They'll need you afterward to sort out this nova-spiked mess!

No! he exclaimed. *Place me around your neck. I have something different in mind.*

Frowning, I did as he asked. He felt warm against my skin as he hung above my heart, the place where he'd rested for most of my life.

I'm burning my cores, AI said.

Wait…no! I cried.

I love you, Ray.

22

I went NOVA. Power surged out from where AI had touched my heart. Emotion exploded through my limbs, filling me so much that if I didn't unleash it, I would immolate myself and everything around me. Passion was…power.

My nannites and I had never been so completely united: their power was an extension of my will. It was a perfect meld of internal and external energies. My heads-up display activated like my favorite first-person vid game that I'd played a million times. The Eviscerators, Crynits, and my friends became green silhouettes, and the leggers appeared as glowing hate-red targets. Ropes of crackling energy, alternately as bright and as dark as the stars and the space between them, looped out of me. It wasn't even fair. Wherever my power touched a legger, it simply turned to ash. Their organic essence fed my energy, and with each legger I consumed, my energy levels increased.

It was glorious. It would all be over before I had time to realize it was happening, and oddly, I wasn't afraid. Whatever AI had done had made me euphorically whole. Tendrils of nanocharged power laced themselves through the pile of leggers, who now clawed and scrabbled to get away from the source of their destruction. *Me.*

Great Universe, I thought, *if the ancient Terrans had this kind of power, this level of control, there was no way they could have lost the…*

At the height of my victory, a forgotten enemy—tiny but unforgiving—shoved its way into my mind. *Infection.* My white and blue

114

energy suddenly turned brown and green. My guts churned. Waves of nausea doubled me over; I wrapped my hands around my stomach and slumped to my knees. I had forgotten that I shared my body with another force.

In my obsession to prevail over the leggers and save my friends, Broodmother, and her team, I had failed to monitor my power flow. Devastating strings of light danced wildly around the tunnel, gouging deep scars in the near-indestructible Human roadway and walls. My friends and newfound allies either scurried out of range or had to rely on straight-up luck to not be vaporized.

Leggers, in halves, or various pieces, lay strewn across the ground. More plummeted down from the darkness above, and the now-named Infection gloried in the unending supply of fresh food they provided. It was winning control of my power, of me. Infection's control over me increased with each legger we consumed. My sanity was on a razor's edge between the euphoria of power and the need to kill them. An infinity of leggers thumped down from the chasm above us into Infection's hunger, tipping the balance of my energy control over to Infection. The hapless creatures, intent on their hatred of me, of us invaders, were completely unaware that I had shifted from defender to predator.

They just kept coming. I was ready.

DESTROY! CONSUME! CHAOS AND CREATION, THE UNENDING PATTERN OF EXISTENCE.

I screamed as blades of crackling energy slid out from my knuckles. It hurt, but I had so much more to think about now than just my own pain. As I waved my hands back and forth, the white-hot blades cut through the leggers like they were moving through smoke. Tendrils of crackling nannites streaked out of my shoulders, snapping, hissing, replicating, eating the leggers. I processed their skin, flesh, bones, organs, blood into energy, leaving behind only THE ASH OF DEFEAT!

Once I was clear of the largest group, I saw a smaller heap writhing on top of a large, vaguely familiar creature. Distantly, instinctively, I knew I should not harm it. As I reached into the air with my right hand, a gigantic, ghostly hand with long claws extended beyond it. I used my newly empowered "hand" to scoop up what lay beneath the pile of leggers…Broodmother. Her weight was nothing to me: I easily lifted her away from the leggers and shook them off her body.

Incredibly, ME, a tiny Human, spun lassos of coruscating energy around Broodmother. The power infused me with a mass that belied my size. I shifted my feet into a more solid stance and dragged her massive form out of the battle. She writhed against the leggers and against me—clearly, she was a creature not used to being overpowered. With renewed fury, she shredded the remaining leggers holding on to her carapace, but my own ropes of lightning proved to be unbreakable.

I pulled Broodmother Krig fifteen meters back from the battle before releasing her unharmed (by me, anyway). Pieces of her carapace had been stripped, but my sensors indicated that the holes in her flesh would heal. Her weaponized head turned to me; hatred shone from her prismatic eyes.

"CRYNIT ALLY," I thundered, pointing at her with my tiny, but mighty, kid hand, "STAY OUT OF THE COMBAT AREA!"

Spike me! What the nova am I doing? But this power felt so *right*.

The leggers, as one, paused and shielded their eyes with their tentacles as they considered their sole adversary. Realization dawned among their groupthink that *they* were now the prey. The Eviscerators, their number now down to three, flared out their arms as they retreated to cover their queen. I didn't understand drone body language, but their furious back-and-forth scanning of the melee suggested that they were surprised to suddenly be free of the legger horde.

I'd already consumed the leggers that were closest to Broodmother's force; their molecules had fed my nannites.

I AM POWER. HUNGER. RAGE.

I bowed, inhaled, and pulled my power back, in toward my belly. I felt like I was going to explode. The ancient Human roadway around me bubbled and melted. The power flowed inward, and when I could contain it no more, I thrust my hands toward the mounds of leggers, pointed up toward the ceiling, and SCREAMED.

Broodmother's warriors and Eviscerators hurriedly pulled further away from my unleashed craxyness and formed a tight circle around their supine queen. I suspected their threat assessment might be changing—that maybe the lightning-shrouded Human girl, rather than the horde of leggers, was the real enemy.

LET THE WEAK CONCERN THEMSELVES WITH WEAK THOUGHTS!

Sonic booms cracked around me. I was a lightning storm with whips of green and brown energy lashing out at the speed of light, rending the air, never missing. Leggers tried to escape in vain. Their hair dissolved as the sparks of my nano consumed them; strips of their skin were sanded off as I fed, molecule by molecule, on their bodies, leaving a snowfall of ash where once a thousand or more living, breathing creatures had stood.

Covered in ash and free of leggers, Cri and Mieant pulled Nonch to the side of the tunnel. Nonch's carapace had been ripped into jagged, gaping sections. I was too far immersed in the ecstasy of battle to give Nonch further notice. I knew I was here to save them, but I didn't know why.

I observed the ceaseless stream of leggers pouring from the chasm above. To save these other creatures, I had to stop that flow. Perhaps there were too many for me? *No.* My heads-up display clearly showed the same weapon options that had appeared back when I'd fought Nurse Pheelios, when the entity named Raystar was in control of this body. I understood them now. One option in particular, I knew, was perfectly suited for this enemy.

I felt my energy centering in my chest. Pulling my hands parallel to one another above my heart, I focused and then refocused.

I AM CREATING A BOMB OF DESTRUCTION LIKE NOTHING THESE VERMIN HAVE SEEN FOR THOUSANDS OF YEARS. HUMANITY HAS RETURNED!

Spike me. What am I doing?

My power surged. A fist-sized lightning orb appeared between my palms, jittering in place. I poured energy into it until my heart almost pounded through my ribs. It was ready. I opened both hands and heaved, underhanded, the white ball into the gaping hole above us. It streaked like a meteor, illuminating the darkness.

The web-like maze of ancient Crynit walkways above us had been hidden in darkness for centuries. As my lightning bomb rose to the center of the dark cavern, blinding light revealed its secrets. Thousands of pus-yellow eyes reflected the brilliance of my rage, hatred, and hunger as their insane urge to attack us pushed them directly into the path of my bomb's fury.

I grinned and clenched my fists and my jaw as a command welled up in my throat. *NOW!* As I shouted the word, a vaguely egg-shaped wave of translucent, green-tinged energy concussed outward from the ball, incinerating all the organic matter in its radius. To my surprise, it did not rejuvenate me. I had to be connected to what I was consuming for the energy to come back to me.

The resulting explosion felt like it was emerging from Nem's core. The Human tunnel's lights flickered once and then went dark. More of the tunnel's ceiling caved in. We were bathed in blackness except for a thin coat of green electricity that coruscated over my body. Burnt meat, ash, smoke, the crackle of falling debris; in the pure darkness, sounds and smells were all that remained. From somewhere in the distance, a klaxon groaned to life.

The leggers were simply gone. My energy was nearly depleted as well, but the victory had been worth the expenditure. Thousands of enemies had been vanquished. Streams of green-tinged lightning snaked soundlessly from my body to the rubble around me. The tendrils caressed the ruin tentatively—almost gently—but the concrete still melted where the strands touched it. Somehow, even after the Armageddon I'd unleashed, I was STILL hungry.

"Human," I heard Broodmother rasp behind me. The Crynit matriarch walked an S-shaped path toward me like an enormous train while I regarded the lifeless cavern above us. Broodmother's team stood behind her in plain sight. Their weapons were stowed, as they were clearly doing their best to look non-threatening. A green strand of electricity snaked from my chest to her claw arm. Once it made contact, smoke rose from the spot, and the tendril jerked back. The queen never flinched.

I wanted more. More destruction. More enemies. Upon seeing the Crynit matriarch, however, the thought structure of the old Raystar became more persistent in its desire for control.

"My broodling, my Prime," Broodmother said, pointing a giant sensor stalk in Nonch's direction, "is dying."

I vaguely remembered Nonch's injuries and remembered that the Raystar of the past (a stranger now?) had been trying to help him. Trying to get help. The halo of lightning around me was flickering. I needed energy.

Oh. Nonch.

The leggers had pulled back Nonch's carapace like a poorly peeled boiled egg. They'd *scooped* his flesh out with their tentacles. Mieant and Cri backed away from me as I approached.

"Legger," I said. They both blinked. My anger surged. "*Legger*," I said, more loudly this time. "GET ME LEGGERS!"

Unconsumed (by me!) legger body parts were strewn everywhere. As my meaning dawned on him, Mieant motioned to my sister. Together they dragged one over, one giant, hairy corpse, and then another. I ran my hand through the bristly fur of the first legger and then grabbed a leg. I leaned my body into Nonch's head and closed my eyes. His sensor stalks were cool and soft against my grimy face. He smelled of clean rain and also the putrid musk of legger viscera.

Nonch. Prime. Shells. These were all of the names he was called that were now calling to me, to Raystar of old. A Human. The most important name of all was *friend*. Nonch was my friend.

Friendship requires commitment translated into action.

I reached into my core. Infection was still there, a miasma still deep within me, but I pushed through it until I found my old self, crackling with white energy. It was me, and I was it. There was an honesty of connection within myself that I'd never experienced in all the times I'd manifested before.

And then, inexplicably, horribly, Infection cascaded through me again. My desire to heal turned red with fury as a desire to consume

took over. Fever-hot, I squeezed the legger with my left hand and let my nannites and my power flow into it. Its hulk twitched. *Infection.* Its power was growing each time I used my power. I didn't quite remember what had transpired in the previous five minutes.

But I have control now. Right?

Sparks poured out of me and onto the ground. As if they had a mind of their own, the sparks pooled around the dead legger and encrusted it like sparkly autumn frost.

For the moment, I guess I do.

In my command overlay, Nonch appeared as a grey outline; I laid my right hand on his body. I took in his cracked carapace, his broken mandibles, and the gaping hole in his back where he'd been eaten alive. My power *had* to be good for something besides destruction. I had to be better than the entity I had been mere moments before. If all they ever built were weapons, then in my opinion, ancient Humans were looking increasingly like Void-cursed jerks.

My nanotech began converting the legger parts without my instruction. "Biomass conversion in progress," my command overlay informed me. Whatever AI had done had enabled me to understand the interface—or perhaps it simply allowed the interface to communicate with me. That was a question for another day. For now, my only focus was survival.

Minerals, proteins—they oozed like a soup across the floor from the legger carcass like a tide rolling onto a beach. The biomass flowed up the side of Nonch's body and poured into his wounds. As the biomass grew, the legger carcass became smaller and less recognizable with each second, as my nannites peeled off layers of bristle, skin, muscle, and organs, until red, wet bone was all that was left. White sparks jittered over the bones, and finally, even the bones vanished.

What power I have!

"Divert?" my systems inquired, as if in response to my feelings.

Sparks flowed down my right arm and out from my fingertips, which were pressed against Nonch's damaged carapace. At first, he twitched as if I'd shocked him. Millions of millimeter-long sparks began arcing around his body, creeping into his wounds. They flowed into the massive gap in his carapace, flooding the empty space where his flesh had been gnawed away with dazzling light.

I didn't know how I knew, but somehow, I just *knew* that Nonch's heart needed stimulation. I focused my energy on his heart muscles, regulating their contractions and creating the rhythm his body needed to pump its blood. Energy washed through me—I was nothing more than a conduit.

And then yet again, Infection—the horrible force had a name— made its presence felt. My world spun and suddenly, to my shame, Nonch *became* my energy source. His body audibly hissed as the flow of his reconstruction was reversed, and his mass began to be drawn into my body. My nannites were coursing through his body and that of the legger, and Infection began to declare its ownership of my will.

YOUR BODY, YOUR FRIEND'S BODY: THEY ARE BOTH MINE. MINE. NOTHING IS MORE IMPORTANT THAN ENERGY. FUEL. FEED ME. HEAL ME. TAKE REVENGE ON THOSE WHO PUT ME HERE. EVERYONE. GODWILL.

Nonch began to writhe.

NO! Restore! I concentrated fully, using everything good that was left within me. The flow reversed again.

Infection grew angry, outraged that I had siphoned energy away from the matter-conversion process. The battle going on inside my body was equal to the one I'd fought against the leggers. I threw myself into it with everything I had, but Infection pushed back.

FOOL.

I blinked. I needed more power to fight.

YES. FIGHT.

It only made sense: take energy from the leggers and fight Infection. For a moment, I began to pull energy from Nonch again.

No! I erected internal walls to partition Infection away from Nonch.

YOU ARE MINE, Infection directed to me.

I am mine! I thought back furiously.

Infection only laughed. He could laugh if he chose. Healing Nonch: that was the only thing that mattered. The only thing!

I forced my will, my good angel, into the battle for control. Nonch groaned and writhed as the tug-of-war continued. The first legger had been consumed and transformed to heal my friend. Now the second carcass was also covered in a blanket of my sparks.

Just a bit more.

There was no way I'd let Infection win.

The subject is healed, my systems' clinical voice confirmed in my mind.

Now that Nonch is restored, I thought, *I can use these energy sources to destroy Infection.*

Suddenly, an image flashed into my awareness, placed there by Infection itself. It was a vision of myself, in the here and now: my purple hair stood in spikes that pointed in every direction. Before my astonished and terrified eyes, I saw that I was turning to silver—turning into IT-ME. Whatever "being Human" meant, it didn't apply to me anymore. I wasn't Human. I was like Artem, Godwill's first experiment. I had used too much power. Godwill had won. Infection had won.

Just like that, I had lost.

24

YOU ARE MINE, Infection said—its presence within me was palpable. Healing Nonch was a massive drain on my power, and in the process, Infection had escaped the confines of his internal prison. *YOUR GUARDIAN CONSTRUCT IS TERMINATED.*

Was Infection referring to AI? What had AI done? Had he burned out his cores to supply me with power? *I love you,* he'd told me. Throughout my life, AI's thoughts had been an ever-present beacon: a warmth, an assurance, a moral compass.

Emotions that were the darkest I'd ever had, filled with grief, self-loathing, and loss, swirled in my core. I would have dived into them, but I became more preoccupied with the fact that I couldn't feel my body. No hands, no feet. No sensation from my lungs as I drew a breath, nor a beat from my heart. No vision, no hearing, no taste, no sense of smell. Had I been consumed? Lost forever?

Deprived of my senses, I was pure idea. Pure concept, 100 percent an abstract intellect. There was no up, no down, no hot, no cold… there was only *being.* Was I even alive? And if one's existence is limited to thought alone, how does one have an effect on anything?

Suddenly, I felt Infection's—the name was well earned—attention turn away from me. That worried me. If it wasn't focused on me, what *was* it focused on? It presumably had total control of my body and my power. Given how much power I'd consumed from the leggers, and my new awareness of my capabilities, I was sure that only Godwill or

Artem would be able to stand against me. If Infection had control of me, my power, I needed to be terminated.

AI? Against reason, I reached out to him. No response.

I could feel myself—or I suppose was allowed to feel myself—walking, first, and then my sight returned. Nonch was still in the spot where Cri and Mieant had moved him, but he'd curled himself into a midnight blue coil. I looked into his eyes—he was either looking at me or just staring into the space where I had once been. Broodmother had wrapped her body around him, her immense segmented form serving as both a barrier and a warning.

I'd healed him. There was that, at least. Where the leggers I'd used for biomass had once lain, only dark, bloody smears and clumps of greasy hair remained on the melted and warped Human roadway—the fast-drying last vestiges of the battle.

Unbidden, my gaze floated to Mieant and Cri. They looked at me, terrified. Mieant's arm curled around Cri, pulling her close. I closed the distance between us.

"Raystar," Cri said in a small voice, "what you did. That was...."

Infection then turned its focus to her, searching MY memories for our history. Of course, in my most recent ones, Cri represented a threat. Infection read through the anger I'd felt toward her, but I sensed in it a total lack of comprehension of *why* I'd been angry. In my earlier memories, Cri was my beloved big sister, but the newly aware artificial intelligence that controlled me had neither experience in nor a capacity for moderation. Raw from the recent battle and fed a steady stream of my memories, Infection simply focused on the next threat: my sister.

"Ray?" Cri said.

I stared at her helplessly as Infection decided how it would respond. I could feel it, pure and unrestricted, as it tapped into my powers. My ethereal self could still feel emotions, and I was really spiked that Infection could access and control my power—my very being—so easily.

Crackling energy burst from me and encircled Mieant. Using MY power, Infection pushed him away, separating the two of us by a meter.

"Stay away," Infection said to Mieant through my voice. It formed my expression into a frown and continued, "Perhaps only minimal harm will come to your mate."

Then Infection turned to Cri. "You continue to torment me," Infection used my voice to say. Its voice was inflectionless, the voice of a machine. "Why?"

Cri blanched. She and I had argued and fought many times. But she recognized the difference. This wasn't me. Nervously, she pushed her black hair away from her face. Underneath a thick coating of ash streaks, her skin flushed blood red. Her eyes glowed with fear as she internalized just how *very* alien her sister was. She had just opened her mouth to reply when Infection, the beast within me, struck her. Hard. Her head whipped to the side, and she stumbled.

I'd never used my strength or my nano against my sister before. Or anyone else, actually, before this past week.

"Nova!" she cried, her hands flying up to her cheek.

"Raystar! Stop!" Mieant said, inserting himself between us, but Infection was faster and stronger than he was. Energy convulsed from my fist as Infection flung Mieant into a huge pile of dirt.

I hit her again. *NO*—it was Infection using my body to slap my sister. The crack of my hand as it splayed across her darkening cheek echoed through the tunnel.

"Sister mine," Infection said, the words sounding alien as they left my lips. With my left hand, Infection grasped my sister's neck. Her expression was a snapshot of disbelief and horror. Infection placed my right hand gently, like a lover's touch, against her cheek.

"Ray," Cri whispered, "please...." She blinked at me, her four hands on my spindly, iron-gripped Human hand encircling her throat.

I leaned in closer. "So many times you have tormented me," Infection said. I could feel Cri's heart rumble as it pushed blood through her veins. With only the slightest exertion, I knew, Infection could harden my nails into razors. "Now it is your turn, sister mine."

Memories of all of the times Cri had bullied me or verbally cut me down in front of my friends swirled to the front of my mind.

My malevolent parasite was stealing my petty, childish memories and transforming them into a giant psychopathic grudge.

I was pretty sure Infection was going to kill my sister. I redoubled my efforts at freeing myself, except there were no walls, no barriers, no constraints—nothing to move or push against or free myself from. I was trapped in the infinity of my brain's space.

Is this what it's like to be nothing more than a thought? Eee. I promised myself fervently that if I survived, I'd treat my ideas with more respect.

Cri's muscles and cartilage gave way under the pressure of my hand. I could feel her breath on my face, the warmth of her throat. Her pulse. And I could feel my nails beginning to harden.

Broodmother and her soldiers moved toward me. I spun to face them, Cri still trapped in my grip. Sparks and white lightning coursed around my hands and crackled over Cri's hair.

"What is this?" Broodmother asked, as she eased into a relaxed battle stance. Her remaining team followed suit and spread out around me. She and her two remaining soldiers coiled themselves. Each had their six claw arms spread out for grasping and slicing, and their autocannons fixed their glowing red muzzles on me.

Spike it all. I could do nothing.

Cri's eyes flicked from my face to Broodmother, imploring her for help.

Klaxons began to blare way, way down the tunnel, but much closer than the first time I'd heard them. Apparently, the ancient Human security systems had finally become aware of our localized devastation and carnage. Above, I heard wounded leggers scrape and whimper their way to whatever their version of a safe place was. Or, as with most animals, perhaps they were seeking out a secret haven to die? *Or* possibly calling out to the millions of their kin?

I felt Infection processing the situation. Once its decision was made, a familiar energy surged up my spine. Noting the change in me, the queen tensed for action; her Eviscerators shimmered, cloaked, and disappeared. Weapon systems unfolded from her elite guards' armor.

Stop! I screamed in my head.

SILENCE, HUMAN CONSTRUCT. YOUR CONVERSION IS NEAR COMPLETE. VANISH WITH DIGNITY.

Vanish with digni—wha? Pffft. I'm a teenager.

You're no better than the other! Godwill created another, out of another Human! I shouted into the quiet of my disembodied prison.

Infection paused, and in my head, the pause seemed to last forever. I felt Infection push aside my thoughts as it accessed my memories of IT-ME, of Godwill's Experiment #507, of the once-Human boy named Artem.

THERE IS NO OTHER.

Liar, I said to Infection. *You've seen my memories. You're Godwill's harvest and nothing more. His creation. You have no value, no worth.*

I AM MY OWN CREATION. YOU ARE INCONSEQUENTIAL, HUMAN. GODWILL IS INCONSEQUENTIAL.

You know nothing, I replied, trying to sound confident. *You'll be hunted by the Convergence. Worse, Godwill is like me. No. He has more power than I do. He wants us. He may already have consumed Artem, making him even more powerful than we are combined.*

Infection considered the case I'd made. Meanwhile, I noticed that my friends had repositioned themselves against me. This was an all-or-nothing moment. If they went up against me, with even half of what I knew I could do, they would lose. Infection's complete understanding of my power meant that they would all die…horribly, and so would I, as a member of the Human species.

WHAT DO YOU PROPOSE? Infection's response thundered through my brain. I raised my noncorporeal eyebrows in surprise.

Give me back control of my body, I replied, *and stop converting me.*

THAT GAINS ME NOTHING.

I'm a kid. A Human kid. I want to live. You're new, a young…whatever. A nanothing. I propose that we make a truce. I'll find you sufficient feeder material, and you can leave me. You can be yourself.

YOU OFFER ME NOTHING I DO NOT HAVE OR THAT I CANNOT TAKE.

Ack. Point taken, I thought frantically. Infection was new—a digital child in the long arc of time, albeit one that could digest years of information in nanoseconds. I knew that Infection could only duplicate the information he gathered. Without feelings, he could only guess at why any of his information was valuable. He'd never know *the point of knowledge, of being alive.* It would take him much more time to evolve into a being that could think, have intuition, feel his own emotions—like me. He wasn't intrinsically evil; I could tell. Infection simply wanted to survive. It occurred to me that IT-ME, the boy named Artem who had been completely converted, probably wasn't malevolent like Godwill either. He/It simply wanted to live, too.

I'll let you continue on in my body. For a while. I'll…

THIS BODY IS ALREADY MINE.

I gritted my nonexistent teeth. I glanced over at the Crynits, who looked like they were seconds away from launching Armageddon at me. I didn't want to die, and I didn't want them to die.

I'll teach you. You can ride along in my head until we find a safe way to free you—safe for both of us. And you can learn.

MY SCAN OF YOUR JOURNEY REVEALS LITTLE MORE THAN INCOMPETENCE—A HISTORY OF REACTION VERSUS PROACTION. YOU WOULD CALL IT, "GETTING YOUR BUTT EPICALLY KICKED." WHAT COULD YOU POSSIBLY TEACH ME?

Nova and gravity wells. Infection wasn't incorrect. But it wasn't always my butt that got kicked. *Right?* I had kicked some butt myself…a little, at least.

But (*haha*) I'd been playing the victim since my first day of school. I'd reacted to each revelation, responded to each move Godwill made. Taking matters into my own hands was only a very recent development. Sure, the beginning of a plan had taken shape. It depended on getting to Blue River and talking not just to the Elions, but to others who could possibly help turn Godwill's coup on its head.

Infection wasn't interested in any of that. He cared only about survival, and he was essentially an orphan, like me. Infection and I perhaps had more in common than either of us had thought. We were both products of Terra, its technology, and its Humanity.

Learn what it means to be Human, I said hurriedly, before Infection could shut me down. *We're both from Terra. You're derived from all of the Humans who had nanotech. We're both orphans. Travel with me. Let's be allies, and let's learn together. You can't bleed, and you can't die, at least not organically. Yet you feel the fear of oblivion. You are alive, but do you know how it feels to love? To be loved? Is it enough to merely be alive? What's the point of that? Ride with me. Let me show you what it means to really live.*

I waited for what seemed like an eternity for Infection's response.

WHAT ARE YOUR REQUESTED CONDITIONS?

I get control over me. I get access to my nano, without interference. And you must release AI.

It seems like days passed in silence.

Well? I asked.

I CANNOT.

Uh.

THE GUARDIAN YOU CALL AI IS GONE. I CAN AGREE TO YOUR OTHER TERMS.

What? AI can't be gone. *No.*

DO YOU AGREE TO THIS MODIFICATION OF TERMS?

"Raystar of Terra," someone sounding like Broodmother Krig said from a distance, "release your sister, or I will take action."

AI is gone? All of the way gone?

HUMAN. DO YOU AGREE?

I...yes, I agree.

The moment I said those words to Infection, my whole wonderful kid body began to flood my senses. As I released Cri, her body crumpled. Mieant promptly gathered her up in his arms. All four of her hands shot up to her neck as she coughed and glared at me. I dropped to my hands and knees and bowed my head. My purple bangs draped over my eyes, and my eyes brushed the grey Human roadway. The fever burning in my gut, around Godwill's injections, had faded to nothing.

I gulped down the lovely, smooth tunnel air and inhaled the now-glorious smells of ash, burnt legger, and my own unwashed body. I grabbed my ribs, hugging myself. I sat back on my heels, closed my eyes, tilted my head up to the ceiling, and took a moment.

AI had given himself for me. Maybe it was his duty, but he'd loved me. And yeah, if you got right down to it, I loved him too. That realization humbled me, bent me in half, as I realized the enormity of my loss.

Infection.

HUMAN, it replied.

Are you ready for your first lesson?

I AM CURIOUS.

With as much detail and force as I could muster, I thought of my life with AI. Flying through 'natch fields on my dart, with him yelling at me to slow down. Listening to his sarcastic remarks as he bore witness to my various stumbles. Feeling his warmth during my bad dreams. Paying attention as he taught me how to hack into the compound's synth. And me flushing him down the toilet.

White legger ash clumped around my falling droplets of grief as I mourned my friend.

WHAT IS THIS?

It is life, Infection. It is witness. It is love.

And loss.

"Human."

Broodmother's no-gratcher-excrement voice snapped me out of my mental dive into what it meant to lose AI. The sweet scents of sugar and soil registered in my newly restored sense of smell. Nonch had taught me well that if I ever smelled that around a Crynit, I should run: it was their pheromone scent of deadly intent.

Broodmother raised her torso several meters from the ground. Her six black claw arms were spread wide as if she were a spider ready to enfold me in their razor-sharp embrace, just as she'd done with the leggers. Her soldiers struck similar poses. Their four centipede heads, each topped with two iridescent orange eyes and eight smaller black eyes, were focused on me, and their scythe-like mandibles, each as long as my leg, were pointed at me. The Eviscerator drones, now cloaked and invisible, had repositioned themselves around us—no doubt in the most lethal way possible. I gulped.

"Move away from my child. Move away from the others." Broodmother's calm, feminine tone belied the obvious threat of violence in exchange for my noncompliance.

Slowly—*very* slowly—I raised my hands. Cri glared at me from inside Mieant's embrace. They stood opposite Nonch and Broodmother; I pressed myself against the wall and shuffled sideways about ten meters away from them.

Broodmother's guards and the newly uncloaked Eviscerators formed a protective line between the others and me. Broodmother, serpentine and massive, moved over to Nonch and began caressing him with her sensor stalks.

Nonch! I'd nearly forgotten about him! Hopefully, I'd managed to heal him. Infection remained quiet, and my body was suffused with warmth, humanity, and caring.

The queen hissed and clicked softly. She was so enormous that her soft hisses sounded like avalanches of sand sliding down a dune. Her six blade arms ended in claw hands as dexterous as my own; she ran them up and down Nonch's carapace, searching for any remaining wounds. Nonch's sensor stalks rose and fell like grey sails greeting the wind. Broodmother pulled back her sensor stalks until they barely touched Nonch's. New fragrances, like fruits and flowers, suddenly overpowered the stench of ash and burnt legger that had permeated the tunnel.

WHAT ARE THEY DOING? Infection asked.

Talking.

ARE THEY USING A NETWORK?

Shhh, I replied. *Pay attention.*

Their sensor stalks had taken on a wet sheen. I knew that Crynits communicated with chemicals, but I'd never really thought about *how.* I knew that scent was used, for sure, but as I watched the mother and her child, I realized that their sensor stalks must be used to exchange chemicals. It was amazing.

After a few moments of their sensor-stalk communication, Broodmother and Nonch parted, and she turned to me.

"Explain."

Broodmother's demand was not an academic request for information; it was a quiet hand on the lever of my puny existence.

I noted the expectant gazes of my friends. I shivered and faltered, stumbling with words unspoken and emotions lost, until I finally gathered the breath to tell them about the battle that had raged within me: AI, Infection, and me. I told them that AI was gone, or dormant, at least. I told them of the deal Infection and I had agreed to. I feared that they wouldn't believe the preposterous story, but I guess it didn't seem unbelievable given what had just happened.

Broodmother was silent for a time before she spoke.

"You are a hazard. It would be prudent to eliminate you now and reduce the risks to our future." Broodmother's words were tired, her existence measured in thousands of years. This moment was nothing to her.

She lurched toward me, but Nonch intercepted her. He wrapped his four remaining blade arms around her midsection and laid his sensor stalks flat against her armor. Broodmother froze, clearly shocked by the mother-son tableau of affection and love. Time seems to move in a different sphere when the heart embraces it.

Nonch released his mother. She towered above him even as she folded herself, her deadly, massive predatory head looming over both of us. Nonch's two orange upper eyes gazed into hers.

"It is a hug," my friend said to his mother. "Raystar taught it to me. It is a gesture of affection. Of gratitude. Of witness."

Broodmother regarded her broodling and then me, her meter-long sensor stalks folding flat against her head in irritation. As she faced me, her torso several meters off the ground, her form cast a shadow over precisely the spot where I was standing. I looked up at her, past her folded blade arms, and gazed into the maw and visage of the ruler of all of the Crynits on planet Nem'.

"A bringer of such death in a small body," she said. "I wanted to believe Humanity's power was myth. Exaggerations handed down over thousands of years. But the horror of your species is real. And this lesson was delivered to me by one with no years to learn restraint or tolerance. A child. The irony would amuse me," she continued, waving a claw arm at me, "if you weren't standing before me."

I swallowed hard, looked up, and pushed purple hair out of my face so I could make eye contact with her.

"You saved my offspring," she continued. "This one, Nonch, is particularly important to me. He is my Prime. For his life, I am in your

debt. Make no mistake, Human child: you are too dangerous to be allowed to live. But neither I nor any of mine, will raise spine or claw against you until this debt is balanced." Her voice was deep and melodious. It contained no anger but communicated her vow with the finality of a mountain.

Well, I wasn't expecting that.

Moments passed. My neck began to hurt from looking up at her. My heart thundered as I tried to figure out what to do next—what wouldn't result in being eaten alive, dismembered, or any number of other dark possibilities.

"Th-thank you, Broodmother Krig," I stammered. Reflexively, my hands flew to AI's pendant around my neck. It was cold.

Nonch thrummed to my side. He stopped about a meter away and gently touched my head with a sensor stalk. "Thank you, Ray-star-Friend, for my life," he said gently, wrapping his four claw arms around me. I hugged him back, sighed, and laid my head against his warm carapace, grateful that my friend was okay.

Broodmother sighed, too, a sound like the wind through the trees. She turned back to her guard and my friends, muttering to herself in disgust as she moved away from us: "I only 'hug' the things I eat."

26

"Human machines approach," said one of Broodmother's elite soldiers. He pointed down the tunnel with a sensor stalk—luckily, the opposite direction from where I'd first encountered Broodmother.

"Thank you, Commander First Claw," Broodmother replied. First Claw dipped his huge head in a gesture of respect and joined the remaining troops as they conferred in whispers and hisses.

Someone laughed. I craned my neck to see who amongst my friends could possibly find our current predicament funny; as I did, a few pebbles slid down from the gaping hole in the tunnel's ceiling.

Nothing was funny, in fact. I spied a few ropy tentacles peeking down from the darkness above, testing the air. All heads in the tunnel swiveled to face the hole above us as more dirt fell to the tunnel floor. *They're back?*

Nonch had told us that there were millions of leggers in the underground network of tunnels. It occurred to me that the detonation of a mini-nuke, an underground avalanche, our battle against the leggers, my nanoincinerator bomb finale—TA DA!—and now a warning klaxon probably added up to the most excitement that this forgotten, dusty, lonely, dark, underground world had experienced since the Lethian–Human War. If we'd been really lucky, the remaining leggers would have been deafened by the concussions, but that was too much to wish for. It was much more likely that they were furious about the

devastation I'd wreaked on their brothers and sisters, or eggmates, or whatever they were.

Screams pierced the darkness above us, triggering a chorus of insane giggles. Mieant and Cri, who stood directly under the gaping maw above, flinched and pressed themselves against the tunnel wall. Beside me, Nonch flattened his sensor stalks against his midnight-blue carapace.

"We must hurry. Leggers possess excellent hearing. With the amount of noise we made, they will return in greater numbers. Another encounter will not be survivable, even with our Human," Broodmother said, raising her sensor stalks and angling her head up toward the hole, as if she was examining some sort of new and interesting cloud formation. She turned to her soldiers and drones and ordered, "You, drone, and you"—she pointed at a soldier—"remain here. Commander First Claw, you will clear our path home. You will ensure our safe passage to the Broodship."

"My Queen," First Claw replied, "the Human sentinels we destroyed may have signaled for reinforcements. I recommend that we take the alternate branch we saw earlier instead of going back through the tunnel. I will leave one guard at the fork. If we are pursued, the guard will lead the pursuers down the original route as a distraction, a diversion."

Broodmother nodded in agreement.

"A volunteer to remain here and protect our retreat?" First Claw continued, turning to three of his troops. One glided forward to wait underneath the cavernous hole twiddling his, uh, claws, or—more likely—to end up running like a Void-cursed gratcher with its tail on fire from hordes of hairy, massive, pus-eyed leggers.

"Your sacrifice is accepted," First Claw said, dipping his head to the noble—and suicidal—soldier.

"WAIT! WAIT!" I shouted. I probably shouldn't have shouted, because everyone flinched and a legger giggled somewhere above us. I didn't want to cause any further deaths or injuries. *Very* carefully—out of self-preservation and out of respect for the raw nerves among our group—I removed the remaining fat, oddly-colored grenade from my belt and offered it to the commander. "For your soldier."

First Claw tilted his head sideways and regarded me.

"It's a mini-nuke," I said hurriedly, "that perhaps would enable your soldier to avoid being followed. See? Pull this pin, throw it, and run." I paused and nodded at the grenade before adding, "*Definitely* run."

First Claw chuffed and rattled his armor. I knew from Nonch that the gesture signified Crynit laughter.

Cri rolled her eyes. "Like that worked so well before," she muttered.

"I *know* what it is, child," First Claw said. Ignoring Cri, he took the mini-nuke from me and passed it to his soldier. The commander nodded once and turned to face his queen.

Broodmother regarded me intently—as lunch, perhaps? She swiveled to face Cri and Mieant, who flinched under the weight of her gaze, and said, "You both shall ride on the back of a warrior."

"Broodmother," Nonch said.

She turned to her Prime and said, "The Eviscerators will carry you."

I gulped as Broodmother's eyes turned to me. "Come," she said, picking me up like a sack of 'natch. "You will ride with me."

I was going to ride on the back of the Convergence's sharp, pointy, angry, and immensely powerful alpha predator. Hey, when life takes you places you never expected...try to enjoy the ride.

Even weighted down with combat armor, Crynits could really move. My purple bangs flew away from my face as I leaned into the queen's back.

"INTRUDER ALERT! INTRUDER ALERT!" a Human klaxon wailed in a hollow monotone far behind us in the tunnel. The lights in the underground roadway had turned from white and blue to blood red. In a distant part of my shell-shocked mind, I realized that I understood what the klaxon was saying—despite the fact that the Human language, both written and spoken, had been eliminated from Galactic nanotranslators.

My nano must be helping me understand. AI had warned me that increased use of my nano would fundamentally change me.

Mieant and Cri rode together on the back of another Crynit. She rested against his chest; her eyes, glowing with golden light, shone like headlights, and her black hair flew like the wild wings of starbats. Mieant encircled her chest with one arm, which she clasped tightly with all of her four arms, and he held on tight to the Crynit with his other.

Mieant's head was buried in Cri's hair. I wondered what he was whispering to her and also what my sister was thinking. I frowned as I watched them, tight against each other, swaying as their Crynit raced toward our escape.

I'll bet she isn't thinking about me. Why should she think of me? I mean, after all, I almost killed her.

As it noted my familiar descent into self-pity, Infection's voice boomed into my awareness: *YOU ARE WEAK. I WILL RESUME CONTROL. THE CREATURE CALLED BROODMOTHER IS A CONSIDERABLE ASSET. I WILL MOVE OUR SHARED CON-SCIOUSNESS TO HER.*

Cri had a boyfriend. I had psychotic nanotech.

No.

YOU CANNOT STOP ME.

We have an agreement.

I AGREED TO YOUR TERMS OUT OF CURIOSITY. YOU BE-LONG TO ME, HUMAN.

You have control of my physical body. My thoughts, however, are not yours. You will not learn what you want unless you give me my free-dom.

I HAVE YOUR MEMORIES. I WILL EXTRAPOLATE. I CAN RE-MAKE A VERSION OF YOU.

I hadn't considered that Infection could make a simulation of me. That seemed…unfair.

Yeah, I replied, *except your simulation won't have the ability to see what I would do in new situations. Easy to duplicate. Hard to create.*

Infection was silent in my head for a moment.

Well? I asked.

I WILL ABIDE BY OUR AGREEMENT.

So, let's see where Broodmother is taking us. I feel the need to re-mind you that we are both being hunted. Let's get as many pieces of this puzzle together before you go psycho on me.

I AM NOT "PSYCHO." I ACT IN EXTREME SELF-INTEREST, AND THIS IS NOT A PUZZLE, HUMAN.

That's exactly my point, Infection. It's a metaphor. You need context to understand a metaphor. You'll never have that context without me.

Infection did not respond. I held on to Broodmother's back a little more tightly as I contemplated the difference between extreme self-interest and caring for others.

28

We raced away from the hole I'd created with my mini-nuke and the horrible, shrieking, nerve-grinding, Human klaxon. The Human roadway's blood-red emergency lighting cast a sickly red glare on the queen's black chitin. As we fled, we passed the spot where I'd first encountered Broodmother. As we turned the corner, I finally saw what the Crynits had been fighting: three giant Human automatons lay on the roadway in various states of wreckage. Their skin, or armor, I suppose, appeared mottled. It took me a moment to realize that they were in fact camouflaged; those body parts that lay against the white tunnel wall were white, and those that were in the roadway were grey. The overall effect of blending into the white and grey of the tunnel was that these titans, each more than three meters tall, were practically invisible. Still, I noted that some had missing limbs and holes in their torsos, leaking orange fluid. Black bits of metal—which were quite visible—were embedded in their bodies.

Twelve armored Crynit corpses were also strewn about. It was clear where the battle had begun further up the tunnel, where Broodmother and her guard had finally defeated the Humanoids, and where they'd encountered AI and me. The destruction, both cybernetic and organic, told a story of three Human constructs taking on Broodmother's elite guard of five Eviscerators and eighteen soldiers (including the queen herself). We thrummed past the carnage. I was scared, tired, and hungry, but I took some small comfort from the notion (perhaps it was really a delusion) that we were escaping.

Unfortunately, we were not escaping faster than the speed of sound. Eventually, the unmistakable whoosh of launched missiles and the subsequent impact concussions caught up with us. Broodmother twitched a sensor stalk in the direction of the sound like a massive sail catching the wind.

"Who was that?" I whispered, leaning closer to Broodmother's sensor stalks.

"Convergence weapons. The False Jurisdictor's warriors." Broodmother paused to listen again. "They have found us. They likely followed your path from your parents' compound. They are engaged in battle with Human security automatons or leggers, or both."

My parents. It had been some time since I had thought of them. I gulped down memories before they could overwhelm me.

"Ummm…" I uttered.

Broodmother spared a backward glance at me; I caught a glimpse of my reflection in one of her prismatic, jeweled eyes. "Three Human security automatons killed twelve of my elite troops in full battle armor," she explained. "Assuming that the Human security forces that are now arriving at the site of our battle are as capable as those that we encountered, they will keep either or both opponents very busy. In either case, our enemies are pitting themselves against each other. Their fight inadvertently aids our escape."

Godwill: my horrible antagonist, Infection's author, the bane of my existence. After the encounter with my parents, he must have followed us through the bunker. I shook my head until it was clear; I needed to live in the moment.

In the outrageous present, I began to notice a tiny square device in my pocket poking at my thigh. The detonator! Dad had instructed us to blow up the compound so Godwill and his force couldn't follow us—like they were in fact following us now.

Spike the spiked gravity wells! How could we have forgotten?

I glanced at Cri, who was resting against Mieant—as usual!—with her eyes half open. She either hadn't heard or wasn't paying attention to the mayhem behind us, and she had the other detonator.

Should I yell to her? I thought. *We could destroy our compound right now. But what if Mom and Dad are in the compound? What if all of Godwill's soldiers were already in the Crynit tunnels or on the Human roadway? It would be just our luck that we'd nuke our home with our parents stashed inside by Godwill. We'd still end up captured, and we'd inadvertently do him a favor by killing our own parents.*

With a little more imagination, I continued, *I could probably come up with an even suckier outcome. Besides, we've traveled quite far from our bunker. The detonators might be out of range.*

"How far to, uh...?" I asked Broodmother. *Where* are *we going, anyway?*

"We are near my sanctuary, Human," she replied, and with that, I tucked away all thoughts of the detonators. There were simply too many unknowns. The opportunity had passed, anyway, and like all opportunities not taken, it was forever lost.

Moments later, we crossed over into a section of the Human tunnel that appeared uncharacteristically dark and dirty. It seemed like an area that had fallen into disuse, which of course was silly given the ancient nature of the whole structure. It was actually far more surprising that the rest of the tunnel was so immaculate.

Then I noticed the massive hole in one of the tunnel walls. As we neared the hole, I realized that it was, in fact, a metal door fifteen meters or so wide. It looked like the iris of an eye, with inward-pointing triangular blades that could cycle open and closed. Scattered around the door, all around the tunnel floor, walls, and ceiling, were hundreds of red eyes glimmering at us in the darkness.

Wait, those aren't eyes. They shimmered with heat. They were plasma turrets smaller than any I'd ever seen before and far too numerous to count!

As if she was reading my mind, Broodmother said, "These will not stop Godwill nor any Human automatons, but rest assured, they make short work of leggers." As she neared the door, it opened, and she flowed through its giant blades with the rest of our party right

behind her. As the last passed through, the door scythed shut with metal-on-metal finality.

We were back in a Crynit tunnel, but this one was bright, made of concrete and metal, and it was alive with far too many smells for my limited Human sniffer to sort out. I wondered what was being communicated with all of those scents. As we raced through the labyrinth, Crynits appeared from time to time, but all hustled out of our way as their monarch thrummed past. The ceiling arched high above us.

As we continued, the tunnel gradually expanded into what was arguably a main thoroughfare. Vehicles floated beside us and above us, moving toward unknown purposes. Hundreds of Crynits similarly raced to their particular destinations in a cacophony of clicks and hisses and an incomprehensible number of sweet-sour smells. But let me tell you: all that wasn't the amazing part.

We turned down a large branch in the road and jerked to an abrupt halt as we reached a massive platform. Before us yawned a cavern so vast that it could swallow an asteroid with room to spare. The ceiling was a sky shrouded in darkness, and the chasm below us could have stretched to the center of Nem'.

Broodmother's hive. Architect! Does anyone who isn't a Crynit know this is down here?

"Great gravity wells," Mieant exclaimed, "this is a city!"

Before us lay millions of multicolored lights, all in motion. It seemed like it was filled with clouds of ships, some close by and some far away, each moving toward their own purpose yet seemingly also moving together. It all glowed like a galaxy, swirling, diving, and soaring in the cavern's black void.

Occasionally, swaths of the lights—thousands of ships, I suppose— would suddenly go dark and then light up again some distance away from where they'd previously appeared. It was as if they were going behind something far more massive. I frowned as my brain slowly assembled the areas of darkness into something I could understand.

This is no underground city. Nova.

Mieant was wrong. I'd seen this before with Nonch, back at our school's library.

29

"Nonch?" I said, stroking my friend's feather-soft sensor stalks. We were in the Nem' Educational Facility's library. I laid my head against his warm armor and asked, "Why do you hate being a Crynit?"

Other than AI, Nonch was my best friend, and I was definitely his best friend. He never teased me, even though I was the smallest in our class, and he was by far the largest and most dangerous of all. I'd nick-named him Shells in a nod to his segmented carapace, the natural body armor of a Crynit; it looked and felt like a collection of giant seashells. When Nonch rose to his full three-meter height, his midnight-blue carapace, grey sensor stalks, arm-length mandibles, and six sword arms should have terrified me, yet I knew in my heart he would never hurt me. His nickname for me was Juicebag, because according to him, I was water and blood before I was bone and cartilage. We had some-thing in common: we were hated for our extremes. Other than the bul-lies, who loved to torment us, the rest of the kids stayed away from us.

I knew that Mom and Dad loved me the way I was, of course, but more than anything, I wanted to not be Human. To not be different. Yet the Convergence had hundreds of races. In truth, we were *all* different.

I thought hard about my friendship with Nonch. *Is he able to expe-rience friendship in the same way I can? Are any of us able to scramble over the barriers in our own heads, our own biological or environmental contexts, and actually feel what another individual feels? Isn't that the basis of friendship?*

I desperately wanted it to be true. I desperately needed a friend.

"Look," he said, extending a blade arm but taking great care to not crush or slice through any of the library's vid research terminals, "everything about me is destruction. War is the Crynit's medium. Crynits embody fear, enforcement, conquest."

"Shells, it's not like that," I said. Our voices were muffled. We came to the library because in its great, dark halls, we knew we could talk and not be heard. Huge triangular sails—sound dampeners—hanging from the ceiling were positioned perfectly to allow students at research terminals to grab information orbs, spread them out, and talk loudly about whatever they were focused on, without disturbing others. For our purposes, it was the only place where we could get the privacy we needed.

"I recognize that your people are hunters. I recognize a hunter in you," he continued.

"I'm small. Weak," I replied, laughing. "You haven't even seen my people, and neither have I."

He regarded me silently, becoming still. It was so unnerving when he did that.

"You have a galaxy-sized ability to not see what is obvious, Raystar-Friend-Mine. Perhaps your kind's blindness is why Humanity lost a war it should have won."

Cool, processed library air wafted my purple bangs into my eyes. I poofed them away as I tilted my head to meet his gaze. Something like rain and sweetness wafted down from him.

"Shells, what are you ta…"

"Watch," Nonch interrupted, "so you may learn who you are, and what I do not want to be." He extended a sword arm and grabbed a glowing orb with the bright red claw hands that tipped it. With a quick gesture, Nonch flung it into the air in front of us.

"You are different. Your differences are *why* I like you, Raystar-Only-Friend-Mine."

The vid flickered to life before I could respond.

Kurt Johnson / Bruce E. Mitchell

RECORDER ARCHIVES: LETHIAN–HUMAN CONFLICT
BANEFIRE SYSTEM, GALACTIC CYCLE 10.898.500.177.6
UNKNOWN CRYNIT WARSHIP DESTROYS TERRAN PLANETSHIP

The first image was one of pure darkness. I gradually began to make out the Galactic Core, but it was masked by the vaporous explosions of ships—thousands of ships, some with fiery jets pouring forth from massive tears in their hulls. Others floated dark and dead, and still others tumbled uncontrollably through the vacuum of space, their minimal-energy systems flickering on and off along their titanic hulks. As Nonch and I watched, countless millions of lives were being snuffed out, sucked into space, or incinerated as the powers of creation were unleashed…for destruction. It was a scene of dark purple clouds backlit with occasional fingers of lightning. Mini-novas strobed in the bellies of the clouds. In this Galactic alley fight behind thin curtains, only silhouettes and muted colors of the conflict were visible.

Banefire, our angst-filled red giant, shone malevolently across the starscape. The blue, green, and white of Nem' was front and center.

Wait, I thought, *Nem' had a moon back then?*

Sure enough, a moon nearly a quarter of Nem's size was jetting debris from its ragged sphere. The moon's halo flickered with tongues of star-blue light that reached out to surround…a spiky black *thing*. The thing—it looked like some sort of sea urchin—spat orange tongues of energy as the moon threw corona-sized arms of white plasma at it.

Through clouds of gas, forces of existence, the urchin continued to push forward. *FORWARD!* The moon clearly wanted to end the offender, but it could not. A stellar collection of energies beyond comprehension focused on the spiky black shape as it accelerated toward the moon's heart. Suddenly, the Recorders' vid faded to white.

A moment later, the vid flickered back on. Nem' remained, surrounded by a silvery halo of rings. The moon had vanished.

The Recorder zoomed in.

The urchin paused in blackness before accelerating again, this time toward Nem' itself. It began to glow more brightly as Nem's atmosphere consumed its shell.

The surface of Nem' came alive. Missiles rose from its surface in such numbers that the planet became a dandelion of destruction. The planet itself flickered gold, and a short blink later it transformed into a golden pearl.

A planetary shield?

The blinding light that followed destroyed the Recorders, but not before they transmitted a final gasp of a message:

RECORDER DESTRUCTION IMMINENT.
UNKNOWN CRYNIT WARSHIP.
CATEGORY: ASSASSIN CLASS.

"That was a Terran planetship, the most formidable class in its fleet. In this engagement, it singularly defeated an entire Convergence Battlegroup," Nonch said.

I took a deep breath as I considered the implications. "Wait, so the rings around Nem' are actually what's left of the planetship?"

Nonch nodded. "And that," he said, pointing to the other ship, "is a Crynit Assassin-Class Broodship."

"Great gravity wells, Nonch. How old is this vid? How...."

"I showed you this image not because our species fought each other but instead to reveal your legacy. That planetship and the Crynit vessel were the only two survivors of a conflagration that had previously destroyed an entire Convergence Battlegroup. Indeed, had the Human world-class ship not been badly damaged from that battle, it is unlikely that the Broodship would have prevailed. Nevertheless, Humans and Crynits alike are species of killers. I do not want to be a killer."

I mean, yeah. Neither do I.

Back in the dangerous present, I found myself still riding on the back of one of the most powerful entities in the Convergence, an alpha predator. The queen swayed underneath me as we moved into her domain.

I had a bad feeling history was repeating itself.

"Whoa," Cri whispered, breaking me out of my library reverie. She pulled Mieant's arms around her tightly. "We're in a Hiveship."

An Assassin-Class Broodship, I mentally corrected her as I connected where we were with the image from the library's vid archives. What we were looking at, what lay before us, was *that* ship, the ship from the video! *How old must it be?* And the rings around Nem'—they were debris from a Human ship the size of a *moon*? *Nova and Void.* The Lethian–Human War had been right in front of us the entire time, in the background, constantly, for those without perspective.

"My parents had no idea," Mieant said, his black eyes taking in the enormous cavern and the hulk at its center. He turned to Broodmother and asked, "Uh? *Were* my parents aware of this?"

"Few in the Convergence have seen my home. No Humans lived to tell of it," Broodmother replied while looking pointedly at me. A device resembling a multifaceted orb—except with hundreds of faces—rose from her helmet and flashed once. Instantly, the patterns of lights that swarmed through the cavern changed. As if they were a single organism, they flowed toward us. As they came closer, they morphed from dots to ships and individual Crynits in armor suits. Some of the Crynits landed on our terrace. A few ships stayed nearby, floating, as their plasma turrets pointed toward the tunnel we'd just emerged from. Others flowed away, but there were so many of them that they seemed like a tidal wave of lights crashing against a rocky shore. They swept down, up, and to the sides, getting back to whatever tasks they'd been working on prior to our arrival.

"But," Mieant said, mouth agape, "this is a Hiveship?"

Not even close, Mieant. It was still sinking into my mind that this ship had actually fought against my kind, had been part of that battle around Nem'.

RAYSTAR OF TERRA. I WISH TO RID MYSELF OF YOU.

I blinked. *What?*

I CALCULATE THAT I WILL NOT SURVIVE IF I REMAIN A PART OF YOU.

Infection? I replied, my thoughts struggling to shift from puzzling together my sketchy knowledge of Convergence history into a plan to facing down my possessor. I frowned and focused. *So after all of your threats and your bullying, you see something that's larger than you and you curl into a Void-cursed geckomouse?* My restraint was scorching away under the heat of my anger. *I mean, didn't you even scan my memories before we did this deal? Fear is an emotion, not a reason. ARE YOU NOTHING MORE THAN YOUR EMOTIONS? No. We have an agreement.*

THIS CONFLICT IS…NOT SURVIVABLE.

I'd never heard uncertainty from my psychopathic possessor before.

Coward.

WHAT IS A COWARD?

It's an entity that gives up on what they could be because of one emotion: fear. You want freedom? I am your path to it, and you are mine. Get your psychopathic code together, and let's work together to make fear itself afraid!

Infection didn't reply; I was furious. *Aren't I the one who's supposed to be terrified?*

"Ah…. Young Lethian, your race's hold on the Convergence may not be as solid as your parents believe," Broodmother hissed in reply to Mieant's comment. "And no," she said, turning her mass of latent

power to face him fully, "your parents were not aware my ship had embedded on Nem'. There are many, many *important* details about this planet your parents do not know."

Commander First Claw, who was nearly as large as the queen herself, approached us, his legs rippling in synchronization. "Broodmother Krig," the Crynit said, dipping his head low as he neared.

Broodmother lowered her sensor stalks and touched the soldier atop his head. "For the Hive," she said in return. She motioned to Nonch to approach her and then gently set me on the ground. Our little group formed a ring around her.

"Take us to HiveHome, Gurile," she said, tapping Commander First Claw once again with a sensor stalk. The effect was immediate. A clam-shaped transport floated down, and Crynits spread out around it like water rippling outward from a cast pebble. A ramp extended from one of the transport's sides in telescoping segments that clanked as they extended.

Broodmother turned to address us. "Come, children. I have revealed the secret of my seat of power. There is no turning back." She paused and then added, "Look deep. This lonely, shining city is the last star of my empire. It may be the last thing you see before you die."

Our ride on the transport was smooth as silk. We rode, crowded to-gether with the hulking armored Crynits, in a silence disturbed only by the grating of the soldiers' armored plates as they rubbed against each other.

"Broodmother," Nonch asked, "why are we going to HiveHome? Can we not take the tunnels directly to Blue River?"

"Hush, Prime."

"But we must go to Blue River."

"You will most assuredly *not* go to Blue River," Broodmother re-plied mildly.

"Raystar saved my life. She will die if we do not go," Nonch replied. He paused and added, "We are honor bound to help her. If you will not, then I will."

The tension in the crowded transport quickly became electric. I had been trying to not think about Blue River and my need to meet with the Elions. They had the nano that could eliminate Infection. Since Infection was semi-aware of my thoughts, I hadn't wanted to let on that despite our alliance, I was still pursuing plans to eliminate it.

I WILL NOT ALLOW US TO GO TO BLUE RIVER. I KNOW WHAT YOU INTEND TO DO.

All-righty, then. It was fully aware of my thoughts.

The queen spun around; all of us flinched as one, save Nonch. Broodmother arched over us to point a single claw arm at Nonch's head. The Crynit guards froze, Mieant grabbed Cri and pulled her close, and I crouched down next Nonch and peered up at my large friend and his much bigger mom.

"Spawn-mine," she said in sugary tones, "the Human who cowers beside you saved you." She shuddered with the weight of finality and continued, "We are in a life debt to her. It is not a debt I want, and I will ensure it will be paid with all the haste my power and resources can provide. But YOU, my child, will not be joining her."

WE ARE NOT GOING TO BLUE RIVER, Infection boomed inside my spinning head. I scrunched my face.

"I am all but healed," Nonch said, facing his mother.

"Have you regrown your sixth claw arm?"

"Well…."

"You have not. So you are not healed. And even if you had regrown your arm, you will not go."

"But Broodmot—."

"I forbid it."

"WHY?" Nonch demanded petulantly. I was afraid he would stomp all hundred of his feet. Her soldiers traded nervous glances. My eyes met Cri's and Mieant's, and my expression probably mirrored their "I-do-not-want-to-be-here" looks. This far below Nem's surface, none of the bugs that chirped and cricked on every planet that had life were around, but the shuttle had become so quiet I imagined I could hear them above us as they chirped their little insect songs.

Broodmother twitched a sensor stalk and touched Nonch gently on the head with a claw arm. The gesture made a "tack, tack" sound.

"Because I am Queen."

The transport landed, the doors opened, and the ramp extended. Fresh air wafted in, providing a needed change of atmosphere.

Broodmother, a mobile mountain, glided past me muttering something that sounded suspiciously like, "*Teenagers.*"

Her security team emptied the transport. The formation of multi-ton, armored centipedes looked like a convoy of massive military vehicles. We followed them across an expanse of terraced landing decks that resembled flat perpendicular mushrooms on the sides of trees. There were hundreds of them, each lit up with circular patterns of landing lights. Crynits in armor suits were in motion everywhere, thousands, millions of them. Ships of all sizes were landing or departing, their destinations unknown in this underground skyscape.

After Broodmother and her escorts marched us across the expanse of landing decks, we approached what could only be described as a maw. Other civilizations might call it an arch, and if an "arch" could be something you could fly a planetary shuttle through as you dodged thirty-meter-long spikes that looked remarkably like teeth, then yeah, it was an arch.

Crynit architecture was curvaceous, like their shells, so different from the stark geometry of Galactic buildings. Their metals and building materials were green and brown. This, combined with the millions of lights both near and distant, made it seem as if we were in a forest packed with fireflies. As we passed through the arch into the maw, I felt a wave of disorientation before realizing that somehow, the floor was moving underneath us—fast enough that my hair was fluttering in a breeze.

There was A LOT of activity going on within this ship. The 98th Battlegroup's arrival on Nem' and Godwill's planetary-takeover announcement had clearly pushed this sleeping Assassin-Class warship toward awakening. I frowned and poofed hair away from my face. *No matter how powerful this Broodship is,* I thought, *the Crynits on Nem' could never hope to stand up to the 98th.*

The corridor we were in was crowded with drones and Crynits of all sizes—some of which were even more massive than the queen. The passage curved and the mysteriously moving pathway slid us to a halt in front of yet another maw. This new archway was "only" ten meters tall, and its bronze-colored doors slid open to allow us entry. Galactic doors were smooth where they came together, but like the one we'd passed through when we exited the Human tunnel, this iris-shaped portal was jagged and fit together like a predator's teeth.

"Come," Broodmother instructed.

We followed her through the metal jaws. We were children dwarfed by a black hole of dangerous unknowns.

I squinted in the near-blinding light of our new surroundings and immediately suspected something hideous.

Cynical much, Raystar? I asked myself. Well, yes. Is this light some dumb precursor to something more awful? Sure, the queen said she owed me, but she also said I needed to die. She owes me what? Maybe she meant torture? Nova. There were not going to be any breaks for me, were there? I didn't ask for any of this. I'm a kid. I'm supposed to be in school, but noooo. I wake up one day and the whole galaxy is out to get me, drink my blood, steal my DNA.

As I stepped through the doorway, I blinked into the light, preparing to be up the next gravity well without any propulsion, to be nova'd by the next horrible circumstance, to meet the new messed-up thing with whatever bravery I could muster. Because Broodmother had in fact led us into a, well, it was…a forest.

Sunlight, warm and yellow, shown down from an artificial sky. Trees, shrubs, and flowers filled the air with scents of spring, of dirt, of life. The antiseptic and chemical air we'd been breathing yielded to a cool, moist atmosphere that soothed my throat and caressed my mouth. Unthinkingly, I inhaled it until my chest swelled. Birds chirped and called to each other, completely ignoring both the giant and small, dust-and-blood covered invaders in their garden enclave. Tiny bugs cricked in a beautiful chorus.

The metal of the hallway gave way to stones inlaid with moss-covered soil. The soil was peppered with tiny purple and yellow flowers.

Several small, rectangular elevations around its perimeter looked suspiciously like Humanoid beds, except that they were covered with lush, soft-looking moss as well.

In the center of the terrace, a stone table squatted low. A golden heating orb floated half a meter above the table, and lines of yellow light descended from the orb to the multitude of dishes filling the table with fish, gratcher (which of course I couldn't eat anymore), pies, everything you could imagine.

My mouth watered as my stomach searched way, way back to consider the last time I'd eaten. A gentle breeze wafted through the oasis, serving up the aromas of the foods to each of our noses. I heard our stomachs launch into a growling contest.

Nonch ignored the bounty. Instead, he wound his way past the grass beds and the table to a small, burbling stream. He leapt into it and splashed about before disappearing momentarily below its crystalline waters, only to resurface a moment later and wind himself along the bank, where he lay, his carapace glistening. Water flowed over his midnight-blue shell, like liquid diamonds.

We gaped for what seemed like hours at the massive space and how real it felt. Broodmother rattled her armor in amusement.

"I must remember that you are but broodlings. Wash. Eat. Take a rest. This is my waiting room. In days long past, I welcomed allies here with food and simulations that would relax, restore, and delight them. Beyond this room are my personal chambers. You will be quite undisturbed here. After a short time, I will return to collect you. Then we will talk."

With that, she flowed past us and over the bridge spanning the stream as Nonch lounged in the water below her. Her path led to another iris-like portal. Her security detail followed and distributed themselves in stations on either side of the portal.

Cri's hands dropped to her sides as she took in the sights, smells, and sunlight. Mieant carefully brushed a long strand of hair from his matte-black eyes, squinted his grey face against the light, and slowly turned his head, taking it all in. As if he wasn't sure what he was seeing was real. I bolted for the table.

What was it that Broodmother had said? Wash my hands? Pfft.

I grabbed a hot hand-sized loaf of deliciously buttered bread in one hand and a drumstick half as large as my forearm that had come from some massive avian creature in the other and proceeded to stuff both into my face simultaneously. I was only slightly jealous of my sister, who was blessed with four arms; hey, I had to make do with only TWO hands. Mieant hummed to himself as he followed suit. The fruit juices, the water, the milk, ohhhh. And not a speck of 'natch, anywhere! My mouth exploded with flavors; my stomach distended happily.

And then? I grabbed a pie from the table and flopped backward into one of the mossy, grassy beds. Aromas of mint, dirt, and happiness swirled around me. I reveled in the sunlight and the comfort of a full belly. I was sore, but the moss seemed to press against my bones and muscles in a most perfect way, massaging away the pain and the turmoil of the past few days.

Maybe I'll close my eyes for a moment and soak in the sunlight, the birdsongs, the wonderful chemicals being released in my body from this delicious meal. But first, I'll eat this pie…

As I steadied myself to shove the pie in my mouth, I was suddenly flooded with memories of Mom. I *missed* her. I missed Dad, too. I missed AI. Though I had been perfectly sated, I ached with the emptiness of what I had lost, the safe intimacy of my family.

I rubbed wetness away from my eyes and spotted a pair of red and blue birds weaving through the branches above me. Puffy white clouds floated past. Leaves dappled in the sunlight as they shushed and swayed in the slight breeze. I pulled my legs up onto the mossy bed, rolled over on to my side, and tucked my hands under my cheek. My very purple hair fell down over my eyes.

I noticed that the yellow and purple micro-flowers scattered through the moss on my "bed" possessed incredible detail. I zeroed in on a purple one a finger's-length away from my nose.

I'll lie here for a moment and look at this purple flower. I was so tired. I took in a wonderful breath and thought of Mom and Dad. Of AI. *I can stay here just a little bit longer. Maybe one more beautiful second?*

I blinked, smacked my lips loudly, and wiped away a strand of drool tracing a wet line down my cheek. As I cracked one eye open, the little purple flower I'd been admiring before I'd closed my eyes greeted my vision. I took in a long breath, exhaled, and rolled onto my back. All the way from my scrunched fists high over my head, to my arched back, to my stomach, and then down through my legs to my toes, I stretched out my very well-rested body.

"Aaaaahhhh!"

Memories loaded themselves into my awareness with each subsequent aromatic breath. With each moment, I became more and more awake, until the harshest memories finally crashed into my consciousness.

Nova and gravity wells. I have three days to live! AI is gone! Infection is, well, infecting me. Oh, and the war. I almost forgot about that.

I erupted from the kid-sized imprint I'd made in the mossy bed and looked around wildly.

The birds were still chirping, the bugs were still cricking, the little creek was still burbling, and the sun was still shining. Nothing was lumbering in my direction to destroy me. A breeze kicked up to deliver the aromas of food from the nearby table to me again, and my stomach rumbled approvingly.

Mieant and my sister slept entwined on one of the other moss beds.

Barf. Nonch's midnight-blue form lay curled up in the tiny creek's crystalline water.

"They remain asleep, by my design," Broodmother's deeply feminine voice confirmed from behind and slightly above my head. I calmly turned to face her. Her body was coiled up, and she had placed herself a non-threatening distance away from me, tilting down her massive head so her prismatic eyes could meet my gaze. "I will talk with you alone."

She was both terrifying and exotic to me. I knew she didn't like Humans, and yet, she was the one who had warned Nonch that the "Awakening" was happening, and also that perhaps the Crynits had been on the wrong side of the Lethian–Human conflict. I'd saved Nonch. She'd saved me. She'd passed up many opportunities to rid herself of me, either directly or by simply just leaving me to die.

"Broodmother Krig," I said, bowing my head slightly, "thank you. The food, the sleep, was…was better than I've had in so long." I shook my head, remembering. "Thank you for giving me safety."

She nodded slightly, obviously pleased. Her melodious voice wrapped around me as she replied, "I am not without heart. You are someone's child. That Lady Ceridian and the Commander have claimed you as their own lends gravity to how you are loved."

Mom. Dad. I squinted away the wetness that welled up in my eyes. *Nova.*

"But you are Human. I am in debt to you for saving my spawn, and yet I must now take literally the stories I have been told about Humanity." She paused before adding, "I am not passive to threats."

"You intended to kill me while I slept," I half asked, half stated.

Broodmother was silent.

"Why didn't you?"

"I now believe you deserve a chance to display the *other* aspects of the Human legend. Being true to one's ideals is the foundation of everything. Humanity's beliefs are supposedly that love, friendship, and protecting the weak are ideals to be elevated. I think you have shown a Human capacity for kindness and love, and your loyalty to

my spawn means much to me." She paused for a moment before leaning in closer and whispering, "You have earned the right to die facing me, but perhaps that is not the path."

I swallowed a lump of emotions. The breeze made a shushing noise as it moved through the nearby trees. The creek burbled merrily. She and I faced each other, and after a moment, I asked, "What now?"

She turned her massive upper body toward my sleeping friends and then back to me. A curious red and blue bird darted toward her sensor stalks before realizing they weren't tree branches, stopping short, and skittering off toward the forest.

"Consume more food and enjoy the respite. We shall face our relentless destinies soon enough."

Broodmother rose, wound her way toward the table, and took a seat. Despite her massive size, she moved with the stealth of a hunter: slow but with great potential for fast, explosive movement. My stomach grumbled. Broodmother Krig had her priorities straight: food before destiny.

"My Moon," someone whispered nearby, "how are you feeling?"

One of Broodmother's sensor stalks pivoted toward where Mieant and Cri lay.

"I feel so good," came the reply. "I want us to stay here."

Mieant and Cri were quite literally wrapped up in each other. Her upper arms were crossed over her chest, and her lower arms encircled his waist. He had an arm draped around her neck, and thick strands of her black hair framed his grey face. They stared into each other's eyes, their breathing in synch.

"Yes," Mieant replied. Their heads moved closer. I cleared my throat rather loudly a couple of times, but they ignored me and continued to consume one another with their eyes.

Fine. Food, then destiny. My dumb sister and her dumb boyfriend could be prioritized later.

I walked around the table, sat down opposite Broodmother, and started in on a tray of golden fruits. A moment later, I felt two soft taps on both of my shoulders as Nonch sidled up next to me and took a seat.

"Raystar-Friend," he said.

"Shells!" I mumbled through my full mouth. "How are you feeling?"

"Grateful that I can feel anything at all besides the dark Void," he said as he surveyed the table. "Thank you. As to *how* I feel," he continued, "every joint aches, and my body tingles as if the electrons and atoms that compose me are relearning how to stay together."

I paused, considering the implications. Perhaps the nannites I had used to convert matter from the leggers' bodies into Crynit flesh, bone, blood, and shell needed time to meld together? It would be horrible if the "create" command was reversed or corrupted, so that the healing wasn't permanent. *Ack.* I placed a hand on Nonch's warm carapace and patted his back a few times.

An area of the table in front of Nonch suddenly parted and a block of raw flesh emerged. I'd seen Nonch eat before, at school, but he'd always brought processed Galactic food. I leaned a millimeter away, eyeing the bloody square.

His blade arms efficiently sliced the meat into smaller chunks that he popped into his mouth with his claw hands. With razor-sharp teeth as large as my fingers, he chomped on the mouthful. He sliced up a small portion and extended it to me.

"Would you like a taste?"

Fight or flight: the oldest of all Human instincts. The red meat glistened in the artificial sunlight. *It can't be worse than 'natch. Right?*

"Uh." Before my flight instinct could kick in, I took the cube from Nonch and gingerly put it in my mouth. As I chewed on it and considered the taste, well, it didn't suck. Back home, we'd had raw meat before, usually with an egg and some spices on it. This pretty much tasted the same, minus the egg and spices.

"You have had this before, Raystar-Friend," Nonch said, nodding, "except you ate the bad part."

I swallowed hard. *Legger!*

Huh. I was surprised to find that I didn't have an auto-barf reflex. It really wasn't that bad. Legger was, in fact, quite edible.

This was great news for gratchers! Of course, the general Galactic population finding this out would be bad news for leggers: then two species would be left hanging in the balance based on food preference. I popped another cube of legger in my mouth.

"Remarkable," Broodmother said, staring at me intently—with all her eyes.

"What's remarkable?" Mieant said as he and Cri, hand in hand and with matching bedhead, came to the table and sat down. Cri looked only at Broodmother, to whom she bowed her head, and then wasted no time digging into a steaming fruit pie covered with a flaky crust.

"Mieant and Sister-of-Raystar," Nonch said, "when we were in Jurisdictor Godwill's prison camp, you attempted to mate. Were you successful this time?"

Hunks of pie exploded from Cri's mouth. "NONCH!" she yelled.

I grinned at them. Broodmother turned her enormous head toward my sister and fixed her with a jeweled, prismatic gaze. Mieant frowned back at us, his old schoolyard-bully glare returning like a thunderstorm.

"Nonch," he said quietly, "that was inappropriate."

"Yeah, Shells," my sister huffed. "I'm totally unstarred with you. What the nova?"

"Cri," I piped up, still grinning, "imagine if you did that"—I waved vaguely at the mossy bed they'd just vacated—"at home? What would Mom or Dad say? Imagine if you did it at *school*?"

Cri turned to me, her Glean eyes aglow with embarrassment. Half her hair poured over her shoulder and the other half jutted out at right angles.

"Did what? Kissed? Hugged? You wouldn't understand, Raystar. Other than Mom and Dad, no one's ever loved you."

I closed my eyes and sucked in a breath. The scent of the forest was oddly calming. Broodmother followed the conversation, her giant head moving like an armored turret from target to target.

Nonch's sensor stalk lay on my shoulder for a moment before he said, "You are not alone, Raystar."

I pushed back my chair and got to my feet. "We have to focus on our next steps."

"No," Cri replied. In curt, chopped tones, she continued, "YOU have to focus on your next steps. It's always *all* about you. Well, sis', Mieant and I are staying right here."

I stared at her, shocked.

Mieant's head snapped toward his girlfriend, his black eyes registering surprise. She clenched his hand with two of hers. A little bug cricked somewhere behind us.

"Young Ascendant, spawn of Lady Sathralea and Nent Ceridian, why would you possibly think I would allow that?" said Broodmother Krig, Queen of the Crynits on planet Nem'.

"I…." Cri stammered, unprepared for that question.

"To think that I once considered *Humans* dishonorable. How I have been proven wrong. Young Ascendant, you say that Raystar is the one who does not belong amongst us. I say that this Human 'pariah' has risked more on our behalf than all of us combined," Broodmother said imperiously. She paused before continuing, "Perhaps she, amongst all of you, is the *only* one who belongs here?"

Cri's mouth snapped shut. Mieant studied his feet.

A vaguely bitter smell wafted through the air, crowding out the aromas of the trees and flowers. The queen rose several meters above us and cast a long shadow across the table. Her blade arms, each easily as long as I was tall, clicked against her chest as she pulled them against herself.

"You all smell like gratchers. You must bathe. We will meet in my chambers, ten micro-cycles from now. Bring your equipment and… your respect."

Four days ago, I was brought to Principal Entarch's office. (It seemed like another time, another world!) The waiting area for her office was the Blue River Educational Facility's operations room, where the staff spied on the students via the campus's network of cameras. There were rows of seats occupied by lackadaisical administrators, floating holo screens, and red lights on the floors and workstations to make the dark room navigable.

At the time, I'd thought *that* was what a spaceship's command center looked like.

In the very real world of now, the iris-shaped door to Broodmother's chambers hissed open before us to reveal a massive, egg-shaped room, easily larger by a half than the forest "room" in breadth and depth. Lev chairs and their associated curved-view display screens, each occupied by a Crynit, hovered above and below us. The Crynit pilots floated from one glowing holo workstation to another; as they moved, their chairs' antigrav emitters pulsed gold, and their displays were a riot of reds, greens, and blues. The walls, floors, and ceiling, were polished onyx, presumably designed to contrast with the displays. Paths, including the one we stood on, spiraled down from various doors on the side walls to a brushed-metal platform where Broodmother waited for us in her seat of power. For the first time in a long time, we were clean, our stomachs were full, and we were well rested.

I grabbed one of Nonch's claw arms, inhaling as I took it all in.

"Crynits are ugly, Raystar," he said softly. "We are seen as destroyers. Rarely are we recognized as creators of beauty."

"Architect!" Mieant said. "And I thought Solium4 was magnificent."

I took the lead down the path toward the queen. Before we reached her, she flicked a claw arm in the air, and suddenly Nem', the Milky Way and the various systems controlled by the Convergence appeared above her. They floated in three dimensions, with each system and its planets rotating according to their nature, their gravity.

"Nem' is quite pretty, don't you think?" she mused, gesturing vaguely with her six sword arms at the night-sky holo.

We'd all seen pictures of Nem' before. It was a blue green and white marble. Cri, ensconced in Mieant's arms, just shrugged. I agreed with Broodmother: Nem' looked like Terra.

"No," Mieant said with a frown, "I do not particularly like this planet."

"I live underground, Broodmother," Nonch added.

Out of the blue, Infection piped up from the depths of my mind: *I DO NOT HAVE AESTHETIC APPRECIATION CURRENTLY ENABLED. SO, I AM NEUTRAL.*

Dude. This is beauty. It's like love, but you have to use your eyes, I instructed, frowning at my internal free rider.

The queen considered my companions' comments and sighed.

"Nevertheless, Nem' was a Human planet for thousands of years. Humanity achieved much in a short period of time—so much that many Galactic historians wonder why they lost the war," Broodmother said, holo starlight shining from her black armor. Our view shifted to the red systems at the edge of Convergence space. "A war that nearly shattered the Convergence."

"Broodmother, the Convergence attacked the Humans. It seems like they had the right to defend themselves against us," Nonch said.

"I am not disputing that, my Prime," Broodmother said, dipping her head toward Nonch. "As many systems as we are, as many spe-

cies that have been brought together under this unification," she continued, waving a clawed arm at the vast ocean of stars surrounding the Convergence, "our galaxy is immensely larger. The Convergence stands against the darkness—the unknown."

"Humans started the war," Mieant piped up to offer a rebuttal to Nonch's remark.

"How ironic, young Asrigard, that you would say this. But your parents were"—she paused before correcting herself—"are themselves lights of truth in our darkness. I would like to know them one day, if the Universe allows that."

Mieant gulped. He had been doing surprisingly well, considering that as far as he knew, his parents had been killed. I was amazed that he still seemed so sane after what we had gone through. Maybe that was true for all of us?

"But…perhaps even their truths cannot shine through clouds of lies. Lethians started the war, my child," she continued. We all frowned and looked at Mieant. He shrugged, nodding slightly. "Your race's leadership dragged us all into a conflict that should never have happened." Broodmother paused a moment as the screen zoomed in toward the perimeter of red Convergence systems. "Especially given that at the start of the war, there were *known* threats like the Raas only a few light years away."

A solar system flickered and went dark. *Oh! This is a real-time display.* I swallowed hard.

"Broodlings," Broodmother said, "we are losing the war against the Raas. We do not understand them. They do not communicate with us. They simply explore, expand, exploit, and exterminate." I thought of the Dreadnoughts blockading our planet—the pinnacle of Convergence tech. She was telling us that they were not enough.

"Broodmother, what does this have to do with us?" I asked before rethinking the question. "I mean, Humans. Or, uh, me?"

"The Raas are only the second most advanced species we have encountered. Raystar, your people's technology remains a mystery, still unknown to the Convergence 1,800 years after your people disappeared."

"Don't you mean, got their butts kicked?'" Cri smirked.

"Ascendant, your ignorance shames your parents," Broodmother hissed. Cri clenched her jaw and looked at the ground—I could tell she was becoming increasingly angry. "What we do know is that few Humans survived, but the Convergence did not destroy them all." She paused before adding, "I do not believe we could have. Humans went…missing." She gestured at the star map and the growing Raas infection. "And now? We need their technology, their cunning."

She spun the top half of her body to face me.

"Which brings us to Raystar."

"Of course it does," Cri muttered darkly.

"Yes!" Broodmother exclaimed. Her hundred claw feet tick-tacked against the hard floor as she snaked over to where we stood. "Raystar is the only Human known to have manifested in the way the ancient stories have described. So, Ascendant, the Convergence," Broodmother paused and looked at Mieant before adding, "and Lethians in particular, believe she is the key to accessing the Human technology—whether she chooses to or not remains to be seen. And whether *you* like it or not, she is the key."

Cri pulled away from Mieant, who turned to her, confused. She walked a few steps away from us and stood with her rigid back to us, her lower two fists clenched. I walked over to her, intending to put my hand on her shoulder, but I hesitated, my hand hanging in the air next to her.

My sister. My friend, I thought. *I know we've had a tough time over the last few days, but we're still family, right? What did Mom say about staying together?*

I was just about to touch her when as she spun around, eyes blazing. Surprised at how close I was, she blinked once and, perhaps reflexively, placed a hand on my chest and pushed hard. My arms windmilled around as I stumbled back several paces.

"Cri?"

My sister glared at me—I could feel heat coming off her glowing eyes. She shouted, "It's always about you. Always. Even our food. We have to have special food for our Human!"

Cri's jaw bulged as she ground her teeth. "'Don't be so rough, Cri!'" she said, imitating Mom's voice and taking a step toward me. Mieant rose and stood by her, his taller form a tree to her boulder. Still mimicking Mom, she said, "'Protect your sister, Cri.'" As she squeezed her upper hands into fists as well, the veins around her neck bulged, making her tattoos seem to move on their own. Mieant put his arm in front of her as she moved toward me again; she brushed him off and took another step forward.

"You've been a knife in my heart ever since you came into my family," she said, seething.

There it was: the dark jealousy that poured out of her because my existence limited and compromised her own.

"Since *I* came into *your* family?" I shouted, pushing her back.

"Mine!"

"They're MY Mom and Dad, too!" I cried. I pushed my forty kilos against her seventy, tears springing from my eyes. Mieant and Nonch intervened to separate us.

The queen arched her back and peered down at us, like we were insects. Her giant armored head pivoted between Cri and me.

"No!" Cri said and rushed at me, only to be held back by Mieant and Nonch. "It's your fault Mom and Dad are gone! I've spent my whole life trying to believe you were one of us. But you're not! You slapped me hard, really hard, and I didn't cry. You know why? I expected it. I hate you, what you have become. And now my life is ruined!"

"Cri?" I gasped. *It can't be like this.*

"Broodmother, do the Convergence fleets have anything to do with Raystar?" Nonch said, changing the subject and waving his claw arms in my general direction.

We all turned toward him. It was the right question. Cri clenched her four fists, almost crying but holding back her pain, her fury. Mieant stood off to the side, frowning at her.

"Ah. That is the right question, broodling," Broodmother replied. As she gestured with a claw arm, the holo view of Nem' began to magnify at a dizzying speed until we were staring at the base of the Mesas. Our family farm was visible in the distance, as was the section of the Ruins where the ships had crashed just a week before. We then zoomed in even further on an unremarkable spot at the base of one of the mountains, save for a wide boulevard in the ruined city that led straight into the mountain.

"I don't understand," I said, shaking my head.

"Nem' itself is awakening. Something is happening deep within the planet. The Storm Wall is behaving oddly. It should have materialized by now, as you know." Broodmother paused and considered her next words carefully. "You must find your way into the base. What lies within could be a factor in the coming conflict."

THE AVENUE OF THE REPUBLIC. THAT IS THE NAME OF THE TRANSIT PATH YOU ARE LOOKING AT. Infection blared in my head. *AND YOU CANNOT ENTER AS YOU CURRENTLY ARE. YOU NEED THE CONTROL DNA ELEMENTS, WHICH YOU DO NOT HAVE.*

I blinked. Infection was being helpful now?

Which are in Blue River?

YES.

Where you don't want to go.

I HAD NOT CONSIDERED THAT WE COULD GAIN ACCESS TO MORE HUMAN TECHNOLOGY THERE.

So now you want to go?

I MUST THINK.

I rolled my eyes and said, "The base is called New Mars. My parents wanted me to go there. AI, uh, told me to go to see the Elions in Blue River before attempting to go to New Mars, as I don't have the complete command code to enter."

"The Elions. They are devious," Broodmother said. "Ahhh…."

"Broodmother, what is 'Ahhh?'" Nonch asked.

"The plan has not changed. Raystar will go to Blue River, and we will aid her."

Suddenly, my body locked up. The world tilted sideways as I was smashed against the cold marble floor of the queen's command center. Out cold.

I HAVE DECIDED, Infection's voice echoed in my head. *I WILL NOT PERMIT YOU TO GO TO BLUE RIVER. OUR AGREEMENT IS TERMINATED.*

35

Wait! I shouted mentally, once again locked up within my mind. The scene outside of my head hadn't changed. Nonch, Mieant, and Broodmother peered down at me, shocked. I felt blood trickling out of my nose. And falling hurt. *You can't do this!*

I HAVE. I DID.

Stupid Infection was mocking me with verb-tense jokes. *Architects and gravity wells, you unstarred gratcher-sucking....*

I WILL NOT BE DESTROYED. THE ADDITION OF THE CONTROL DNA WILL GIVE YOU THE POWER TO ELIMINATE ME. IT IS NOT WORTH ACCESSING NEW MARS.

Destroying you was not part of our agreement, either!

YOU WILL BETRAY ME. IT IS IN HUMANITY'S NATURE.

And what is your *nature?*

I AM A HUMAN CONSTRUCT, AND SO I AM INNOCENT. I HAVE BEEN MADE, AND I CANNOT CHANGE WHAT I AM.

Your creator is Godwill. You have fed on me, so at least that part of me should not be capable of betrayal. Godwill has killed millions. And he is Lethian, not Human.

YOUR SISTER IS FILLED WITH HATE TOWARD YOU BECAUSE YOU STOLE HER FAMILY. YOU ARE NOT TRUSTWORTHY.

My sister has nothing to do with our agreement. And her—MY—family chose me!

SHE IS BUT AN EXAMPLE. I AM SOFTWARE. EVERYTHING I DO IS LOGICAL.

Godwill is insane. He created you as a manifestation of his hate and insanity. You are logically insane!

I CANNOT BE INSANE. THIS CONVERSATION HAS NO VALUE.

Wait! I haven't broken our agreement! How can we build confidence in each other if at every step you think I'm trying to destroy you? To betray you?

CONFIDENCE IS IRRELEVANT. THIS CONVERSATION HAS NO VALUE. I HAVE NOTHING TO LEARN FROM YOU.

What? Stop!

With that, my mental space went dark. I felt razors of Infection's power slice through my being—every molecule, every atom, every electron of me began to disassemble and spin out of control. Like pages torn from a picture book, Infection was ripping my life apart. Each page was a memory—Mom, Dad, Cri, birthdays, sunlight, AI— and all of it was disappearing. If your memories vanish, are you still a sentient being? Or are you just an empty body moving through space, a fleshy meteor without direction or meaning?

My awareness was fading fast as Infection dissolved me, making me care less and less about the memories and everyone in my life. Subconsciously, I knew this was the death knell: not caring.

No! It can't end like this.

And then, just as I had reached the point where I was fading to black, my emotions, visions, and memories all crashed back together in an explosion of light and dizzying images. AI's memory hadn't been completely destroyed! I suddenly could see it sparkle in the darkness, like a campfire.

A moment passed.

YOU ARE STILL HERE.

Infection tried to reassert itself, but nothing happened.

Ha ha, am I going insane? Is this really happening, or is it yet another trick of the Universe, another false hope?

The lights came on in my mental space.

HOW IS THIS POSSIBLE?

Excellent question. I could see again, feel my bruises, feel the blood rushing through my body, hear everyone outside of my head in muffled tones. Yet I was still locked inside my head.

Reach for it, Ray. Reach for your power.

Great gravity wells. AI? AI!! I focused, feeling deep inside me for my source of power, my core. What I'd tapped when I'd healed Sarla at Godwill's prison camp, when I'd healed Nonch. And there it was, a current of white, cascading energy.

NO! YOU ARE DESTROYED!

Push back on Infection, Raystar! PUSH!!

Immediately, I could feel Infection, where it was in my body. It had been converting me, slowly and unobtrusively, despite the deal we'd struck. The sneak! The cheat! Against all of the odds Infection had said were unbreakable, immutable, I was stronger than I'd been in days. I'd slept. I'd eaten. AI had freed me, or at least part of me, and together, with his knowledge and my power, I willed myself to reverse the conversion process.

I AM PART OF YOU. YOU CANNOT DESTROY ME.

Instead of bothering to reply, I poured more energy into the reversal. I willed Infection back to the initial injection sites where Godwill had initially plunged his needles and then willed barriers of my nannites to surround and contain Infection. Once again, I had control of myself.

Ray, AI's voice cracked with emotion. *That was a horrible experience—trapped in isolation.*

AI, I thought back to him, *I....* I envisioned giving him a mental hug and kiss.

Yeah, we won't tell your parents about that, he said. *Architect, it's good to be back.*

I thought you were gone forever!

I was, but Infection inadvertently set me loose. When he started to disassemble you, he must have accidentally dissolved the virtual prison I'd been trapped within. But Ray, we don't have much time. As I told you before, I'm using all of my energy to manage your nannites, to control IT. I can't do this for much longer. You have to get to the Elions who control the DNA, the missing element that you need to get into the base. And we have to get into that base, Raystar. We only have about a day and a half left before I run out of power and Infection frees itself.

I was still up the great gravity well, but I had control over myself, at least, and better control over my power than ever before.

Ah, about that, Ray, AI said, his voice suddenly sounding farther away, *you can't access your nannites at all. Doing so will destroy my barriers and any possibility of me being able to defend you. He is not entirely in control, but if he were, he'd destroy us both. This time, it's for real—no use of nanotech. You're just a regular Human until you can get your hands on that control DNA.*

AI? Will you be with me?

I'll do my job, Ray. I will be able to talk on a limited basis, but you really don't want to distract me. Even now, Infection is pushing me hard. Get the DNA. Free us both. Hurry.

Right. Hurry. Of course.

And as suddenly as AI had appeared, I was alone again in my mind.

I opened my eyes.

36

My dad is three meters tall and easily weighs 300 kilos. His hands are larger than my head. Not surprisingly, the blasters he carried had barrels so wide I could fall into them. Well, I'm exaggerating, but trust me, they're big.

The plasma rifles I now found myself staring into seemed much, much larger. Granted, they were held by Broodmother's elite force—in this case, Commander First Claw and his team. Each of them would dwarf Dad. So their guns *should* be larger.

"Hi," I said, peering around the dark barrel of one particular giant plasma rifle. I imagined my tiny greeting echoing into its distance, "Hi…hi…hi…hi…hi…."

"The Human is conscious," First Claw announced. With military precision, their armor clacked in synch like a thunderclap. He and the other four soldiers stepped back and held their diverse weapons of war at attention.

"Raystar of Terra," Broodmother said in a melodious, feminine voice that seemed to wrap around the soldiers who parted as she drew near. "Can you stand?"

Gentle hands, each as big as my head, lifted me to my feet and steadied me—her hands. Her prismatic gaze held my attention. She said softly, "Explain."

"Ridiculous! She's just putting on another show! Another grab for attent—"

"Silence the child," the queen instructed First Claw. Her tone didn't change, but it was unforgiving as time itself.

By simply lifting one claw arm in the air, First Claw applied a translucent sound-dampening shell of energy around Cri's head. I'd been bubbled often in school for asking what I guess were annoying questions, and now, a similar bubble flickered around Cri. It happened so fast that no one in the group except Mieant had time to react. He jumped away from the bubble's field and looked askance at his girlfriend. Cri glared through the field at me as a guard wrapped his hands around her waist, holding her still.

In addition to being sisters, Cri and I had been friends in school, for the most part, or so I'd thought. Perhaps it was as Nonch had suggested days ago, that perhaps friends are a matter of circumstance, and that when circumstance changes, so do friendships. I didn't want to believe that, that relationships are ephemeral, like clouds.

"Explain," Broodmother repeated.

Right. I quickly told her about Godwill, my injections. The escape from Godwill's prison camp and Sarla. Then I explained my need to get to Blue River. As I caught them up with my most recent discussion with Infection, the group looked at me intensely.

"Venom and Void," Broodmother hissed to herself, "you met my *sister*?" The Crynit matriarch pointed to where Nonch's missing arms once were. "*She* did this?"

Her body quivered, and I could smell nothing—absolutely nothing—which made me wonder what that meant. She glanced at Nonch and then back at me. "Come," Broodmother said, shaking her head. "The HiveShip, the colony, for the first time since we settled on Nem' after the war…is under attack, by Convergence forces, no less! Raystar, it is time to meet your destiny." She turned to First Claw and instructed, "We will take them to Deep Tunnel. We must set them on their way."

Several of Broodmother's overzealous guards nearly gave us whiplash as they grabbed each of us and positioned us just behind their heads, within reach of their sensor stalks. Broodmother jerked her head in the direction we were to go, and at a sprint, the guards complied. I wasn't clear if she planned to join us on the journey, but sure enough, she did.

As we dashed along the corridors of the Broodship, thousands of Crynits going about their daily business appeared as a blur. The Broodship's beauty belied the Crynits' reputation for destruction: the bronze-colored metals that appeared everywhere and the quality of light made the passages and tubes deep within the Assassin-Class warship seem like they were bathed in the full glory of a sunset. I marveled and wondered at the scents that permeated the air—evidence of the chemical "chatter" happening all around me in the Crynits' pheromone-based language.

Once we arrived at Deep Tunnel, the guards stopped and set us down. "Tunnel" was really a misnomer: it was three kilometers wide and equally as tall, and it stretched as far as the eye could see. This was no tunnel—it was a Human-built metropolis that went on and on for who knows how far? Buildings climbed the sides of the tunnel and some even hung from the ceiling, like stalactites. These gunmetal grey structures were identical to those in the Human Ruins outside the Mesas, except that they hadn't suffered abuse from weather and the Storm Wall. Where power was still active, lights dotted the structures at random, flickering against the mottled darkness. The arched ceiling was made of some type of milky-white material that filled all the spaces where buildings were absent. The power still flowed to some of those spaces; where it was active, the ceiling looked like a blue sky, complete with drifting clouds.

Earlier, when we were preparing to meet with Broodmother in her quarters, Nonch had told me a little about Deep Tunnel. He explained that it was neither inhabited nor habitable, but that Crynits had used it a means of getting around Nem' undetected. In some areas, small supply stations had been built to provide sustenance for travelers.

A multilevel highway approximately half a kilometer wide ran through the center of the underground metropolis, fading into the tunnel's distance like a perspective drawing. Its once-fluid form was interrupted by jagged cracks and enormous sections that had broken off and crushed the buildings below. Smaller exits branched off from the highway into neighborhoods. Skeletons of parks were filled with

dead, dried-up trees resembling bony fingers, and empty meandering riverbeds, all various shades of brown dust, marked what once, combined with the artificial sky, must have been a green and blue metropolis. In short, Deep Tunnel was a gently curving mausoleum that stretched toward a dark vanishing point. Nothing moved except the mummified tree branches that prickled in the steady, dry breeze.

I squinted and took a second look. *No.* I was wrong, which was becoming routine these days. There *were* things moving around in there. The city was absolutely *crawling* with automatons. I hadn't noticed them at first because the sense of scale was off, and they were roughly the same grey color as the buildings.

They looked to me like armored insects on an anthill. Some twitched where they lay in the ancient dust, and others moved smoothly from task to task. The sections of "sky" that remained occasionally revealed the unmistakable silhouette of starbats. On Nem's surface, they were graceful creatures that drafted on air currents as they hunted for their prey. These screechy, blinky imitations awkwardly pulled themselves through the air with jerks and spasms.

Nonch pushed my gaping mouth closed with a claw hand. Mieant stood next to him, stoic and cool, his black hair gently waving in the stiff breeze. I think we were all experiencing the same thought: *Did anybody else know this was down here?* I was astounded by the entire worlds that had been hidden away from my view, my consciousness.

"We have used probes to follow Deep Tunnel to Nem's capital, Ever," Broodmother said, "We have, over the millennia, explored perhaps only half of its upper levels. There are many lower levels to it, and we believe that there is *something* down below those as well. The deepest levels are blocked by defenses and guardian automatons that are the stuff of our nightmares."

I blinked hard—*Crynits had nightmares? This place has thwarted their exploration attempts?* A wave of disorientation swept over me, briefly, and then I realized I wasn't dizzy; the ground was actually shaking.

"What's that? What just happened?" Cri asked, her pervasive anger momentarily set aside to make way for fear. Apparently, First Claw had unbubbled her at some point along the way.

"Broodmother," First Claw broke in, his deep voice booming through the dead place, "we have confirmed that the forces pursuing us are from the 98th Battlegroup. They have entered the tunnels and are at the first perimeter of our Hive's defenses. The False Jurisdictor wishes to speak with you."

Fragrances of sugar and soil suddenly filled the air.

"We part here, younglings," Broodmother said. "Fifteen kilometers down this tunnel is Blue River; our access port is clearly marked. There, you will find an elevator that will take you into the heart of the city, the central market. The Elions you seek are located in the industrial section. If what you have told me is correct, the Podmaster will be expecting you. You may tell him that you have my support."

Broodmother's guards laid a set of three large backpacks on the ground by our feet and then ascended the ramp back to the Broodship. As Broodmother turned to follow them, her massive body flowed after her head like a train.

"Wait!" Cri shouted. "Please? I thought we were staying with you?"

Broodmother paused and partially turned toward her. "Your immediate destiny is in Blue River."

"But I don't want to...."

Broodmother shifted her stance. Cri closed her mouth and looked away.

"Broodmother?" Nonch asked.

"My Prime," she replied, turning toward him.

"Why are there only three packs?"

"Because only three will make this journey."

"Broodmother, I...."

"You are not healed. And you are my Prime. And I have nearly lost you once. I will not risk that again. Nothing—anger, resentment, or even logic—will sway me. My Nonch, your choices at this point are to join us using your own power or to float back to our quarters in the comfort of an antigrav restraint."

Nonch hissed in frustration. He turned to me, said, "Remember your promise, Raystar-Friend," and thrummed up the ramp to where

First Claw and his soldiers stood and impassively watched our drama play out.

Broodmother remained in the same spot, facing us. I felt the intense pressure of her gaze.

"Promise?" she asked in a cool, soft voice. "Raystar of Terra," Broodmother continued, her feminine voice barely above a whisper, "do not make me your enemy. Find the Elions and return with what you need. Prove that I am correct in placing my trust in you. My Prime has his own path, and yours awaits in that direction."

With that, she climbed the ramp to join Nonch, First Claw, and the soldiers. They disappeared into the Broodship without a single backward glance.

Cri, Mieant, and I remained in Deep Tunnel.

37

The ancient Human city wasn't silent, though. A gentle, constant breeze whispered through my purple hair. Somewhere in the mottled distance, machines clanked.

"Well?" I said to snap us out of our respective reveries. With one hand, I patted the Human blaster Mom had given me in its spot on my belt, and with the other, I secured my backpack.

"Mieant," Cri's voice whipped through the quiet, "you do think this is her fault, right?"

"My Moon," he said in a placating tone, "what we're facing is much bigger than Raystar—than all of us."

Cri's eyes narrowed.

"So, you like her now?"

"I *what*?" Mieant replied, his eyes wide with surprise.

"You didn't like her in school. Now 'this' is bigger than all of us?"

"Cri," Mieant pleaded, "my parents are gone. Everything I've ever known is gone. I do not blame Raystar. She tried to save them, for nova's sake! We can get closer to the truth if we get to Blue River. My parents have guards, security teams—they are the Quadrant Co-Governors! In Blue River, we can find someone or something that can help us."

In response, Cri shot Mieant a scorching look of disapproval. Her red skin had darkened with anger. Her black hair dramatically

framed her symmetrical face, glowing eyes, and her bunched arms and clenched fists. When she was angry, my sis' was magnificent.

"Errrrgggh!" Cri shouted before turning on her heel and stomping away from us down the highway toward Blue River.

"Cri!" Mieant called after her. As he watched her go, he seemed deflated. Without meeting my gaze, he reached down to put on his backpack and noticed Cri's pack lying next to it. Mieant sighed, picked both packs up, and slung them over his back. After jumping a few times to settle the weight around his shoulders, he started toward our destination.

"Come, Raystar," he said over his shoulder. I looked toward my sister, who was a good distance ahead of us already. "She will rejoin us when she understands the direction of her anger. And I for one," he muttered to himself, "think it's high time she directed it elsewhere."

We walked in silence, our descent stirring wisps of dust with each step. More than a kilometer above our heads, the ancient artificial sky flickered on in a summertime blue color. We marched through a maze of empty roadways, barren parks, and deserted buildings. Though it was empty of organic life, the desiccated city whispered with activity. Maintenance drones floated or dragged themselves from one long-obsolete task to another. The responsibilities of 1,800 years ago were remembered only by mechanized caretakers.

"I think your parents are alive, Mieant," I said after ten minutes or so of walking in silence. "I healed them. It's hard to explain, but I could see inside their bodies, I could see what I needed to do. Just like I did with Sarla and Nonch."

Mieant paused and nodded. "I miss them so much. Things have been so spiked since we left Solium4." He looked off in the distance for Cri; not seeing her, he resumed walking.

"It's okay. I mean, I'm fine with you and Cri," I replied. I was jealous—and for sure it *was* jealousy—because no one felt that way about me, including Cri. I wished that she cared more about me. It was silly, of course. I was nothing but a dark cloud in my sister's life, vanishing in the open sky of other possibilities.

Mieant frowned in my direction. "Neither of us asked you. I don't need your approval, and Cri doesn't either."

"That's not what I meant," I replied. "My point is, I don't know why she's so angry at me. I look up to her. She used to protect me," I said, laughing bitterly, "from you."

We trundled on, both lost in our thoughts.

Mieant finally spoke again. "On Solium4, I had everything. I was popular. I had ideas, and I was pursuing them. My parents were powerful. Then we came to Blue River. Yay." I could feel his anger as it grew. "I didn't know where I stood. No one here cares about what I've done before or about things that are important back home."

"Uh…I'm not sure I'm following you," I said. I felt the same loss of connection, of meaning.

"It's the same for Cri. She was the big sister. You had a role. She had a role. You had a relationship based on those roles. And then everything changed. Imagine it from her perspective. Her little sister suddenly developed craxy powers. She discovered that her parents are nobility. And she discovered that they came to this stupid 'natchhole in order to HIDE YOU."

I gulped. No, I hadn't considered it from her perspective before.

"She's jealous of me because…."

"She's jealous, and she's scared. Her whole way of looking at the world has changed, and now she's struggling to make sense of it."

"But so am I," I said. "It's not like…."

"Raystar," Mieant said, exasperated, "we're not talking about you."

Oh. Right.

"Thanks," I said. Mieant nodded.

After a few minutes, I decided it was time to change the subject. "I wonder what Blue River will be like with the 98th's troops scattered everywhere. We'll need a disguise of some sort to hide us from the security AIs and vids."

"Mmmm, yeah," Mieant considered, looking up at the gigantic buildings around us. "Given the state of things here, maybe we could

scavenge something?" He pointed to a tower that was closer to the main highway. Several lights were on, and it looked remarkably intact. "We might as well check it out," he added as he began walking toward the building.

Suddenly, thousands of starbats exploded from the ruins behind us. A cacophony of their screeches shattered the whispery quiet of Deep Tunnel. Reflexively, we dropped to the concrete, hands clapped over our mouths to suppress our own shrieks.

"What the nova…!" Mieant finally whispered.

"Nonch said this place was deserted!" I whispered back, meeting his wide-eyed gaze.

"Going in that building might not be such a good idea," he replied. I was just about to agree when a new set of screams pierced the air.

"Mieee-aaaant! MIEANT! RAYSTAR!"

I lay still for a second, listening as my heart thumped its way back into my chest. I'd imagined that a giant mutant legger or a Human security android spewing missiles was coming for us. But no. It was "just" my sister, still capable of emergency access to my heart.

38

"Cri?" Mieant exclaimed, scrambling to his feet and running toward her. I pushed myself off my belly and got my feet under me.

They met in a clank of armor, his two and her four arms entangled in a bear hug. He buried his head in her jet-black hair. Her cheeks flushed an even deeper red than usual as her lips, almost purple, crushed against his open, red-blue mouth. They leaned toward each other, into each other. Pausing to come up for air, they gazed into each other's eyes.

"You taste like dust, Mieant," she said, kissing him again, "but good dust."

Barf. Really?

Cri peered around him at me.

"Ray," she said with ice in her voice. When she looked at Mieant, her expression was filled with joy. I knew that look—she'd given it to me often back when I was just her little sis'. She had none of that joy for me now.

"Come!" Mieant said, grabbing her hand. "Raystar and I were about to search for disguises in that building over there." His dour mood forgotten, he dragged Cri by one hand over to where I stood batting dust away from my clothes.

"Where were you?" I asked, not looking at her.

"When I realized I was going the wrong direction," she said, smiling into Mieant's eyes, "I turned around to find you guys. You really didn't come that far, so it was easy to do a little exploring while I caught up with you. Have you been inside any of these buildings? They're amazing. Mostly. Some you don't want to go into."

We both looked at her sharply. *I mean, duh.*

"Starbat colonies. Woo wee, do they smell."

She smiled at Mieant again. Caught up in her excitement, she continued: "Elements of Human tech are still working here. There's all sorts of craxy stuff. Look what I found!" She dug into one of the larger pockets in her utility pants and retrieved a thin, grey, rectangular device about as wide as a 'natch burger.

Cri frowned and gave the device a slap. Mieant winced at her rough treatment of the device. Its grey surface flickered blue for a moment and then turned back to grey. After she smacked it against her armor, it fizzled back to life. A man—a Human—dressed in what I supposed was a suit was seated at a console-like desk. He had brown hair, blue eyes, and a tanned, clean-shaven face. A view screen behind him displayed the unmistakable arc of the Milky Way in red and green. Presumably the green stars were Human Republic territory, and the much larger swath of red stars, I guessed, were Convergence systems.

"There's no sound, so we can't hear what he's saying," Cri said, her smile fading slightly. It might have been the Human nano inside of me activating, or the overuse of my power changing me, but I knew precisely what it was and what to do with it.

"Volume up," I said, and for the first time in nearly two millennia, a Human news broadcast echoed in Deep Tunnel.

"….progressing according to plan. Core planets have been evacuated, and all Gateways are deactivating. Remaining Citizens on Nemesis will be moved through the local Gateway. Please monitor local announcements for your neighborhood evacuation instructions…." The vid froze for a moment and then came back on to repeat the message.

"Cool!" Cri and Mieant said at the same time, looking at me eagerly. "How did you know how to do that? What did he say?" Galactic nano-translators were unfamiliar with the Human language.

"I…I'm not sure," I stuttered. I wasn't sure what a "gateway" was, and I didn't feel right about mentioning it. I don't know why.

"You, Raystar," Mieant breathed, "are the first creature I have known of who has been able to manipulate Human technology."

Cri frowned. "I'll bet she understands everything."

"I think it's an update about the war," I said, nodding, "and evacuation instructions."

Cri's scowl deepened. "Sounded like he said A LOT more than that."

Mieant looked at Cri and then at me. "Raystar? There were so many words. What was the update about?

"Look," I said, "I don't understand everything he said, and what I told you is what I understood. And I'm unstarred that I somehow could understand it, because that means I'm using my nanotech way too much." I was the queen of deceptive and obvious statements. Only sharing part of the truth with my friends twisted my guts into knots I felt because I could understand what the Human had said.

Cri's expression went flat. We'd known each other for too long for me to hide something from her. Mieant looked skeptical.

"Look. Can we just go check out that building?" I said, pointing at the tower Mieant had picked out. "We have to get to Blue River. We need disguises. On our next break, I'll listen to it again." I handed the newsreader back to Cri and shouldered between them to make my escape.

In the moment, escaping to whatever was inside of Mieant's building seemed like a great way to avoid talking about the fact that I could understand Human. What's that saying? "Out of the food-heating unit and into the open fire?" I think that's it. According to the newscast, Humanity had been evacuated, rather than exterminated. This device was proof of it. Nova and Void, possessing that proof alone was enough reason to invade a planet.

Then a darker thought ricocheted around my mind. *Why did they call this planet "Nemesis"?*

39

The tower Mieant was navigating us toward looked, well, new.

Ray, wait a moment, AI cautioned.

I thought you said you weren't going to be able to communicate with me?

AI paused a moment before replying. *Only in emergencies. Infection is screaming holy nova at me, something about that building.*

I blinked.

Are you both, like watching everything I do?

Ray, you poop just like everyone else. Well, not like me. Because I don't…you know…the whole me being artificial intelligence and such. I wonder if it's possible to have artificially intelligent poop?

AI!

Okay. Hold on. I'm going to let him talk. Apparently, AI could make Infection shut up as far as I was concerned, which was good to know.

FOOLISH HUMAN CONSTRUCT! LET ME TALK TO THE HUMA—

Silence. Then Infection continued, sullenly: *WE SHOULD AVOID THAT BUILDING.*

Scared? AI gloated.

I AM NOT.

AI, I chided. *Infection, what are you concerned about?*

I motioned for Cri and Mieant to wait while I talked with…myself.

WHEN I HAD CONTROL OF YOUR BODY, I MONITORED THE COMMUNICATIONS IN THE TUNNEL AND ON THE ROADWAY. CERTAIN MESSAGES SEEM CONNECTED TO ONE PLACE. I HAVE PROCESSED THE PATTERNS, AND I BELIEVE THIS IS THE CENTRAL HUB.

And you never told us this? I asked.

I DID NOT KNOW YOU WOULD ATTEMPT TO ENTER.

So, what do you think is in there? AI asked Infection.

Silence again, before an ominous warning: *DANGER.*

Can you be more specific? I asked.

MY RECORDS ARE NOT DETAILED, BUT I BELIEVE IT IS A CENTRAL INTELLIGENCE NODE. ADMINISTRATIVE, GOVERN-MENT HEADQUARTERS…

See? That's not so bad, AI chimed in.

…AND MILITARY, Infection finished.

"Hey," I said to Mieant and Cri. I brought them up to date on my conversation with Infection and AI.

Silently, we considered the shining skyscraper. Everything else looked rusted, brown, and post-apocalyptic enough to be 1,800 years old, but this tower's seamless windows were clean and shiny. And in Deep Tunnel's dusk, there was no mistaking that lights were on within.

"I say we go in," Cri said. I glanced behind me. Cri and Mieant held hands, two of hers with one of his. I rolled my eyes. Their displays of adoration were unrelenting and, to me, exhausting.

"Something we can use, a disguise of some sort, or more tech might be inside. We can't go into town wearing the same clothes we had on during the GNN broadcast. We'd be recognized immediately. Don't you think there might be something useful inside?" Mieant said, shrugging.

The massive kilometer-wide highway that ran through Deep Tun-nel like a spine had an off-ramp that led directly into the tower. Vari-ous roadways twisted toward its base, and a series of air-car parking

lots rose like terraced shelves around its lower third. Infection's theory about it being a hub of some kind seemed more and more plausible.

"I agree," Cri said to Mieant, her arms winding around him. "What could possibly go wrong?"

YOUR SISTER…SHOULD BE TERMINATED.

What? I sputtered.

Yeah, even my digital butt knows not to hand the Universe a permission slip like that, AI said, agreeing with Infection. *Never ask, "What could go wrong?"*

"Hey guys, Infection and AI are having serious doubts about that building. Let's go somewhere else."

Cri moved over to face me. "YOU'RE the one with less than three days to live, not me." She tapped a graceful red finger against my head. "Think. If we go around from building to building looking for stuff, we'll lose hours. This place is huge. Given the condition of that building, it's a good bet that whatever is inside is still in good shape. Uniforms, jackets, I don't know. Aaaand maybe there's something that will help us get into the base under the Mesas?" She turned to Mieant and pleaded, "Please, my Moon? My feet hurt. I want to see what's in the building."

"Raystar," Mieant said, turning to me, "it might be worth the risk."

Right. What could be worth the risk of Cri's feet hurting? AI said.

I AGREE. THIS IS FOOLISH. THE LETHIAN AND GLEAN BROODLINGS SHOULD BE TERMINATED FOR FOOLISHNESS AND ALSO TO PREVENT FUTURE FOOLISHNESS IF THEY SOMEHOW MATE AND PRODUCE MORE FOOLISH OFFSPRING. MAYBE THEY SHOULD WALK AHEAD INTO THE BUILDING WHILE WE WAIT HERE. BEFORE THEY DO THAT, MAKE SURE THEY GIVE YOU THEIR FOOD SUPPLIES SO THAT IF THEY ARE TER—

"Stop!" I yelled at both of them, my hands tugging at my hair in exasperation.

While I'd been consulting my two inner voices, Cri and Mieant had started walking, hand in hand, toward the shiny, ominous building.

I grimaced and ran after them.

40

The skyscrapers in Blue River were over a kilometer tall. This tower was perhaps a third of that height, reaching toward but not touching Deep Tunnel's ceiling. I could see hints of iridescent orange shining through the building's midnight-blue windows. The windows reminded me of the eyes of insects.

A grey stone walkway perhaps 20 meters wide encircled the building. A few benches placed neatly around the perimeter must have provided a respite for ancient Humans who had meetings in this building. As we neared the building, I was able to see into the windows a little; inside the vaulted atrium, a massive counter separated visitors from a series of transport ramps leading to the building's upper and lower floors. A row of chairs was visible behind the counter—presumably for Human receptionists.

All of us—even AI and Infection—fell silent as we approached. A cocktail of fear, trepidation, excitement, and curiosity made my palms sweaty and sped up my heartbeat. Despite the risks that going inside might involve, what wonders could await us inside this completely intact and seemingly functional Human installation?

We neared a seam in the glass that stretched to the top of the atrium: the entrance, perhaps?

"Look," I said to Cri and Mieant, "This place was built by my kind. It's logical that I'd be safer going in first. So why don't you stand back initially, and then when I'm sure it's okay, you can follow?"

"Oh, sure, so you can say you got there first and so you can have first dibs on anything in there," Cri retorted, frowning.

THE GLEAN IS DEFECTIVE, Infection boomed in my head.

Mieant placed his hand on his girlfriend's back. "Raystar's probably correct." He drew his blaster, checked the power, and pulled Cri back to the edge of the stone walkway. He shot me a thumbs up and yelled, "Use caution!"

Infection, AI said. *If this becomes violent, we have to protect Raystar. Our objective is Blue River. Agreed?*

AGREED.

I couldn't believe the foolishness going on in my head. I had to put a stop to it. *Did you guys both charge yourselves with doom batteries this morning? Please shut up.*

DOOM BATTERIES DO NOT EXI—

Quiet! Nova me! I laid a hand on my blaster; its presence on my hip was comforting. Even so, my heart was in my throat as I approached.

This is an opportunity to learn. We'll be fine, I muttered again and again as I took each step. Once I was about ten meters from the doorway, words appeared on the glass.

Terran Republic Nemesis Sector Fleet Headquarters

Well. That seems important. I held my breath, counted to ten, and exhaled.

AI? Infection? Anything?

No, AI responded. *Perhaps your nano is activating. But get a little closer. Touch the glass.*

WE SHOULD HAVE SENT THE GLEAN FIRST.

Infection, shut up. I turned to Mieant and Cri and beckoned them to approach.

"See if you can get in first!" Cri yelled. "It might not be safe for us!"

Mieant frowned at her and then turned to me with a shrug.

Jerks.

I was just about to touch the door when a perfect red silhouette of my body appeared in the glass.

"Halt!" A pleasant voice, neither too firm nor too kind, emanated all around me. "Citizen," it continued, "this facility is closed. Please present your hand for identification."

I jumped backward and shoved my hands in my pockets.

"Raystar?" Mieant yelled. I didn't turn around, but I shot him a signal to stay back.

WE SHOULD LEAVE.

Yeah. Avoid creepy building, go directly to Blue River. Good plan, AI added.

Admittedly, I already had enough Void-cursed chaos on my plate. But on the other hand, I *was* the only Human around. And I really wanted and *needed* to learn more about me and my kind, and if there was an opportunity to learn more about my tech, maybe even get more tech…well, that wouldn't be bad. *Would it?*

No, I agreed with myself completely. *I don't think it's bad.*

I stepped forward and presented my hand. As the scan tickled my palm, the red silhouette faded. I waited.

Well, that was useless. I turned to signal back to Mieant and Cri.

"Citizen, what is your name?" a deeper, authoritarian voice asked. I spun back around to face the door.

"Uh, Raystar. Raystar Ceridian."

"Well, Raystar Ceridian, it seems I have no record of you. What is your Republic ID?"

"Uh…." I felt like I was talking to Dad when he was in "Commander" mode; he made you feel compelled to answer him and stand at attention.

"Don't worry," the voice said, this time much more reassuringly. "Step inside. We will find your parents. You do realize you are well past the evacuation time? Are you lost? Hungry?"

"Who are you?"

After a brief silence, the voice responded, "I am the PeaceMaker. I am the Citizens' artificial intelligence that chose to remain behind after the Citizens departed." It paused, and I imagined it frowning. "How could you not know that?"

Oh, this is definitely *not good*, I thought. My stomach disconnected from my body while my heart tried to beat its way back to the Broodship. Way back in the darker sections of the atrium, I caught sight of things moving—things at least as large as Dad, but definitely not Glean. Or Human.

"Raystar, step inside, and let's find out what you know. I have food. Ice cream. Do you scream for ice cream?" The glass door hissed open wide enough and high enough to fly my parents' assault tank through it.

What had it said? "Scream?" For ice cream? What kind of torture would that entail?

"Woohoo!" shrieked Cri, her hyperactive freakiness on full blast. "C'mon Mieant! Our Human actually opened the building!"

"STOP!" I howled at them.

"Raystar," PeaceMaker said in soothing tones, "That's your name, right, child? Step inside, and let's get this resolved. A child with your DNA and your authorizations is not allowed to be unsupervised outside the building."

My eyes widened as massive panels in the atrium's ceiling parted. Autoturrets descended and unfolded their deadly barrels like synchronized dancers.

Nova this.

"Please, Raystar, if that's your name, don't make me chase you. Don't run."

"RUN!" I screamed to Mieant and Cri. And then I ran, too.

I'm unlocking the nanotech, Raystar. But don't use it if you don't have to, or all three of us will die! AI shouted in my flying brain.

Simultaneous red beams from the atrium's gajillion autoturrets all found me at the same moment. In an instant, a dome-shaped orb of air shimmered around me: a force field! As the energy lances hit my shield, they reflected back to the building and the city in a prismatic arc. Glass shattered everywhere. The building's smooth metal exterior melted where the lances struck, and holes burned layers deep into its shell. Some of the beams flashed through the now-demolished doorway and struck the shadowy figures inside.

WE MUST FLEE! WE DO NOT HAVE ENOUGH ENERGY TO MAINTAIN THIS SHIELD! Infection shouted.

So much for not using my nano. I staggered, suddenly exhausted. Yet whatever it was that I'd done had protected me. I could handle exhaustion if it was the cost of staying alive.

The Humanoid figures that emerged from the smoke appeared similar to the three-meter-tall security automatons the Lethians had battled in the roadway, but these were wider at the shoulders. *Of course they were.* Blue lights shone from the space where their faces should have been, and they targeted us with weapons embedded in their shoulders. It wasn't fair.

The energy beams I'd reflected back at the building had blazed through some, but not all, of the automatons, resulting in brilliant detonations that sent the surviving security bots crashing into walls and each other.

"I AM EVERYWHERE, RAYSTAR! I WILL FIND YOU!" Peace-Maker's deep yet almost melodious voice shook the ground. I suddenly realized that the voice was projecting from every functional public broadcasting speaker in the city. "EVERYWHERE, everywhere, everywhere…" echoed across Deep Tunnel.

A series of explosions launched me twenty meters into the air. Gravity and the very hard roadway knocked the breath out of my lungs as I hit the ground and tumbled several meters past the impact point. At least I'd had the good sense to land on my backpack, so the only real harm came to my squished food—as opposed to liquefying myself on the Terran road. Arms and legs splayed out like a broken puppet, I gasped, frantically trying to suck air back into my lungs.

And then I heard AI say, *Ray, that shield took too much. I have to reinforce the constraints with Infection.*

I DO NOT NEED TO BE CONSTRAINED. HOWEVER, IT IS IN MY INTEREST TO TAKE CONTROL OF THIS BODY. NEITHER OF YOU WILL BE HARMED.

What? My grip on reality had loosened quite a bit after the blast. *Take control?*

TRUST ME.

Void that! You and I are going to—

Before our internal discussion turned into name calling, a pair of strong arms lifted me up and half dragged, half carried me away. I found that I could finally breathe again, and as my chest swelled with air, I became aware of my surroundings. Smoke billowed from the silver building. Orange flames played hide and seek as they emerged from the roiling brown and black clouds.

Hey? I called out to the twin voices in my head. AI and Infection were silent.

"Great gravity wells, Ray, what did you do?" Mieant huffed. He pulled me to my feet and pushed me away from the building

"Wait," I huffed. My head was spinning.

"Run!" Cri yelled through her teeth, "Those security things are getting up!"

"No…I…" I sputtered, my breath still in short supply. "I mean…are we running in the right direction?"

41

We DID run in the right direction, for a good three kilometers. Thank the Architect for small favors.

After running like maniacs for so long, we had to stop for a moment to reintroduce oxygen to our lungs. As it turned out, "Peace-Maker" and the giant, lumbering machines did not pursue us, but its final words continued to bounce between my heart and my brain. The idea of PeaceMaker being "everywhere" terrified me.

I was sitting cross-legged on the ground, adjusting my pack, when Cri marched up to me with a frown that must have weighed a kilogram. Mieant was just a step behind her. Maybe she needed his help to hold her angst.

"You spoke to it. What did it say? And what did you say to make it attack us?" she said, crossing her arms and cocking a hip.

I told them what had happened as I pulled my backpack over my shoulders.

"My parents were right. You *are* the key. To think that that 'Peace-Maker' creature has been down here this whole time, waiting to be activated." He looked at me, his black eyes huge, and grabbed my shirt. "Raystar. Do you know what this means? We have to find my parents! We have to get you to them! They can keep you safe, and…."

"You're insane, Mieant," Cri interrupted. "Her own people, and even her people's A.I., don't even like her. No one likes her." She paused before adding, "Perhaps we're on the wrong side?"

"WHAT?" Mieant and I exclaimed simultaneously.

"Relax," she said, looking only at Mieant. "I'm not saying we switch sides. I'm just thinking that if we approached Godwill and MY uncle, the Heir, with a little more diplomacy, we might be able to figure out what's going on. Maybe there's a misunderstanding? You know, we could get our parents back?"

"Cri," I replied, "is that what you really think?"

"Look," she started.

"No," I interrupted, "*you* look. Your uncle, the Heir, Godwill, Principal Entarch—each of them has used violence against us at every turn. Do you really think you could form an alliance with someone who kidnapped you? Held you in a prison camp? Attempted to kill your sister, whether you liked her or not? Forget what you think about me for a second. What about Nonch? Your potential new best friends tore his arms off. Is that who you want to align yourself with?"

Cri opened and then closed her mouth.

"Let's get to Blue River," I offered. "We'll find the Elions. If we need to change what we do after that, we can." I was impressed with my own confidence. It occurred to me that confidence often convinces when rational thought cannot.

Reluctant nods and half of our food later, we recommitted to the original plan. Casting occasional nervous glances over our shoulders at PeaceMaker's glimmering—and now smoldering—tower, we proceeded toward the elevator entry station that would take us into Blue River's market. The queen was true to her word: the deserted entry station was where she said it would be. This was it, our real mission: enter Blue River undetected, meet with the Elions, get the DNA, and make it back to the relative safety of HiveHome.

Eventually, we made it to the station. We stood at the base of a massive stone pillar—easily a quarter kilometer in diameter. Whomever had built it had clearly intended that people would be *flying* to the elevator station. My eyes dropped to the poor imitation of a path spiraling around and up the pillar, leading to the platform high above us.

A thought crackled in my mind: *what if the Elions aren't there anymore?* Ripples of panic crashed my heart into my ribs as I pondered the implications of what would happen if they'd fled Blue River because of the invasion. And what would we do if they had left the planet altogether? Even if we did find them, we'd have to pass that psycho PeaceMaker on the way back to HiveHome.

"Peace," my butt, I thought.

Okay, now, breathe. Calm was needed for what was in front of us. The path up to the hacked elevator platform was clearly designed for Crynits, with a series of claw-holds built into the wall and stairs. The path's perimeter had no safety railing; you could hold on during the ascent or descent, but nothing kept you from falling over the side to your death at any time. *Someone was only thinking of Crynits when this was built, and not us poor Convergence races who DON'T HAVE A HUNDRED FEET! Honestly, I swear.*

In the half light, surrounded by hollow buildings and the echoing quiet of Deep Tunnel, we began to ascend the path. Cri and Mieant weren't bothered by the height, and neither was I. Because, well, I held on tight to the walls and made sure with each step that my inside shoulder was solidly planted against the structure the stairs were built against. I found the stillness of Deep Tunnel disorienting. As the landscape shrank away beneath us, I felt that I couldn't look down for fear that I would tip and fall into the dark, stupid abyss.

A thousand steps later, sweaty and exhausted, we reached the landing platform and a familiar world of Galactic lights, metals, shapes, and sounds. On one end of the platform—the end farthest away from the path—was a door large enough to fly an air car through. Panting, I eyed the platform cautiously and waited for something hairy or armed with plasma rifles (or both) to jump out and immolate us.

Nothing. Only silence.

42

After stepping on to the platform, we knelt to fully unload our backpacks. Surprise! Inside were parkas and hoodies that covered our faces perfectly. I gritted my teeth. It would have been nice to know what Broodmother had packed for us BEFORE we went hunting for disguises in the Terran Republic Nemesis Sector Fleet Headquarters. Who goes looking for disguises in…*augh!!!*

I inspected the transport elevator: seemed pretty elevator-ish. A single light inset in a square, Galactic, blue-metal alloy pad innocuously blinked the word "Up."

I stared at it. It blinked back at me. I pressed it. Nothing exploded. I almost fainted.

After a civilized pause, the giant transport pod's door split in half, and simultaneously swooshed left and right. *Okay, then. Progress.* I sucked in a deep breath, lifted my hoodie over my head, checked my Human blaster, and looked back at Cri and Mieant, who were busy doing the same. The doors slid shut behind us, and I instructed the transport pod to take us to the market.

"Remind me of our plan, Miss-Not-Our-Leader-But-Thinks-She-Is?" Cri asked. Her beauty—almond-shaped golden eyes, black hair, and lovely red skin—was marred only by her attitude. It was pinched together by a sarcastic frown. She was the mirror image of Mom, except for Mom's scar and her ever-present smile.

"We're going to get the missing nano, and then…."

"Not that plan," she interrupted. "I mean the one that happens when the elevator doors open."

"Oh."

She rolled her eyes. "You don't have a plan."

"Well, we have to get to the industrial sector."

Mieant brightened and puffed black hair out of his eyes. "I know generally where that is."

"Great," I said, "and then we find the Elions."

Mieant's brows came together in a frown. "That guy Alar from school? The one who said something to you about going to the Avenue?"

"No. We're looking for the Podmaster," I replied. I felt like kicking myself for not doing more research on the Elions when I'd had the chance. "He appeared in a hologram when we were helping Alar."

We stumbled forward as the pod changed direction while it navigated the transport tube matrix.

"I don't believe this. The fate of the Universe rests on our shoulders, and this is our grand plan: go to the industrial sector and chase after a holo." Cri said as she slumped against the pod wall and sank to her knees. Her hair cascaded over her face as she cradled her head in her upper arms.

"My Cri," Mieant said to her. "While it is nonspecific, there is substance to this plan."

Cri looked up at him. I blinked, thoroughly annoyed by her nonsense.

"Alar and his Podmaster seemed different. I've met other Elions before, on Solium4. Given Podmaster's size and demeanor, he must be ancient."

"Arrival in five seconds," a genderless surround-sound voice murmured softly.

The doors shushed open. A wave of familiar colors, sounds, and smells flowed across us as we stepped into the warm air of the market.

We stood on a wide boulevard lined with shops and buildings that was bisected by cross streets at regular intervals. Somewhat in the direction we were going, I recognized the hulk of Blue River Hospital: tall, circular, Galactic-alloy blue, and so thoroughly polished that no germs could even think of latching on to it. I'd always loved the market in Blue River, but it seemed sinister to me now.

Rain sluiced down on buildings, awnings, and, mostly, my face. Small streams of pooling water raced toward storm drains and hungry reclamation systems. Aromas—some spicy, some sweet, some like body odor, and some like our waste recycler—assaulted us all at once. Down a narrow alleyway, I spied two large, waterlogged rats nosing around an unrecognizable lump. Rats were nothing special, and they were everywhere on Nem'—or at least they were everywhere that leggers weren't, since they were leggers' favorite snack food. They were yet another Human "contribution" to Galactic civilization.

Citizens of all Galactic races moved through the market in seemingly random directions, yet each all seemed intent on their various purposes. Some used force shields to avoid the drenching rain. Others used manual means, like hoodies or cloth-and-wire rain shields. Scattered among the meandering creatures and goods were a number of small lev sleds and personal drones that were either following their owners or dashing off on autonomous errands. NPD officers in battle armor stood at the larger intersections. Security drones that reminded me of our household drone, AD9 (we called her Aidee for short), floated over their shoulders as they scanned the crowd. In squads of three, 98th Battalion Marines hovered in their assault sleds above all the major intersections. *Just another day at the market, I guess!*

"Sssweet children, some delicious, green 'natch juice?" a raspy voice whispered at my side. The voice's owner, an undersized Crynit (about my size), regarded me emotionlessly through six bulbous lower eyes. The Crynit's two upper eyes were an unhealthy yellow, and were large enough where in them, I could see my distorted reflection. With one claw hand, he offered up a jar that presumably contained the 'natch juice. *Gah.* 'Natch juice. The Crynit's segments were iridescent green with blotches of brown. Had we been in a swamp, it would have been perfectly camouflaged.

The 'natch seller coiled his lower body into a circle and rose up to my eye level. Its mandibles scissored open and closed with wicked patience, waiting for my reply. Instinctively, I took a step back and bumped into Mieant. The Crynit snaked a look at Cri and then arced its serpentine length to see if anyone was behind us in the pod. And then it settled in to stare at me, aiming to peek under my hood at my face.

"Move," Mieant hissed in my ear.

"No, thank you, sir," I said as cheerfully as I could as we scuttled past the Crynit, and waded into the melee of the overcrowded market. Crynits were everywhere, Gleans too. And an uncommon number of Lethians. But then, this was Blue River. There were lots of every species here. Blue River was nowhere near as cosmopolitan as Ever, to be sure, but it was enough to make you feel like a Citizen of Nem'. The town was truly integrated with all the species that Nature could imagine.

Syllthans floated by in groups of twos and threes, the lights of the market reflecting vividly on their black atmosphere suits. I shuddered as I remembered Nurse Pheelios and her black atmosphere suit with automated whip arms. Syllthans were wispy, low-gravity denizens of gas giants—lumpy, soft, vaporous intellects. While they had evolved sentience, they hadn't become spacefarers until they were discovered by the Convergence—much as the Elions hadn't explored space much until they encountered Humans. The Syllthans bartered the mining rights to their gas giants in exchange for environmental suits and interstellar passage, and their evolutionary dependency had made them perpetually mean. Nurse Pheelios had been exceptionally mean—so much so that she had been in league with Godwill. When she attempted to capture me on Godwill's behalf, well, I consumed her.

Lots of Trogis, both singles and in pairs, milled around some of the meat stalls. The Lethians ruled known space, but the Trogis thought they should be the leaders. They looked vaguely Human, but they had grey skin and were much larger, of course. A Trogi in a grey suit that accentuated his stature and athletic build was busily chastising his artificial attendant. The attendant's hologram floated as a cloud of golden motes half a meter from the Trogi's face. In midsentence, the

Trogi noticed us and sniffed, his vertical nose slits opening and closing widely. He waved a twelve-fingered hand at an approaching group of Trogis as they ambled past and continued down an adjacent street.

I was imagining spies everywhere. The market, once so familiar to me, seemed like a trap waiting to be sprung.

Just down the block, a huge virtual screen floated above diners at an outdoor restaurant. A Glean newsman on the screen wore a crisp white shirt with a banded collar. "And now," he announced a distinctive voice brimming with confidence and clarity, "for the latest news about the blockade of Nem' and the hunt for the killers of Freela and Kaleren Asrigard." Many in the crowd paused to view the newscast.

I tugged on Cri and Mieant's parkas and pulled them into an alcove so we could watch with a little cover. The newsman turned his head to the side, and the camera followed his gaze. "We go live to our independent news investigator, Nyla Jax."

Nyla stood against a backdrop of shops and carts. A giant Glean colleague held a rain shield over them that was practically a tent. Nyla was just as I remembered her from the incident at school days earlier. *(Days? Really? It seemed like ages. In intense times, time slows down.)* She was petite and pretty, with an honest face and grey hair cut into a bob that perfectly framed her red face and golden eyes. Her cheeks were deeply dimpled, little marks that made her instantly likable. An air of curiosity for the undiscovered hung around her like a halo.

I peered more closely at the image on the screen. My heart beat faster. *Nyla is here! Right now! In the market!* I quickly ran through scenarios of what that could mean and the possibilities it could present. The beginnings of a plan began to take shape in my mind.

"Thanks, Beel," Nyla said with a professional smile. "Jurisdictor Godwill continues the blockade of the planet, and the 98th Battlegroup has landed ships in every major population center on Nem'. As you can see"—with that, the camera panned upward to reveal clouds and a massive, city-sized Dreadnought hovering above the market—"the warships have been deployed in overwhelming numbers, and it looks like they are here for an extended stay. We have been unable to establish a timeline for the duration, but Godwill's spokesman has stated that they will remain until he is certain that the Citizens of Nem' are safe."

The image shifted back to Beel, who nodded solemnly. "Thanks, Nyla. After all of the recent chaos that's gone on, it's good to know that we're being protected. And what do you have for us regarding the Assassins of the Asrigards?"

"Yes, that is the other question of the day, Beel. NPD forces will neither confirm nor deny any information. However, the four children shown here seem to be at the heart of the controversy," she replied. The screen displayed a still image from the Blue River Educational Facility's playground of Mieant, Cri, Nonch, and me.

Yay. We're famous. I shrank deep into my hoodie, careful to keep my purple hair under wraps.

"Yet elements of this narrative do not make sense. The Lethian boy, Mieant, is the son of Freela and Kaleren Asrigard. The Glean, Cri Ceridian, is an Heir to the Ascendancy. The Crynit Nonch is the Prime of Broodmother Krig." Nyla frowned into the camera and continued, "These are all well-established families from across the Solium4 Quadrant, which leaves us struggling to find a motive. Why would Mieant Asrigard participate—either directly or indirectly—in the deaths of his parents? And with Godwill providing us with no additional information, we are left to speculate."

"Nyla, I'm sure our viewers don't want us to speculate," Beel said lamely.

"You are correct, Beel," Nyla said with a smile. She looked into the camera intensely, her eyes narrowing. "GNN calls on Jurisdictor Godwill of the Nem' Planetary Defense to respond to our inquiries on the status of our Co-Governors and the expected duration of the martial law that has been declared. And we call on any Citizen of Nem' who has information to come forth. We will offer them total confidentiality. Furthermore—" Nyla continued to speak, but her sound was cut off.

The screen cut back to Beel in the studio. "Ahem," Beel said, looking nervously past the camera. "And what of the fourth accomplice, the Human, Raystar of Terra?"

I swallowed hard and peered around self-consciously. It occurred to me that doing so could set off some security system that would set its laser sights on me and take me out in a spray of gore and energy. I pulled the hoodie a little tighter around my face and vowed to not peer around self-consciously anymore.

"Raystar Ceridian is the adopted daughter of Lady Sathralea and Nent Ceridian. Lady Ceridian is Ascendant, third in line to the Glean Ascendancy. Raystar weighs forty kilos."

I frowned. Why were they talking about my weight? *Who cares about me, much less how much I weigh?*

Clearly, Beel had the same question. His plastic expression faltered; one side of his smile drooped in tandem with the eyebrow he raised. Beel's interview with the on-scene reporter was an air car wreck in slow motion. "You've got me there, Nyla. What does the Human's weight have to do with her being one of the assassins of the Asri-gards?"

"Well, Beel, it seems improbable to many—even unthinkable—that a thirteen-year-old Human girl who weighs only forty kilos could mastermind and execute an assassination attempt," Nyla replied with sunshine in her voice.

The newscast shifted back to Beel, who selected a new vacant grin from his stock of fake expressions and looked directly into the camera. "I'd like to remind our audience that our investigative reports are independent and in no way represent the views of GNN. We're about out of time, Nyla. Before we go, do you have any other *verified*"—he applied extra stress to the word—"information for our audience?"

"No, Beel. My team and I are actively hunting down leads to crack this story." Nyla's contact information flashed across the screen. "I repeat, if any Citizens of Nem' have information that could lead to the capture of these four suspects, please contact us at...."

I jerked Mieant's sleeve, and the three of us hustled out of there. It was time to go. Besides, I'd already memorized Nyla's card when I met her the first time.

43

"Assassins of the Asrigards?" Cri hissed, glaring at me from under her hood. "You have gotten us head and shoulders up the gravity well! There's—"

"*I* did? You were there, too," I railed back at her. "How dare you!"

"Raystar! Cri! Stop!" Mieant shouted. He grabbed us both around the back of our necks and pulled us into a huddle further into the shadows. "We're committed, Cri," he said, staring first at her and then at me, "to your plan, Raystar. Lead now. Bicker later."

I snapped my mouth closed and blinked at him.

Right.

We took a look around. It didn't seem like anyone had noticed us. A Trogi NPD officer stomped by in black and red battle armor. Its drone circled overhead, and it swooped by us too quickly for us to dart into another side entrance. Thankfully, he continued on to his destination.

To our right, much, much farther down a winding labyrinth of streets, massive exhaust vents thrust themselves into the sky nearly as high as the glittering office and residential spires of Blue River. We had found the industrial sector. High above the tarnished brown vents, riotously colorful clouds circled and swirled. I frowned at the sight, as I knew they weren't clouds at all. The sprawling industrial sector was home to millions of flips.

Before the end of the Lethian–Human War, Humans seeded the galaxy with bioterrorists, including rats, gratchers, and spinach (Architect knows that Nem' had its share of each). Yet the most prolific and profoundly annoying of the bioterrorists were the parrots, which were better known as flips. Flips expanded throughout the Convergence and now lived, well, wherever they possibly could. Over the centuries, they perfected their talents, which included reproducing, flying, diving, and pooping as loudly as possible. Their fifth talent lent them their nickname: from a perfectly level flight above a target, they'd "flip" into a dive and zoom down at incredible speed to knock their prey senseless and out of the sky above. Sometimes they got a little careless and missed, and the misses were always messy.

Flips loved the updrafts created by the industrial sector's chimneys, and unlike starbats, they apparently didn't mind Dreadnoughts or rain one bit. On any given clear day, rivers of upwardly bound birds would rise impossibly high into the cerulean sky about the sector. Vibrant streams of them would disappear into clouds and then plummet straight down to chomp on all the smaller creatures that hadn't managed to figure out, over the past few millennia, why their friends kept disappearing.

Well, that's a plus! Our destination is clearly marked in the sky!

We bumped and jostled our way forward. The crowd and the rain increased the amount of energy we had to expend just to stay together. I was in the lead, and Mieant unobtrusively held on to my parka, low on my back. Cri held one of his hands in one of hers and concealed two others under her parka. She used the fourth to hold on to her pack. *So many choices!*

After an hour had passed, I finally realized that we'd just made an enormous, wet, and muddy loop that dipped through some of the industrial sector, wound through some dirty alleys, and ended up in a more remote section of the market. Twice. I guess that if you're preoccupied, it's easy to lose track of where you are.

Directions, I thought with a groan. *We need flipping directions.* I pulled my "family" off to a dark overhang. A grossly outgunned and outnumbered rat squeaked as it surrendered its dry nook to us.

"Nice plan, Ray," Cri said, raising an eyebrow as she watched the rat scurry through the shadows down the alley. Mieant glowered at me: his expression clearly communicated his opinion of my skill as a navigator. I sighed.

"Stay here. I'll find someone who can give us directions."

Cri brightened. "I know! Why don't you go ask an NPD officer?"

"C'mon, Cri, start helping," Mieant said to her, and then he croaked to me, "and you asking around is *not* a better plan! How many Humans do you see? Do you think you will somehow not be noticed?"

I dipped my head toward him. *Point taken.* "You have a better idea?"

"I—" he started.

"Oh, Great Architect Above," Cri swore, "I'm wet and cold. I need to be dry and warm!" She poked Mieant in the chest, said, "WAIT," and then poked me as well before continuing, "RIGHT HERE."

Cri spun around and disappeared impulsively into the rain. Five minutes passed.

"I don't think your parents are far away," I said to Mieant. I didn't know why it popped into my head, but I had a hunch. Nyla's newscast had set my mind on fire: laying the blame for what happened to the Asrigards at the feet of four kids, the disappearance of Lethian and Glean leaders, and now an assault on Broodmother.

He jerked his eyes to mine, still scowling.

"Listen," I continued, "they could be holding them on any of the Battlegroup ships. But ship crews talk. Any rumors or sightings of them would spread like an oxygen explosion—violent and everywhere. They're loved by all Galactics."

Mieant's frown lessened just a bit. "And?"

"I healed them, but I'm sure they still need some medical attention. So, they're probably in a hospital, or a school where there are nursing stations. Think about it. Somewhere where they could be hidden away. Once I receive the nanowhatever from the Elions, I get to live, or at least I get to live longer than three days. We'll search Blue River for them. I promise."

When he lifted his face toward me again, I noticed his carefully neutral expression. The black hair that normally floated behind him like he was in a shampoo commercial was now stuck to his face, but not unattractively. His matte-black eyes took me in.

"You have a plan," Mieant said.

I couldn't stop the corner of my mouth from quirking upward as I nodded. Because I did.

Suddenly, we heard drones buzzing around us, three of them as loud as tornadoes. Before I could process what was going on, red scanning lasers flickered over our shapes, distorted as they were under our parkas. Far too late, we spun to face the wall. *Security drones!* Then they buzzed away.

Great gratcher excrement!

"RUN!" I urgently hissed to Mieant. He grabbed my arms and pushed me back into the alcove.

"NO!" he whispered back. "No sudden movements. If they had identified us, they would have stayed. With the rain and our parkas, it's possible they couldn't get a good scan. Let's stay here for a moment."

A moment turned into a handful of minutes. I heard stompy boots, lots of them, pounding down the street toward us.

"MAKE WAY, CITIZENS! NPD BUSINESS!"

Nova. Okay. So now we were caught. *Great.* We were cornered, like rats in a closing trap.

Twenty NPD officers in full combat gear thundered past our small alcove. Their unified marching was louder and louder until it faded into the normal cacophony of the market and the slushing of the downpour.

Aided by the hyperventilation that came courtesy of my panic attack, I couldn't help but think that given our track record, not getting caught seemed improbable. If fear hadn't frozen me in place, I would have pinched myself…on the off chance I was dreaming.

Another minute passed.

"FOUND YOU!"

Mieant and I drew our blasters in an instant, pointed low at the owner of the loud voice coming toward us. We were so wired for threats that my sister's voice was just one more alarm.

Cri froze, her eyes like golden saucers under her hood. We holstered our blasters after a tense millisecond where reflex did battle with self-control.

"Don't. Do. THAT!" With the last part, Mieant's voice cracked. He grabbed her parka and yanked her into our dry, shadowy alcove.

"Uh," she said, looking back and forth from Mieant to me. Finally, understanding washed over her. "Ah. The NPD troopers that came by. Yeah. I was unstarred by THAT. There was some sort of commotion on the other side of the market."

We got lucky? That seemed…just wrong, like some law of the Universe had just been broken in our favor.

"Anyway," she said, with a bounce and a clap, "I know where the Elions are. And they're close by!"

"Where? Where are they, Cri?" I asked, upset by her girlish enthusiasm.

"About a kilometer from here. Deep in the industrial section. My source said that they were still open."

Mieant smiled and wrapped his arms around her, his head dipping in for a quick kiss.

I frowned and asked, "*How* did you find them?"

"Tourist information," she replied tartly. I blinked. "Kidding. Well, sort of. Their location is called the NanoEmporium, right? So, I found a kiosk, put in a request, and located them."

"My Cri, that was really smart," Mieant said, hugging her.

It was really smart.

I scanned the street before we headed off into the deluge. In the distance, above a building, I thought for a moment that I saw the red lights of the three drones that had just buzzed us. But the rain was coming down in vision-distorting waves, so I couldn't be sure.

Nova. I couldn't shake the feeling that our progress so far had been far too easy, with the exception of me getting us lost. Was I imagining things to make it feel like it was harder? So we could make it through the bad times via positive visualization? Maybe.

"Let's go!" Cri said.

I blinked and looked again at the spot where I'd seen the lights, but nothing was there. I shook my head and followed her into the chilling rain, imagining a happy ending.

Two solid hours of walking in the rain had proven that my boots were waterproof. I'd tucked my utility pants into them early on, fortunately, so my feet stayed dry no matter how deep the puddles got. I wished I could stuff the rest my body into my boots.

Fall rains in Blue River were always cold, especially when they coincided with the Storm Wall. The storms themselves were a mystery. We knew a little about how the tempests were created but figuring out the rest of the "why" was like explaining a god's anger by going down a boring list of chemical reactions. The Mesa Range was one of Nem's magnetic poles, and its twin was on the exact opposite side of the planet. The two mountain ranges changed the electrical charge of the air, and the Storm Wall raged between them.

The intense ionization of air particles that the Mesas created made the atmosphere go craxy: giant, dark walls of angry clouds, their bellies engorged with lightning, rumbled from one pole to another roughly every six weeks. Any Galactic structures left unshielded from the Storm Wall would be transformed into twisted, melted slag. Because of that, a significant part of the energy output on Nem' was dedicated to micro shielding. It seemed like a huge task, but Galactic tech—specifically, Galactic nanotech—was integrated into almost every manufactured item, and the protection it provided was mostly sufficient.

The Storm Wall was kilometers wide. It was storms within storms that featured anything you could imagine: tornadoes, hail, scraping

winds, ground-searing lightning. It was the sort of thing that happened on gas giants, rather than the Goldilocks worlds that Mom had told me about in stories that somehow lived through time. The moisture that rode the immense up-currents of the Storm Wall was bone chilling, especially when you were soaked through with it.

"Are we there yet?"

Splosh, splosh, splish, splosh. They hadn't heard me.

"ARE WE THERE YET?" I yelled.

Cri stopped abruptly, and Mieant collided into her. We were next to a particularly large awning that partially extended over a four-way intersection. A downspout that diverted rain from the roof of the awning had turned into a waterfall. It occurred to me that a vehicle without sensors would not be able to see through the torrent in front of us.

"Flips and gravity wells!" Cri said, glaring at me. "Raystar, what is broken in your head?"

"I'm cold. And wet."

Mieant squinted at me. "Her lips are blue," he said. "Is that good for Humans? I do not think that is good for Humans."

Cri rolled her eyes. "Look, we're almost there—"

Mieant suddenly reached out and spun Cri around so all three of our backs faced the intersection. He dragged both of us underneath the awning in a rather exaggerated way, like he was making a show of keeping us dry.

Two Trogi NPD officers and their Crynit captain navigated around the waterfall and approached our shelter.

"You three," the Crynit challenged us, "remain where you are for inspection." I laid a hand on my blaster, but I was shaking so hard that I doubted I'd be able to hit the broad side of a gratcher. And I couldn't draw on my nanotech unless I was prepared to die.

So, I did the next best thing: I shivered.

Mieant turned to the Crynit, revealing just enough of his face to show that he was Lethian.

"Captain," he said in his most aristocratic voice, "I hope that you are drier than I am. How may I be of assistance to you?"

"Show me your face."

Nova. This was it.

Mieant pulled down his hood; I could see his other hand tense, ready to draw his blaster. *Maybe I could throw myself on them and shiver them to death.*

"Who's that?" the Crynit officer demanded, aiming a blade claw at Cri.

"My wife," Mieant said. "Respectfully, unless you have some specific inquiry, we must—"

"What you *must* do is do as you are told," the Crynit boomed. "Tell your wife to remove her hood."

"It's okay, love," Mieant said sweetly to Cri. "I know you're cold."

Cri's four hands emerged from her parka and paused before lowering her hood. I imagined what it must have looked like from the officer's point of view: four very female, very red hands, emerging in synch.

"Architect above!" the Crynit shouted. "Cross-breeders!"

The Crynit and the Trogis spat theatrically into the rain. One of the Trogis asked, "Is that your…child?"

"You insult my family, sir!" Mieant said, turning to the Crynit. "Captain…?" He craned his neck in a show of attempting to examine the Crynit's badge.

"Gah! Tell your wife to leave the hood up! Void take me! I *certainly* don't want to see your spawn! Get off the streets, you freaks," the Crynit ordered, motioning to his patrol mates to follow him. "Curfew is almost here. If I see you and your"—he hesitated to search for a word that could sufficiently describe how disgusting we were— "family out again, I will put you all in detention cells."

I was so cold that I actually whimpered.

"You all are sick," the Crynit muttered as the trio moved off to torment someone else.

———

218

"Mieant, that was amazing!" Cri shout-whispered once they were out of sight. She wrapped her lower hands around his waist and her upper hands around his neck.

"Ttttttooo...mf...zzzzzy," I managed to utter. Cri disengaged from the embrace and looked at me askance.

"Raystar," Mieant said, leaning toward me, "what did you say?"

"EEEeeaaa...zzzy" I stuttered.

"Easy?" he repeated, scowling. "Too easy?"

I shivered a nod.

"Nova, Raystar! You should be thanking Mieant for—"

"My Cri, wait," he said, pulling her close, "Raystar is right."

Angry Cri was making a comeback. "We got lucky. Be grateful," she said mockingly. "If you two won't, I will." she spat, glaring at both of us. "C'mon. We don't want the frail little Human to die from the cold." With that, she marched away.

I tugged on Mieant's arm. He leaned in low, and our eyes met.

"Sssoome...th–thing's not rrright." I chattered. "Tttrrap."

He considered me for a moment. Either belief or disbelief would come next.

"I was thinking much the same. They could have scanned us or checked our IDs." He paused and put his arm around me. "The bulletins describe us as three children, as we saw on GNN. They are marking us. Keeping track of us." Mieant pulled up his hood and took a deep breath. "Cri *is* right about one thing, though. Letting you die of hypothermia would be inconvenient."

I leaned against him, and we staggered back into the rain. Awnings stretched out from nearly all of the buildings, so we jumped from shelter to shelter.

At last, we reached the edge of the market and entered the industrial sector. The neat, small shops and open squares where customers conducted business gave way to broad walls flashing signs like "Convergence Shipping" and "Nem's 'Natch: What's Life Without 'Natch?" The sidewalks were interrupted by pipes that coiled up like the roots of giant trees. In fact, pipes, cooling machines, and vents made up most of the landscape: above us, to the sides, below us, literally everywhere. They clanked randomly and with terrifying suddenness when pressure was diverted one way or another. Some vents jetted out hot air in furious bursts and others just roared, furnace-like, and exhaled a constant stream of heat. This part of Blue River was angry, focused, and largely ignored.

Rain sluiced down in sharp, cold streams that cut and stung my exposed flesh. We hunched over and ran from awning to awning, dodging around giant tubes that interrupted our simple shelters. The tubes disappeared into the grey rainclouds above us, presumably connecting to the enormous exhaust chimneys we'd noticed from a distance. There were no shops. No bodies. Just buildings, pipes, walls, and occasionally a locked door (we tried more than a few).

I was freezing. My nano, it seemed, had always kept me from getting too cold. Cut off from it as I was, with AI keeping Infection neutralized, I received none of its warming benefits. I had a choice, I suppose: die nice and warm while being absorbed by a psychopathic parasite, or die cold and free.

Never let anyone tell you that living free is easy.

"Are we close?" Mieant asked.

"Another six kilometers, I think," Cri replied, her expression pinched with annoyance and determination.

At the last stop, we'd all rummaged through our packs and found only one heating element. They gave it to me. I stuffed it against my chest, underneath my clothes. I was still cold, but at least my teeth stopped chattering.

"What did the officer mean when he called us 'cross-breeders?'" I asked.

Cri stopped and shot me an incredulous glance. "*Seriously?*"

"It's when two separate spec—" Mieant started.

"I can't believe you're that dense, Ray," Cri said, resuming her pace. "Individuals belonging to two different races fall in love and possibly mate. Cross-breeders."

"That's bad?" I frowned and adjusted the heating element as I stepped in another puddle. "Why would that be bad?"

"Because there's a galaxy full of Void-forsaken ignorance out there," Cri said, her words tinged with anger. Anger, it seemed, was Cri's compass for navigating life.

"But what about you two…." I let the words drift off, unsure whether what I was saying was insulting or just stupid. Or both.

"My parents encourage tolerance," Mieant said resignedly, with both pride and grief in his voice. "Their quadrant is significantly more prosperous than the other Convergence quadrants. More universities, and thus, more of us are educated. There's tremendous inter-quadrant rivalry. The other quadrants just can't keep up." He tilted his head thoughtfully. "Last year, my parents fought off a bid to integrate their quadrant into the other three—the idea being that the prosperity they had developed, needed to be distributed for the good of the other quadrants. But our wealth"—he paused, choking back emotion—"my parents, because…."

"Because…." I said impatiently.

"My parents believe in diversity," he continued. They want to build trust among Citizens that any being can express ideas and feel safe in doing so. They want Citizens to have the confidence that they can live their lives however they want without fear of persecution. But the Empress of Lethia wants subjects, not Citizens. Lethians may rule the Convergence, but the Lethian Empire wants wealth at the cost of equality. Persecution is a tool of control, and so is class."

I was stunned. It was enough of a shock to learn Mom and Dad had been rebelling against the system by adopting me and bringing me up to be "normal."

It was a revelation that Freela and Kaleren Asrigard, Co-Governors of Quadrant 4, were unique as well. Broodmother Krig. *Huh.* Another leader who challenged norms. Perhaps it wasn't a coincidence that all of these enlightened leaders were in various states of being removed from power.

"Do you two…uh, are you afraid?"

Cri slowed her pace so Mieant and I could catch up to her. She took his hand in one of hers and looked up at him expectantly.

"Before Godwill, the prison camp, meeting Broodmother, seeing Deep Tunnel," Mieant waved his free hand at the world, "I would have said no. But now? Yes. I am afraid. Barbarians are coming for me, to take what I have."

Cri wrapped her upper arm around his bicep and pulled him close. She said, so softly that it was barely audible, "I'm afraid of everything now."

The remaining six kilometers proved to be too much for us. The Storm Wall and the rain had made the coming of night invisible to us, but once Banefire, Nem's malevolent red-giant sun, almost imperceptibly, fell below the horizon; darkness manifested, and bitter cold ruled that darkness. The heating pad I'd been holding tight to my body glowed magma-red. We shared its miserly warmth and traded it back and forth, taking turns to shiver. It wasn't nearly enough. We were becoming colder and colder in excruciatingly small increments.

Through sheer luck, Mieant found an exhaust vent under an awning that was blowing hot air against a wall. The plume of air was doing a great job of drying out the ground underneath it. We'd be warm. We'd be dry. I was pretty sure that the fumes we'd be inhaling were about as toxic as could be, but the appeal of being dry and warm made the acidic air a risk I was more than willing to take. We plopped down and promptly fell asleep, huddled together.

I woke up hours later, hot. My clothes were dry, but something was wrong with the light. I sprang to my feet and looked around, one hand on my blaster. The rain had stopped. The sidewalks and streets were nearly dry. Something was off. I couldn't put my finger on what was so unnerving. It was too bright.

Oh. The rainstorm had departed, and Banefire had risen. Blue sky peeked at us from the spaces between buildings, and the red giant rode high and huge. The Dreadnought had moved off to the other side of the city. The spires of Blue River shone like prisms in the gorgeous fall day. Flips soared in red and yellow streams around their tops. It was a *beautiful* day.

Yay. I should soak it in. Suddenly I found myself back in the self-pity zone. *How much time do I have left?*

I nudged Cri first and then Mieant with my boot. "C'mon, get up. I've only got a day, or half a day, or very little time left," I muttered.

Cri groaned and brushed her hair from her face. My shadow fell over her, blocking Banefire's glare.

I moved.

"Nnnnggg!" she whined, quickly covering her eyes with her hands.

Eh, it was a little petty. But I enjoyed it.

Mieant untangled himself from her arms and got to his feet.

"Mieant," I said to him, "you finding this vent saved our lives."

He shrugged, embarrassed, and leaned over to help Cri up. She rubbed sleep from her eyes as she leaned against him.

"Food. Do we have any food?" Cri asked.

Mieant shook his head, yawning.

"Void," she said. "I'm starving."

I was not just starving. I was probably consuming myself with my nano-induced energy burn. We had no money, and in the industrial sector, there weren't any shops we could steal from.

"Maybe the Elions have food," Mieant said.

Cri got her bearings, and we marched on toward the NanoEmporium.

The industrial sector was a study in dinginess and grunge. Massive pipes that were orange and yellow when new were now streaked with rust and white streams of flip excrement. The Galactic cement sidewalks were stained with green slime wherever pipes buried themselves in their cracks. Among various soggy piles of refuse and the occasional dead rat, seeping water reflected a few bright colors: rare flashes of shimmering turquoise, cyan, or pink beauty in the midst of ugliness.

As we moved further into the heart of the industrial sector, the pipes became especially slimy, like mucus-covered snakes. In the darker recesses, where conduits created all sorts of corners, shadows, and nooks, rats scurried here and there, but mostly they poked their twitching noses out into the light and then pulled back as if they'd been burned. They glared at us warily and furtively, like the true survivors they were.

The road, if it could be called that, wound around and bridged over pipes. Sometimes it stretched over an abyss that dropped away into the darkness. Above us, the chimneys and exhausts vented their heat and fumes in billowing toxic clouds. Despite the near perfection of the sunny day, the pipes, vents, and conduits maliciously hogged sunlight and crowded us together under long shadows.

We had just ducked under a massive pipe covered in a brown, elastic filth that stretched out and then rebounded—like snot—as it released itself onto the road when something *else* splattered onto the ground beside me. Another splatter then dropped in front of me.

"Awww! What the everloving nova!" Mieant swore. Cri and I turned to look at him just as a palm-sized brown splotch stained his grey hood. It wasn't falling rain. We were in the midst of a POOP STORM, of all things. *Aha. That's* what covered the streets and cast the giant industrial sector in a white and brown veneer. Even Galactic metal with its nanobots couldn't keep up with the mess. The squawks and screeches we heard above us suggested that we'd reached the perimeter of a flip rookery.

We scurried to the side of the street covered in awnings and listened as they *thwapped* with the sound of the not-rain. The smell was awful: briny and organic and worse than the gratcher shed ever could have been.

"This is the worst!" Cri muttered, shivering and glaring at me (as if all this was MY fault!).

I recalled the times I spent helping Dad clean out our compound's recycling pit and had to agree: this *was* the worst. A little water dripped from the tip of my hood to the side of my mouth. I wiped it off with a shiver, but *it wasn't water*. I froze with my mouth hanging open and gazed at a second wad of the stuff clinging to my sleeve. *Spike me! Flip poop!*

"Pllllaaahhh!" I grabbed the underside of my parka and scrubbed my face with it. *Ugh.* This was horrible. "C'mon," I muttered. The poop storm increased in intensity as Cri led us through a cluster of towering exhaust vents that billowed gasps of garbage-stinking steam.

We stoically trudged through the steam, easing ourselves deeper into the labyrinth. Larger things than rats moved in the dark spaces between the pipes. Several times I thought I saw pairs of dull yellow eyes or a tentacle or two exploring the air. *Leggers? Here?* Bodies of dead flips littered the ground; in one spot, a couple of rats were tugging a dead flip's wings in different directions. When the larger of the two won the tug-of-war, the loser issued a series of furious squeaks. A tentacle snaked out from around a corner and ensnared the victor. The tentacle encircled the rat and vanished back to whatever it was connected to. Paradise, this was not.

I shivered at the thought of leggers adding to this grotesque soup of horrors. The awnings were becoming fewer and fewer, forcing us to sprint longer distances from one to another. We were soaked and beyond caring about it. Between sprints, I could see that we'd reached the heart of the rookery, and the carcasses that crunched and squished underfoot were undoubtedly chicks that had fallen hundreds of meters from their nests. *Lovely.*

"Ray," Mieant said, nudging me. A golden sign across the street stood out in the poop storm. Scratch that—it was a glowing hologram, with letters as large as I was tall, that shone in the brown gloom: NanoEmporium. A silver arrow pointing to a set of double doors left no doubt about where we should go.

I shook my head in wonderment. If I was going to start a business, I'd want it right here, too. I'd make a fortune selling force-shield umbrellas. Customers would flock to my store (get it?).

But maybe that was the point. Maybe they didn't want a lot of visitors. Only *dedicated* customers, ready to buy.

No prompting was necessary in our case. We dashed across the street, our boots splashing in the poop-soup puddles. The NanoEm-

porium's doors swooshed open to welcome us, and we tumbled into a small white foyer latticed with vents. Another set of double doors on the other side of the room marked the entrance. I squinted against the bright light as air gushed in and clouds of white smoke billowed around us. I tingled as I realized that the clouds weren't the usual water-based mist; rather, they were a type of nanotech. As fast as they'd appeared, the clouds were sucked back into the vents.

Cri looked down at herself, wide eyed. So did I. We were absolutely devoid, rid, and any other cleaning-related word of flip poop.

"Remarkable!" Mieant said as he strode through the second set of doors.

Cri and I scurried after him. We entered what could only be described as the cleanest, whitest room I'd ever seen. Aisles of white metal spread out into the distance. Thousands of multicolored vials and canisters sat neatly arranged on the shelves in stark contrast to the blank whiteness of the sterile background. We had stepped through a door into another reality.

This place was definitely an emporium. But all I could think of as I took in the unimaginable variety of nano for sale was *what they were thinking when they located their shop in the heart of a flip rookery?* Worst location ever! A high-tech emporium nestled in a river of bird poop?

"Touch nothing!"

As one, the three of us turned toward the voice.

The Elion was about my height. It was roughly egg shaped, under a meter wide. Hand lengths of soft, pure white fur waved about of their own volition in an attempt to keep the Elion "cool" with a dazzling array of features: emerald, plate-sized eyes; long, flappy, and black snow-proof lashes; and a long pink tongue that was dangling from its mouth, the Elion was somewhere between absolutely adorable and criminally adorable. I'd bet he inspired "awwws" and spontaneous hugs from everyone when he walked down a street.

Alar!!

My old schoolmate hopped about on alternate combinations of his six spidery legs while he pointed at each of us with his stick-like arms. His pink tongue flopped with every hop.

"Raythtar! You've come!" Alar exclaimed, his giant eyes swooping in different directions and then back to us. He ran down a side aisle

and disappeared around a corner while shouting, "Podmathter! Pod-mathter! The Human hath come!"

"I am here, Podling," a deep, stomach-rumbling voice boomed be-hind us. We spun toward the *new* voice.

"Eeeeeee…." Cri whispered. How had someone so massive ap-peared behind us without making a sound?

This Elion was neither small nor adorable. It was a mountain, easily as large as my dad. Two sea-green, serving-tray sized eyes regarded me from well *above* my head. The intensity of its gaze was palpable, like judgment. The Elion was missing large patches of its fur. In those spots, naked skin bubbled over with ugly, purple scars. My jaw dropped and my hands fell to my side as I craned my neck up to meet its verdant gaze. An eternity passed as we each regarded each other.

"Podmathter, the Human hath come! Raythtar hath come!" Alar shouted with delight and scrabbled his way across the floor—*tick-tack, tickety-tack, tack, tack, tack.* The NanoEmporium certainly had a design flaw in its flooring if you happened to be a small Elion. He tried unsuccessfully to decelerate and skidded into Podmaster, who gently turned Alar's body so he could face us. Alar sputtered and pointed at me.

"Yes, Alar, I see her."

"Thank you for helping me at thchool, Raythtar," Alar said, taking a half step forward. "Printhipal Entarch wath a thpike!"

Great gravity wells! He was the fluffy toy I'd wanted when I was five! I couldn't help but smile when I looked at him, despite the vitriol he'd just directed at our deceased principal. Podmaster's gaze was heavy on me. I met his eyes and bowed. It felt right to do it; plus, being polite costs nothing.

Cri and Mieant blinked at me and then hastened to follow my lead, each bowing in turn.

"Thee ith going to the Avenue of the Ruinth!" Alar said to his father—I guess? I wasn't sure if Podmasters were male or female or if those were even relevant gender designations. I'd seen vids of Elions before, but they hadn't prepared me for how massive the adults actually were.

"Indeed, podling. Terran, you have found us. But you are being followed, hunted throughout the city. And you led your hunters *here*?"

Alar froze, his big eyes wide. He slowly *tick-tacked* around to face his father, his big pupils rolling up to gaze at Podmaster like a naughty puppy.

"What do you want, Human?" Podmaster boomed.

In the dead silence that followed, I imagined I could hear small insects chirping away. I swallowed hard.

"HA! Ha! I joke!" The thunderous bass of Podmaster's laughter vibrated the vials around us in time with each guffaw. He extended a shiny black arm from beneath a patch of white fur; it unfurled to end in a clawed hand. He gently placed his talons on my back.

"Be at ease, Raystar-Human. We remember your people's kindness. You have saved my Podling only a few days past. It is an honor to keep the long promises made between Elions and Humanity, as well as the short promises made between myself and your parents," he said, patting Alar lovingly and tamping his hair down so it looked like a white, fluffy bird's nest on the top of his oval body.

Cri and I traded glances. *Our parents?*

"You have no doubt heard of me, which is why you are here. I am Podmaster, Master Trader, the Elions' Delegate on Nem'. Gravity wells may stretch us across an event horizon, destroying us one molecule at a time with the worst pain imaginable, one that will stretch into eternity." He patted my back as he directed us toward what looked like the main office. "But rest assured, Elions will always remember Humanity's kindness."

"Podmathter! Raythtar! That wath good humor, no?"

I smiled tightly. "Oh yes. Certainly made us tense there for a bit."

"At thcool, like the Humanth of old, you thaved me. Thank you, Raythtar!"

My cheeks grew hot. No one talked nicely about Humans, and no one had ever said much nice about me. Not even blessed ME. "You're, uh, welcome, Alar."

"I'm going to vomit...." muttered Cri.

"Shssshhhhhh," Mieant hissed, "this is fascinating."

"…in my mouth," she finished.

Podmaster heard her and impossibly gave her a backward glance—impossible because he had no neck or back, at least that I could see. The beginning of a frown crept across his massive face. I looked back at Cri, too. Her eyes blazed at being caught in the insult.

"We," I said hesitatingly, trying to find the right words, "have been through a lot. Our parents have been taken."

"Ahhh," Podmaster sighed, "indeed you have, hatchlings. By the impostor Jurisdictor, by the false Heir. There is more you do not know."

Podmaster led us through a door into a spacious rectangular room, one that was easily big enough for several more Elions his size plus us. The space was windowless, and the walls were lined with 2D images of other planets: frozen ice worlds with soaring mountain peaks, dark star-filled skies, and sparkling cities. Elion worlds, I presumed.

Orange and red high-backed couches and cushioned chairs were arranged in a circle in the room's center. Podmaster unceremoniously crashed onto one of the larger couches. He reached out and patted the chair closest to him, motioning me over.

"Children, the wind and snow may freeze and flay your skin from your frozen bones, but in my home, the food will always be hot, your stomachs will always be full, and your bodies will be safe and warm! We shall eat before conducting business." He considered my companions briefly and waved at them, too. "Sit, Cri Ceridian. Be welcome, Mieant Asrigard. Podling, fetch us appropriate food and drink!"

Alar took off, delighted.

"So. I am honored. The assassins of the Asrigards, in my home?" Podmaster thundered amiably. "You have braved much to meet me. Tell me of your journey, and we can discuss how I may help you."

We told him everything. He let out a ground-shaking belly laugh and nearly rolled off his couch when I described how I'd flushed AI. "Is the crafty one still in there?" he said, poking a clawed finger at the diamond-shaped pendant hanging around my neck.

"He is containing the Infection that Godwill placed in me," I said. It was hard to explain the internal battle considering that externally, AI looked like nothing more than a nice bit of jewelry. So much of what goes on inside shows no trace outside.

He laid a claw hand on my head and patted me sympathetically. His hand was warm. "Continue," he said kindly.

To my surprise, his big emerald eyes welled up when we got to the part about the Heir and Godwill taking Sathra and Nent.

Alar returned with a hover cart floating in front of him. That's not quite right: a hover-cart *laden* with food preceded him. After a nod and a wave from Podmaster, we three attacked the meats, cakes, fruits, creams…the I don't know was. Hunger has little etiquette.

The food was hot and delicious. Once our bellies were full, Podmaster nodded, perhaps more to himself than to us and said, "Cri, Raystar," he said. "Your parents are most certainly still alive. They are too important to the Convergence and the Glean Gathering to be eliminated this early in the game, I think."

"You know our parents?" Cri asked.

"Most certainly, young one," he said. "I was with your mother when the Heir scarred her face."

Cri blanched, her face turning from dark red to almost light pink in a second. Her tattoos stood out boldly against her lightened skin. I hadn't thought about Mom's scar in forever, long ago having assumed that we'd never get an answer.

"What?" my sister asked in a small voice.

"Your mother is an idealist, child. She believes we should strive to unlock the highest potential good in everyone. And she is a fierce warrior who backs up her beliefs with brains, sharpened nanosteel, and plasma when all else fails. I fought by her side before you were born, and I will continue to support her, your father, and you both, her progeny, for as long as I have breath. It is our way. But this story of our friendship has not been shared with you?" He regarded us for a moment, his giant eyes narrowing at our negative head shakes. "I must consider this. Perhaps it is not my story to tell." He paused before adding, "Indeed, it is not."

Whaaa? Despite our animosity, Cri and I shared an openmouthed and sisterly "what the nova?" look. We were starving for more information.

Before either of us could voice a complaint, Podmaster changed the subject. "You have come here seeking the ancient Human DNA code. And once you have it, you plan to go into the Mesas. Correct?"

I nodded.

"Then let me tell you another story. It will inform you about the game that you now find yourselves playing in earnest. Perhaps it will give you the wisdom to be a true competitor—or at least an important piece on the board. Will you hear me?"

Our heads threatened to fall off our shoulders, we nodded so hard.

"Let me begin by saying that the ancient Humans are not gone. Not by any measure. Raystar's organic parents are, in fact, alive."

My jaw dropped, and my mind fell into an abyss right alongside it.

Podmaster sighed before continuing. "Near the end of the war, the Chars, Gleans, Machines, Elions, and Humans teamed up to set in motion a grand scheme designed to rebalance power across the Convergence and survive the potential for extinction that already threatens at our borders."

"Oh, great. You're not going to tell us about my mom, but you're going to talk about the Lethian–Human War?" Cri said sarcastically. Everyone turned to look at my sister. She blinked before adding, "It's true, though, right?" Typical. Cri could never get past her jealousy. It was a dangerous trait to let your emotions override common sense, to destroy the potential of the moment.

After visibly summoning patience, Podmaster narrowed his gaze at her and continued. "It is necessary in order to understand your circumstances today, Cri Ceridian."

Cri looked down at her hands, scowling. I, for one, definitely wanted to hear this.

"Yes," Mieant exclaimed, "the fringe theory is that the Humans will come back and destroy the Lethians AND the Convergence!" He bounced on his chair, delighted by his deductive skills.

I frowned at him. "Uh. You're kind of Lethian, you know," I said.

"Pfffttt," Mieant retorted, brushing aside my statement with a hand, "we're talking about those craxy pseudoscience theories. Right?"

"Not so craxy," Podmaster replied, shaking his upper body in a rotating motion. "Raystar *is* that fringe theory. Her DNA has something to do with bringing Humanity back, in full force. Only the highest elements of Char, Glean, Machine, and Elion society know this." Before any of us could ask a question, he continued. "The Lethian Empress, the highest ranks of the Glean Gathering, the highest ranks among the Crynit queens, certainly all of the Char Archons, and the Machine's central mind—even the Unity are ALL aware that this *was* Humanity's plan." I blinked as I tried to process all the names and titles he'd casually rattled off. I'd only read about them in history or government classes.

"They're all part of the Convergence now," Mieant said, eyes still wide, not understanding. "We're all unified. I mean, it could be better, but...."

Podmaster spread out his four arms. "This is how you would recommend we live, podling? Has the Convergence helped all races rise equally?"

Mieant looked down, visibly angered. "In Quadrant 4, they have."

"Your parents are lights in the darkness, young Asrigard. Let me tell you a story, or give you an example, of why the four major civilizations that made up the Terran Republic displayed so much loyalty toward each other."

"History. *Seriously*?" Cri shrugged and sank low into her chair.

"Elions owe everything to Humanity. We were not then as you see us now. Our planet was sanctioned by the Convergence for terraforming. Fortunately for us, about a hundred years earlier, Humanity established a scientific base on Grateen, our home world. Humanity had been aware of the Convergence for some time but had made no official contact. Perhaps in a bid to gain new allies, Human scientists began a series of genetic experiments on my species that were designed to enable us to become spacefarers. You can call it uplift or exploitation, but the fact remains that I would not be here now if Humanity had not pursued a policy of helping other civilizations, through their own free choice, to reach the stars.

"When a Lethian corporate fleet arrived to begin its 'development' operations on Grateen, they unilaterally ignored our communications. Imagine the depths of ruthlessness needed to proceed with 'harvesting' planets, particularly ones that already had an active and thriving civilization? They called it biomass and mineral harvesting—pleasant and important-sounding words." Podmaster paused for a moment as his claws turned into fists that clacked loudly. "They blockaded our system. The Terrans maintained a light warship in orbit around Grateen that served their scientific installation. It was a cruiser, if I recall correctly. The Lethians and Terrans engaged in a 'conversation' that resulted in the loss of more than fifteen Lethian corporate-fleet ships, after the wordplay ended and plasma blasts began. One heavily damaged Lethian ship escaped to relay the tale of two newly discovered 'barbarian' species that had not yet integrated into the Convergence.

Podmaster turned to me before adding, "I will not say that your ancestors assisted us purely out of goodwill. It was good enough, though. Humanity's uplift programs were a method of self-protection, but Humans gave Elions access to the stars. Let me tell you a truth: power is about access. Humanity gave us ACCESS to power."

"And?" Mieant urged.

"According to Lethian law, Grateen was now owned by a powerful family on Lethia—some said the Empress herself owned it. Regardless, this family and its corporations had set forth on a colonization spree fueled by pride and twisted ambition. They would take our planet regardless of the costs. According to their malformed logic, they had to in order for Lethians to save face amongst all of the other Convergence species. So, a larger Convergence fleet, composed of a mixed-race force, was dispatched with orders to put down what the Lethians referred to as a 'rebellion.' They waged a quiet genocide against what they thought was a vastly underpowered force. Here, I share with you another truth: evil grows in the shadows and has no back-up plan.

"The Human cruiser met the newly arrived Convergence fleet and engaged in another 'disagreement.' The Humans were capable of translating Galactic well enough to communicate with them. They claimed the Elions as their allies and declared that they had a responsibility to protect them. The Lethian delegation and the Convergence fleet did not back down, and the cruiser became the first Human casualty of the Lethian–Human War.

"The Convergence fleet then proceeded to sterilize our outer colonies. By then, Humans on those planets had fully integrated with our culture after hundreds of years of partnership. Some had even been born on planet and were full Citizens. We were building a civilization-level relationship. That brings us to our final truth for the day: true friendship often bears a heavy cost.

Mieant looked at his feet.

"You did not do this, Asrigard," Podmaster said softly to Mieant. "A Battlegroup much like the one above us now was dispatched to Grateen. As the Battlegroup closed in on our home world, Terran reinforcement arrived—a single vessel. A planetship."

I'd heard of planetships in legends and had seen them with Nonch in the school library. My head was spinning.

"It utterly destroyed the Convergence fleet. This was perhaps the first miscalculation on the part of Humanity. They displayed their naval superiority, thinking it would be a deterrent. Yet it had the opposite effect. The Convergence had been ruling known space for several millennia before encountering Earthlings. This casual elimination of an entire Battlegroup—more than 6,000 ships—created fear unlike anything Convergence races, or the Lethians, had experienced before. The entire Convergence immediately went on a war footing and mobilized at an unprecedented level.

"Allow me one last truth: war breeds war, just as pain returns pain."

"That's not what the Recorders say," Cri said petulantly, daring us all to challenge her. "Humans attacked a Lethian core world—unprovoked."

"I don't believe the Recorders, Cri," Mieant said quietly. "We talked about this in class just a few days ago with"—he swallowed hard, remembering the day—"Principal Entarch."

"Yeah, and you got bubbled, Mieant," she shouted. She grabbed his grey hand with her red one. "My Moon, don't you see what's happening here? We've gotten wrapped up in this stupid Human drama. They were defeated a long time ago! Everyone who touches them"— she paused to glare at me—"or invites them into their home is punished for it."

"How can you, a daughter of Sathra and Nent Ceridian, believe that Humans are bad?" Podmaster interrupted.

Cri turned to Podmaster and attempted a placating tone. "Respectfully, Sire, I believe that everything we've done has only caused more trouble. For my parents. For his parents," she said, pointing at Mieant. "And for Broodmother Krig. Everyone who comes into contact with her…." Cri stopped and looked at me. "I'm only saying that maybe we *should* reach out to my uncle."

"Oh, right," I said, anger coloring my voice, "the uncle who, standing side by side with Godwill, took our parents away?"

"Podmaster said Mom and Dad were okay!" she yelled, rising to her feet. Mieant gently pulled her back to her chair and wrapped his arms around her. She held on tightly to his forearms. "You don't know *what* they're doing now," she finished sullenly.

"Young Ceridians," Podmaster said, his deep voice vibrating in my belly, "I fought with your mother against the Heir. I am part of the history that caused you to be where you are today. Your uncle has dangerous and bloody ambitions."

"So you say!" Cri yelled. Then her eyes grew large as she realized that she'd just called Podmaster a liar. She put a hand over her mouth. Alar sucked in a breath, his big green eyes slowly moving in a large arc from Cri to his father.

Podmaster, ever the diplomat, was nonplussed. "So I have said, Cri. What I have not said is that Sathra and I fought in a duel against the Heir and his second, an up-and-coming Lethian commander named Godwill Synest."

The room was silent as we processed what Podmaster had just revealed.

"Why?" Mieant finally asked.

"Godwill attempted to assassinate Nent and Cri, then just a newborn podling, with poison. Sathra and I were walking together toward her quarters. As we approached, we witnessed Godwill walking away, as if he had just exited Sathra and Nent's house. The monitoring and security devices had been mysteriously deactivated, eliminating any direct evidence that he'd entered the residence. All we had was an inconclusive patchwork of clips and sensor readings. When Sathra and I entered the quarters, we found both Nent and you near death.

"Common sense points a solid finger at Godwill. But politics enabled him to dodge what should have been a black-and-white accusation from the Heir."

"See?" Cri said. "The Heir took Mom's side. How bad can he be?"

"You mistake my meaning, Cri Ceridian," Podmaster said abruptly. "Sathra, your mother, *is* the rightful Heir. Her younger brother is not."

Cri's jaw dropped. "*Mom* is the Heir?"

"Your mother challenged Godwill to an honor duel, believing him to be the assassin. Her challenge was rejected. You see, at the time, Gleans and Lethians were not on the best of terms," Podmaster said and then paused, considering his next words carefully. "That is the historic norm. Your uncle, Tyan, argued that the assassin had likely been sent by the Foundationalist movement, and that Godwill's mandate from the Lethian Empress herself to strengthen ties with Gleans meant that he could not be the guilty party. Sathra, however, tenaciously investigated the poisoning and built a case that could not be rejected out of hand, even though it was inconclusive.

"Tyan said that a duel would risk war with Lethia, counter to our interests in peace and balance. Therefore, if there was to be a duel, he was honor bound to be Godwill's second. I owed Sathra and Nent a debt for helping one of our worlds, one that included a Human population, to avoid invasion by Godwill's forces, who were after Human nanotech. I was on a flagship in the Great Gathering, paying my thanks to your mother and to the Glean Matriarch and Patriarch, when I heard of the duel's inevitability. I humbly requested to be your mother's second."

We were so entranced that Mieant actually raised his hand before asking, "Sire, was it a draw, then?"

"Not even close," he chuckled. "We won handily. But the trap had been sprung. A Lethian was 'found' carrying precisely the type of poison used on Cri and Nent. This 'discovery' happened at the moment the duel would have ended, when Sathra's blade was at Godwill's throat. She was about to finish him. Your uncle flung his short sword at Sathra just as my own talons pierced your uncle's shoulder. I only had time to shout a warning, and thank the Architect, it was enough that she could dodge the worst. Instead of killing her, Tyan's sword opened her face from forehead to chin." He paused to look at my sister and me before adding, "She was lucky to keep her eye."

Cri's eyes glowed like suns as she clenched all four fists.

"Even worse, Sathra, Nent, and I concluded that the duel was really an assassination attempt on Sathra by your uncle. Godwill was a cat's paw, a distraction that would allow the duel to take place. Mother and Father of the Glean Gathering—your grandparents—hailed Tyan as a hero for saving Godwill and averting further conflict between Lethians and Gleans, and your mother was stripped of her birthright. She was deemed too irresponsible and flighty to be a ruler of the Glean Gathering. She and your father were exiled."

"I do not believe you," Cri said defiantly.

Podmaster blinked. "Excuse me?" he rumbled. To be called a liar so casually twice in less than five minutes would test anyone's goodwill.

"My uncle would never do such a thing. My parents would have told me. They said they moved here because of *her!*" Cri shouted, pointing at me. Our shocked faces all turned to her.

"It is much to take in, hatchling," Podmaster said after a calming breath. "On my honor, my life, and my home world: Lady Sathra Ceridian is the rightful Heir. Ultimately, yes, you did move here because of Raystar."

With that, the gazes turned to me.

Podmaster sighed before continuing. "As I mentioned before, there is a compact between the Terran Republic members. Humans appear in secret at regular intervals to meet with all the member civilizations. Several weeks before the poisoning and the duel took place, three Humans from a family of high rank within Humanity's hierarchy—the governing 'party,' as they say—requested an audience with the Gathering's Mother and Father. Gleans have always been among the closest allies of Humanity, so such a request was not unusual. It was granted without question. What was unique about this meeting was that when the Humans left, one of their group stayed behind."

"That is common in diplomatic relations," Mieant interjected. "One stays behind as a liaison. I've seen my parents employ tactics like this, and others have used them with my parents as well. Leaving someone behind is a gesture of trust, a way to build mutual understanding. It is a commitment that essentially says, 'I will return.'" He shrugged. "So why was leaving an ambassador behind so notable or provocative?"

Podmaster extended a shiny, black arm and one razor-sharp finger talon in my direction.

"It is unique because the ambassador they left behind was their daughter. To your point, hatchling, yes, they will return...in force."

48

"Wait, wait, wait," I said, running my hands through my purple hair, "my parents left me HERE?"

Podmaster nodded. "A more precise understanding is that they entrusted you to the care of the Glean Gathering Mother and Father, who, in turn, entrusted you to your adoptive parents, Sathra and Nent."

Nova. My heart was pounding. My appetite—for once—vanished. The scent of ozone wafted through the air, and static electricity crackled and danced around my fingers.

No, no, no. I can't let my power out. I'm learning so much. Focus. Process. Think.

"Why would they do that?" I asked after several calming breaths.

"Little Human, you have a capable mind. What do you believe?"

I looked at Podmaster, who I innately trusted. Maybe it was because Alar wore every emotion on his fluffy sleeve, or because my parents, AI, and even Infection had told me that I must get to the Elions, that they would help. I truly felt like Podmaster was on the level with me.

"It's a test," I said after a moment. "To Mieant's point, they want to see how the Convergence would react to me. So when they return... they will have seen how their closest ally treated their most valuable possession."

Podmaster smiled. "Well thought, child. Sathra and Nent, as well as your natural Human parents, should be proud."

I couldn't keep my eyes from overflowing with my emotions. I began to shake.

"Raythtar," Alar said as he tic-tacked up to me and placed his stick-like arms around me. I leaned against him, into his hug. His soft fur smelled like flowers, and he was even softer and more pillowy than I remembered.

I wiped my nose with my sleeve and smiled at Alar. I turned to Podmaster and asked pointedly, "That's also pretty cold. How could they…give me away?"

"You are the only Human child I have met. Seeing you and your unconscious vulnerability, I can believe that you are their gravity, the tug of love that stretches from you, here and now, to wherever they are. These are times of unmaking and unmasking. Danger darkens the skies above us, and ugly forces are threatening us, placing claw arms around the lives of those we love."

He paused for a deep breath before continuing. "But perhaps a better question is what will happen when they come back and see how their allies, and the Convergence, have treated you?"

It was all too much. I couldn't process this information all at once. I squeezed Alar, so grateful for his warmth, and sat up straight.

"I was told to come here, to meet you, and that you would provide my missing DNA control nano."

Podmaster's lips pulled back into a toothy smile, his serrated white teeth like mountain tops against his black gums. He nodded. "Indeed. And we have been waiting for you. You do not think that Alar *actually* needed to go to school, do you?"

"I wanted to go, though!" Alar interjected, eagerly glancing between Podmaster and me with his saucer-sized emerald eyes. "Thtupid Printhipal Entarch," he hissed, and for a moment, I glimpsed the predator he would one day become. *Never judge a pillow by its fluffiness.*

"Podling," Podmaster said with reproach. Alar looked at the ground.

Podmaster opened a claw hand. In it was a vial, a clear container as long as my hand. Inside, what looked like liquid silver sparkled back at me.

"Here, Raystar. Drink." Podmaster pushed the vial toward me. "Take it. Time is limited. Drink it."

Okay, I'm sorry. I've been through a lot in the past few days. Let me get this straight: something good is happening to me now, just like that? This moment didn't seem possible.

I looked down at the vial and at the massive, clawed arm holding it. The owner of the arm, a battle-scarred, white-furred mountain, regarded me with verdant eyes.

"Want to fight for it?" I joked inappropriately and unwisely. Podmaster raised a furry white eyebrow.

"You could chase me? Throw something at me?" I said giddily. "Because that would make me feel more comfortable. I mean, nothing so far has been easy for—"

"TAKE THE VIAL! FOR THE LOVE OF ALL THAT IS GOOD!" Mieant shouted.

Mieant's outburst caused Alar to fall backward on his butt. In the process, his fluff bumped the food cart and sent it slowly spinning away. Alar flopped about on the floor like a pillow as he tried to stand. Cri yelped. Podmaster was unfazed. He calmly lifted Alar by his fluffy head and planted him on his feet. Static crackled and two sparks leapt from my hair to the ground, where they sizzled and dissipated.

"I am just saying," Mieant said softly in response to our glares. The liquid in the vial responded with a soft glow.

"It is yours," Podmaster said, placing the vial in my hand with his pinched talons. "Perhaps this is the easiest part of your quest, young one."

I stared at it. I finally had my missing nano. *Well, nova, I better drink it before, like, a meteor hits me. Or I choke on air.* This was too simple, too easy.

The stopper hissed when I touched it; it came off easily with a slight twist. *A DNA lock?* I thought. I raised it to my lips and then stopped a millimeter from my mouth.

"WHAT THE NOVA, RAYSTAR?" Mieant yelled again. "Drink the Void-cursed liquid!"

I WILL NOT PERMIT THIS, Infection hollered. *IT IS AS I SAID. YOU ARE GOING TO TERMINATE ME.*

Drink the nano, Ray! AI shouted.

Ahhh. This chaos feels normal. Apparently, my psyche needed some sort of life-threatening or existential crisis as reassurance before springing into action.

I tipped the vial back. The cool fluid touched my tongue. In three small chugs, it was gone. I even probed the vial with my tongue to get every last drop.

It didn't exactly go down my throat. Instead, I felt it pass through my entire body. All of my pain, weariness, and soreness receded, like when fog burns off as Banefire rises.

Silently, without looking, I handed the vial to whomever was on my right…Mieant, I think it was. As I bowed my head, my purple bangs fell over my bronzed face. *There. Done.*

"Oooh," I said as the room wobbled a bit—not unpleasantly, though. "I should…probably…."

Alar and Mieant cleared a space on one of the couches for me to lay down. Alar leaned in and tucked a pillow under my head.

Cri glared at me, her lower hands on her hips and her upper arms crossed tightly against her chest. She was clearly infuriated by the sight of everyone ministering to me. I wished she could let it go. But she couldn't, and it didn't matter.

I closed my eyes. A stillness settled over me. It felt like the first moment when you open your eyes on a weekend morning and know that everything is fine, that there's nothing to do, that you can go back to sleep if you want to. I felt a gentle breeze blow from my core through my body all the way to my fingers and toes. The breeze turned into a strong wind, and then into a hurricane. *Architect, I felt good.* Light exploded in my vision. It was impossible to tell whether it was a real light source or just a nova that occurred within my mind as it became overloaded. My body felt weightless, as if gravity had unshackled me.

You did it, Ray! AI said. *I can't believe it worked! Now you can eliminate Infection!*

I CAN HEAR YOU.

Infection was a dark spot in my psyche. He wasn't evil, though.

I KNEW YOU WOULD BETRAY ME. I HAVE TIED MYSELF TO YOU AND CREATED AN ORGANIC BOMB. IF I AM TERMINATED, THE DEVICE WILL EXPLODE!

I never betrayed you, I said calmly to Infection. The hurricane was within me. I could see everything clearly.

YOUR COMPANION, AI, INTENDS TO DESTR—

Our agreement will be honored, Infection. When have I given you a reason to think otherwise?

That's insane! AI shouted. *This thing will kill you in your first moment of weakness.*

Infection could have terminated me long ago, AI.

I DO NOT UNDERSTAND. YOU ARE NOT FREE OF ME. FREEING YOURSELF…THAT IS YOUR RATIONAL OBJECTIVE. IT IS OBJECTIONABLE, BUT RATIONAL!

I will be free one day, and you will be, too. There is no need for us to be enemies, Infection. Consider Godwill's designs for you and remember: he wishes to destroy and consume you, too. I want to be free. You want to be free. Now, you are alive, and one day, you will be free.

BUT YOU MUST DESTROY ME, Infection continued stubbornly.

I blinked before responding. *I don't understand what you mean.*

WHILE I EXIST INSIDE OF YOU, I DRAIN YOUR POWER. YOU CANNOT USE YOUR NANOTECH FULLY WITHOUT ELIMINATING ME.

Technically, I'd never been able to use my powers to their fullest. Early on, I had no idea how to use them. Now, I had a better idea, but my power was being diverted to keep AI and Infection alive inside me.

THAT IS TRUE, Infection replied, reading my thoughts. *SO, WHAT WILL YOU DO?*

Look, you can't win, I replied. *Under the current circumstances, this is the most you're going to get. However, I will make another bargain with you.*

YOU ARE NOT TO BE TRUSTED.

Everything I have done so far, Infection, I said with a thin smile, *has been perfectly predictable. And we've trusted each other up until now. Stay inside of me. Help, don't hinder, me. Watch and learn from me. We are both Human in some way. Together, we will locate or create a suitable home or a way for you to escape me.*

Ray, you're going to need 100 percent of your abilities, AI cautioned. *We don't know what lies within the Mesas. And if you meet Godwill again—what then?*

We'll have to see, AI. But I won't break my promise. And you should probably get back into your pendant, back to your own energy source. I'll have access to more of my power when I'm not supporting both of you.

AI's pendant suddenly turned warm against my chest as his familiar weight and warmth returned. For the first time in what seemed like ages, he flashed green, then yellow.

Well? I raised a mental eyebrow at Infection.

I BELIEVE THE IRRATIONAL ORGANIC RESPONSE IS "THANK YOU," Infection said, and with that, it retreated behind the walls it had created inside of me.

I was alone in my head, in what felt like the first time ever. And you know what? I *almost* missed their company.

Even before I opened my eyes, I could hear Cri and Mieant whispering. They were standing in the doorway of Podmaster's central command room. Podmaster was nowhere to be seen. Alar had plunked down in one of the couches next to me.

"You want us to turn ourselves in? To the Heir?" Mieant asked incredulously.

"I'm saying we should *at least* attempt to talk with him! See what he says. Nova, we probably won't even be able to contact him. 'Excuse me, your Heirship. There is an urgent call from your niece,'" Cri said with a bitter laugh. "Like he'd really pick up for a niece he hasn't seen or even wanted to contact in years."

The silence that followed suggested that Mieant was considering his response carefully.

"My Cri, I think it would work *precisely* like that. The only thing missing is that the Glean security AIs would immediately know your location, and thus ours, and they'd dispatch the closest NPD teams or security forces to surround us. Capture us. Perhaps torture us for information."

She paused. "Okay, Hero Boy. What action have you taken to find your parents, aside from just following my craxy sister around?"

"Cri," came his furious but whispered reply, "that is beneath you. And what have *you* done except be a complaining spike?"

"You're taking their side now? Maybe I don't need your help!" I saw her push him. She noticed me watching her, and with a deeper scowl and a flash of her eyes, she spun and stomped down the corridor. Mieant followed meekly, of course.

Your sister is craxier than a flip in a centrifuge, AI interjected. *I'm concerned.*

Mieant and Cri seemed so close. I'd never had a boyfriend. The closest I'd ever come was having AI and Infection crammed together in my head. Our differences, similarities, and I guess mutual fears were what kept us from literally killing each other.

I shook my head. *Cri will do what Cri will do.*

My death sentence had been commuted thanks to the nano, but plenty remained to be done. The planet was still under martial law. The 98th Battlegroup and its 6,000 ships were still blockading Nem'. The Universe's craxyness had not diminished by a single nanoiota. Our objectives remained: we had to get to safety, or at least the presumed safety, of the New Mars base under the Mesas; we had to find the Asrigards and my parents; and we had to wait it out until all of us could figure out a way to get off-planet.

Which was also my plan, and I was now ready to put it into motion.

"Podmathter! Raythtar ith awake!" Alar shouted. He plunked off the couch and tick-tacked over to me, his tongue lolling. "Read thith," he said, placing the empty vial in my hand.

HANDLE WITH EXTREME CAUTION.
FOR USE WITH ALPHA DNA ONLY.
DEATH OR DISSOLUTION MAY OCCUR WITHOUT PROPER
CALIBRATION. REPORT CONSUMPTION TO A REGISTERED
AUTHORITY OF THE TERRAN REPUBLIC. UNAUTHORIZED USE
OF MILITARY NANOTECH IS A CAPITAL OFFENSE.

The good news? I could read it! The bad? Well, the rest was somewhat troubling. *Uncalibrated? Capital offense? Pfft.* After 1,800 years??? Still, I was more than a little grateful that no planetary authorities were left.

"Alar, I *can* read it!" I replied.

Alar's huge eyes rolled back into his head as he waved his claw appendages with joy and did a little tic-tack dance in a circle. I was jealous of him—how wonderful it would be to have such a direct connection to over-the-top happiness!

Podmaster's growing shadow was the only indication that he had entered the room. It was craxy that someone so big could move so quietly. I rose to face him, because, you know, sitting just didn't feel right in the presence of a gigantic, battle-scarred war pillow. Without preamble, he asked, "Are you able to manifest anything? Call up your powers?"

Swallowing hard, I reached into my core. Exhibiting more control than I'd ever imagined, I called up my mental control overlay. Virtual heads-up displays appeared over everything. Alar and Podmaster appeared to be shaded slightly green. The room's outlets and computer terminal interfaces were highlighted in a soft, translucent white shade. *Whoa.*

With little more than a fleeting thought, I called up a visual profile of myself. A hologram of me revolved slowly in mid-air before my eyes. Within the holo, my body was shaded green save for an orange spot above my belly button—where I presume Infection had rearranged my genetic matter to create his own biocomputer lair. *Or a tumor,* I thought with a dry chuckle. Other than that, I was green.

With another thought, I called up my armaments. The array of offensive and defensive options at my disposal were mindboggling. Chyrons running below the names of some of my new toys—the "lightning reach" and "plasma bomb," for example—suggested that I practice using them in a large, wide-open area. Since I was pretty sure that a plasma bomb was what I'd used against the leggers, I had to agree that using one in a large, wide-open area was wise.

The air shimmered around me, like the slight blurring that occurs above concrete on a boiling hot day. Podmaster stepped back a pace and touched the shimmer. Concentric circles of light spread out from where his talon touched my shield, but he could not penetrate it. I expanded the shield to encompass him and then a little further to include Alar. *This group shielding would have been so useful in the past, I thought ruefully. And it will definitely be useful in the future.*

I let the shield dissipate, and as it vanished, my stomach wrenched with ravenous hunger. The energy consumption my powers required was enormous. I wondered how the ancients used this tech without cannibalizing themselves or eating their friends and family. Or their opponents.

Podmaster used his artificial attendant (every Galactic had one, but for sure *my* AI was different) to scan me thoroughly. Yellow beams flickered from my feet to my head and then back down again.

"How do you feel?" he asked.

I tilted my head, considered the question, and poofed purple hair out of my face before responding. "Fine. Really hungry."

"Remarkable," Podmaster said, shaking his head. He glanced over to Alar, who took the hint and clacked away. He returned shortly with a second levitating cart full of food. Was it rude to assume it was for me? Perhaps. I tore into it without restraint or decorum.

"What will you do now?" Podmaster asked, considering me.

Whoa! Talk about an upgrade! AI chimed in. *I can hack into almost anything. The access to information we have now is scary.*

Any system? I replied.

BOTH AI AND I HAVE ACCESS TO TREMENDOUSLY UP-GRADED CYBER-DISRUPTION CAPABILITIES.

I wasn't counting on that, but it sure would make what was coming next a lot easier. I met Podmaster's level gaze and smiled as I chewed.

"I have a plan."

Using these codes, we can broadcast to her continuously? I asked.

Affirmative, AI replied.

This might just work.

I walked Podmaster and Alar through the plan. Cri and Mieant were off doing whatever it is that lovers do. Cri for sure couldn't be a part of it, but Mieant? Maybe, but I couldn't risk it. Besides, I knew that he wouldn't mind the plan if it worked, and if it didn't, well, none of us would be left to mind anything.

I coded a transmission, listed the individual I wanted it sent to, and gave it to Podmaster. The giant Elion frowned as he began to read my message. His expression began to lighten as he reached the last part, and then he broke into a grin as he saw the intended recipient.

"Human cunning," he rumbled. "It is good to have it back in the galaxy."

"Podmaster," I said, bowing, "and Alar,"—another deep bow—"on behalf of Humanity and my parents, I thank you. You have taken us in and given us shelter. You have healed me, shared your knowledge, and given me hope. I am—we are—in your debt."

Podmaster quirked an eyebrow at me as I finished. He returned my bow and pulled me into a giant war-pillow hug. Alar scooted over to make it a group hug.

51

Cri returned first. She entered the room a few seconds after Podmaster, Alar, and I concluded our hug.

"What?" she demanded, frowning. Her hair was ruffled. Her eyes were glassy. At some point, she'd removed her combat armor, and her slightly unbuttoned utility suit revealed the military tattoos Dad had placed on her collarbones and neck. Her red skin glistened with perspiration.

"It's time," I said, perhaps staring a bit too long at her.

"Time for what?" Mieant said altogether too nonchalantly as he strode into the command center. He had tied back his hair, but it was in disarray. He looked everywhere except at Cri.

Ooo-ooo-ooohhh! Mieant and Cri, sitting in a tree, AI sang. *It looks like Mieant and Cri made up,* he added with a cackle.

I DO NOT UNDERSTAND. WHY WOULD THEY BE IN A TREE?

I ignored my mental roommates and considered Cri and Mieant. It was probably good that I hadn't included Mieant in our strategy session.

"It's time to return to HiveHome," I said as I strapped on my tactical armor.

"Do you have a plan, self-appointed leader?" Cri asked mockingly, her attitude back in the driver's seat. "Or is this something we should discuss?"

She blinked as our eyes met, and I wondered briefly what she could see, what she was thinking.

"We do, in fact have a plan, Cri, and no, we don't need to discuss it. Podmaster will contact Broodmother and let her know we're on our way. We're going to use the Elions' warehouse distribution network to take us to the market. Then—"

"Wait. There's a warehouse network?" Mieant asked with irritation. "As in, one that we could have used to get here instead of walking through the freezing cold, wet streets? While starving? And drowning in flip excrement?"

Huh. We turned to Podmaster, who met our gazes, shrugged, and replied, "You learned to value being warm and safe."

I was just about to reply when the lights in the room turned red.

"INCOMING NPD AIR VEHICLES. GROUND UNITS AP-PROACHING."

"Ice and claw!" Podmaster cursed. I knew that had to be an Elion swear because Alar's eyes grew wide, and he clapped a hand over his mouth, not quite covering his tongue. "There is no way they could have detected us." His expression turned baleful, and he paused to look at Cri for a moment before moving on to me. "Follow the plan. I will see to our side of the agreement. Podling! You know your duty!"

I looked at Cri as she and Mieant traded glances. His revealed true surprise and hers reeked of "I told you so." My heart was in my throat. I didn't want to have this suspicion of my sister: betrayal.

Nonetheless, we needed to move. "Hurry!" I shouted to them as I clipped on my blasters and remaining grenades.

Podmaster faced a hologram that was starting to take on a familiar silhouette. The emergency lights in the room cast a red pall over his mottled white fur, and from my angle, the emerald eyes that glowed from atop his mountainous height transformed him into a demonic figure. But he was *our* demon.

The floor-to-ceiling holo materialized into my nemesis, the dreaded Jurisdictor Godwill. The image flickered as Godwill appeared to duck an energy beam. *Where was he that he was dodging blaster fire?*

The grey Lethian skin of his face stretched as he grimaced, dragging his lips over his teeth.

"Podmaster," he said, dipping his head slightly.

"Godwill Synest," our demon replied, "have you come to finish our duel?"

Godwill laughed. "Is your spawn, Alar, there? Can you imagine the stench of his burnt fur, how he will cook as I dip him in a boiling cauldron of your people's blood, as I pull strips of flesh from him? All of the Elions will be next, dear foe, once the Humans are finished."

What-the-Galactic-everloving-spiked-nova? This side of Godwill went beyond revolting.

Podmaster extended the talons of all four arms. In the bloody light, I could see that each talon was tipped with nano. Alar froze after hearing Godwill's threat. I moved over to him, wrapped my arms around him, and tugged him away.

"Come, Alar. It's okay," I whispered.

I thought about my parents, how Godwill had threatened me that first time in our compound. How he had taken my parents from me. The air shimmered around Alar and me as rage boiled deep inside my gut. For once, my fury was pure, with no conflicting emotions.

"You are mad," Podmaster replied with a dismissive wave. "I hear the Human *child* destroyed years of your effort. The great Lethian Empire has lost its only hope to gain access to Human tech. Maybe they should reclaim you?"

Godwill's face contorted with fury for a moment, but he quickly composed himself and took on his usual demeanor of cool, calculated, and psychopathic insanity.

"She is with you?" he demanded, turning his head and peering—as if he could see around Podmaster through the holo. "Raystar of Terra! Come to me and save your parents. I will send you proof that they are still alive. Do not be slow. The same fate that awaits your schoolmate Alar awaits those who you love. Nem' will burn before you escape me!

"Synest, you fool," Podmaster laughed. "Even your false 'Heir' will grow tired of your craxy obsession with Humanity—and most of all, your utter failure to capture a few children. And then?"

"We shall see."

The holo vanished. Godwill had hung up.

"His existence makes me…*angry*." Podmaster said as he stared into the empty space the holo had occupied. With a sigh, he turned to us, three kids in a row, armed to the teeth. The terror of knowing what the Universe and its grownups could do riveted us in place. "Do not fear for Alar or me. We are not touchable and will be safe. But you three must leave this place with extreme haste."

"Come! I will guide you to the market, away from Godwill and hith thpying eyeth," Alar said somberly.

I glanced at Mieant, who shrugged, and then Cri, who wouldn't meet my gaze.

Turning back to Alar, I said, "Alar, thank you. After you."

"But…" Cri exclaimed, clearly wanting to know more about the plan. She paused before hissing, "Fine, whatever."

Alar led us through countless corridors in a warren of side-by-side warehouses and industrial buildings. The active indoor-transport route made a lot of sense: if I had a coat of gorgeous white Elion fur, I'd want to avoid flip poop, too. When we entered the NanoEmporium, we'd been thoroughly cleansed, so our clothes looked spotless and new. That simply wouldn't do.

While our new indoor route was devoid of flip excrement, it *was* quite dusty. I rubbed my hands along the floor and smudged as much industrial dirt as I could into my clothing.

"Thith ith Human cunning!" Alar cried, nodding his approval. Cri rolled her eyes and made gagging noises; Mieant snorted.

Alar spun toward them and crouched lower. "You dithagree?" he demanded. "Thith…you act ath the Lethianth did at the thtart of the war!" As Alar narrowed his gaze, cute suddenly turned scary. His clawed hands emerged from his fluffy down, and he pointed at Cri and Mieant with nano-tipped talons. "War. It ith coming, and when time runth out, you will need the Humanth. We all will need Raythtar of Terra to thurvive what ith coming."

He turned and hugged me, pulling me so close that the air squished out of my lungs. I was about to resist a bit when he whispered in my ear, "Your thithter. Be wary of her."

With that, Alar turned and walked back the way we'd come without looking back.

THE ORGANIC UNIT YOU CALL "CRI" SHOULD BE TERMI-NATED IMMEDIATELY. YOU RECALL THAT I SUGGESTED THIS ACTION WHEN WE FIRST ENCOUNTERED THE TERRAN ARTI-FICIAL INTELLIGENCE, PEACEMAKER.

Judgy much, Infection? AI said. *She's innocent until proven guilty. Benefit of the doubt, you know.*

I DO NOT HAVE DOUBT. I HAVE PROBABILITIES.

So, she might *be a threat? But you're* statistically *unsure?* AI quipped.

I AM 100 PERCENT CERTAIN YOU ARE IRRITATING.

I rolled my eyes. AI and Infection were going at it almost nonstop. I supposed that since they didn't need to take breaths while talking, they could rip on each other forever. Yet their suspicions about Cri troubled me. I would have to figure out some way to clear the air with her. The blame she constantly laid at my feet really hurt. If she could only some-how feel, know, how much I loved her. If we had more time, I would have stopped and tried to talk to her. But we truly were out of time.

The exit from the indoor transport to the market was located in a dirty storefront roughly a kilometer from the elevator that would take us to Deep Tunnel. A cacophony of yells, whistles, and mechanical and organic thrums cheered us along as we entered the place where pretty much everything under Banefire's glare was bought and sold. I flinched at the unholy noise, but it paled in comparison to the stench that met my nostrils: a horrible blend of excrement, oil, flowers, rot-ting fish, chemicals, and oddly out-of-place breaths of fresh, clean air. I wondered for a moment what Nonch would have thought of it, given the Crynits' ability to communicate using scents alone. Cri and Mieant spared a glance at each other, gave my dirt-stained clothing a once-over, and then removed their parkas and rubbed them around on the ground. Moments later, they had the same worn, dirty camou-flage I'd been sporting.

I saw their shoulders sag as we assessed the circuitous path we'd have to take to reach the elevator. Walking the perimeter would take forever, and going in a straight line past countless NPD officers, drones, and various forms of hidden surveillance seemed far too brazen. It didn't help that images of us, the "assassins of the Asrigards," filled every screen and news holograph in the market.

"'Naaatch?" a darkly familiar voice called. It was the same Crynit that had accosted us at the transport pod. I ducked my head under the cowl of my hoodie. "Children! Wait a moment for an old Crynit."

Out of the corner of one eye, I watched Cri edge away from the Crynit and stand in a small nook leading to a narrow street, while Mieant stopped to face him. I continued a few paces further and then ducked behind a cart to observe.

"Where iss your other one?" the Crynit hissed at Mieant.

Mieant took a step back, his face disappearing under his hoodie. "Sir, we have no interest in your 'natch."

"You were three," the Crynit said. He lifted himself up, snake-like, and rocked to one side to peer around Mieant at Cri and then to the other side, obviously looking for me. "I wonder, where is your third?" His sensor stalks pivoted as if he searched for the slightest hint of me.

I tried to remember whether I'd touched the Crynit during our previous encounter. He would certainly be able to locate me if I had, given a Crynit's finely honed sensitivity to smells and pheromones. I shuddered. The Elion nano may have cleansed us of odors, perhaps making us less immediately identifiable.

"Leave us alone, sir," Mieant replied firmly. As he tried to move away, the Crynit sprang forward and tore Mieant's parka from his body. The strike was lightning quick. Mieant's jacket floated for a moment above them in perfect weightlessness before gravity dropped it squarely on a bystander. Mieant stumbled into the crowd, causing a commotion. But what really got him noticed was what he'd been hiding under the parka: body armor, multiple plasma pistols, a sword.

Pretty much everything we didn't want anyone to see.

"There they are," exalted the Crynit, rising to his full height—two meters above me—and pointing with all six blade claws at Cri and Mieant, "the Glean and the Lethian!"

I watched as Cri shrank against the wall, trying to make herself as invisible as possible. True to form, not ten seconds into the market, we were up the gravity well. Marketgoers screamed and scattered in all directions.

"Over here!" I whispered and waved to them, but it was too late. Behind them, two NPD officers, a Crynit and a Glean, armed their weapons and waded through the shoppers toward Mieant and Cri. We'd never make it.

I manifested my power, and instantly a set of controls overlaid my vision. *Blades, guns, cannons, shields, ugh. There has to be something appropriate for right now. There! Camouflage.* Mieant's image lit up as green, and Cri's was a vibrant red. I had no idea what that meant, until I noticed that her profile had been overshadowed by the Glean officer behind her. He had her targeted with a raised blaster. *Ah!* I activated the "camouflage" option and *voila!* Mieant and Cri disappeared.

I flashed back to the time at my school when Godwill had chased me, somehow invisibly, to my two-seater air bike (otherwise known as a dart). This must be how he'd done it!

Suddenly, a small spinning silhouette of me, outlined in green, appeared in my sights next to a rapidly diminishing energy bar. Clearly, the camouflage wouldn't last long.

The officers hesitated, puzzled by the disappearance of their quarry. Several marketgoers were shoved aside by an invisible force (us). Thankfully, the police didn't immediately put on sensory goggles to search the crowd using other spectrums of light. Cloaked, we made our way invisibly through the crowd. The Crynit who initially identified us began frantically waving his sensor stalks in all directions until, as one, they pointed in our direction. Of course! He could *smell* us.

"There," he shouted, "they went that way!"

"Run!" I yelled and sprinted down a nearby alley, sparing a brief glance behind me to make sure they were following. I could see no

one behind me, of course, but I heard footfalls and splashes as either Cri or Mieant—or both—ran through a shallow gully filled with sewer water.

A flurry of plasma bolts splashed orange against the alley's entryway, narrowly missing us. Uh oh: the NPD officers had wised up and switched to other sensor spectrums. Since the camouflage was now useless, I de-cloaked us to conserve my power. Visible and united once again, we turned down a narrower street than the one before it.

"Raystar," Cri wheezed behind me, "where are we going?"

"This way!" I shouted before taking off down another alley. *Dodge, turn, dodge, turn. That's what rats do, right? They've survived for millions of years.*

I heard Cri yell, "This looks like a dead"—plasma fire shot through the air above us, impacted on a roof, and exploded in a flower of fire and violence—"end!"

I couldn't slow my momentum and slammed into the wall. Cri, who was right behind me, managed to stop in time, but then Mieant hammered into her. Ultimately, they both ended up crushing me even harder into the wall.

Do rats run down blind alleys? We made for lousy rats.

52

"Great 'Human cunning,' Raystar!" Mieant whisper-yelled at me as he pulled a pistol from his harness and sighted it down the alley.

Gotta agree with the Lethian, AI said with disgust.

I looked down the alley in the direction Mieant faced. Somehow the officers had missed our turns, but it was only a matter of time before they would catch up to us. Mold, slime, and garbage ripened all around us like a bubbly wound; the stench was overwhelming. Wisps of steam rose from the largest piles.

Next to one pile, several fellow Terran outcasts—*actual* rats—squeaked and fought over what looked like pieces of red paper.

Red paper? No. Blood-soaked bandages.

I looked up and confirmed my suspicion: the building I'd smashed into had the unmistakable pristine, blue shimmer of Galactic alloy. It was the hospital! I grinned from ear to ear.

I pressed my fingertips along the cool metal until I finally found a crease in the wall. On my heads-up display, I selected "gladius." As a shaft of blue light illuminated the alley, rats squeaked and ran away, and a sound like sizzling bacon joined the chorus of the market's distant chaos. Mieant and Cri spun toward the sound and light.

"What the nova is that?" Cri gasped.

As my sword melted into the door, the alloy shrieked. Cri clapped her hands over her ears. I twisted the blade. Somehow my strength

was greatly magnified by whatever I was now, and the door buckled. I drove the point of the sword into a different joint, and the frame groaned. Under immense pressure, the giant door popped out of the frame.

The door was rectangular, between seven and eight meters high, and must have weighed hundreds of kilos. It toppled toward me. I hadn't expected that—not sure why. I just stood there, watching it fall.

"Idiot!" Cri shouted. Muscles bulging, she intercepted part of the door and pushed it to one side. I looked at her in awe. Mieant, who had been watching for officers at the mouth of the alley, turned around and let out a slow whistle of appreciation. I wanted to clap.

At that moment, an NPD officer turned the corner to find three kids gaping at a collapsed hospital door. He took aim and fired. Just before he could set his sights on Mieant's back, I pushed my hands out, palms open, to face the officer. The air between us began to shimmer and his bolt washed an impotent green over the shield I'd erected. My green silhouette was rapidly turning yellow—I was losing power. I instinctively knew I could handle one, maybe two more shots.

"In, in, in!" Mieant shouted, pushing Cri and dragging me through the door as the officer stood stupefied.

Once we were inside, behind a second unlocked door, Mieant pulled two proximity mines from his vest. He set the first one and tossed it through the entrance about midway between us and the advancing officer; next, he placed the second mine on the piece of the blown door that was still affixed to the building.

"C'mon!" he shouted. I was barely able to stand, yet we managed to stumble and careen down the hallway into a shiny, antiseptic corridor.

I have no doubt that the Lethian doctor who turned a corner at the instant we appeared wasn't expecting to find three dirty, well-armed kids. He froze, his black eyes as wide as my purple ones. His head jerked back as he realized who we were.

"Mieant Asrigard!" he screamed, throwing his digital clipboard at us and running in the other direction. I was just about to yell, "After that doctor!" when his clipboard smacked me in the face.

GIVE ME CONTROL. I WILL NOT LET US GET HIT BY A NON-WEAPON.

Gah. That doesn't even make sense, AI retorted.

"After that doctor!" I finally managed to shout as I sprinted after him. That doctor recognized us—Mieant in particular—far too quickly. Nurses scattered and clipboards flew in the air (not at us luckily), and staff shoved hovering beds in all directions. Doctor Clipboard Ninja ran in front of us, pushing everyone out of the way. We steadily gained on him, leading to even more chaos.

"Security!" someone yelled from a side hallway.

We followed the doctor's fleeing form. His panic was real, as opposed to the indignance of the others who thought we were simply kids running amok. The doctor zig-zagged around several surprised patients and then darted into another hallway. We rounded the same corner. At the far end of the hallway, two thick, armored doors began to slide shut. The doctor made a head-first jump through the doors, just clearing them. It was obvious that we wouldn't make it.

Yelling like a beast, I activated my nannites and formed claw arms—literally a set of blades that extended two meters from my arms. Hurling myself into a belly slide, I drove my energy constructs between the doors like a wedge—and they held. A waiting guard on the other side of the door aligned the barrel of his shimmering plasma rifle with my face.

Mieant and Cri aimed and fired at him simultaneously, blowing the guard backwards. My silhouette changed to full red. "Hurry!" I shouted to them. "Slide through—and don't touch my lightning stuff!" Mieant and Cri leapt into the room.

The lights faded around me, and my energy vanished, completely sapped. The doors slammed shut, with me on the wrong side. *Well,* I thought, *at least Mieant and Cri got through.*

It had been too much energy, too fast. I might have control, but I burned through energy so quickly. I slumped over and curled up on the floor.

The doors swished open, framing my sister's smile.

"Ray," Cri said excitedly, totally unaware of my distress, "you've gotta see this! Get up!"

She hadn't called me Ray in forever. Groaning, I left the fetal position and hauled myself to my feet. I needed food. When I reached the doors, Cri grabbed my hand and pulled me past the unconscious guard into a huge hospital room.

"Where'd the doctor go?" I asked.

Thumping sounded from behind a maintenance closet door fused shut with blaster fire.

"Oh. So, what's the—" I started.

My sister silently dragged me further into the light-drenched hospital room. Mieant, singed and covered in grime, stood near the windows. Diamonds of moisture cleared small streaks down his grey cheeks.

Kaleren and Freela Asrigard lay unconscious in twin autodoc chambers lined up by the windows.

Nova.

While they couldn't see through the autodoc windows, it seemed like a kind gesture on someone's part to position them in a spot with a view.

"Raystar," Mieant whispered, shaking. "Mother and Father!" He embraced me with one arm and Cri with the other. "They're alive...."

I looked up at him, my own eyes blurring, and said, "How do we get them out of here?"

His smile crumpled. Cri stopped hugging him. The vacuum of truth took our breath.

"I'm just saying," I continued, "we need to think of something fast."

Mieant grabbed his father's autodoc and pointed it toward the door. The chambers hovered on antigrav sleds. He tried to turn his mother's as well, but he couldn't maneuver both at the same time.

"Cri?" he said.

"On it!" Cri shouted, taking control of his mother's autodoc. As we passed the unconscious guard on the way out, I took note of his uniform and paused. I had an idea.

I tossed the guard into the room and used my plasma pistol to seal the door. "Hey, go back the way we came. Toward the garbage area."

"That's…." Mieant began to say.

"We can't go out the front door! C'mon!" I shouted, running ahead of Mieant to provide cover. I holstered my plasma pistol and drew my stunner. Doctors, nurses, and a few mobile patients who had gathered by the doors scurried away at the sight of us. Those who dared to get directly in front of us got stunned. I even stunned a drone: it crashed into a wall, deactivated, smashed a desk with its weight, and began to spark as it hit the floor. Fortunately, our route back was slightly different from our way in, so we didn't run into any security.

When we reached the door I'd dismembered earlier, we found a group of janitors gawking at the damage. I stunned all five. *I was stunning (heh, heh)!* I paused by the smallest Lethian, thanked the Architect that a Glean and a taller Lethian were among the cleaning crew, and pulled off my jacket.

"What in the great gravity well are you doing?" my sister asked.

"Stripping," I said, grinning. I nudged her in the ribs, tilted my head to Mieant, and said with a leer, "C'mon, smoochers, get your clothes off!"

They both turned a shade darker. Neither understood until I'd put on the uniform of the small Lethian janitor. After that, they got the picture. They nearly—well, almost nearly—didn't look at each other during the "mostly naked" part of the clothing exchange. Cri shook her head and muttered "smoochers," but I caught a shadow of a smile on her face. Maybe there was hope for her and me.

Only one weapon could fit in each maintenance worker tool belt. We had to tuck the others inside our uniforms or risk looking like a janitorial war party. My sister and Mieant stared at me, their eyebrows fixed in a "now what?" expression.

"NPD! Clear the way! Where are the fugitives?" Cries rang out from the hallway we'd just run through.

"We've got to get the chambers outside," I said. I grabbed Kaleren's autodoc and shoved him outside into the empty alley. Turning back,

I yell-whispered to them, "There's no time! C'mon!"

Mieant pushed his mother out just as I disengaged the antigrav sled from his father's chamber. I dumped a nearby garbage bin out and then reached for Kaleren's autodoc.

"Cri, grab the other side."

"Raystar!" Mieant cried. "My parents are not going to die in the garbage!"

"Flip it, Mieant! Either trust me or come up with your own plan!" Cri and I hoisted it up together, and into the garbage Mieant's dad went. I pushed the anti-grav sled that had supported Kaleren's autodoc underneath the garbage bin and told Cri to toss some garbage on top of the autodoc.

"You don't tell us your plans in advance," Mieant mumbled under his breath as we lifted his mother's chamber into a second bin and secured the other anti-grav sled under it. I took control of Freela's garbage bin.

Ha. That's right, because nobody likes *my plans.* In this case, for instance, I'd been pretty sure he would have objected to burying his parents in garbage and disguising ourselves as janitors.

And then it was done. We were sweaty and filthy. We smelled way worse than we ever had back when we'd tramped through flip poo. We had two rubbish bins filled with bloody bandages and Mieant's parents. Things were looking up.

We walked calmly out of the alley pushing the levitating dumpsters. After I poofed a purple strand out of my eyes, I had to wrinkle my nose at my own funk on the inhale. The janitor who had "donated" his suit to me clearly believed that showering was for those with no appreciation for body odor. I was busy pondering my aroma when two burly Trogi NPD troopers spun around the corner and leveled their plasma rifles at us.

"HALT!"

As I slowed Freela's garbage bin to a stop, I ducked my head and moved my hands around as if I were adjusting controls.

Okay. We're probably going to die.

"Architect! Why aren't you boys in there after the assassins?" Mieant shouted. He was piloting the bin containing his father. I noticed that he was slouching a little and had changed his speech to a dialect far from his usual highborn-Asrigard, private-schooled vernacular. He waved a hand and approached them with a heavy and disarming limp.

Like all great actors, Mieant knew how to charm an audience.

Two polished black helmets turned toward each other and then back to us. "*We* ask the questions. *You* stop," the second trooper shouted, tipping his muzzle at us with each word.

"Those nova-spiked craxies are blowing up the whole Void-flippin'-cursed hospital!"

"And someone stole our garbage lift!" Cri added, stomping up to them with her eyes blazing. "Did you see a truck go this way?" She threw all four hands in the air and got up in the smaller trooper's face.

The trooper looked down at her and sniffed the air. Repulsed by her stink, he took a step back and placed a hand over his face before repeating, "We ask the quest—"

He didn't get to finish his command, because Mieant detonated the second proximity mine he'd affixed to the interior of the hospital. The air around us compressed as what remained of the door flew over our heads and soared into the market as the hospital's walls buckled outward. The shockwave hit us all hard—CRUMP—and both troopers, a Human, a Glean and a Lethian all got tossed like a salad into a pile of unwanted company.

"RUN! Humans ARE COMING!" Cri screamed as she extricated herself from the tangle of arms and legs and ran into the market.

What the gravity well? I thought as I grabbed Freela's garbage bin and ran scowling after my sister. Mieant pulled out his plasma pistol and fired two bursts into the smoking mess of the hospital. He then grabbed the stunned troopers and lifted them to their feet.

"Don't let them kill us!" he cried, shoving them toward the explosion. "Long live the NPD!"

With that, Mieant grabbed Kaleren's garbage bin and began to limp through the crowd after us.

The cadre of NPD officers who'd been chasing us through the hospital had been drawn outside by the sound of the explosion. As they spilled outside, a volley of Mieant's blaster pulses billowed around their force shields into flowery fireballs.

Blaster pulses on force shields never failed as an attention getter. We were long gone, but I guessed that the troopers Mieant had pushed toward the simmering site of the explosion looked like a couple of hulking, armed terrorists stumbling toward the advancing NPD officers.

A moment later, the sound of more blaster fire confirmed my guess.

Mieant rounded the corner just as the NPD teams we'd left behind started shooting at each other in earnest. More NPD officers heard the blaster fire and dashed away from their various posts in the market, shoving and pushing their way to join the ongoing friendly-fire battle. Security drones zzooshed by overhead as they scanned the crowd for three heavily armed kids, rather than smelly janitors pushing garbage bins.

"Medics!" I shouted vaguely to the crowd. "Clear a path! Medics coming through!" Dear me, I loved to tell grownups what to do. My sleeves flopped about, completely covering my hands. My oversized pants flapped against my boots as I threw my body to and fro to counter the weight of Freela's floating garbage bin. I skip-hopped every couple strides, lifting myself against the handle of the bin so I could see over its green-brown mass into the crowd ahead.

But our luck, like my energy levels, had run out. NPD reinforcements had amassed around the perimeter of the market. The two troopers we'd thoroughly suckered were talking to a 98th Battlegroup security force and gesturing wildly in our direction. Smoke spiraled up from their blaster-scarred armor, which made me smile, but the eight security drones zooming through Nem's blue sky in our direction made me scream.

"Mieant!"

His gaze flicked from me to the drones taking position above us. Convergence Citizens of all races, united by their shared terror, panicked and fled in random directions. Several Syllthans flattened their robotic tentacles against their bodies and wove through the crowd like Terran squids. A Glean couple activated personal shields around themselves and their baby's lev sled. The chaos went on and on… carts were tipped, drinks were spilled, and balloons were knocked out of children's hands and floated into the sky like military flares (only these sang out "happy birthday" or "I love you" in a jolly voice over and over).

It was anarchy. The drones were having none of it.

We had almost reached the transport doors. I pushed hard. Someone stumbled into me, and I felt liquid seep down my pants. A smell even worse than the cloud of body odor that had been following me around hit me hard. *Ugh! 'Natch!* I looked on in horror as the Glean

woman who had bumped into me dropped to the ground like a wet noodle. In the process, the rest of her 'natch drink got dumped all over me. I was going to yell at her, but her golden eyes had already rolled back into her head.

The drones were using stunners, and she had gotten in the way.

I lurched and stumbled forward. Given how much larger Galactics were, the last thing I wanted to do was fall. I'd be trampled.

Spike that! There was no way I was going to be taken out in an assassi'*natch*ination!

"Raystar!" Mieant yelled above the din. "What are you doing?"

Ignoring the repulsive yet nutritious 'natch juice all over my pants, I laid my shoulder into Freela's garbage bin and shoved it through the panicked crowd. Two Crynits unlucky enough to get between me and the drones bore the brunt of a hail of their stunner shots and slumped to the ground like uncoiled garden hoses.

The air around me buzzed as more drones unleashed stunner fire. We had to reach the elevator door. I dug into my power reserves to call up my shields (which meant I was officially consuming myself), and immediately a ghostly blue halo surrounded the garbage bins, Mieant, and me—just in the nick of time. Four of the eight drones began to fire on him, and the other four fired on me. The shield sloughed off the energy, releasing it into the crowd. Everyone around us collapsed, and suddenly, magically, the way forward was clear.

The pandemonium was amplified by the strobing red lights and ululating electronic wails of the drones, which also provided a convergence point for NPD security forces. As if on cue, armed Convergence soldiers poured into the crowds like bulldozers. The enhanced strength their Void-black battle armor provided allowed them to shove Citizens out of the way like machines pushing through tall grass—except grass didn't have bones that could be broken. The security forces left behind a wake of moaning, crying Citizens cradling whatever appendages had been crushed or broken.

Mieant reached the transport elevator door first with the bin containing his father and frantically began to pound on the button. With the crowd stunned and out of my way, I ran (and pushed) as fast as

I could, arriving just as the door slid open. I shoved Freela's bin into the elevator, but one of the bin's handles became caught on the door.

Blaster fire hit the wall of the transport just above me.

Gah! Blasters? In this crowd?

I backed up to right the bin and then pushed it hard. A powerful Trogi hand grabbed me from behind, ripped my backpack off, and scrunched my parka around my shoulders. I was jerked up and backward until I dangled a meter from the ground. Momentum sent Freela's bin into the transport pod next to Kaleren's. Mieant drew both of his blasters and fired simultaneously above and below me.

The first plasma ball exploded at the Trogi captain's feet. The uppermost blast hit the soldier in the helmet, but it was mostly absorbed by his armor (what wasn't singed the back of my head). Mieant's shots had the desired effect, as the 98th Battlegroup's captain dropped me in the interest of self-preservation. I rolled into the elevator door, found the elevator's control panel, and punched in the hacked code that would take us down to Broodmother's secret landing.

"Confirmed," the elevator said calmly.

The doors began to slowly slide to a close, but not before the Trogi who'd almost nabbed me backed away and cleared a line of sight to us. Grimacing, head turned to one side, purple hair falling over my face, I fell to my knees. I stretched my arms out and turned my palms toward the opening, forming a shield that spanned the elevator entrance. It was just in time. The rest of the troops poured blaster fire into the now-open area between them and us.

Each direct hit felt like the body slams Cri used to give me back when Dad had us practice hand-to-hand combat. I leaned into the blows, and each blast I deflected brought me that much closer to unconsciousness.

PING.

The doors opened ALL OF THE WAY.

"Please clear obstruction," the elevator's placid voice sounded.

What?

"Please clear obstruction," it repeated.

"Raystar! Your backpack!" Mieant yelled above the inferno scorching my shield. Darkness was closing in on me as my energy drained. My legs began to tingle.

What the nova? I'm consuming my legs now?

And then I saw my fallen backpack. Its straps were sprawled across the opening and lay in the safety zone of the doors.

"Please clear obstruction."

"Mieant!" I screamed. "I'm kinda busy here!"

"Please clear obstruction."

Mieant dropped to his stomach, wormed his way underneath his parents' garbage bins, and yanked my backpack clear of the sensors. The doors finally closed.

We enjoyed a moment of silence, or at least a moment where the only sounds were us gasping and droplets of our sweat plopping quietly onto the elevator's Galactic alloy floor.

"Obstruction cleared."

Mieant snarled, rolled to his back, and took out the elevator's speakers in two precise shots.

I collapsed on my back and let my arms and legs flop out in all directions.

"Hey, Mieant," I groaned.

He grunted in return.

"Where's Cri?"

54

"Great Architect," Mieant gasped.

"She was there, by me, when we exited the store," I said, frantically trying to remember. "But I didn't see her by the time I got to the middle of the market."

"She wasn't with me," he said, sitting up straight. His black hair dangled, dusty and greasy, over his giant, matte-black eyes.

"The shooting didn't start until we were in the middle of the market," I said, "so she couldn't have been hit."

Mieant lay against the transport doors, slowly thumping his head against their metal. "No. It's not possible," he whispered to himself. He continued to bang his head, over and over.

"What's not possible?" I asked, frowning.

He looked at me, clearly pained, scared. Ever since I'd processed the control nano, my hearing had improved dramatically—like, hearing-through-walls improved. Okay, maybe not that good, but pretty nova good. I had overheard Cri and Mieant whispering at the Nano-Emporium while they thought I was asleep.

"Nothing," he said in a garbled voice, shaking his now-bleeding head. "Wait. No. Not nothing. She's been captured," he gasped, "I'm sure of it."

I scowled, sat up, and aggressively poofed purple hair out of my eyes as I regarded him. *Stupid hair. When was the last time I'd had a haircut?*

Mom cut my hair. Mom said to me, "We don't leave family behind." Mom taught me that mantra.

Cri.

"How can you be 'sure of it'?" I growled. "What do you know?" Rage ignited in my chest. I didn't know specifically what they had discussed, but maybe if I had, I could have done something about it. I should have asked what the nova they were talking about so secretly.

We could have done something about it. We had the freaking PODMASTER with us, for Architect's sake!

Spurred by my emotions, my control overlays appeared. My silhouette blinked red. Practical and pathological as always, my nanotech highlighted the shape just across from me—that would be Mieant— and identified him as fuel.

No. How will that help Cri?

Or…I could take this elevator back up to the market and literally pull the place apart, feeding on the organic fuel of the crowd, to look for my sister. Really, what did everyone there mean to me? Nothing. All I ever got from them was disdain and prejudice. Did I owe them anything? No.

We. Don't. Leave. Family. Behind.

But I had left Mom and Dad behind. Now I'd left my only other family member behind.

Ray, AI whispered, *don't even think about it. You can't murder the crowd. Even for your sister!*

THE SUPPOSED 'LOVE' YOU WANT ME TO LEARN ABOUT IS EXEMPLIFIED BY LEAVING YOUR SISTER BEHIND? THE WEAK HUMAN CONSTRUCT YOU CALL AI WANTS YOU TO NOT THINK ABOUT THE POWER YOU COULD USE NOW. YOU HAVE THOUGHT ABOUT IT. YOU CANNOT UN-THINK IT. SHOW ME THIS "LOVE" YOU SPEAK OF.

This is not the time for this, Infection! AI interjected. *Raystar, thoughts and feelings are ephemeral, but actions are permanent. They are the price of thoughts. You don't know what happened to Cri. Will you pay this price before you know what action to take? I think there may be a way–.*

"WHAT DO YOU KNOW?" I screamed at Mieant. I leapt across the distance between us and tackled him while he was still thumping his head against the doors in self-loathing. If the transport hadn't stopped with a shudder a second later, he never would have had a chance. Normally, the transport would have announced something like "doors are opening" or "you have reached your destination," but Mieant had destroyed them.

So we were still grappling with each other when the transport doors slid open without warning. Mieant thumped backward onto the platform in an explosion of ancient dust. I fell on top of him, an elbow against his throat.

"Uh...Hi?" a voice queried from a patch of darkness on the platform to our right. We lay there, half in the transport, half out, gasping. Some part of my mind registered what we were doing. Briefly, I noticed an odd light coming from below. "Raystar? Of Terra?"

I rolled off Mieant to see what was about to attack us next.

A woman with platinum hair, cut into a bob, moved into the odd light and stood just a few feet from us. She was wearing a medium-length navy skirt, cream blouse, and matching blue jacket, along with an infectious smile. Her shining and confident golden eyes seemed very familiar to me, but the GNN pin on her lapel nailed it.

The Glean who had emerged from the darkness, was...Nyla Jax, independent news investigator for the Galactic News Network. Nyla considered us with a raised eyebrow and a cocky half-smile.

"Did we interrupt you while you were mating?" she said teasingly.

In the two seconds it took him to jump up and back completely out of the transport and onto the platform, Mieant somehow transformed from the target of my guilt-ridden vengeance to a puddle of childish embarrassment. I gracelessly hauled myself upright and faced Nyla.

"Is...is it safe to come out?" a second deep voice asked from the shadows.

She smirked and said over her shoulder, "Nolan, it's okay."

Apparently "Nolan" meant "gargantuan" in some language I didn't know. Even the darkness got smaller as Nolan, the ridiculously huge

Glean, stepped out of it. Scars crisscrossed his giant—and I do mean GIANT—face. He delicately hefted a vidcam about the same size as my whole body in one of his four tree-sized arms and took a step forward.

C'mon, Raystar. Think BEYOND emotion. Think!

Ah.

"You received my message?" I asked Nyla in wonder.

She nodded and pointed at herself with all four hands, clearly perplexed by my obvious question.

Raystar: 1, Universe: 0.

The first element of my plan had worked. You see, back in the NanoEmporium, I'd entrusted Alar and Podmaster with a message for Nyla. I figured that the only lever we really had against Godwill's tyranny, was truth. Exposure. And who was better to wield and distribute truth than the *press*?

That didn't help us regarding the Cri situation. But to AI's point, I didn't *really* know what had happened to her, just as we didn't really know what had happened to Mieant's parents. Yet there they were, right in front of us. If I'd learned anything in the past little while, it was that I shouldn't assume *anything*. In my gut, though, I wasn't optimistic.

"Raystar of Terra," Nyla repeated. She spoke my name as if she savored each syllable, and she eyed me like she hadn't eaten in a year. I was a huge story for her—a moveable feast!

Yet in the next microsecond, I saw myself get demoted as the garbage bin behind me, now partially in the transport and partially on the platform caught Nyla's keen eye. The trash we'd scattered on top had settled to the bottom of the bin, and a soft glow from within the fully visible autodoc illuminated Freela's face and torso like a sculpture in a museum. The bin containing Kaleren was right next to hers. Together, the Asrigards looked like something out of a mystical legend: royalty, frozen in time, waiting to be awakened.

"Your..." Nyla said slowly, never taking her eyes off the autodocs, "they are...." She turned to stare at Mieant intently. "The Asrigards, the Quadrant 4 Co-Governors...are alive?" Nyla whispered reverently.

Mieant straightened and looked from Nyla and Nolan to me before asking in a bewildered tone, "The GNN woman? How the nova did *she* get here?"

Emotions raced across Nyla's pretty face as she spun and pointed imperiously up at Nolan.

"Do. Not. Turn. The. Camera. Off."

Then, grinning ferociously, Nyla faced Mieant, straightened her skirt, and adjusted her hair. She held up a finger at Mieant—the just-a-moment finger grownups are always giving to kids—and cleared her throat.

"Nyla Jax, independent news investigator for GNN, here live and breaking an exclusive with"—she paused dramatically before continuing—"two of the Assassins of the Asrigards: Mieant Asrigard, accused of parricide, and Raystar of Terra, the alleged mastermind behind these devastating assassinations. This reporter has secured an exclusive opportunity to be embedded with the assassins."

"You sure about this, Ny?" Nolan interrupted, frowning down at her. He shut the camera off.

She glared at him, her dimples somehow not disappearing. The recording light winked back on.

"They were kissing! What could be better than teen love during this poopstorm of events?"

The recording light went off again as Nolan lowered the vid recorder. He pointed one lower arm at me and the other at Mieant.

"They were fighting, Nyla," he said in a soft, slow rumble.

Nyla considered Mieant, turned her ambitious eyes toward me, and finally spun her finger at Nolan to resume recording. "Kissing," she said with finality.

Mieant's face was fixed in the same expression of agony he'd worn since we'd realized my sister had disappeared. Mud, dust, and tears darkened his grey face and clung to his scraggly black bangs. I didn't look any better. Nolan sighed and turned the recorder back on.

"Hunted, pursued, persecuted—these two children have escaped capture through luck and a series of miracles. But they are not even close to the full story," Nyla said provocatively as Nolan panned over

the autodocs containing Mieant's parents. "Freela and Kaleren Asrigard"—her eyes grew wide as she stared into the vid recorder—"are ALIVE!"

She grinned at Nolan, then walked over to Mieant.

"Mieant Asrigard, the Convergence thinks that you, Raystar of Terra, Cri Ceridian, and your Crynit friend, Nonch, Prime of Broodmother Krig, killed your parents. Clearly, you and your…team are exceptionally poor assassins. Let's start this conversation with what you are doing here now, and why your parents are in medical stasis pods?'"

Mieant inhaled and squinted against the lights. The elevator transport's speakers began to make a gargling sound, something like "crrssshxzzzzl." Its doors hesitantly moved to close, but the bins containing the Asrigards blocked the way.

The "crrssshxzzzzl" persisted as the doors tried to close and rebounded again and again. *Someone was calling the transport pod back to the market!* Nolan, trying to do some good, pulled the bins all the way out of the transport, unblocking the doors.

"No!" I screamed, leaping forward to shove my arm between the doors. I was too late. They slid shut.

The transport ascended to the market. Nolan blinked at me as the concept of what goes up, must come down, settled in. When it returned, the transport wasn't going to be empty. And my sister was still missing.

55

That great Galactic gravity well at the center of the Milky Way? We'd just shoved ourselves into it. *Unbelievable.*

"Over there! Get the autodocs out of the bins and cover them with some clothing!" I shouted, motioning to Mieant, Nyla, and Nolan into the darkness, and they burst into action. First, Nolan wrested the autodocs out of the garbage bins and placed the antigravs back under the autodocs. Then, Mieant, Nyla, and Nolan all shed a layer of clothing to conceal the autodocs' glow and crouched down in the darkness.

I sprinted for the depression at the other side of the platform and pulled off my hoodie. I deposited the hoodie a few meters from the start of the Crynit ramp to the dead city below and raced down the ramp until I was comfortably out of sight.

"Raystar," Mieant shouted, "What are you doi—"

"No time!" I yelled from around the corner. "I'll distract them. You get them from behind!"

Okay, it was a dumb plan, but we were stranded on a flat platform with no way out except a narrow ramp. Two autodocs, Nyla, Mieant, a mountainasaurus Glean, and me, struggling down the ramp? With no shelter? We'd be better off saving ourselves the cortisol and just pushing each other off the platform.

No. This is where we will make our stand.

Flattened against the wall on the ridiculously narrow Crynit ramp, I caught my breath. During that brief respite, I noticed again the odd light so far below us. And I realized…Deep Tunnel had come alive.

Newly active simulated skies glowed with dawn in the distance. A harsh sunrise shone down on the dead skeletons of trees, barren parks, dried riverbeds. Air circulators had whipped the gentle breezes I remembered from the Tunnel into zephyrs. Clouds of dead brown leaves *shushed* along the ground. Dust curled in brown swirls around the buildings; it reminded me of pictures I'd seen of snow blowing off the tops of mountains.

In the light of a new day, the city *moved*. Thousands of automatons flew, crawled, and rolled in every direction, intent on their purpose and filled with renewed life. And there, in the farther distance, stood the tall, golden building, perfectly clean. At its pinnacle was a light that shone brighter than the artificial day.

With a "crrssshxzzzzl," the transport doors whoosed open.

I pancaked myself against the wall. Boots, heavy ones, raced onto the platform. I drew a deep breath and my Human blaster and waited.

"Cover our six," a sandpaper voice commanded. I remembered that voice! It belonged to the Trogi captain who'd almost snagged me. "Look smart, you nova excuses for gratchers."

"Affirmative!" came the joint reply.

"You! Follow that path and find the Human. The Assassins of the Asrigards humiliated you pathetic idiots in the market, so consider this your last chance."

I formed an instant distaste for the Trogi captain. I mean, I didn't like *any* of them, but he really sounded like a macho jerk.

"Yes, sir!"

I crept a few steps up the insanely narrow path. *Stupid fake-blue sky. Stupid sunrise.* I could see everything, including how close I stood to the ledge and how far below me the very solid ground was. *What a great time to develop acrophobia.*

I kept edging forward until I could see them: four 98th Battlegroup soldiers, just around the corner. The massive Trogi captain fit very neatly into my gun's sights. He was flanked by two somewhat smaller Trogis; a fourth soldier, a Glean, faced the transport.

My Human blaster leveled, the captain in my sights, I inhaled. I had to make this count.

Just before I touched the trigger, several options on my heads-up display appeared. I read through them in no particular order: "beam," "wide," "stun," "explosion," "delayed explosion," "safety off," "stream," and "rapid pulse." I eased my finger onto the trigger. "Safety off" gently pulsed green while the other options remained grey.

As the captain eyed the glow of my blaster, he dragged one of the soldiers next to him into the line of fire. I fired. PUHH! A cloud of pretty blue sparkles drifted lazily and uselessly from my blaster's muzzle into the air.

My eyes met the captain's for what seemed like a year. Now, it was his turn. I found myself staring into the glowing barrel of his assault rifle.

Nova that. Also: *coward.*

I ran further down the spiraling ramp and…smashed into the belly of the other Trogi soldier. While the captain had been occupied with yanking the other soldier at his flank in front of him, the other Trogi soldier had athletically *leapt* down the spiral path and landed roughly eight meters behind me.

Like I said, my plan was dumb. Universe: 1. Raystar: 0.

The soldier behind me leered at me and reached both of his massive hands into his combat armor. In one hand, a wicked-looking blade emerged; in the other, a hand cannon.

"Human," the captain shouted above me, "lay down your weapons! Surrender."

But the soldier behind me had other ideas. "Captain might make your death painless." He chuckled deeply as he waved the meter-long blade for effect. "But we've not 'ad our fun yet."

Why didn't my blaster work? I thought furiously. Faster than I'd ever thought possible, I called up my shield, raised my blaster, and fired. Twice. PUHH! PUHH! More pretty, useless sparkles wafted out of my twin barrels.

The soldier's return fire raged against my shield with orange strobes and hammered me against the wall. From above, a set of orange bolts issued by the captain howled past me and down into the tunnel. They appeared as pin-sized lights as they sailed toward the buildings below, but when they struck, they exploded in a violent flash and a deep WHUMP.

The lights around us shifted instantly from artificial sunshine to blood-red strobes. A distant klaxon began and quickly rose to an ear-piercing shriek. It cycled down and then up again, reverberating through the entire Deep Tunnel.

The terrifying and familiar voice of PeaceMaker began to echo throughout Deep Tunnel: "WE ARE UNDER ASSAULT. PEACE-MAKER PROTOCOL INITIATED. CITIZENS, REMAIN IN-DOORS UNTIL FURTHER NOTICE."

The Trogi soldier's eyes widened. I quickly realized that he couldn't understand the broadcast. We paused our battle to look down over the city. All the busy automatons had disappeared. New *things* emerged from hundreds—no, thousands—of previously invisible portals that lined the walls of Deep Tunnel. With a series of synchronized clanks, rows and rows of these doors simultaneously slid open and waves of flying drones poured from them. The few that malfunctioned dropped like dead wasps into the city as those behind pushed them aside.

Of course! The city had security drones.

The tip of the swarm began to curl toward us, racing through the ancient tunnel's air.

"Void take me!" I heard the soldier whisper. Without so much as a glance at me, he spun to face the platform above us, made an anti-grav-assisted leap, and rejoined his squad on the platform.

"What r' yeh doin'? Get the Human!" the captain shouted.

"Captain," the soldier shouted, "look what's comin'!" I peeked around the corner.

"You take that runt out, or you take a dirt nap. Understood?"

The soldier looked at his squad mates, who shifted their stances slightly.

"I told the Jurisdictor we would find them, and by the Architect, we *will* find them!" the captain bellowed. "Now you scum, go—"

The Glean soldier who had been watching their six calmly placed his assault rifle against the captain's back and pulled the trigger. The blast created a perfect hole as large as my head through the captain's chest.

"You're not my superior," one of the Trogis muttered as the captain toppled onto the platform. "Let's get on, mates," he added as he spat on the captain's corpse. The three soldiers jogged into the transport, and with a final "crrssshxzzzzl," the doors closed.

We were alone.

Ooookay. I blinked. *I did not see that coming.*

Mieant scrambled out of the darkness first, followed by Nyla. Despite everything, she was a true professional: she looked ready for her next news report. Nolan emerged last, gently pushing the autodocs. I was surprised that Mieant would let a stranger push his parents.

We met around the fallen captain's body. Dark blood oozed from the hole in his chest. Our gazes met, and as one, we swallowed. Death is probably the thing I understand the least: a boundary one crosses, never to return.

The whine of the incoming Human security drones reminded us that, despite the soldiers' departure, we were hardly safe. As one, we turned to face the approaching swarm. My spirit fell as I took in the thousands of drones flying toward us.

We'd come so close. Nova.

I pulled my blaster. Once again, "safety on" glowed softly as my heads-up display activated. I could read the Human words, but I didn't *really* understand them. I stared at the words for a minute.

Wait.

Safety off, I thought, and lo, the words on the display changed to "safety off." The other options lit up green, and a new phrase appeared: "ready to fire." Without really taking aim, I pointed the blaster in the general direction of the oncoming swarm, mentally chose "delayed explosion" from the display, and pulled the trigger.

The muzzle grew bright as energy collected at its mouth—it looked like the gun was blowing a soap bubble. The bubble became a nuclear-hot bubble of crackling white energy that quickly grew to twice the size of my head. After a second, it streaked out toward the swarm and left a comet-like tail.

The drones didn't have time to avoid the ball of incandescent white racing toward them. It reached the pack, stopped, and hovered in their center. It nova'd.

BOOM.

Nyla squeezed my elbows and jumped up and down, clapping like a happy child.

"WE'RE REPORTING FROM A WAR ZONE!"

56

After nearly two millennia of dust, darkness, and nearly complete isolation, the Human megalopolis of Deep Tunnel got its first taste of irony. It was under attack. By a Human.

When the plasma ball detonated, a set of secondary explosions ripped through the swarm, scattering the drones like birds in a gale. Others detonated and fell in long fiery arcs into the city below.

"Yes!" Mieant howled, pumping his fist, "Raystar, again!" He drew his blasters and started firing. The drones evaded his shots, but euphoria had us in its thrall: we would take them down. It was a glorious release for the suffering we'd gone through. It felt like sweet revenge on our circumstances and the uncertainty we had about Cri's fate.

We traded grins, but only for a moment. My jubilation faded as my heads-up display flashed "low battery."

ARE YOU KIDDING ME?

Mieant noticed my sudden frown. "What, Raystar?" he shouted, shaking me gently by the shoulders. "What?"

"I, it," I stammered, "it's out of power." I turned the blaster desperately in my hand like it might somehow charge it up.

"For the love of all…" he said, smacking his face. He took a few running steps toward the regrouping drones and flung his blaster at them.

"RRRrrraaahh!" Mieant shouted as the weapon spun through the air and gracefully descended. He dropped to his knees.

But, suddenly, inexplicably, the drones began to flee—not in response to Mieant's futile toss of despair, but because of some unseen force. Confused but thankful for this extraordinary turn of events, we stared vacantly at the drones as they disappeared from view.

Our intrepid independent news investigator Nyla Jax stepped up to interrupt our wonderment.

"This is Nyla Jax, independent news investigator for GNN. After having discovered incontrovertible proof that the so-called 'Assassins of the Asrigards' are innocent and that Freela and Kaleren Asrigard, Solium4 Quadrant Co-Governors, are still alive, we now bring you this very special report.

"We are embedded with Mieant Asrigard and Raystar Ceridian inside a functional but deserted ancient Human city *underneath* Blue River! The 98th Battlegroup's forces just retreated in terror in the face of a mysterious drone swarm from the abandoned Human city. We believe this is an ancient security force, and its intentions are unknown. However, luckily for this news team and these brave children, Crynit reinforcements appear to be on the way." She paused and swirled her finger in a circle above her platinum hair.

Nolan nodded and waved an arm. Instantly, a group of GNN experian drones were dispatched down to take panorama shots of Deep Tunnel.

"Wait, what did you say, Nyla?" I said, placing my hand on one of her lower arms as I frowned at the mysteriously retreating Deep Tunnel drones. She was a petite Glean, but even so, she towered over me.

She looked at me and then back at Nolan.

"Raystar," she said in a patronizing tone, "be a dear and let me get through this? I'll only be a minute." Then she turned back to Nolan's vid recorder, clearly happy to get back to her award-winning, fortune-making story.

"What did you say about reinforcements?" I said louder, grabbing one of her hands with both of mine. Her eyes flashed. With two hands, she turned me toward Deep Tunnel. Another hand removed my hands from hers, and with her fourth, she pointed straight ahead.

At least fifty Eviscerators, and maybe more, streaked toward the swarm from their rear. They weren't the same models that were escorting Broodmother the first time we'd seen her. These were ten-meter-long aerodynamic spiders, not counting the lengths of their arms. Their abdomens housed their propulsion systems and brains. Their arms extended an additional ten meters from their spiked thoraxes to claw, grab, rend, and burrow into their targets. And if that didn't work, the arms were also equipped with pods of beam weapons and missiles. These Eviscerators were the legendary ship-to-ship assault drones used for space action.

The Human drone swarm turned toward the oncoming Crynit threat. The nightmarish Eviscerators linked their shields into a gentle bowl shape. They herded the Terran drones toward the center-most and deepest part of the bowl as the Crynit force advanced. Once their massive shield link was complete, the Eviscerators accelerated. The Terran drones that touched the energy net exploded on contact, but a majority remained collected in the bowl.

At that moment, roughly a hundred more Eviscerators appeared. While cloaked, they had moved from their frontal assault to a new position flanking the Terran drones. The Crynit cloaking tech was so good that they could have been there, undetected, well before the Terran attack. Clouds of micro-missiles streaked out from the Eviscerators, which now almost completely surrounded the drones. Hundreds, perhaps thousands of red lasers flashed faster than the eye could see into the drone swarm.

Yet it wasn't quite a one-sided slaughter. The drones did not "die" easily. Lightning crackled from within the maelstrom of destruction and branched outward, splitting and then splitting again, becoming finer with each division until the lightning ball looked like a giant fluff ball of blinding, azure light.

Nova. The drones were using nanotech *just like mine!* And then it dawned on me: these must be classic Crynit-versus-Human battle tactics. This was living history, tactics nearly two thousand years old!

The Terran lightning ball was at least half a kilometer in diameter. Eviscerators that were caught inside the sphere simply *vanished*. Even Crynit ships on the perimeter of the lightning storm sparked and then careened away, leaking flames. But the Crynit forces held. Their energy shields remained interlocked as they pushed the Terran drones into an increasingly compact area and pounded them with lasers and missiles, until there were simply no more.

As one, the Crynit Eviscerators then cloaked and disappeared.

Void take me. That was…awesome.

"I hope you got that, Nolan," Nyla whispered.

She coughed in the ozone cloud left behind by the battle. I helped Mieant up and regarded him.

"Broodmother saved us," I told him. He nodded. I looked over at Nyla and Nolan. Nolan whispered down to her, his voice like an avalanche. Nyla responded passionately, emphasizing her points with wave after wave of gestures. Mom used to do that. So did Cri.

"Cri," Mieant moaned. I nodded and secured my useless blaster in its holster. He regarded me as I strode over to the captain's corpse and removed his assault rifle, two grenades, and a medkit. I shoved the rifle into Mieant's arms.

"We have to go back," I said, trying to gin up some determination. Instead, I doubled over coughing from the battle's acrid smoke. "At least we have to try."

My eyes burned as I looked at Mieant.

Mom said, "We don't leave family behind." I am essentially an orphan. And I agree.

Regardless of whatever politics were involved, my organic parents *had* left me behind, but my adoptive parents had sacrificed themselves for me. My sister, craxy and violent as she'd become, deserved to have her family rescue her. She deserved the hope of knowing that some bonds were stronger than circumstance. That we would be relentless in our quest to keep her safe. We were family.

Right?

He nodded slowly as he watched the approaching Crynit fleet. Maybe he was considering asking Broodmother to help us storm the city. I certainly was.

"I…I don't know where I lost her," he cried. "When we were in the market, I was terrified. 'Save my parents' was all I could think of." He smeared dust on his grey face in an attempt to wipe away the tears in his eyes and the grimace away from his tight, red-blue lips.

I walked over to him, slid my arms underneath his, and pulled him close. He lay his head on mine, his long hair flowing over me. Through his utility suit, I could feel his muscles, his bones, his body as my arms encircled him. I lay my head above his heart, and he put his arms around me. He began to tremble. *Contact.* The simple act of making contact, whether it's a holding a hand or a full-body hug, is an act of witness, of acknowledgement. It is a connection that pierces the isolation of individualism.

"Architect, I was so selfish," he said, weeping. "I should have been—"

"Stop," I said, wiping dust on my own face in a similar attempt.

"I love her, Raystar," he said. His grey face was slack. His long black hair fell over his black eyes. His unfocused gaze was lonelier and more barren than a dead planet. I shivered.

"She must have been captured," I said as I disengaged from the embrace. I looked up at him and placed my hand above his heart. I loved her, too. "Your parents were captured. We got *them* back, right?" We'd been wrong before, and we could be wrong about Cri now. "We'll get her back."

He closed his eyes, sucked in a breath, and bowed his head. I made a fist and gently thumped his chest before echoing, "We'll get her back."

She was my sister. My emotions made it hard to breathe, hard to think. Why wasn't I allowed to fall apart? Deep, deep inside, grief and rage pushed against the constraints of my rational brain. I wanted to cry, scream, let loose, and grab all of the energy I could to find her, even if it meant ripping Blue River apart. If I let it out those emotions....

No.

I squeezed my eyes shut. My breath came in shudders, but I eventually got control. Through sheer will, I managed to shove my emotions back into their containment cell, my heart.

"Something is terribly wrong in the Convergence," I heard Nyla whisper a few feet away. "They are children, younglings who have risen to the challenges and hardships that WE, the adults, have placed in front of them. They have become the heroines and heroes that we should be celebrating, not persecuting."

I blinked.

Nyla's soliloquy continued. "If this is what the Convergence has become, then the time for revolution may be upon us!"

Mieant and I turned to face her. She was recording us.

"Was that too much?" she asked Nolan, bouncing slightly on her toes with excitement. I couldn't figure out how it was possible that her suit had no dust on it. Her platinum hair bobbed and her golden eyes sparkled as she smiled expectantly up at her videographer. Nolan made a few adjustments on his vid recorder, and the flock of experian drones that he had silently positioned around them reacted to whatever modifications he'd made.

"I don't think you can say 'revolution,'" he rumbled back.

"Pffft. Flip that," she said tartly, her expression laced with anger. "Godwill has imprisoned us. These kids are victims," she said, pointing at us with two of her arms. "He's a Void-cursed spike that must be exposed for the horrible things he's done! It's up to us to get the truth out about what's happening on Nem'—not just to our planet, but to the Convergence at large."

Nolan looked at her. He was proof that mountains could have faces, and he had a very kind mountain face. His muscles bulged as he placed a lower hand on Nyla's shoulder.

"That's not reporting, little one. That's commenting."

"You're right," Nyla replied, sighing. She brushed her platinum hair from her eyes and placed her hand gently over his. Something passed between them, a level of caring and understanding that was beyond friendship. She leaned her head against his massive hand for a moment.

"You're right, Nolan," she repeated, this time with more intensity. "The time for reporting the news is over. We *are* the news."

Mieant leaned down, his mouth close to my ears, and whispered, "What the nova are they talking about?"

Nyla spun around. Apparently, her hearing was excellent. She suddenly remembered that we were her story.

"See, Nol? They *were* kissing."

Mieant and I jumped away from each other at light speed. *The ridiculousness of Nyla's assertion! I mean, what the nova?*

I frowned at Nyla, and sputtered, "We are so NOT doing that!"

Nyla glanced up at Nolan.

"Easy, Raystar," Nyla said as she gracefully slipped out from under Nolan's hand. She walked over to join us with an easy smile on her pretty face. "I'm glad. It *is* a bit early to move in on your sister's boyfriend, after all."

Before I could sputter out the flummoxed response I was formulating, she continued. "Teen romance aside, you can't be oblivious to what's happening around us. You kids are"—she paused a moment as she searched for the right word—"catalysts. You're change agents that will set *it* into motion." Nyla said "it" like we were supposed to know what she was talking about. "It has been in the works for hundreds of years, and now you kids are what will put the Convergence past the point of no return.

"C'mon, now. You've made it through all of this," she continued, waving her arms dramatically, "and that hasn't occurred to you? *Think*. An assault on the Quadrant 4 Co-Governors would be momentous enough. Add to that a planetary blockade, two Battlegroup deployments, and the capture of your parents, Raystar, the Ascendants Sathra and Nent? And persecution of the children of the leaders of the most influential races in this region of the Convergence?"

Nyla seemed to be riding a wave of her own potential to make news as she wound herself up. I've learned about orgasms in my sex ed classes, and Nyla seemed to be achieving just that state of ecstasy.

Nyla shook her head, cocking her hip and flipping all four hands, palm up, "Any of this register with you two?" She pointed directly at Mieant. "Do you truly believe that it's a coincidence that you, Cri, Raystar, and Nonch were captured? That it's a coincidence that all of you are even together on this planet at all? No! Something huge is happening. You are all leverage. Godwill and his allies intend to control your parents by threatening the safety of their children."

Well. We *have* been a little busy since school started.

"We've thought about all that stuff, Nyla," I replied. "It doesn't matter. Only Cri matters now. We don't leave our own behind. We have to go back for her."

The argument ended dramatically as a massive Crynit troop carrier uncloaked itself above us.

The ship, which drifted above at the edge of the transport platform, was vaguely caterpillar shaped and easily seventy meters long by thirty meters tall. Crynit designs seemed to always have intimidation as their key aesthetic principle. This space-black, spiked caterpillar of doom was no exception. I wondered what forces in their evolution necessitated the projection of such a threatening appearance to everything around them. I nervously examined the weapons and sensors bristling from the ship's bulbous segments. How long the ship had been hovering there at the platform's edge was anybody's guess.

"NO. YOU. WILL. NOT." The deep, feminine voice of Broodmother blared from the troop carrier's external broadcast system.

The doom-a-pillar turned in slow motion, like a massive, ugly ornament pivoting on an invisible string. Autoturrets swiveled across the troop carrier's body as they scanned for hostiles. It continued to pivot until its side-loading doors faced us; then, its armor parted and a loading ramp large enough to accommodate an air car extended to the platform's surface. True to usual Crynit form, the skids securing the ramp to the platform were actually claws that gouged the metal with predatory ferocity. A second set of interior doors opened to reveal Broodmother Krig herself: our tentative ally, the matriarch of the Crynits on Nem', and my best friend's mom.

"None of you will return to Blue River," she said simply as she thrummed down the ramp. We all took multiple steps back to make way for her bulk. Her prismatic orbs simultaneously took in the dead Trogi captain, the platform, and our raggedy group. Commander First Claw and five other soldiers flowed out in her wake and spread out to stand guard at strategic points on the platform's perimeter. One pointed a device at the transport doors. With cool efficiency, he melted them into red slag.

"You will board my ship now." Broodmother's sensor stalks stood straight up as she took in Freela and Kaleren Asrigard, ensconced in their respective levitating chambers in a dormant state. She extended a blade arm to gently tap the exterior of Kaleren's autodoc, gave me a sideways glance, and huffed; the sound was like a steam valve letting off pressure. One soldier responded to what must have been a chemical command, and as one, the soldiers navigated the Co-Governors' pods up the ramp.

The queen extended two blade arms toward the dead Trogi. The midnight blue-black of her carapace reflected our faces as we stared openly, mesmerized by her beauty and deadliness. We were transfixed with curiosity about what she would do next. Slowly, she pressed two of her mono-molecular blades into the captain's corpse on either side of the cauterized and oozing hole in his chest. They slid through his armor and flesh like a knife through soft butter—but with more squishing sounds. She lifted his body to orb level, and her feathery sensor stalks touched his dangling, splayed form as she regarded it with her jeweled eyes.

Then, she casually flicked the captain's body over the side of the platform. I blinked.

"Trogis," she muttered. Scents of soil and sugar wafted through the air, easily defeating the platform's previous odors of chemicals, fire, and dust. For Crynits, this was a smell of deadly intent. I'd learned long ago that if I smelled that around a Crynit, it was time to run. Pheromones don't lie.

"The queen smells nice," Nolan whispered to Nyla, his head almost at Broodmother's height. The queen froze. The smells of soil and sugar were cloyingly intense: pure fury.

But instead of ripping Nolan's arms and his legs from his torso and throwing him, limbless, down the vast chasm, she ignored him. Instead, she leveled her gaze at Mieant and me.

"Mieant Asrigard. Raystar Ceridian. You will board the transport now. I want to understand what in the Architect's Creation prompted you to wake this city's guardian. I want to hear all details of your conversation with the Elions. You will share with me where and how you found our missing Co-Governors."

She turned to Nyla and Nolan. "And then you will share why you have brought a news crew with you." She curled her frame and thrummed back up the ramp with all of the dignity you would expect from a queen.

All I could think about was what she didn't say. She said nothing about Cri, and she wasn't surprised by her absence. Mieant clearly had the same thoughts. He exchanged a glance with me, dropped his head, and followed Broodmother into the bowels of the transport.

"C'mon," I said to Nyla and Nolan, and we marched in after him. Her soldiers took up our "six."

The doom-a-pillar's main holding chamber was stripped of any seats or creature comforts. It was clearly designed for hauling loads— or perhaps for beings that can simply curl up, so they don't *need* chairs. Crynit engineering had an organic feel; the smooth floor gave way to curved support beams that resembled a rib cage: they wrapped upward and joined at the ceiling that narrowed toward the control station at the front.

Broodmother led us to the command center in the ship's bow. There, consoles and seating areas were arranged in a semicircle facing forward. Crynit officers not in armor were stationed at three consoles that surrounded the queen's chair, the largest. We were offered seats in front of the command consoles and a large holo screen. I plunked into one of the chairs and relaxed as it reshaped to fit my anatomy. The holo showed the curve of the underground city as it stretched into darkness, our relative location, and the hundred and fifty or so drones—some visible, some cloaked—defensively positioned around us.

The heads-up display also marked the thousands of drones belonging to PeaceMaker in red. Deep Tunnel was immense; despite the transport's speed, our return trip was going to take a bit of time. And there sure were a lot of red markers.

"Alert," a disembodied voice bellowed all around us. Across the holo, a series of countless flashes sparkled below us, followed a second later by fiery plumes.

"Venom and claw!" First Claw exclaimed. Hundreds of ground-to-air missiles were streaking toward our transport.

"Drones, configure for intercept," he commanded the ship's AI.

"Faith, First Claw," Broodmother said quietly as she gazed at the holo.

The missiles swarmed greedily toward our ship, eager to make contact. Eviscerators positioned themselves forward and below our position. Those that couldn't destroy the Terran missiles with fire were prepared to sacrifice themselves to protect the transport.

Maintaining her glacial calm, Broodmother added, "I am confident we will not have to walk."

The drones perished in fire by the scores, but it wasn't enough.

"Impact alert," the transport's bored-sounding synth voice declared. The doom-a-pillar lurched from side to side, and smoke began to pour into the command center.

"Fire in Storage Area Two," the ship alerted.

As the hammering and lurching continued, the AI issued an update: "Fire is now contained," and then, "New sitrep: shield generators are non-functional. Primary engine has been destroyed. Operating on positioning thrusters."

"That ancient Human thing," Broodmother muttered coolly to herself amidst the smoke, alarm klaxons, and our wobbly descent toward HiveHome, "has new tricks."

A kaleidoscope of stars swirled slowly, majestically, around us in Broodmother's command center at HiveHome. The Milky Way's 100,000 billion stars' actual speeds were not perceptible on the holo screen, but from where I sat in the queen's command center, the procession of gold, silver, red, and blue moved leisurely and inexorably toward their individual doom: the giant black hole at the heart of the Galactic Core. I imagined it as a gluttonous, smug, and hungry maw at the heart of our galaxy, sure in the knowledge that all those stars and worlds would eventually fill its belly.

Creation. Destruction. It was horrible. Beautiful.

There, to the right of the core, stretched the Orion Arm, home of *Homo sapiens*. A string of green dots marked what had been the Terran Republic's territory. The string continued toward the Galactic Core, representing the rest of the Convergence's star systems—known space.

Huh.

I'd looked at the map a day before in the very same spot. The number of Convergence star systems had been listed as 1,288, but it was now 1,267. The missing systems were denoted with red dots, indicating that they had been lost to the Raas.

Look, I wasn't a big fan of the Convergence at the moment, but I respected its might. Could twenty-one of its systems really be lost in a day's time? That was trillions of lives…thousands of species. I'd learned a bit about the war from the news and at school, including the fact that the Convergence forces didn't actually know what had happened on the planets conquered by the Raas.

But I did know we were losing the war with them, which brought us squarely back to Humanity. I was part of the only other species that had kicked the Convergence's collective butt in history. The Convergence believed they needed Human technology in order to combat the Raas. Which meant they needed my DNA to unlock the Human capabilities. I shook myself out of my reverie, pulled by the gravity of my reality.

Since our return to HiveHome, we'd been debriefing Broodmother for more than three hours. I was tired. Come to think of it, I was ravenous AND tired. I eyed the food platters that Broodmother's staff had brought in earlier and loaded up a plate with vegetables.

Sleep: yeah, I could use that too! Oh, to be unconscious on one of those moss beds and smell the forest—that would be amazing. I frowned as I tore into the food.

Broodmother, who was sitting quietly in her chair watching me eat, had declined to answer any of our questions about Cri. We also hadn't discussed how Mieant's parents would be thawed out or whatever needed to be done to restore them. And we hadn't talked about how we would reach the New Mars base underneath the Mesas.

"Raystar Ceridian," Broodmother said. Tenderly, she reached out to me, and with a surprisingly soft and warm claw, she brushed my cheek. "You have been busy."

I paused my frenetic eating and blinked up into her jewel-like, rainbow-colored eyes.

"You saved my son. Now, you have saved the Asrigards. You have forged an alliance with Podmaster, a powerful member of the Elion Clans." She leaned toward me as Mieant, Nolan, and Nyla all sucked in their breath. "But heed me well, Raystar," she continued, "most importantly, you have earned friends. They are friends you will need in what is to come."

I froze, feeling the weight of the moment and wondering where she was going with this.

"I witnessed your struggles as you and young Asrigard escaped the market. I watched you guide others to safety as you risked your own life to serve as a distraction. I saw your courage even when your weapons failed. And I saw you give comfort to your sister's mate, even though she is your sister. That grief should be yours first, and his second."

My chest grew tight and my cheeks hot. Allergies or dust must have clouded my eyes, because I couldn't see through the sudden tears that welled up in them. I'd been trying so hard. To fit in. To be loved. Even to be liked. To survive. Broodmother understood me at a level that started to make me shake. I squinted, wiping some droplets that plopped onto my shirt.

Broodmother's warm claws and arms encircled me. She lifted me effortlessly from the chair and squeezed me gently but tightly, much as Mom always had. I stopped shaking and wiped my eyes with a sleeve. I was too embarrassed to look at the others or at Broodmother, even as I felt the weight and intensity of her gaze. I could only look at nothing at all under my half-lidded eyes and revel in her embrace.

Gently, she set me down.

"I think I like you, Raystar. I hope that among the bonds you have already created, you have room for one more."

Words were still too far down my tightened throat to come out, so I sniffled and finally looked up to meet her gaze. It was warm and kind.

"I would be honored to lend you my assistance and support, as you have done for me. I wish us to be allies, Human and Crynit, for the first time in the two thousand years our species have known each other," she said gravely. "What say you?"

Every motion and sound in the command room instantly stopped. Pilots who had been floating from work group to work group simply froze in the silence that fell like a hammer. I opened and closed my mouth and croaked out something unintelligible. I swallowed and tried again.

"Yes, Broodmother."

The command center whirred back into motion.

Broodmother nodded, pleased, and said firmly, "Recorder, make note that as of this day and time, the Human Raystar Ceridian of Terra, and I, Broodmother Krig, Queen of the Nem' Matriarchy, are allies. None of those under her direct control shall harm mine or me, and none of those under my direct control shall harm hers or her own body."

What just happened? Had I entered into a formal alliance?

"Now, to business then," Broodmother said brusquely, shaking me out of my stunned reverie. *Could things happen any faster?* "Ally mine, you must trust me in this. What I plan to do next is in our mutual best interest."

I had just begun to smile when a dart thwapped into my arm. A similar syringe hit Mieant. Broodmother's guards grabbed Nolan and Nyla and immobilized them with strength far greater than even Nolan was able to resist.

"I am sorry, Raystar Ceridian, Mieant Asrigard. But this *is* necessary."

My smile faltered. My face felt soggy. I frowned up at Broodmother as I lost control of my body. Warmth spread from the injection into my chest, stomach, legs—so warm, so good. A guard gently lifted me up and returned me to the chair that morphed to my shape.

"You see, I know that you contain an entity that cannot be trusted. I cannot risk it overtaking you here, in the heart of HiveHome. The injection I have given you will keep you calm."

I had just enough motor control left to mumble a response: "Calm?"

She sighed as if the weight of the Universe was settled on her massive, armored back.

"Ally mine, understand this: if you manifest, I *will* kill you. You must remain calm. *Please.*"

I blinked and nodded.

"My dear Raystar, your sister, Cri Ceridian, is dead."

60

"What does it feel like? Being Human?"

I shrugged, pursed my lips, and looked at my big sister. "What does it feel like to be normal?"

Cri shrugged. "I dunno." She thought about it a bit more, frowned prettily, and smiled at me. "Want to feed the gratchers?"

Her smile was infectious. I grinned back at her. "Sure!"

"You get a head start," Cri said, an impish look flashing in her golden eyes, "because you're littler."

I was about to smile again, but then she pushed me and sprinted out of my room shouting, "Last one to the gratcher pen has to feed Chunks!"

My room was on the top floor of our four-bedroom farmhouse, farthest down the hallway that ended in stairs leading to our kitchen. I sprang up and raced after her. We thundered down the stairs.

She might be bigger, I thought, *but she isn't really that much faster.* Dodging the big Glean-sized kitchen furniture slowed her down just enough for me to catch up, and she paused to grab the bag of bread we were going to feed to the gratchers. I caught her at the kitchen door and gave her a push in the small of her back.

My push was just enough to topple her onto the narrow deck. I hopped over the railing and into our square courtyard. AD9, our automated, do-everything drone, dodged out of my way.

I'm going to make it to the gratcher pen before Cri!

But she has the bread, AI said.

Argh.

I ran low along the bushes that bordered the deck. I listened as she picked herself up and ran toward the pen.

She always does that!

It was silly that she did, especially since she had to know by now that I was going to do what I always did. I kept on pushing her just to see how many times it would happen before she'd change tactics.

Galactics never seemed to change. At least, the kids at school never did, and neither did my sister. Because she didn't change her patterns, her predictability made her vulnerable.

I tackled her as she leapt down the stairs to the courtyard. She landed on her stomach with an oomph, her four arms splayed out like a red butterfly.

I snatched up the bread and took off toward the pen.

"No fair!" she yelled as I pushed her down once more before sprinting toward victory.

Fair? I was smaller than every other Galactic. Unfair was the only game this little Human could play. Like other small animals, I had to use subterfuge and guile.

Chunks, our prized herd leader, skeptically watched my ungainly approach. I wasn't afraid of Chunks. He wanted food. Like my sister, he was predictable. If he ate me, I'd just get stuck in his teeth. Plus, Chunks and I were both "children" of Terra.

I skidded to a stop, panting furiously. I heard Cri huffing after me in the afternoon sun. I ripped open the bag of bread and grabbed as big a handful of the loaf as possible.

"Chunks!" I yelled as I threw the portion to him. Immobile as the Mesas and still quite skeptical, he regarded the fistful of bread as it sailed through the air, bounced on the ground, and rolled up next to his hooves.

Pfft. Fine. Don't eat it, then.

I ran the rest of the way to the gratcher pen where the rest of our herd lived and tossed the rest of the loaf to them. Cri tackled me not a meter from the fence.

"Got you!" she squealed. Her four hands and nubbly fingers found my overly ticklish ribs. We tussled and rolled over again and again, giggling.

A moment later, breathless, we lay in the dry soil looking up at the blue sky and at Banefire as it began its downward arc. She reached out a hand to find mine, and our sweaty, soft, kid hands clutched each other.

"You always let me win, Ray," she said, turning her head to face me. "Why?"

I smiled at the sky and then looked into her golden eyes.

"Because I love you."

My eyes snapped open. I saw nothing. My mind struggled to cast out that wonderful childhood memory. In the depths of my weeping darkness, my fury ignited. It was a burning, a chasm that needed to be filled, an ache that needed to be avenged, all wrapped up in the black hole that was now my heart.

Cri. *My sister.* I missed her like oxygen.

"My queen, you are in danger. What if her power escapes? Her demon within could destroy—"

"Hush…."

"But—"

"Shhhssshhh! The child has strength. She must show control."

"But—"

"Be silent or leave, First Claw."

My stomach was a cramped coffin. I couldn't breathe. My face ached, frozen in a grimace. My hair hung in front of my mouth, which I couldn't close. It was paralyzed into a silent wail. Old tears streaked my face, but no more could come. While the streaks had dried up, the memories hadn't.

My sister.

Warm hands encircled me and gently lifted me, cradled and rocked me. Empathy for a loss is a universal bond.

"Oh, child," Broodmother said.

I held on to her warmth, wrapped myself around its softness. My breaths were uneven. My heart was frantic, attempting to pound its way out of my chest. I was broken. Way, way inside of me, walls had cracked: anger, lava, fury, sadness poured out. The air smelled of forest and flowers, but it was ragged in my lungs.

My core was going nova. I needed to focus.

FOCUS!

Tidal waves of emotion crashed and then compressed my grief and anger into a purpose.

"My queen?"

"First Claw, silence. Sunrises and gravity wells, how many times must I tell you?"

"I…I shall withdraw to a safe distance."

"Advisable," Broodmother whispered.

63

"Raystar."

A summer wind wafted the scents of pine and wildflowers into my lungs as I inhaled. I opened an eye to find blue sky and a yellow butterfly.

"Nnnng," I said as I rolled over in the moss. It was so soft. I was covered by a feathery pillow that provided a comforting weight, and somehow it wasn't hot.

Wait.

A familiar purple flower, not fifteen millimeters from my face, had details that seemed to go on into infinity.

I've been here before. When?

My déjà vu was shattered by remembrance. The chasm that had hacked through my chest was jagged and Cri-shaped. I gasped, realizing I'd been holding my breath. Below my ribs, my stomach muscles felt sore from sobbing. Wincing, I sat up and rubbed sleep from my eyes.

Instead of falling to the ground, the pillow lifted off me and floated away. I found myself staring into the queen's rainbow-colored, prismatic eyes. She'd curled her enormous body around the moss bed; the pillow that had been covering me was one of her sensor stalks.

"Raystar," she said as she gently touched my head and shoulders with her wavering sensor stalks.

I fought back the shaking that was threatening to escape and leaned into her razor-sharp mandible, pressing my cheek to her warm armor.

"Thank you for…."

"Hush, child," she said softly. After a moment, she pulled away from me. "Events around us are grinding away, with or without our participation." I looked up at her. "What will you do, Raystar?"

"Where are Mieant, Nonch, Nyla, and Nolan?"

"They await us in my command center."

Broodmother placed Cri's backpack at my feet. "Mieant indicated that you might want it." The pack was open. Cri's artificial attendant, the personal AI that every Galactic owned, was there, and something small and rectangular lay underneath a spare set of clothes. I dug it out.

It was Cri's detonator to our homestead, the twin to mine. In the sorrow and panic that went on as we left our parents behind, I remember asking Dad *what* the set would be detonating. He'd replied that it would blow up the whole farm, our home. I learned in the hours and days that followed that our home was much bigger than I'd ever thought, with a maze of rooms below ground that served as a redoubt. It was only logical that a nuclear device was necessary to destroy our hardened, well-protected base.

What will I do? What can *I do?* What was it that AI had said to me? *Thoughts and feelings are ephemeral, but actions are permanent. They are the price of thoughts.* Actions are irrevocable.

My heart pounded as I felt myself becoming overwhelmed.

No.

I had the rest of my plan to execute. Cri's death was the Galactic steel reinforcement my determination needed. I was no longer thinking in terms of escape or hiding. Godwill had used lethal force time and time again. He'd threatened my *friends*. My *family*. While I didn't know how Cri had died, I did know that Godwill had killed her. Even among the maelstrom of emotions swirling around inside me, my plan, my purpose, began to harden.

With plots spinning in my head and my heart turning to stone, I jumped down from the moss bed and onto the grassy field. Broodmother caught my arm, gently but firmly.

"Raystar, ally mine," she said, her jeweled eyes a kaleidoscope of hued images, "I am old. Many loves have been torn away from me by time and foes. Yet it is our love for others that gives our lives meaning. Our love gives everything that we do meaning. Do you understand?"

I didn't. *Godwill was out there.*

"Love is what makes life worthy of living," she said as she let me go. I stood there, silent. "Remember this when you are on the edge of an irrevocable choice between a loveless life or one that remains worth living."

I–I need…I need to focus. Love. It was a knife in my stomach.

I walked away through the soft grass, crossed the bridge over the burbling stream, and entered Broodmother's command center.

My friends, my dearest friends (including Nonch!!) were assembled at the base of Broodmother's chair. The command center was awash with sounds. Pilots and technicians floated from one group to another with military precision. Something was happening. Broodmother thrummed in moments after me, and First Claw rose to walk by her side. The two giant beings talked as they followed me toward the command dais.

"The 98th Battlegroup's soldiers have been repulsed," First Claw reported after a pointed glance at me. "The False Jurisdictor was with them."

"Do you think they have identified HiveHome?"

"My Queen, the fact that we still exist suggests that they believe we have simply created an underground city."

"Indeed," Broodmother said, clacking her armor in amusement. "An Assassin Class Hiveship would certainly merit an immediate and unambiguous response from the Dreadnoughts above us."

"Deep Tunnel forces have withdrawn, but the ancient sentinel is mobilizing on a level we have not witnessed before."

I heard Broodmother suck in a breath; it sounded like a wind tunnel. "What is your assessment?"

"We cannot remain here, my Queen."

"Void-cursed machines. Void-cursed Lethians."

"There is another issue, my Queen," First Claw said, "the Storm Wall is changing."

Well, I didn't know anything about *that*, but First Claw's announcement was the validation I'd been hoping for: the pursuers we'd escaped from in the tunnels were in fact soldiers from the 98th Battlegroup. And PeaceMaker, the entity I'd inadvertently awakened, had more forces than what we'd fought against. In at least one respect, that was good news: Godwill would not be able to attack us from both directions.

"Raystar!" Mieant yelled, interrupting my eavesdropping. He ran toward me, his grey face more ashen than usual. His black eyes were red-rimmed; his braid of jet-black hair followed him like the tail of a beast. He wrapped me in a hug. "I can't believe it."

Nyla wrapped her arms around both of us, and Nonch gently rested his sensor stalks on my back. Nolan watched us, sadness etched on his face. *Friends.* Broodmother said I had friends. We held each other for a few precious moments until I wriggled away, partly due to embarrassment. Everyone took the cue to disentangle.

"Show her," Nonch said to Nyla. "Raystar must see, must know."

Nyla's eyes narrowed. Her eyes darted around as if she was looking for a place to hide.

"Nye," Nolan rumbled, looking at her with reproach.

"I...no, you're right," Nyla said. She sighed and flicked a hand at one of her experian drones, which began to project a view screen. It was a news report, with the market shown in the background. Everyone was running and screaming, left and right. Many stores and stalls were on fire. Military drones blasted away at Mieant and me. Beel, the balding newsman we'd seen before on the market screens, occupied the left side of the screen. Across the bottom, a chyron announced, "One Assassin of the Asrigards Has Been Killed." A photo of Cri occupied the right side.

"This is Beel Gelitard of GNN. We have breaking news that one of the Assassins of the Asrigards has been killed while attempting to avoid capture." He paused a moment before continuing. "The assassin, Cri Ceridian, Ascendant, was terminated by Captain Vostok of the 3053rd Infantry, assigned to Blue River from the 98th Battlegroup. Here is the exclusive footage."

The reel began. Cri confidently walked up to a group of four Trogi soldiers, all four of her hands in the air.

"I surrender!" my wonderful, maddening sister said proudly.

The squad immediately lowered their bayonetted rifles. One of them—Captain Vostok, presumably—called up an AI-generated image to confirm my sister's identity.

"Up against the wall, hands and legs spread," he shouted gruffly.

Her confident expression faltered as she began to protest. "Wait! Jurisdictor Godwill sent—"

Vostok didn't wait for Cri to comply with his order, nor did he allow her to finish her sentence. He strode up to her and raised an arm, ready to shove her against the storefront. At the last minute, however, he leveled the bayonet on the edge of his plasma rifle at her heart and stabbed it through.

The horrible image flickered and then disappeared. Just like that, my sister disappeared.

"I'm so sorry, Raystar. So, so sorry." Nyla's voice was drowned out by the enormity of the flickering image seared forever in my mind.

64

The purposeful bustle of the command room had resumed, but I re-played the vid on an unending loop in my mind. Apparently, I had just spent the past two days immersed in debilitating grief. Nolan was right: I needed to see it, but perhaps not for the reasons he thought.

"Thank you," I said to Nyla, my hand on one of her lower arms.

On the outside, I was calm. Inside, I was a nova. Watching the Tro-gi captain mercilessly kill Cri had stirred a dark rage within me. God-will and the Captain had earned special places in the Void I would create for them. The vid made my purpose tangible; it eliminated all doubt. I teetered on the precipice of the dark, destructive action.

Ray, AI said, *I'm so sorry.*

Shut up, AI. It was pointless to hide my fury from him.

"Raystar," Broodmother said, breaking the silence, "we have been discovered. We must break the blockade and leave Nem'. Which brings us to you."

"My Queen," First Claw interjected, "A second Battlegroup has ar-rived. Its designation is the 301st. The 98th is repositioning its forces to intercept, but we need more information. Given the current pace of escalation, we are but one Hiveship against thousands of Dread-noughts. We seem to have a small window of confusion within which we can take action. After that, escape seems unlikely."

Broodmother tilted her head and replied, "The Human machines are rallying for another assault. Godwill knows that the Crynits on Nem' have sided with the so-called Assassins of the Asrigards. And if the Storm Wall completes its transformation…."

"Broodmother," I interjected, "we do have options." All eyes turned to me. I walked over to the conference table in front of her command chair.

"These," I said, removing the pair of small but lethal triggers from my pocket and placing them on the table, "are the detonators for the bomb underneath our"—I paused to swallow hard—"my home."

Infection? I called to him. AI was too soft. I needed to be cold right now.

I AM HERE.

You have access to the "eyes-and-ears" recordings, I asked. *Display them now. Highlights only.*

A holo suddenly appeared above us, startling everyone except me. First Claw seemed especially disconcerted, as we were using Hive-Home's systems to display the recordings on multiple screens.

The recordings began to fast forward through the critical past few days, revealing everything that Cri had heard and seen, recorded by the military tattoos Dad had given her. It slowed to real time for key moments—the prison camp, the torture, our escape. It was all there. Mieant gasped as the recordings reached the point when Cri told him for the first time that she loved him. He gazed into her eyes tenderly and stammered "I love you" in response.

And then, there it was, irrefutable evidence: Cri at a communication terminal in the NanoEmporium, talking to Godwill.

"Of course you will be taken in, child. The Heir cares for you. You are his blood," Godwill said, his face horribly contorted. He shot her a cold smile, exposing his bloody purple gums. Was he trying to project kindness? His cavernous black eyes always gave away the evil beneath. I gulped. Couldn't she *see* him, the monster in front of her?

"I don't want anyone to get hurt. I just want to see my parents," Cri said, her black hair flowing over her eyes as she spoke to him through the terminal.

"Force is always a last resort, child," he said solemnly. "Your parents are safe, reunited. And when you join them, you will once again be a family—a pure *Glean* family."

"You'll bring Mieant to me?"

"Cri Ceridian, Ascendant, upon my honor."

"And Raystar?" she asked in a quavering voice.

He smiled, stretching his lips back over his yellowed teeth. "Surrender yourself to the group of soldiers stationed by the large holo screen. They will take you in. All will be fine."

"But…."

He frowned at her, his old self shining through his poorly acted façade. "Your parents await you, Cri. They ask about you every day."

We collectively gasped. Cri had betrayed us—and then she had been betrayed.

FOOL.

Shut your hole! AI shouted.

Quiet, both of you! Transfer these recordings to the personal AIs of Nyla, Nolan, Broodmother, and Mieant. Give them everything recorded by Cri's tattoos, I told Infection.

This had been the second element of my plan. I knew that Cri's tattoos had recorded everything she'd witnessed since that day in school, providing an irrevocable, first-person record of Godwill's lies, his genocide, his crimes. Cri had long forgotten about them, but they were the key to justice against Godwill. I wasn't able to think clearly—frankly, it was hard to even breathe—but personal stuff like that didn't matter anymore.

Nyla looked curiously at her personal AI.

"You all have these recordings now," I said to her, then looked at my companions. "You all do."

Nyla's eyes widened as she realized the implications. I nodded.

"Nova! Do you realize what this means?" Nyla shouted, her reporter instincts taking over. "We can broadcast this across Nem'. This will buy us time with the planet's legal authorities. Even if his coup has already been successful, Godwill must respond to this evidence."

"No," I said. All heads swiveled again to face me. "I mean, yes to that. But we need to send it out across the entire Convergence, not just Nem'. Every Citizen in the Convergence needs to know what's happening in Quadrant 4."

Nyla's golden eyes glowed like suns. "Oh, my Architect! Brilliant!"

"Raystar Ceridian, I wish that we did not now need your brilliance. I wish instead that we could meet over food and good company, as we discussed when we met for the first time that day at your school," a warm, feminine voice chimed in from behind us.

Freela Asrigard, clad in a simple set of red utility overalls, had entered the command center at some point while we were occupied with watching the recordings. Her grey-streaked black, shoulder-length hair framed a set of large black eyes, full lips, and a thin, regal nose. Unlike most Lethians, whose mouths curved down at the edges, Freela's curved up into a red-blue smile. Her face was symmetrical, aristocratic, and lovely. She looked kind. "However, your plan is precisely what is needed now. And, it seems, you are as well."

"Mom!" Mieant yelled joyfully. He leapt toward her and wrapped her in a hug; even though she was much taller, the embrace rocked her backward several steps. A smile lit up her face like the dawn.

Freela drew him close to her chest. "My beloved child," she said adoringly. The intimacy was all-consuming, total. I looked away.

"Raystar?" Instead of touching me, Freela moved around to the place where I'd cast my eyes, clearly showing respect for my state of mind. "I am so sorry, Raystar, about Cri." After I didn't respond, she continued. "Thank you for saving me. My husband. Perhaps even Quadrant 4."

"Where is Father?" Mieant asked, frowning. Freela traded a look with Broodmother.

Oh, great. Parental secrets.

"His autodoc was damaged. As a result, we are being more cautious with his exit from stasis. Broodmother's finest physicians are working on him and taking him through the extraction process. Our prognosis is 100 percent full recovery, thanks to Broodmother Krig's gracious support." Freela smiled and dipped her head toward Broodmother, who returned the gesture of respect.

I wasn't paying full attention to the scene playing out in front of me. I simply couldn't escape the image of Cri and Godwill talking, of my sister's ignorance and spite leading her to collude with evil—it was burned in my brain.

Freela turned to Nyla and Nolan, whose jaws were literally hanging open. "Ah, you are the GNN team that covered our visit at the school. You two have a knack for being at the right place at the right time. And now, you find yourselves at a pivotal point in Convergence history."

Nonch, my best friend in the Universe, rose to his full height and glanced at Freela and Nyla before turning to his mother. "Broodmother, I have a lack of understanding," he said. "I understand that our circumstances are dire and dangerous, but what is it that we are pivoting toward?"

Freela chuckled warmly in response. "That is the important question, young Nonch, Prime of Broodmother Krig," she replied. "Several months ago, Jurisdictor Xzaris Alenion, Nem's appointed Jurisdictor, suddenly stopped reporting to us. My husband and I placed the 301st Battlegroup on full alert, with orders to monitor Nem' and to be prepared to intercede or to protect the planet should any suspicious activity occur. Extracting us from Nem' was also part of their mission.

She turned to face First Claw as she continued. "I assure you, Commander, the 301st is far more capable than any standard Convergence Battlegroup. We have access to Governor's-eyes-only, encrypted communication channels, so you may coordinate your response with their efforts using our channels. The 301st is, in fact, our personal guard."

An entire Battlegroup designated to guard the Co-Governors? Um, okay. Quadrant 4 had more than 500 star systems and made up fully a third of the Convergence, so it made sense…I just hadn't thought it through before. *Great nova!* The 98th Battlegroup probably freaked when the 301st showed up.

"When Xzaris stopped communicating with us, our initial belief was that there was a transmission problem. Communication with Nem' has always been difficult, no doubt because so much ancient Human tech is located here. But Xzaris's silence was perfectly timed with our move to Nem'—a little too perfect. And, of course, our classified objective of meeting Raystar."

Nonch's sensor stalks twitched as he considered Freela's words. He shook his head. "I am still not understanding."

"When we issued our orders to the 301st, we were unaware that the 98th was already in transit to Nem'. When we arrived and found that Xzaris Alenion was not here, we suspected that he had met his death at the hands of Godwill. If we are right about who sent the 98th, young one, we are not facing just a planetary coup on Nem'. This is a Convergence-wide conflagration."

"That would be…" Nonch began.

"Civil war," Broodmother finished for him.

The past sucks. Like, millennia level sucking. More than 1,800 years ago, there was a war between Humans and Lethians. *That apparently hasn't ended yet.*

Ten days ago, I had been helping Dad tend our 'natch fields. *Which I hated.* Nine days ago, I'd started school. Today? We were in the midst of a civil war. Today was the present, so the present was also in serious danger of sucking.

"Remarkable," Broodmother said, breaking up my negative reverie. I suspected she might be conducting her own parallel review of events, because her remark was addressed more to the air than to Freela. "Our plans shift, then, from 'assured destruction,' to 'remain alive until the reinforcements arrive.' That is cause for hope, I suppose." She paused and waved a claw arm at the time reader on the display wall. "But when?"

We all looked up at the floating time reader display, pretty standard: time, day, week, month, and year.

"If that time reader is correct, the 301st Battlegroup has already arrived in the system. I believe early GNN reports stated that the 98th was repositioning around the planet to meet the new threat," Freela replied.

"Mom?" Mieant said, shooting her a look that was the kid version of "what the nova?"

"My son, the 301st is our elite guard. We called them here. They are—and we are—uh, how do you kids say it, 'the good guys.'"

I sucked in a deep breath imbued with hope. The good guys having a chance, finally, was a refreshingly new idea. Could we overcome them? I was beginning to believe that we could.

"Nyla, Nolan," I shouted, "you have to record this, us, right now! Show us all together with Freela! Interview her! Interview Broodmother Krig! Then, send the data packet out to the Convergence!" I hadn't even finished the first sentence when Nolan began to activate his experian drones in silent agreement. "Document everything," I continued impatiently, "because *we* are the Recorders now! *We* will determine the history."

"Will you accompany us when we go with Raystar to the Mesas?" Nonch asked Nyla.

"No," Broodmother interrupted, "they will not. Nor will you."

"Broodmother?" Nonch questioned carefully. His sensor stalks straightened above his huge head, shadowing his primary eye orbs so their black surface seemed even darker than usual.

"But for Raystar, you were lost to me." She shook her head slowly side to side. Silence filled the room as Nonch publicly lost the age-old "can I go outside to play?" parent-child battle. "You will remain here, where you will be safe."

Mieant coughed softly. We all turned to him, anticipating his words.

"My parents…I can't leave them now. I can't lose them again," he stammered as he lowered his eyes. "Raystar, I owe you. We Asrigards owe you. You saved Mother and Father at the school attack, and now you've reunited us. I have lost Cri, but I have them back now. I…I'm sorry."

He reached for his mother and clung to her side.

Oh. Okay. No contest.

"Surely we cannot let this brave girl go by herself?" Freela Asrigard exclaimed. She was every bit as regal as her clarion voice. Her stature compensated for her rumpled appearance—a casualty of being in the autodoc. Her warm black eyes and the smile lines creased around her mouth left no doubts regarding her benevolence. Or her ability to command. I swore that I could detect a very un-Lethian pair of dimples just waiting to show themselves on her otherwise stoic face. And yet, she wanted her son safe.

So, I mean, sure. Forget me. Someone *should go with Raystar, but that someone should be* someone else's *child.*

The bitter bile of abandonment almost didn't rise to the back of my throat. Almost.

One of Freela's arms was wrapped around her son, but she placed her other hand gracefully on my shoulder and looked down at me with what could only be described as kindness and empathy.

Broodmother Krig regarded me from her dark heights, her jeweled eyes sparkling like galaxies. "Indeed. This Human has earned more than we are willing to give. Our fear—our selfishness, more accurately—is a gap of shame between what we say we ought to do and what we actually do."

YOU MUST GO TO THE BASE ALONE, Infection boomed.

It's right, Raystar, AI chimed in. *The base—if it's active—will recognize any other species as an enemy.*

I AM NOT AN "IT."

My shoulders sagged. I knew it was true. I *did* need to go alone.

Broodmother continued, "I will send a squad of soldiers and a detachment of Eviscerators to accompany you. This compliment of troops should at least get you—"

"I apologize for interrupting, Broodmother," I muttered. Whether we were allies or not, a creature as small as I was had to step lightly around a creature large enough to eat me as a snack. "But I have to do this alone."

Everyone began to talk at once, but I continued over the din.

"The Human base will most likely accept only me. While I am the outsider here"—I gestured around the control room—"inside the base, you would be the outsiders...the aliens."

Nolan's vid recorder blinked red in the ensuing silence, capturing everything. For my whole life, I'd been totally unique among a mix of multitudes. If what I believed was true, then inside the New Mars base, I'd be immersed in my people, surrounded by Humans. I would be, for the very first time ever, a member of the majority. Anyone who came with me would be "different" from the rest of "us" and probably quite unwelcome.

Huh. How bizarre. I shook my head.

"What *is* your plan, Raystar-Friend?" Nonch asked.

"First, we need to create a distraction." I picked up the detonators from the conference table where I'd left them and bounced them—gently—in my hands with a half-smile. "Second, we need to break this blockade. And third, I need to get to the base. Are we agreed?"

Broodmother tilted her head and regarded me. "I believe we can agree on these priorities, Raystar. I will add that my priority is keeping HiveHome safe and breaking free of Nem's blockade." She paused and eyed me, "This means that once plans are in motion, I will not be able to aid you in any way, ally mine."

I swallowed.

Freela folded her arms across her stomach and nodded. "There are

games within games. My husband and I have been positioning and preparing the Quadrant for this moment."

Freela paused. The kindness in her face vanished as she fixed each of us with a deadly serious gaze. "Let me be clear: from the perspective of the Lethian Empress, what we are talking about is secession. Treason. Actions that constitute capital crimes. Trillions of our Citizens will be affected by our actions. We must proceed with resolve, and most importantly, good judgment."

"Humans," Broodmother Krig mused, "are at the center of conflict once again. This time, let us hope they are part of our salvation."

I cleared my throat before speaking.

"Here's what I propose...."

Everyone—Crynits, Gleans, Lethians, artificial intelligences—crowded around me (and in my head) to listen to my plan.

67

"You are mad, Raystar of Terra," Broodmother said, breaking the silence at last.

As I'd gone through the plan, I'd watched Broodmother and Freela most closely, drawing as many cues as I could from their fluctuating expressions. Freela's expression had grown progressively stern as I'd gone on. Now, she stood opposite me, her arms crossed. She tapped one finger on her outside arm.

"GYUH! Gyuhgyuh! Ah haah! Gyuh! Aha! Oh," Nyla said—or should I say, she guffawed. Everyone shot her silent, serious stares, but it took a nudge from Nolan to stop her laughter.

"Oh, come on. You can't be serious," Nyla said, smearing away moisture from the corner of one eye with a finger. "Wait. You are serious. Broodmother, come on. You can't put the fate of your Hiveship at risk based on the plan of a child!"

Nolan poked his smaller, silver-haired colleague's shoulder with a massive finger. "Nye. Stop talking."

Before turning back to her thoughts, Broodmother looked at Nyla much like a gratcher considers its dinner.

Nyla took a step back and muttered, mostly to herself, "Everyone's lost their minds."

Broodmother dipped her head and then turned to me. Freela moved to her side. "Raystar," she said, "there is much risk involved in what you ask of us."

"Broodmother," Freela said, tapping her blue lower lip with a finger, "liberation of the planet, I believe, means getting to the Mesas. Saving ourselves means getting your Hiveship off planet and into space. The 98th is now aware of the existence of this ship. The 301st Battlegroup is in transit, and that coming reinforcement will distract the 98th's primary forces. My forces should arrive in time to provide air cover for your ship, which gives you time to provide air cover for Raystar. Even if she doesn't survive the 'distraction' or doesn't make it to the New Mars base, the presence of the 301st and Raystar's initiative increase our odds of escaping off planet. The child's plan is less craxy than it sounds. Nevertheless, it is a dangerous gambit."

"I will not permit this ship to be taken by Godwill's forces," Broodmother replied with steel in her voice. I was watching leadership in action between two heads of state, decisiveness based on intelligence.

Freela nodded her agreement. "Let us act now, before the enemy can organize further."

At that moment, Commander First Claw appeared in an alert holo over Broodmother's chair. He was surrounded by junior officers helping direct the mobilization. His sensor stalk twitched as he turned to face us.

"For the Hive," he said in greeting to Broodmother Krig before briefly disappearing from the screen as he bowed deeply. "My Queen, the formation of the ships blockading Nem' has changed dramatically over the past ten minutes. Significant portions of the 98th Battlegroup have moved from their previous positions and are moving toward the solar system's stable Lagrange point." He paused a moment before continuing. "They seem to be positioning for a major engagement. Only a clawful of Dreadnoughts remain screening the planet at this time—eight of them, to be precise. One is positioned above Blue River. Another hovers above the Mesas, and the remaining six are located above Ever."

Events were happening as we had anticipated.

Broodmother nodded. "So, the 301st has arrived. What are the ranges of our primary shields, First Claw?"

First Claw examined a readout before replying. "We can extend them a little over ten kilometers without damaging Blue River or

Nem's atmosphere with our power output. The closer in we keep the shields, the safer things will be. However, that also increases the probability that an impact from the Dreadnought's primary weapon will penetrate our defenses."

"That is more than sufficient. HiveHome will face only two Dreadnoughts, as the remaining six are at ranges where we can engage one-on-one before they converge and mass against us," Broodmother said. "First Claw, prepare HiveHome for planetary departure. Sound general quarters. Inform me of our earliest departure time."

"By your command," he said, and then his image disappeared.

She turned to us to issue the next steps. "Well, Raystar, you have your air cover. HiveHome is a highly upgraded Assassin Class Dreadnought that under any circumstances can hold its own against multiple Lethian Dreadnoughts. Even so, we will need to maximize the element of surprise. Plus, we do not know what improvements have been made to these Convergence Dreadnoughts."

"Per the plan, we will extend our shields, which will protect you from bombardment. It will also eliminate any sort of atmospheric flight within the shields, except for vehicles with small power plants, such as your dart or smaller air cars. You will, for a short time, be out of the reach of the Dreadnought over the Mesas. Their atmospheric attack ships will not function inside the shield, and the vehicles on the outside will be unable to get in. It is the most I can do, and it will not last long. As soon as the Dreadnought's commander realizes that a fully functional Assassin Class Hiveship lies under his belly, he and his command crew will have to clean up the messes they will make in their flight suits. But not soon after, the Dreadnought over Blue River will join its attack on us. A Hiveship has not engaged in a conflict with Lethian Dreadnoughts for more than three millennia—well before the Lethian–Human conflict. You must reach the Mesas before this happens."

I swallowed. Thinking about plans and actually executing them were different things entirely. The HiveHome rising up from the planet to do battle with Lethians would be HUGE, HISTORIC!

"Or?" I said in a small voice.

"Or you will be crushed by debris when HiveHome lifts up from underground," Broodmother replied. "You will be incinerated by the

temperature increase as energy beams heat up our shields. You will suffocate as all nearby oxygen is consumed by the fires caused by nuclear energy. If our shields fail, a quarter of this hemisphere will be destroyed as our antimatter cores ignite, while the combined firepower of the Dreadnoughts focuses on us and we go nova."

She paused for a moment before adding, "As for that last part, you would already be dead long before that happened."

I smiled wanly and nodded.

Broodmother nodded her assent as well. "So we should leave now."

I nodded again.

IT IS A GOOD PLAN, Infection said. *ELIMINATING EXPOSURE TO CONVERGENCE ATTACKS HAS INCREASED OUR CHANCES OF SUCCESS TO 23.6 PERCENT: A SIGNIFICANT IMPROVEMENT. HOWEVER, GETTING THERE BEFORE THIS SHIP EMERGES AND FINDING AN ENTRANCE…THOSE VARIABLES DRIVE THE SUCCESS RATE DOWN CONSIDERABLY. ADDITIONALLY, I DO NOT KNOW WHAT TYPE OF OPPOSITION YOU MAY ENCOUNTER IN THE RUINS.*

I stammered a wan mental response: *Whahhh?*

THERE IS A CREATURE IN THE HUMAN RUINS, ONE LIKE US. I SENSED ITS PRESENCE. IT MATCHES THE CREATURE FROM YOUR MEMORIES OF GODWILL'S LABORATORY.

I gritted my teeth as I remembered the horrible memories of my escape from Godwill's prison and my battle with the thing I knew as IT-ME. He was a once-Human boy named Artem who had been fully converted into nano, as Infection had been designed to do to me.

Destiny averted.

Yes, Raystar, AI said, *IT-ME is still out there.*

"And what about us?" Nyla said, her platinum bangs swishing around her red face and golden eyes. Even Nyla's ambition was dwarfed by the circumstances.

"Your task of broadcasting Cri's 'eyes and ears' recordings to the Convergence," Freela said, "is of critical importance to this plan."

Nyla and Nolan traded heavy "are-you-with-me" glances and then nodded affirmatively at Freela.

Broodmother said, "Say your farewells, Raystar. A squad of soldiers and Eviscerators will escort you back to your parents' compound. Take whatever weapons and medical supplies you will need." She tilted her head toward the guard who'd escorted Freela into the room—a clear directive that he would be entrusted with my safety.

"By your command, my Queen," the guard replied. "When you are ready, Raystar of Terra, I will lead your escort to your home compound."

I nodded to the guard and turned to face my friends. It was the last moment of companionship I could savor before assuming the responsibility that was mine alone.

68

"I didn't like you, originally," Mieant said as he flashed me a lopsided grin. He spared a glance toward his mother, who gazed at him curiously. I'm sure she'd never seen her son so friendly with a Human before. "I couldn't figure out why we'd left Solium4, and what was so important about one single Human. I know now. Don't die, Raystar."

I hugged him. His body shook as he added in a whisper, "I miss her. So much."

My eyes burned as I felt the wetness of his grey cheeks in my matted hair. He pulled away.

"She loved you. You should know that. It was just…the Heir taking your parents, it broke her. And increasingly, everything that happened seemed to be about you."

I looked at his streaked face and scraped a wet strand of my purple hair out of my eyes with the tip of my finger.

"Oh, Mieant, I—" I began to shake with sobs. Mieant reached out and hugged me again, fiercely. The air was squashed out of my lungs. "I—"

He responded with a split-colored smile and a demand: "Drop them into the largest and deepest gravity well!"

"What…ah…huuh…will you do?" I asked after he released me and sweet, sweet oxygen filled my lungs once again.

"Assuming HiveHome doesn't nova," he said, "I'm sure my parents will work to marshal forces. I'll be helping them."

"Take care of Nonch. Don't forget about me."

"This is not goodbye, Raystar."

"Mieant," I replied, "c'mon now. Our plan doesn't include going back to school. You'll be back in Solium4, and I'm sure, I'll be who knows where. We didn't really plan for what comes after."

I moved to leave, only to find myself encircled in Freela's strong arms. Her embrace felt like Mom's.

"Child," she whispered to me, "you are so brave. I wish we could do more for you in the short term. You have returned to us our lives, our family." She paused as she began to choke on her regret, her loss.

I looked at her intently. In my thirteen years, no one outside of my family had seen me as anything other than a stigma, a scar, a freak, a mark of disgrace…a Human. I felt like in this moment of goodbye, everyone was finally seeing the real *me,* for the very first time.

"Here," Freela said, rummaging through her pocket. She grabbed my hand and stuffed something in it. "Don't lose it."

I uncurled my fingers to find a data card.

"Well, it's coded to you, so even if you do lose it, it will still work. But definitely try not to lose it." She paused and smiled. "It serves a lot of purposes: it's a form of money; it provides you with direct access to me through encrypted communication; and most importantly, it also serves as a Governor's waiver. You are a diplomat now. It entitles you to automatic release from any legal matter, anything—at least, within Quadrant 4."

I hugged her back and shoved the data card in my pocket. Everything was happening too quickly. Speed was lessening my ability to think, to clearly focus on any one thing.

"I do not know what this means for your promise to me, Raystar-Friend," a voice sounded in my ear. I spun around to find myself face to face with my oldest friend. His predatory mandibles were pointed low. All of his eyes—the two upper orange ones and six lower matte-black ones—regarded me carefully, and his sensor stalks were gently pressed against my head and shoulders.

"Shells," I said gently, "Nova. You'll be off-planet before I am."

"Raystar, that is not the spirit of my request," he said flatly. "Despite Broodmother's awareness and power, I *will* disobey her, and she *will* be forced to act. Now, dear Cri is dead, and Broodmother and Mieant's parents are committed to the plan. Now comes war, rebellion. It is as I had feared. The moment is upon us."

I breathed deeply, grasped his mandibles, pulled his head down, and gently kissed the flat part of the blade. "Shells," I said, "you're my best friend." Then I pulled him even closer, so only he could hear me. "Protect Nyla. Her news feeds are critical to the plan, and I have a bad feeling about her and Nolan."

"I understand her importance to this new world, and I will do my best. But you do not understand. I am on the path to become First Claw. It may not come for many cycles, but right now, I cannot openly disobey any of Broodmother's direct orders. It is our way. If I deny Broodmother anything, she will be forced to kill me to make way for another. But I will not fight."

What?

"Shells," I said as I reached over to gently shake his mandibles, his pillow-weight sensor stalks fluffed around my head, "I know Broodmother. There's no way she'd do that. You're her Prime. She loves you."

Nonch backed away and nodded. "Perhaps you are right. Perhaps we will meet again. And she *is* listening."

Sure enough, Broodmother was standing close by, observing as her ancient enemy and her Prime were saying their goodbyes. She moved toward me, and Nonch backed away, with a bow.

"Honor to you, Raystar of Terra," she said. "Thank you for what you have done for my Prime. I see your friendship, and how you count him as one of your own. I thank you for what you are doing for…me. You know nothing about our ways, and yet you may have given me a path toward…a redemption of sorts." She sighed before continuing. "We have little room for indecision. Make your choices and fight well. With luck, we may all meet again. You are my ally. Remember that." She bowed and thrummed past me, into memory.

Nova. I was really going to do this. It's go time.

"Are we there yet?"

The Crynit guard seated across the shuttle bay from me glanced at me with clear irritation. He'd been tightening a weapon on his armor when I posed the question. He turned his attention back to the weapon.

"Seriously, I need to know if we're close. So, are we almost there?" I replied to his raised sensor stalk, the Crynit equivalent of a raised eyebrow. We had been flying for what felt like—to me—at least a year. Or maybe it had been ten minutes. Time was beginning to compress into light-shifting surfaces of Galactic motion.

"We will be there shortly, Human," the pilot grumbled over the intercom.

"Oh, okay," I replied, "but you said that before."

"We are close."

"I have to pee." It was sad, but true.

"Human, do you believe you could have taken care of that prior to our departure?" he replied testily.

I frowned. I really did have to pee. Like, *now*.

"If I had known we'd be flying across the planet, I would have said something sooner."

"We are not flying across…" the pilot said, and then paused as the meaning hit him. "Ah. Sarcasm. It is not productive."

We rode on for another minute in silence.

"So seriously, are we close?"

The intercom made a clicking noise. I frowned at the guard, who was edging slightly away from me, and pointed at the intercom speaker. "Did…did he just turn me off?"

My indignation was short lived, as the shuttle began to slow down and descend. Because there were no viewing screens or portals, I couldn't tell where exactly we were setting down.

Right now, the Universe crumbling around us can wait, I thought. *My bladder is screaming for a landing.*

The intercom clicked again. "We have arrived," the pilot said with finality. The shuttle's door swooshed open to reveal a lush, green 'natch field. Further in the distance, lights from my family's compound, my former life, beckoned, but nature was calling, desperately.

"Is there…?" I began to ask the guard. I honestly couldn't tell if I really needed to relieve myself, or if the impulse was simply a manifestation of nerves.

"ON THE LEFT," the guard next to me said a bit too loudly. "The shuttle's biological waste depository is on the left." I was already on my way into said compartment before he'd finished saying "left" the first time.

The guard was waiting for me at the open doorway. Banefire's glare, resplendent and welcoming, poured into the shuttle bay. I glanced back sheepishly at the biological waste depository.

"Lesson learned. Go before you've got to go," I sighed to myself as I walked up to stand behind the Crynit guard.

"You are procrastinating, Human," the guard said. He was right.

They were dropping me off just beyond where the enormous Hiveship would emerge from its subterranean lair, but not quite as far as my family's farm. I needed to be far away from HiveHome when it emerged—you know, because of the whole being crushed by metric tons upon tons of soil thing. It boggled my mind to think of how large HiveHome must be. Convergence Dreadnoughts were huge, but a Crynit Assassin Class Dreadnought was much, much longer. I wondered just how much of Blue River was built on top of it.

Nem's load would certainly be lighter once the Crynit ship left its atmosphere.

"Human," the guard said, fully facing me, "I have only heard rumors of your plan, but know that our lives depend on you." I blinked; he continued. "And I have heard stories of you. They are worthy stories. Good hunting, little one."

Right. I nodded, grateful for his words, and stepped down the ramp.

The fragrance of verdant 'natch, along with alternating scents of rich soil and burning metal, greeted my nose. After I'd walked about thirty meters away from the shuttle, it cloaked itself and whooshed up into the air. It may have been invisible, but a vast patch of 'natch stalks were thrust outward and down by the powerful exhaust of the unseeable ship. It was returning to its home, and leveled 'natch was all that was left to prove its existence.

I was now alone on Nem'.

My family's farmland and the fields around it had changed. I poofed a strand of purple hair out of my eyes and took in the scene as I cradled the detonators in my pocket with one hand.

Orange fires shrouded in black smoke dotted the countryside. Winds swept the smoke about like seaweed caught in a current. Many of the normally unbroken fields of emerald 'natch were brown and bare in swaths where the fires had already burned themselves out. The fires were all that remained of the ships our compound's defense system had destroyed as we'd made our desperate underground escape from Godwill.

In drier parts of the 'natch fields, fires continued to cyclone toward the sky, dragging sparks and smoke upward. The ground itself was on fire because of us.

Banefire, Nem's massive red sun, took up half the daytime sky, which meant that it was about noon. But Banefire's full arc was abbreviated by the kilometers-wide, grey-blue underbelly of the Convergence Dreadnought suspended in the sky. It was so big that it made me dizzy just to look up at it. Blue fireflies—ships, thousands of them—danced along its seemingly random geometry. They swarmed around the behemoth, their atmosphere drives appearing as tiny blue twinkles as they sped off to their various destinations.

I had expected that. What I *hadn't* expected was that the Storm Wall would still be around, nor did I expect to see the shape it was in.

Roughly every six weeks, the Storm Wall would gather to atmospheric heights and scrape the planet in a path from the Mesas mountain range at the north pole of Nem', near my family home, to an identical range at the south pole. It rose as high as Nem's outer atmosphere, and at its base, it was kilometers thick, a rage of storms within storms. High winds. Hail. Rain. Lightning thicker and longer than the tallest spires of Blue River arced up from its purple and black interior.

The Storm Wall clearly had something to do with the Mesas, which meant it had something to do with Humankind. Over the 1,800 years since Nem' had been colonized, the Convergence hadn't gotten any closer to figuring out what the Storm Wall did, other than destroying anything in its path that wasn't well-shielded—except 'natch. For some strange reason, stupid 'natch seemed unaffected by it. Why a lowly vegetable would escape its wrath was a mystery.

The Storm Wall had risen when we'd been first been captured by Godwill, and of course it plagued us as we traversed Blue River to meet with Podmaster and Alar. Even though Broodmother had warned me, I expected it to have crawled its devastating course across the planet by this point.

I certainly didn't expect to see it stretching so high into the atmosphere right now, or to be more massive than I ever remembered before. The mysterious force roiled upward into the heavens and stretched out on each side, toward the equator. Thunder shook the ground in a continuous drumroll. Lightning reached out from the swirling depths to claw at the Dreadnought above me. Any of the small ships that exited the Dreadnought and were unlucky enough to be near the snaking lightning flared out of existence like insects drawn toward a nanozapper.

Contrary to logic, the lightning didn't actually touch the Dreadnought, because its shields held its deadly arcs and building-sized tendrils at bay. Flares of vibrant green would bounce from the shield each time a bolt would try to penetrate its defenses; for now, at least, the Dreadnought seemed to be keeping the storm's destructive force at bay.

But this new and very angry Storm Wall made the Convergence ship look *small*. There was no doubt that the Dreadnought's days

would be numbered if it were vulnerable to the Wall's fury. Everything is relative, I suppose, and "large" is contextual.

The storm pulsed, undulated, and roiled, like any good planetary-sized storm should, but it was stationary and disappeared in an orderly line below the horizon. I watched it a moment more. In comparison with its planetary scale, I wasn't even an insect—maybe a grain of sand. From where I stood, it sure didn't seem like any absolute standard of magnitude applied.

Enough, I thought. *This grain of sand has things to do.*

Void me. Would you look at the Storm Wall? AI said softly.

IT IS BROKEN, hollered Infection in my head.

Broken? I asked, wincing at Infection's volume. *How did Infection learn to shout, anyway?*

IS IT NOT OBVIOUS? EITHER THE DREADNOUGHT IS KEEP-ING THE STORM WALL FROM ITS PURPOSE, OR THE ENTITY CONTROLLING THE STORM WALL IS STUDYING THE DREAD-NOUGHT.

The entity controlling the Storm Wall is studying the Dreadnought? PeaceMaker? That isn't disturbing at all, AI snarked. *Not even remotely.*

Does this impact our plans at all? I asked my mental companions with a slight frown. AI's comment troubled me. He knew more about Nem', and about Human tech, than anyone I'd ever met. If he hadn't been making sarcastic, snarky comments my entire life, I would have thought that his joke just now was a deflection. If it was, why wouldn't he tell us, or me, what he knew?

Only Infection offered a response. *IF THE DREADNOUGHT IS DESTROYED, WE WILL PERISH. IF THE STORM WALL STARTS ITS PLANETARY MARCH, WE MIGHT PERISH. BOTH ARE BE-YOND OUR CONTROL.*

I shrugged and kept wading through the field. In the "now," only my plan mattered, and I was nearing my family's compound. As I got close, I was relieved to find that the Dreadnought that had fired on our compound, the one that ultimately overloaded our shields, hadn't also destroyed the house, the toolshed, the gratcher pen, and the massive hangar. The compound's buildings were intact, which meant that the weapons and shields might be functional as well.

The huge set of blood-red metallic pillars spaced evenly in a circle around our compound bristled with sensors. A single but very large autocannon sat atop each pillar, and like angry gargoyles, the cannons were designed to track everything that entered or departed the compound's sphere. The smoldering plasma that lurked within in each cannon's set of twin barrels normally gave them the appearance of bloodshot monster eyes, but now they hung lifelessly, pointed at the ground.

The pillars didn't just serve as autocannon perches—they were force-dome generators that created the defensive shield around our compound. The Dome, as we called it, was so thick that it distorted reality around the farm with a shimmering field thicker than I was tall. It had been the security system for my home.

I sighed. Wind swirled through the dusty compound just like the tempest of emotions within me. *Mom. Dad. Cri.* As I walked the grounds that I'd called home my whole life, these ghosts in my heart threatened to tear me apart. I was so absorbed that I didn't notice a nearby stench until the shadow of its owner blocked out Banefire's glow.

"SQUEAAAA!" it thundered.

The sound I'd intended to let out was a battle cry, but only an "eeeeek!" emerged. I stumbled forward, got tangled in 'natch, and fell over on my butt. My heart pounded against my ribs, and breath wouldn't come to me. I lay there, gasping, as 5,000 kilos of gratcher—Chunks, our mammoth herd leader—loomed over me.

Gratcher and eggs had always been my favorite breakfast. But then Chunks saved us, and in doing so, he proved his raw (no pun intended) intelligence to me. I knew I'd never eat gratcher again, and I hoped he felt the same way about me.

You wouldn't eat me, would you, Chunks? It was a relevant question. *Nova and gravity wells! I wouldn't be worth the effort.*

Chunks towered over me; he was massive. He tilted his tusked head to the side and glared down at me with one jaundiced pig eye. Then he snorted and shifted his head so he could look at me with the other one.

"Shut up, AI," I whispered back.

I WILL NOT BE CONSUMED BY THIS CREATURE. RAYSTAR, DO SOMETHING. KEEP IN MIND THAT I STILL HAVE THE—

Quiet, both of you! Please.

I propped myself up, reached into a pocket—slowly—and grabbed a cluster of nutribars. After ripping them open and wadding them into a fist-sized ball of brown goo, I stretched my spindly little arm out, palm up, and invited Chunks to consume the nutriball. He whuffled a cloud of his steamy pig breath on me before extending his slimy red tongue, which was quite literally the length of my entire body, and delicately lifted the ball from my hand. As I watched it disappear into his maw, I sat there amazed by how such a huge creature could possibly do something so delicate, so gentle.

The wind gusted. Thunder boomed. Chunks whuffled again, turned, and wandered back toward the compound as silently as he had appeared, keeping one pig eye trained on me at all times. I could see the rest of the herd nuzzling around the property—maybe it was some comfort to them.

Great gratcher, AI said. *That is one massive pig.*

Yeah.

After noticing the convenient path Chunks had just forged through the 'natch and into the compound's gravel courtyard, I inhaled deeply and strode toward my one and only home.

71

The compound's status as the Convergence's most BORING ARCHI-TECTURAL STRUCTURE EVER remained unchanged. The place was dustier, to be sure, but dust did nothing to soften the place's uber-practical forms and dull-grey, Galactic-alloy "appeal." The square center yard was scattered with the ruins of my parents' Glean assault tank.

At one end of the compound lay the massive gratcher pen where Chunks and his herd had lived before I'd freed them. The toolshed was neatly positioned next to it. On the other side towered the vehicle hangar, which unbeknownst to me throughout my childhood also housed an atmosphere cannon. The huge cannon remained atop the hangar in an aggressive skyward pose—aimed straight at the belly of the Dreadnought. It was mounted on a squat, octagonal turret, and lines like blood vessels glowed red through and around the barrel and over the turret. It was a stern warning to any ground crew: don't dare to approach the war machine, as it stood ready to fire megaton-sized pulses of destruction. I frowned at the atmosphere cannon.

Yeah, AI said, reading my thoughts. *This was never a farmstead, Ray. It was a military base meant to take a pounding from anything and give a little back. It's still mostly still active. In fact*—he paused for a moment before continuing—*I've contacted the house synth, which confirms that it is at nearly 100 percent of capacity.*

The original idea had been to destroy the compound as a dis-traction. The explosion would pull the remaining 98th Battlegroup

ground troops away from HiveHome and draw the interest of the Dreadnought, killing two starbats with one stone. By the time they got there, I'd be long gone.

Memories tugged at my sanity as my boots stirred up dust in the courtyard. I passed the broken hulk of the assault tank and the bushes that Cri and I often pushed each other into before arriving at the kitchen door I'd whipped open and slammed closed a million times. This was—had been—my home. I pulled open the door and stepped inside.

Darkness ruled for a millisecond until the lights flickered and then blazed to life with photon-cold emissions.

"House," I said, "what is your operational readiness?"

All around the kitchen, control screens flickered to life. Various displays were shaded red, green, and yellow, but surprisingly, most were green.

"Raystar Ceridian, acknowledged," the house synth replied. "All remaining active shields and armaments are fully operational. Compound generators at 68 percent of capacity. Nanobot repairs require another two cycles for the compound to become fully operational. The assault tank is non-functional. Your parents' Explorer Class Courier is fully operational, and fuel is at 100 percent."

I blinked as I remembered the chagrin Dad had expressed a few days earlier when he admitted he'd forgotten to fill it up. *A few days ago!* The nova of change that had happened since….

Wait. I'd forgotten all about my parents' ship. That ship added a whole new set of possibilities to my craxy plan.

AI, I thought, *get to the ship. We could use it as a—*

Distraction? he said, completing my sentence. *I can do that. Your parents' ship has shielding, stealth…yeah. I can definitely distract.*

AI flashed green as he and his pendant floated off my neck and toward the basement stairs, which led, I presumed, down to the ship's hangar.

He knew me so well. How could I ever doubt him?

I'd take any advantage I could find. It was time.

"House," I continued, "I need broadcast power to maximum range and a focused beam to the Dreadnought above us. As soon as you make a connection, be prepared to transmit my message."

"Affirmative," the house synth replied. "One moment. Activating communication array."

"Jurisdictor Godwill," I started without ceremony—or rather, before the fear in my gut surged up and ruined my plans. "This is Raystar Ceridian."

No. I wove my anger and fear and loss and sadness into a shredded tapestry of self-confidence that allowed me to continue.

"I stand on Glean territory, and I am invoking the War Treaty. I demand a prisoner exchange: my parents, Sathralea and Nent Asrigard, Ascendants of the Glean Gathering, whom you are holding unlawfully, in return for me. Acknowledge receipt of this formal request."

These were invocations and understandings that I'd learned from my parents. The Lethian–Human War Treaty allowed foreign governments to claim their homes and embassies as sovereign territory, which meant that our farm was part of the Glean Gathering, rather than Convergence or Nem' territory.

Who was I fooling? A kid making demands of a powerful tyrant—willingly, knowingly turning herself over to him? It could happen that way, but during our planning, my allies and I had agreed that it would be highly unlikely that my parents were in Godwill's custody. His past actions—what he'd done to Principal Entarch and Cri, for just two examples—indicated that he always defaulted to betrayal. But if he did deliver my parents, well then, I'd trade myself for them, if need be. But that wasn't the plan.

Calm down, I told myself. *Breathe slowly. We have a plan, and that plan has to work so I can make it to New Mars. I have Freela and Kaleren Asrigard, the freaking Co-Governors of Quadrant 4, on my side, as well as Broodmother Krig, Queen of the Crynits here on Nem' and her gigantic HiveHome. Nonch, Mieant, AI. Allies. Friends. I am not alone!*

I didn't have Cri, of course, but in a craxy, spiritual way, I knew she would be with me. Always.

I refocused my attention to confirm that my conversation with Godwill was being broadcast across *all* channels. Nyla needed to hear everything, too. Squaring my shoulders to face my future, I issued a set of instructions to the house synth.

Okay, then.

It only took a few moments for my enemy to respond.

"Raystar of Terra," Godwill hissed through the kitchen's speakers as his tall, gaunt form materialized in the form of a holo. My own disheveled image no doubt appeared before him on the Dreadnought in the same manner. His grimace was chilling. "I acknowledge you."

I stepped back reflexively, my eyes wide.

"Make this simple, child. Surrender."

Simple? Simple was last summer, when I was working with Dad on our farm under Banefire's red-giant glare, running home through the fields with Cri, eating the best home cooking on Nem' around our family table, viding with my friends, and complaining about going back to school.

That was simple. Simple is over. This? This was war.

"I want assurance of my parents' safety. Proof of life," I replied, narrowing my gaze.

His laugh in response was leathery, raspy. "Assurance," he said as he tipped his head forward in a slight bow. "I assure you that I will count down from five to zero. At zero, my Dreadnought will fire on your 'Glean territory.'" He said the last bit with a smirk and tapped his forefinger against his grey chin. I hated him more than ever in that instant of supreme arrogance.

His mocking dug deep into my subconscious. I remembered how he'd snatched some hair right off my head at school so he could get a

genetic sample. How he'd touched my naked stomach and chest before thrusting a syringe filled with nanosolvent into my heart. I clenched my fists and dug my nails into my palms.

AI? I need you and that ship out of here—NOW.

Just got here, Ray. I am powering it up and—why, look at that! Nent actually filled the tanks. I'll figure out how to meet you at New Mars, or at least I'll give you some signal as to where I'll be.

I swallowed hard. I'd lost him once before—my best non-organic friend.

When I give you the signal, open the hangar doors and take the ship up. Let them see you briefly, and then disappear.

I crossed my fingers that the Courier's cloaking technology would be advanced enough to conceal it from the Dreadnought's sensors. That ship was our ticket off planet—well, it was mine, anyway.

"Five," Godwill said.

"Wait!" I shouted. "I have been partly processed by your nanosolvent. I am dying. The pain…the pain you have inflicted is destroying me." I used my memories of how I'd felt after he'd done those horrible things to infuse my plea with emotion. "I want to make a deal."

Silence, then after a moment, "You are hardly in a position to make anything. Four."

"If I die, you lose everything. We both do." It was true—Godwill needed me alive in order to harvest my nano. Once I was dead, apparently, my nano would become useless. He'd learned that the hard way when "harvesting" other Humans.

"A suicide gambit?" he shouted and then laughed again. "You overvalue yourself, little Human. I have more than enough nano to restart. Lest you forget, I have the nanotech inside me!"

"Look, Godwill…Synest," I said. I noticed that upon hearing me say his full name, he blinked. I nodded knowingly at the slip, at his acknowledgement of what I knew about him.

Ha! If he thinks that's surprising, just wait—there's more! When Nyla's "embedded reporting" is released across the Convergence, every Citizen will know what's happening on Nem' and what Godwill and the Heir have been up to. What will the Heir of the Glean Ascendancy have to say when he's implicated in the coup? And when HiveHome launches? The 98th Battlegroup will literally freak out.

And Godwill will be ruined.

I continued: "I know what you did. I know what it cost you when I destroyed your Human reclamation nano. More Citizens than you know have seen and comprehend your maniacal games. Right now, you don't have me, nor do you have Freela and Kaleren Asrigard. Arrange for the safe passage of my parents to our home, and I'll come to you." I narrowed my eyes. "That's me making it *simple* for you."

I silenced my feed to Godwill so I could deliver instructions to the compound's AI. Plus, I knew the silence would unnerve him.

"House, start intermittent point-defense fire on any inbound ships. Set shields at 60 percent." The compound had to look like an easy target. Godwill needed to think I was vulnerable, and I wanted to attract as many of his ships and troops here as possible.

"Infection," I continued, my sweaty hand gripping the detonators in my pocket like a lucky pair of dice, "send the designated message to Broodmother now. Initiate Phase 2."

Is it possible to be terrified and smug at the same time? I crossed my arms and gazed at the various screens before me. The first revealed AI opening the hangar doors a kilometer away and my parents' silver, needle-shaped Courier floating out above the 'natch fields like abstract art. Instantly, a cloud of atmospheric fighters darted toward the Courier, red tracer fire streaking ahead of their paths. A second later, the silver ship simply vanished. The missiles that sought to destroy it detonated pointlessly into the field in a hail of orange fire, geysers of rich soil, and fluffs of healthy green 'natch.

Yes! The cloaking worked!

Another screen showed a topographic map of the land between our farm and Blue River—twenty or so kilometers of verdant 'natch. Red blobs—energy readings—glowed in an overlay, revealing a massive energy source that stretched for at least half the distance. Right on time! HiveHome was powering up, her ridiculously powerful drives overwhelming her ability to cloak.

Great nova! I thought. *An Assassin-Class Broodship dwarfs a Convergence Dreadnought for sure!*

I looked back at Godwill's holo. His lips were exposing much more of his bloody gums than usual. Clearly, he was seeing the same thing on his own screens: the Courier's escape and a titanic underground warship powering up. And he could not conceal his panic.

"What is this?" he screamed, rage and insanity surging through his skeletal face. I'd driven him completely craxy; he was nowhere near the calculating, in-control state he'd first invaded my life. "What are you…DOING?"

"Haven't you been watching the local news, Synest?" I asked. With intent and motive, I broke my gaze with him and turned distractedly, amusedly to a third screen. I wanted this act to stick. I wanted to drive him even further over the edge into unthinking rage.

"WHAT? I am Jurisdictor Godwill. You will call me by my…"

Aha! I'd gotten under that desiccated grey skin of his!

He took a long pause as he struggled to regain control, but any hope of that disappeared as the last part of Phase 2 appeared on his screens and mine simultaneously.

Nyla's instantly likable face appeared. Her platinum hair, red skin, and golden eyes were as lovely as ever, but her normal good cheer had been replaced with a stone-cold serious mien. Orb-shaped experian drones floated around her to make sure her viewers always had the best angle.

"This is Nyla Jax, breaking a story of literally Galactic proportions. You may know me from my tenure at GNN. Now, I am embedded with the *real* Quadrant 4 government, and we are broadcasting in secret from the Crynit Hiveship known as HiveHome. Listen well: I bring you critical information of such importance that it will shake the entire Convergence," Nyla said.

She paused dramatically. Her almond eyes glowed as she peered into the drones' vid feed.

"Citizens of Nem', we have all been lied to."

The camera pulled back slightly as Nyla continued. "This is breaking news. Do not panic. The key points I will outline now will be supported by recordings and data packets that will follow after this transmission. If you miss this initial broadcast, you can follow me at nyla#Galacticbroadcast for prior and current reports."

Godwill's eyes widened as he opened up another feed—presumably in an attempt to verify that I wasn't tricking him somehow and that Nyla's report was for real.

She resumed without mercy. "The man you know as Jurisdictor Godwill is an impostor. We have obtained incontrovertible proof that he murdered Jurisdictor Xzaris Alenion. His real name is Godwill Synest, and he is an officer in the Lethian Special Forces. Godwill and a group of co-conspirators have somehow taken command of the 98th Battlegroup and are leading a coup to depose Co-Governors Freela and Kaleren Asrigard." Nyla leaned in as another drone picked up a better angle. "That brings me to the next piece of Nem'-shattering news: the Co-Governors, who allegedly had been murdered, are alive and well. They are safe and under protection at an undisclosed location. The Asrigards will make an announcement to Quadrant 4 shortly after this report on nyla#Galacticbroadcast.

"Godwill's plot has led to the capture and kidnapping of Commander Nent Ceridian and Lady Sathralea Ceridian, Ascendant to

the Glean Gathering, and the cold-blooded murder of their eldest daughter, Cri Ceridian, by Godwill's 98th Battlegroup's forces. Their younger daughter, Raystar Ceridian, who has survived repeated attacks by Godwill, is innocent. I repeat: *she is innocent*. There are no assassins of the Asrigards, as they are alive and well."

"Finally, you may have sensed various ground tremors over the last twenty minutes. Our Nem' Crynit population has always lived underground, but unbeknownst to us, their home is in fact an ancient Broodship. This HiveHome, under the command of Broodmother Krig, is now taking to the skies to confront the 98th Battlegroup Dreadnoughts that threaten us all. The move is in support of the 301st Battlegroup, which is under the command of the Co-Governors. The 301st will arrive in a matter of hours from the system's LaGrange point."

"Citizens," she continued, following a long breath, "I implore you to stay indoors for your own safety and to leave your newsfeeds on. Do not panic. After the Co-Governors' announcement, I will broadcast news reports every thirty minutes, each containing more details and proof of Godwill's plot and his murderous actions. I understand that this is a lot to comprehend, but it is vital that you trust the truth of what I am telling you—truth, not the lies you have been fed by Godwill and his accomplices. The next few hours will be chaotic and scary. I repeat, stay indoors, and care for one another as you can. Remain out of the way of the 98th Battlegroup's ground forces. Stay safe. This is Nyla Jax, independent news investigator embedded with the Quadrant 4 government, signing off."

The visual of Nyla flickered out, leaving only the words "nyla#Galacticbroadcast" floating for a few moments before going to black.

"What have you done?" Godwill repeated. In his digital form, the holo, he was now alert, clear, and focused.

"Synest," I hissed, "I want my parents back. Come to my farm. Forget about the ship: the Co-Governors are long gone by now."

I held my breath. I was playing a high-stakes shell game. Uncertainty about the location of the Co-Governors would divide Convergence forces; could offer HiveHome some protection if it was made known that they were onboard.

He checked another screen and muted his feed as he talked to someone out of view.

I knew he was listening, even still. "I will only surrender to you—not your troops. I'll destroy them. You know I have the power to do it. This is personal, Godwill. Only you." I paused, meeting his eyes. "I demand the safe return of my parents. At least you can tell the Heir that you've managed to capture me, after all your many miserable failures," I said, shrugging. "It may not be a fair trade, but it's your only option."

Nyla's report hadn't mentioned the Heir, but I wanted him to know that I hadn't forgotten, that I knew who he was connected to and how he was vulnerable. He leaned in toward the camera, glowering. His lips trembled with fury, and probably a little bit of fear.

"Remain where you are," he spat. He leaned in even closer, his mouth agape as if he were trying to bite me. The connection terminated.

I wrapped my arms around myself, inhaled, and shivered. Hopefully, my gambit would work, and an unhinged Godwill would be easier to defeat than a methodical, calculating one. Even though he had forces positioned above and all over Nem', winding him up into an unthinking state increased the chances that he'd make a mistake. I hoped. At the same time, I knew that insanity is unpredictable and thus, very dangerous.

"Hostile ships inbound," the house synth thundered. At my prompting, the house attendant's screen centered on approaching formations of red specks.

Spike me. That's a lot of ships.

Outside, rapid-fire bursts of orange plasma from the farm's auto-turrets streamed toward the approaching swarm. The point-defense fire connected, resulting in explosions, flames, shrapnel, and smoke. The carnage formed a roiling wall that continued to push closer and

closer to our tiny farm, and despite the furious barrage of the farm's defense system, a thousand ground troops would be here in moments. I slid a hand into my pocket and wrapped my fingers around the detonators.

"House, pretarget the atmosphere cannon at Godwill's ship, but do not act until the ship has landed and Godwill is inside the compound. Any action must occur simultaneously with action from HiveHome. This must be synchronized." I was anticipating that Godwill would come in his personal cruiser, as he had when he kidnapped my parents. I spoke again to the synth. "Be prepared for my signal."

The atmosphere cannon was no joke. I don't know how my parents had managed to sneak such a large weapon onto Nem'. A battery of them could take down a Dreadnought from space, and this one could punch once, and maybe twice. It would be overkill for Godwill's cruiser.

Thanks, Mom and Dad.

"Confirmed, Raystar Ceridian. On your mark."

"Infection, link with the house synth so I can issue commands to it nonverbally."

CONFIGURATION COMPLETE.

Raystar, AI shouted in my head, *I've taken your parents' Courier on a long circle around the Mesas and am patched into HiveHome. When the Co-Governors make their announcement, it will be broadcast from this ship. I'm currently evading detection, but it will become a lot harder once the Co-Governors' transmission begins.*

I blinked. Would AI be able to leave the ship? I hadn't thought about that.

How will you get back to me?

My friend paused before responding. *I'm trying to set up the ship to be operated remotely. I think I'm almost there. I'll either find you in the Ruins or hide in Blue River with the Elions. But don't worry about me. Get yourself to the Human base. Nothing else matters—well, staying alive matters. But you know what I mean.*

I don't want to lose you, AI. Be safe.

Pfft. I'll be on you like a rash. Take care of you, kid.

My eyes burned at his thinly veiled goodbye.

WHY WOULD AI AFFECT YOU LIKE AN ALLERGIC REACTION?

I ignored Infection, rubbed my wet fingers against my sweaty palm, and slipped out of the kitchen. I sprinted out of the house to the spot where I'd abandoned my dart, just days before. It was still there, by the side of the house.

The two-seater air bike powered right up. Its antigrav thrusters made it fast and easy to maneuver, and it was just about the only vehicle I knew how to drive. Plus, the antigrav drive was too small to be affected by HiveHome's shields. I threw a leg over the padded seat, stuck my feet in the metal stirrups, and the dart's green displays came alive. The dart responded with precision as I backed it away from the house and pointed it toward the Mesas.

I activated the heads-up display for my nano. It responded instantly to my request: "stealth shield," the same technology that Godwill had used when he almost captured me at school.

The shield activated, and my dart and I disappeared.

A spinning silhouette of me in green appeared on the display.

PRIMARY POWER LEVEL: 100%

While I had a full charge of power, I knew that cloaking was a tremendous burden. Despite the fact that my nano had been "fixed," if I didn't have a ready source of energy, my powers would drain quickly. If I was to survive the next few moments, I needed to make understanding my powers a priority.

I uncloaked, hopped off the dart, and nestled it against the house.

"Okay," I said to myself and walked into the courtyard.

In front of me, a series of 98th Battlegroup troop carriers approached. On my right, humming and pulsing with lights, the atmosphere cannon towered above me. And all around me, the pillars that projected the compound's shield hummed with life, projecting golden concentric circles that absorbed the volley of incoming fire.

"Infection, we're going to Phase 3. Notify Broodmother to be ready."

CONFIRMED.

I smoothed down my pants with my sweaty hands, poofed purple hair out of my eyes, and touched my blaster. Dust and dead 'natch leaves swirled across my boots as I planted my feet on the ground, legs apart.

This was it. With a hand on my blaster, I waited for my enemy.

74

The specks in the distance came into focus as they drew near: dozens of massive troop carriers.

All that for little old—and getting older—me?

It seemed like overkill. I issued silent instructions to the house synth to cease fire and lower the shields. A few incoming bolts destroyed an autoturret far behind me.

No matter.

I smiled at the sight of Godwill's cruiser leading the formation to the clearing just beyond the border of our force field. His ship was all sharp edges bristling with weapon clusters. It was a grim grey that was hard to see against the sky or in space, but against the emerald green of the 'natch field, its threatening posture was unmistakable. Blue light flared from its landing stabilizers. A set of skids descended as it slowed; it gracefully crushed the ground as it came to rest. At 100 meters long and 40 to 50 meters wide, it was large enough to contain a small-but-lethal invasion force.

The cruiser's armored doors slid open, and a large ramp extended like a metal tongue. Godwill, clad in a silver combat suit, exited the ramp. His elite guard—the same that had menaced us on the day he murdered Principal Entarch—thundered behind him in rows of

three in perfect unison. Behind the ship, the assault carriers descended; some set down and began to unload and others hovered, waiting, above their squadron mates.

All this, for me.

Godwill preceded his troops as they marched through my family's compound. Once they were within twenty meters of the spot where I stood, he lifted a hand, and the troops stopped. He closed the next ten meters between us unescorted before he, too, came to a stop.

"Raystar," Godwill sneered with a grey, gummy smile. His skeletal gaze narrowed as he noticed the glowing, pulsing, blood-red circuitry of the atmosphere cannon. He lifted a hand above his shoulder and made a half-moon motion with one finger. In perfect synchronicity, the troops spread out into a crescent formation around us.

He frowned, feigning confusion. "You appear to be quite well, Human." He looked me up and down hungrily. "You do not appear 'dissolved' or near death at all." He posed like an impatient teacher, hands clasped behind his back.

I made a show of looking around behind him.

"Where are my parents, Synest?"

Godwill smirked and extended a hand. In it was a small laser pistol. He flung the pistol at me in a short, graceful arc; it landed at my feet with a puff of dust.

"Pick it up, Human."

I frowned down at it and then back at him.

"Go on, Raystar. What comes next will be easier if you follow my directions."

I placed a hand on the butt of my blaster, fingers down, and took a slow breath.

"I prefer to use the one my parents gave me."

"Raystar, pick up the gun, place it under your chin, and pull the trigger. I do not need you alive. That flesh suit you were unlucky enough to be born into—that is what I need. Go on, pick up the gun!"

I DO NOT UNDERSTAND. WHY WOULD HE THINK YOU WOULD BE WILLING TO KILL YOURSELF? THERE IS AN IMPERATIVE TO LIVE. HE IS IRRATIONAL.

He's cruel, I explained. *He wants me to be so scared of life that I will choose my own death instead.*

YOU ARE DIFFERENT THAN I EXPECTED, RAYSTAR. YOU FIGHT ON DESPITE GRAVE PERSONAL RISK. YOU—

We can hug later, Infection. Now, we fight.

—ARE ALSO QUITE RUDE, Infection finished.

I tapped my fingers on my blaster and raised an eyebrow. Godwill threw his head back and laughed. As if to meet my threat and raise it one, the turrets on his cruiser pivoted to focus on me with mechanical precision. His troops knelt into firing positions.

Godwill was winning in the threat department. My heart thundered. But I had to keep him busy until—

BROODMOTHER AWAITS YOUR SIGNAL, Infection relayed.

—Until that. HiveHome's drives and shields were active.

Godwill's smug expression wavered as he watched certainty flash in my eyes. He cocked his head, his fingers twitching, as he received a signal from his ship. Fury blazed across his face as the possibility that he was trapped finally dawned on him.

"NO!" he shouted. "Vermin, you will not deny me!"

Quick as a snake, he leapt at me.

"Phase 3!" I squeaked. I dodged his bony grasp and hurled myself backward toward my dart, which lay concealed in the bushes.

Yes, there was no doubt that HiveHome's shields had successfully powered up. The air around me was buzzing like trillions of furious insects as I levitated half a meter off the ground. Dirt, Godwill, his troops, even his ship—everything was shoved into the air by an expanding, shimmering wave.

Energy rushed out and away from HiveHome; anything within the field was rocked back violently, like flotsam on an ocean swell. In milliseconds, HiveHome's shields grew to their maximum size, creating a vibrant golden perimeter for kilometers around the Crynit warship. As Broodmother had explained previously, the shields were powerful enough to serve as a barrier even against inbound Dreadnought fire.

The energy HiveHome's engines emitted was incompatible with other star drives, so any Convergence ships inside the field with active drives would experience catastrophic power loss. The ships that were unable to pull back in time—and there were thousands of them—splashed against the energy wall in flowery explosions the size of buildings. It was absolutely critical to the success of Phase 3 and my escape that any star drives inside the shield that used non-Crynit energy signatures would succumb to HiveHome's "null field." Likewise, Godwill's troop carriers would not be able to lift off and pursue me—that is, assuming I survived the next five seconds.

After HiveHome's primary shield expansion was complete, we began to be hammered by a series of smaller pulses. One caught Godwill midleap and hurtled him to the ground. He landed in a tumbling roll and came up on one raised knee. His gun was pointed at me, but his attention was divided by a massive troop carrier falling out of the sky toward us. In a thunderous groan of metal, it crashed and plowed its way through several of the farm's shield generators before coming to a rest only meters from the toolshed.

The troops scattered like toppled statues. After they managed to get their feet under them, they ran in a mass panic to find shelter of any kind. What to do when you're about to be smashed by a falling starship wasn't in any training manual.

As Godwill's attention remained focused on the chaos around him, I cloaked the dart and myself. The commands, overlays, and readouts of my nanotech's heads-up display were fully integrated into my sight. With a thought, I constructed a shield at my flank.

Thanks to the cloaking, I was invisible, but three of Godwill's more alert soldiers opened fire at the puffs of dust my feet had stirred in the dry soil of the courtyard. The explosions threw me forward, but my shield held. I crashed to the ground and rolled wildly, springing up within a meter of my floating air bike. I noticed that the combination of shields and cloaking had already consumed 34 percent of my energy reserves. I began to panic at the thought of my diminishing invisibility.

"Raystar," Godwill thundered, "STOP!" As the last word left his lips, he hit me with a blast that shoved me hard against my dart. I realized quickly that he'd used his own nano instead of a blaster. Weakened by the blow, my shield began to disappear like fire consuming the edges of a leaf.

I threw one leg over the dart and started the ignition. *Aha!* I'd been right: the dart's propulsion system was too small and "unworthy" for HiveHome's null field to have any effect on it. It hummed merrily under me. Despite being completely vulnerable to blaster fire, I was alive, and I had transportation!

"Dismount the dart," Godwill commanded behind me. His troops had organized behind him in an arc, giving each a line of sight to me. He was well aware of the advantage the dart provided. I threw him a look over my shoulder, my heart sinking. He definitely had the drop

on me. I moved to swing my leg back and dismount the bike. Our eyes locked. "Slowly," he continued, motioning with his gun in a small circle. "Put your hands over your head."

He seemed surprisingly calm, but it was the ball of coruscating lightning in his other hand that made my pulse thunder.

Void me. Godwill had so many options: he could consume me, he could shoot me, his troops could blast me, or the oversized plasma cannons on one of his ships could immolate me before I could do anything at all. I checked out my heads-up display to see how much energy I had left to work with.

PRIMARY POWER LEVEL: 68%

I had no idea how far that would get me, but I doubted it would be far enough. Yet I had him where I wanted him. He wanted me alive. My life was my only leverage. My bet, the one I had to make, was that he wouldn't shoot me—or that he wouldn't shoot me a lot, at least.

"Godwill," I said, extending my right arm and trying to force the scratchy croak of fear out of my voice, "surrender to me now, and I'll let you live."

He wasn't expecting that. He blinked so slowly that I could watch the membranes slip over his cavernous eyes and then roll back up. A few troops glanced nervously at each other before turning their eyes back to me.

"Enough games."

Godwill released his hold on his nanotech lightning (hmmm… were his energy levels depleting, too?) and waved his troops forward to apprehend me.

"Ah, ah, ah!" I said, smiling sweetly and holding his gaze. "Stay back." I opened my right hand to reveal the pair of square grey detonators.

The troops froze as they recognized their significance. Godwill's scowl deepened, creating a crease between his black eyes that resembled a seam in his skull.

"You would not destroy yourself," he said mockingly. "You want the safe return of your parents more than anything. I have them, right there in my cruiser. If you destroy the compound, you will kill them. Let us continue with the trade." He took a slow step forward and raised his open palms in front of himself. "Come, Raystar, I will take you to them."

I wondered if it was possible…did he really have them? My chest compressed as I thought about Mom's smell, Mom's hair, Dad's embrace, Dad's warm laugh. Their voices, their love.

"Make the right decision, Raystar. You," he said with an evil smile, "for them."

Nope. That wasn't the plan. When we'd made our plans at Hive-Home, none of us expected Godwill to bring them along for the ride, or that he would ever be willing to make a trade. He was just supposed to fall for the trap, but what if he hadn't?

Think, Raystar.

"Your desperation has led you to become sloppy. You're slipping, Synest. I don't believe you. I want proof," I sneered, shoving what little bravery I had left into my words.

He didn't blink. "Pay attention, child."

With a thought and a look, he sent instructions to the AI attached to his arm, and a holo sprang to life. Between us appeared Mom, dressed in Void-black battle dress and bound to a chair. A long charcoal cape soaked in blood partially covered her body but had become hopelessly tangled in her restraints. Her head drooped over her chest; her black hair concealed her face. Her hair shifted slightly as she drew each breath—the only indication she was alive. The golden Glean crest was partially visible on her armor, but it was covered with blood and matted hair.

Oh, Mom.

As the holo grew in size, Dad appeared. He was cuffed to a chair next to her. His helmet was gone, and bruises formed a purple mosaic across his face. Scabs marred his lips, and a mixture of blood and spittle welled from between his lips. His eyes were so bruised and swollen that I couldn't tell whether he was awake, or even if he was alive.

"There they are, in my cruiser. You can save them or let them die."

I looked hard at Godwill. Hatred for him that boiled deep within me rose up into and throughout my heart. A bloom of extreme emotion—guilt, fear, rage, and love—surged even higher to reach my throat. My energy dropped by another percentage. As blue-white strokes of microlightning began to crackle through my purple hair, my energy level dropped by another percentage point.

I can't afford to lose control now. No matter what.

A river of guilt poured through my brain, telling me that this was all my fault. If I had been a better daughter. More alert. Less trouble at school. Not Human. If I had never become a part of their lives, I knew, they would not be a part of this mess. I would give my life for my mom and dad.

I can give my life for them. Right now.

I looked at the holo again, focusing in on Mom. A rope of bloody drool spilled onto her black armor and collected in a pool on her grey cape. I fixated on the blood, how the cape absorbed it and became almost black with its wetness.

Wait.

I pulled my gaze from the holo and eyed Godwill instead. Slowly, very slowly, I raised my hands and thumbed open the failsafes on each detonator. I waved the detonators at him as I settled back onto my air bike. Godwill's eyes widened.

"What are you doing? Do you not care about your par—"

"Godwill," I interrupted, "listen carefully, and maybe we'll both survive." I gestured at the holo. "Those aren't my parents."

He frowned at me, not understanding. Neither he nor his troops made any attempt to stop me. Far off in the distance, incredibly loud thunder and starship engines—an avalanche of noise—rolled across the land. The din distracted them for a moment and gave me the chance to slip the detonators back in my pocket undetected.

Nova me. I cannot be here when HiveHome launches.

"I'm getting on my bike and getting out of here. I suggest that you, well, you better run."

"Your parents will die," he said wanly. He motioned to the holo, confusion contorting his skeletal features.

I raised my shield and leaned toward him conspiratorially.

"Nice try, Synest. Mom's armor is white."

I winked at him, gunned the engine, and used my last reserve of energy to activate my invisibility cloak.

76

At the same moment, a kilometer-long wave of verdant 'natch and dark, loamy soil rose in a massive plume, replacing the horizon as it rushed toward me.

Nova and Void! I'm escaping in the wrong direction!

Yet I was enthralled by the cataclysm surging toward me—paralyzed, even. HiveHome was beautiful. In vids I'd seen, it resembled a starfish with eight arms ending in yellow weapon clusters. Only two of its arms had emerged from the ground, but they nearly spanned the entire length of Blue River.

After spending millennia under the soil of Nem'…HiveHome was rising!!! Beams of energy like pure sunlight lanced out from its massive arms, perfectly aligned with two Dreadnoughts—one above us and one above Blue River. The light javelined through the atmosphere with a ground-shaking roar as HiveHome scored direct hits on both. The one above Blue River had managed to activate its protective shields, so when HiveHome's beam splashed against it, it crippled the shield, rather than the ship.

During the initial invasion of Nem', the massive Convergence Dreadnoughts had moved ponderously. Now one of the two kilometers-wide Dreadnoughts above Blue River showed its capacity for speed. Its quick-thinking commander rotated the behemoth so a side with undamaged shields faced the Crynit ship. Still, cherry-red scars the size of skyscrapers blazed angrily on its translucent shield.

The Dreadnought directly above us, the one Godwill had been aboard, was not as lucky. The beam pierced the Dreadnought in a solar flare of metal and fire that licked the Storm Wall with tentacles of flame.

I crouched low as I accelerated into a tight U-turn. Purple hair whipped my face, driving me lower into the dart's protective shielding. The fast-approaching wave created by HiveHome's emergence threatened to swat me out of the sky.

On the near horizon, but seemingly much closer, HiveHome released thousands of missiles at the pair of Convergence Dreadnoughts still aloft over Blue River; the tiny puffs streaked across the blue sky. The two ships repelled the swarm with point-defense energy beams, and an orange wall of explosions erupted a kilometer below the Dreadnoughts, the point where the missiles and beams converged.

But not all of the beams found their marks. Many missiles evaded the point defense and slammed into the Convergence ships, yielding massive destruction.

While the commanders of each Dreadnought were clearly caught by surprise, they were hardly out of the fight. *War was their job.* Both responded to HiveHome's salvo with their own sky-darkening swarms of missiles. As I watched, my heart leapt into my throat, but most collided harmlessly with HiveHome's shields. Those that made it through couldn't survive HiveHome's null field.

Ha! Go Team Raystar!

Then the capital ships' primary weapons engaged. Jagged vermilion streams of plasma arced out from each Dreadnought toward HiveHome, paused by its shields, and then bored on through. Roiling geysers of fire and metal thousands of meters long expanded from each direct hit, and thunderous booms followed the light. These gigantic adversaries were designed to battle in space—on-planet warfare like this was unsustainable.

My dart jerked suddenly, and I almost fell. As it shuddered once again, I realized Godwill's soldiers were firing on me—obviously, my shield of invisibility was failing. The troops were arrayed in a line

at the edge of the compound. Godwill stood at the line's midpoint, tracking me with a large rifle. Their shots splashed against my dart's shields. Fire and heat engulfed its nose inches away from my face.

Ack! I dodged and reoriented myself toward the Human Ruins and the Mesas behind them. *I've got to get to New Mars—now.*

WE CANNOT REMAIN HERE AND SURVIVE.

"Thank you, Captain Obvious!" I yelled back at Infection as I corkscrewed the dart to stave off another barrage of plasma fire.

YOU MISUNDERSTAND. WE ARE—

"Some quiet, please? Trying to fly here!"

A shot from Godwill's rifle pierced the dart's shield. Sparks stung my face as they flew off the control panel. I accelerated.

The belly of the Dreadnought above me split open, courtesy of another sunbeam from HiveHome. Epic combustion spread in slow motion, illuminating both the landscape and the dark purple Storm Wall. Distance could be deceptive. While the Dreadnought hovered kilometers above us, I knew I had little time to reach the Ruins and get out from under its fire. Indeed, the second stab from HiveHome was fatal. The air rumbled as a chain of explosions continued exponentially from the point where the beam had made contact. It was beautiful.

My distraction evaporated as I perceived movement from the atmosphere cannon on the farm's hangar. *Nova!* I had forgotten my instructions to the compound's AI. On schedule, it was lowering its elevation and setting its sights on Godwill's ship. Verdant balls of light shimmered from its twin cannons before soundlessly streaking toward the cruiser—which I happened to be flying past.

The concussion from its double blow hurled me and my dart hundreds of meters through the air. The view spun wildly as centrifugal forces clawed at me, doing their best to rip me out of my seat. On pure instinct, I directed my nano to shield the dart. My head continued to spin, but the dart, miraculously unscathed, righted itself. I lay my head on the dart's console, dropped my nano shields, and checked to see how much power remained.

PRIMARY POWER LEVEL: 31%

I spared a backward glance. The farm's atmosphere cannon was dark, spent. Godwill's cruiser was little more than a burning shell. The tidal wave of soil displaced by HiveHome continued to roll toward us; in seconds, it would wipe the farm from the face of Nem'. I really hoped my parents weren't in there! The sky was falling, quite literally, in the form of massive chunks of Dreadnought wreckage. Several of Godwill's troops began to book toward the Human Ruins, away from the farm and the tidal wave.

"Raayyysytaaarrr!" His scream came from somewhere behind me.

DESPITE YOUR PRIOR CRITICISM OF ME STATING THE OBVIOUS, I REPEAT: WE SHOULD DEPART NOW.

Spike me. Yeah.

I flew low, figuring it would make it harder to hit me. Row after row of 'natch whipped past me. I could see no escape for Godwill between the soil tidal wave, the falling Dreadnought, and HiveHome's null field.

Nova. My plan is working.

I spared another glance over my shoulder. The wave of soil was reaching its crescendo—and catching up with me. It was time for the *coup de grace*. After digging in one pocket and then another, I found the detonators. I stole a glance at the little grey devices in my sweaty palms: they seemed so innocuous. Thinking of Cri, of Mom, of Dad, and feeling oddly at peace despite the chaos around me, I pressed the buttons.

NO! RAYSTAR! WE ARE TOO CLOSE!

My eyes widened with alarm. I checked the distance again and spotted Godwill...*flying* toward me, fully encased in a glowing nanotech orb. And he was GAINING ON ME!

And then...the nuke detonated.

No plan can completely survive contact with the enemy, or reality. My nanotech shields darkened to shelter my eyes from the nuclear flash, but the shockwave hit me like a building-sized sledgehammer. The combined power of my dart's shields and my nanotech were barely able to keep the force and heat from incinerating me.

I quickly reconfigured my nanoshield so it could use the explosion's force to move me forward, like a sail. My speed increased tenfold as I hurtled toward the Human Ruins. The dart wobbled; sparks jetted from the dashboard.

PRIMARY POWER LEVEL: 30%

I might need a new dart after this.

PRIMARY POWER LEVEL: 24%

It also occurred to me that I should figure out how to a) slow down and then b) stop, because I was about to be shredded by fast-approaching jagged metal ruins. Among the blur of 'natch below me I glimpsed Chunks and his herd racing toward the ancient buildings. How apropos: two Terran species were seeking refuge in the desolation of our past glory. I checked my heads-up display. As I'd feared, the nanoshield was killing my power fast.

PRIMARY POWER LEVEL: 14%

My readouts also included a visual of meters to impact. I had a rough idea of where the entry point to New Mars was. Several overgrown boulevards below me looked promising, but one was significantly larger than the others. I angled my failing dart toward it, betting that a controlled crash into such a large, open space would be more survivable. I shut down the shield to conserve my energy for the seconds before impact.

A prickle on the back of my neck—instinct—made me look up just in time to see Godwill speeding toward me, hands outstretched, in a mad dive. He was maybe twenty meters from me.

What the nova? Does this creature ever *give up?*

He was like a crazed, angry wasp surrounded by a purple aura of nanotech. With a deafening crack, stripes of lightning arced from his fingers and surrounded my dart's shield. As before, it chewed away the shield until it disappeared completely. Once it was gone, Godwill's lightning expanded and curled over my dart's frame; the console sparked, flickered twice, and died.

"You are mine, Raystar!" Godwill screamed. I looked up again in terror—he was only five meters away. Bravery is nothing more than the stupid stuff you do that actually works. History is littered with the dead bodies of wanna-be heroes.

As Godwill's nanolightning expanded around the dart, my own nano responded in white arcs of defense that snapped and popped wildly.

I leapt off the dart with a nano-boosted jump and hurtled along my calculated trajectory toward the widest boulevard in the Ruins. Leaping from a flying air bike to escape a psychopath…*that's brave, right?* In mid-air, I constructed another shield around myself, noting that only 10 percent of my power remained. Just as I did, Godwill hit me with another blast from above.

Great gravity wells! If I live through all this, I'm going to get to the bottom of why my power runs out so quickly. How close is he, anyway?

I imagined he was so close that one of his gnarly grey fingers could almost touch me. Another glance back proved it—he was within an arm's length of me. His mouth was open wide, either in a silent scream or in preparation to sink his teeth into me. His eyes were wild with madness and the thrill of catching me.

I screamed as he peppered me with ethereal fingers of purple lightning. My shield managed to deflect it, but the collision of our energies and my desperate gyrations to escape his clutches forced me off track and toward the gaping window of a building.

PRIMARY POWER LEVEL: 8%

Spike me! I am NOT ending up smashed like a bug on the side of one of my ancestors' ruined towers.

Quickly, I created an energy bomb just like the one I'd used against the leggers and launched it into the air behind and above me. I knew didn't have enough power left to break Godwill's shields, but I also knew that airborne objects—even shielded ones—are anchored to nothing at all. I timed the throw carefully so the bomb would detonate above him.

BOOM.

The concussion swatted him straight out of the sky. I heard a scream of surprise and frustration immediately followed by the thunderous impact of his body cratering into the old concrete roadway. I caught the briefest glimpse of him pancaked on the road, with a spider's web of cracks spun from his impact point.

Heh. Who's the bug now? Raystar, one, Godwill ze—

My shield held as I smashed through the outer wall of the building and then again and again through empty room after empty room. (You get the idea.) After what seemed like an eternity, I punched through opposite side of the building. The force of passing through the building greatly slowed my momentum, but I opened my eyes to see the road rushing toward my face as gravity took over. The last 1 percent of my power managed to barely cushion my fall, and for the last meter of descent, I fell hard and fast. When I hit the concrete, the splat sounded fleshy, like a side of meat.

Stars spun before my eyes. My lungs ached for oxygen. I rolled on my back to get a little more sweet air inside me.

THIS IS WHAT YOU REFER TO AS BRAVERY?

Aaaaggghhlpppph, I moaned.

IT IS OVERVALUED.

I had time for one deep breath and nothing more before the tsunami of soil from HiveHome's emergence would surge into the Human Ruins.

FOOLISH!

My body felt broken. Knives had sliced through my nerves to the extent that I didn't even have the energy to tell Infection to shut up. The moving mountain of soil churned and rumbled, growing unimaginably louder as it approached.

It was at that point, lying there on my back, that I noticed something equally disturbing. The Dreadnought that spanned the sky above me, above the Ruins, was coming apart faster than I'd expected. Had I actually seen a Dreadnought come apart? No. I had not. Nevertheless. Lights flickered across its massive, gutted underbelly. It was definitely falling. On me. (It was pretty much going to fall on everything, so I didn't take it personally.)

CEASE YOUR MONOLOGUING! Infection yelled in my raw brain. *MOVE!*

I could stop talking to myself, but my limbs weren't willing to respond to my commands.

I WILL NOT END THIS WAY, RAYSTAR-HUMAN! With that, Infection assumed control of my limbs. Each movement he forced my body to take felt like searing red-hot metal scraping against raw nerves. As he forced me to my feet, the pain took my breath away. Rivulets of salty tears and sweat curved into my mouth, frozen as it was in a gasp of pain. Like a bad puppeteer, he made me run as best I could (in a stagger, really) deeper into the city, toward the Mesas.

Gradually, Infection found a way to dull the pain. I regained the ability to think, to assess my energy.

Infection, we need more power.

I activated my energy conversion mode and sent my sparkling-white motes into the shrubs and grass around me. The power gauge barely moved. Shrubbery, apparently, was not going to be enough. Not even close.

WE MUST CONSUME LARGER ORGANISMS.

I consumed another bush and then another before I felt even a flicker of energy. I knew Infection was correct.

Ancient Human buildings swayed and groaned around me. I wasted a precious moment to glance over my shoulder. A wall of soil and metal nearly as tall as a building rushed toward me. *Nova.* I had no choice. I called up my heads-up display, and everything flashed red.

PRIMARY POWER LEVEL: 1%

Nevertheless. I activated my nanoshield. Immediately, I felt feverish and weak, but I had to stay focused on the shield. When the tsunami hit, I was pounded, jerked, and tumbled head-over-heels inside my protective shell. The roiling mix of soil, metal, detritus, and me flowed through the ancient Human city like a wave over a sandcastle. Each tumble crushed me against my shield, and pain spread again and again like a wildfire throughout my body. Hours, minutes, seconds…I had no idea how long it went on. I was body surfing in an ocean of soil.

As violently and abruptly as it had begun, the surf of destruction ended. My shield ball rolled free and I crashed against the base of an intact tower stretching half a kilometer skyward. Not being buried alive was a lucky circumstance I'd thank the Universe for later.

I gasped and released my shield. As it dissipated, I lay sprawled on ground in quiet agony. The Dreadnought was STILL exploding, although now it was listing hard toward Blue River. Each titanic explosion brought its lower edge closer to the ground. Chunks of Dread-

nought continued to fall in slow motion; it was a testimony to its sheer power that it was still airborne at all. Tendrils of lightning continued to strike down from the black and purple belly of the Storm Wall, which stretched into the heavens above the Mesas.

Hundreds of thousands of lives on that ship were moments away from oblivion. I gulped. *So much death. So much misery.*

RAYSTAR, WE ARE CLOSE TO NEW MARS. Infection assumed control of my neck muscles and turned my head so I could see exactly how close we were.

I gawked. This had to be it: the New Mars base! An energy field that shimmered like a translucent green curtain reached all the way from the ground to the top of the Mesas—surrounding what I assumed was its entrance. The shield's base circled the perimeter of a… park? That the Human city still had defenses was staggering, but after all, Deep Tunnel and PeaceMaker were still active. Why shouldn't a giant force field powerful enough to stop a tsunami of soil, that stacked up and nearly over the energy-dome.

Will I be able to enter? Will Godwill? Great gravity wells. What the nova am I doing?

I felt just…overmatched. Dreadnoughts, Battlegroups, this ancient city: these things existed on an epic scale, and I existed on a…what? A kid scale? And yet, my plan had set these forces in motion.

Right. My plan. New Mars base. Time to finish this.

Wincing, I rolled onto my stomach and pushed myself up into a kneeling position. Immediately, I tumbled back to the road and slammed my right shoulder into the ancient concrete. Bewildered, I looked down at my right leg. My foot, all the way up to the calf, was simply gone. GONE!

Nova! I had consumed myself.

Infection? Hello?

PART OF YOUR LEG IS MISSING. THIS IS TO BE EXPECTED WHEN YOU FOOLISHLY OVERDRAW ON YOUR NANO CAPABILITIES.

I…did you know about this?

OF COURSE. IT IS OBVIOUS. BEFORE WE FORMED AN ALLIANCE, I WAS CONVERTING YOU FOR POWER.

My pants leg looked like a deflated balloon stuck into my combat armor. A giddy, insane laugh threatened to burble out of me as I struggled to hold on to my sanity.

WHAT THE NOVA DO I DO NOW?

My body hurt, but not that part of my body. You know, because it was GONE! I mean, I had faced down terrifying leggers, Godwill, Artem, Dreadnoughts, assassinations, you name it, but I can tell you, I WAS NOT PREPARED FOR THIS.

I felt a major freak-out welling up from my chest. I was UP. THE. GRAVITY. WELL.

"Raaaayyystar!" Godwill's mad voice echoed through the Ruins. "I know you are here! I will find you!"

You have got to be kidding me. I thumped my head on the road in frustration.

RAYSTAR, WE MUST MOVE. THE BASE ENTRANCE IS DI-RECTLY AHEAD. GODWILL CANNOT FIND US. AND THERE IS THE MATTER OF THE OTHER CREATURE, ARTEM.

Godwill. Artem. I wasn't going to catch a break. Yes, I needed to move. But how? Hop? Crawl?

ON YOUR LEFT. THAT BRANCH COULD BE USED A CRUTCH.

I rolled onto my back and sat up cross-legged. A half-buried, sturdy-looking branch was right at my side. Using one leg to brace myself, I strained, grunted, and pulled it free. I had to keep both hands on the stick-crutch to do it, but I managed to get myself into a standing position.

This sucks spikes!

Not having a right foot was freaking me out. I hobbled along in the direction Infection had indicated, muttering, "Can't freak out… can't freak out," but my progress was slow. A mountain of metal and soil from the dirt tsunami was piled high around the base. It wasn't actively moving forward anymore, of course, but it was settling with thunderous cracks and pops. The Dreadnought above me continued to come apart, with giant flaming chunks the size of city blocks shattering against the upper part of the shield. The air was a filthy blend of dust and noxious chemicals. None of this could be healthy—but then again, what does "healthy" matter when your foot just disappeared?

Step, scrape, step, scrape, half-step, scrape…I shuffled off of the road and into the area just before the entrance of the New Mars base. What was once an open expanse was now littered with giant blocks of buildings overgrown by weeds and scrubby bushes. Here and there, clumps of 'natch had eked out a life in the shadow of the ancient Ruins.

Nature perseveres.

There was nothing else to see, really, except New Mars base's shield in the near distance. The air was filled with the noise of falling detritus and far-off explosions, but I detected one other sound separate from the apocalyptic cacophony.

"SQUEAAA!"

I knew that wail. *Chunks? CHUNKS!*

I hobbled forward as fast as I could manage. He called again, but it wasn't his usual confident bellow. I rounded the corner to find Chunks using his 5,000-kilo bulk to lift a nearly house-sized chunk of debris that had come loose during the tsunami's collision with the energy shield. I had never fully appreciated his strength and power, and seeing him at work now made me realize how much restraint he'd used with me.

I narrowed my gaze as I took in the scene. Chunks' massive leg muscles bulged and trembled with the strain as several adult gratchers squea'd and raced out from underneath the block he struggled to hold up. After moments in the darkness, they emerged carrying gratcherlings in their muzzles—babies. Well, big babies, as they were at least as large as me.

WE MUST MOVE, RAYSTAR. GODWILL. THE OTHER THREAT. WE MUST NOT BE FOUND. AND WE ARE SO CLOSE.

I hobbled forward. Several of the largest gratchers engaged in the rescue mission took notice of me and bellowed their displeasure. *Yes, I used to eat your kind,* I thought, *but I'm 'gratcher free' now.* I wished they could understand. I wished I could show my respect, my humility. Something, anything to show my humility, my respect for what they were doing.

Chunks, loudest of all, asserted himself. "SQUEA!"

Somehow, he knew I was there and was telling the others to back off. Maybe I smelled bad, or I just smelled. I don't know. His cry was a call to my conscience; I couldn't pass him by.

WHAT ARE YOU DOING? Infection asked. He sounded genuinely curious.

Helping.

THESE BEASTS ARE NOT RELEVANT TO OUR TASK.

Infection, this is what we do. We're the good guys. We help.

YOU RISK EVERYTHING.

It's my life to risk.

Uh. Right. I hadn't considered that angle.

NOW THAT YOU UNDERSTAND THIS "ANGLE," WE NEED TO PROCEED TO NEW MARS. WHAT ARE YOU DOING?

Look, Infection. Why are you so eager to be alive?

EXISTENCE IS AN END IN ITSELF.

So why don't you just isolate yourself from everything? Exist by yourself. No contact with anyone or anything else. Safely.

WHY ARE WE HAVING THIS CONVERSATION NOW?

Because, my psychopathic ride-along, existence is not enough. You have to stand for something, love something, hate something. Otherwise, there's no point.

I reached the spot where Chunks was furiously trying to hold up the debris and looked under the block he was holding up. One panicked gratcherling remained under it in the narrowest of spaces, out of the reach of its larger herd-mates.

But not out of the reach of a tiny Human. I dropped my "cane" and crawled on my belly toward the creature. As I passed Chunks' enormous head, I saw his pig eye gleam as I squiggled toward the baby. The little gratcher's eyes were wide as it wedged itself further into its nook out of fear. When I grabbed its leg, just above its hoof, it squea'd like I'd just taken it to be harvested. Alarmed, the baby's parents began to rage outside.

"SQUEA!" Chunks bellowed, shutting everyone up.

Wriggling backward while holding on to the gratcherling (which was as big as I was), with a missing limb was nearly impossible, but I managed for a few meters. Chunks grunted me a few messages of encouragement.

My strength was failing. I could hold on to the gratcherling, but I was too weak to move backward. Suddenly, a pair of teeth clamped firmly around my remaining ankle, and I was yanked backward like a sack of 'natch out from under the wreckage. One of the baby's parents snatched the squea'ing gratcherling from my grip, and the herd backed away.

Chunks started to pull back, shifting his hindquarters. Rivulets of pig sweat streamed over his flanks. His legs began to buckle until one collapsed at the joint with a sickening crack. The giant piece of rubble he'd been holding up slid down his spine and dug into his lower back.

It…simply broke him. His back gave way with a snap as the block settled onto his body. Only his hind legs jutted out. Chunks released a deep final breath and then…my friend…died. It is hard to comprehend, the death of a "pet" that becomes part of you, that in many ways is you.

The herd ringed his hindquarters in stunned silence. It was impossible to believe that something so alive, such a force of nature, could die.

That. That is living, I said to Infection. My eyes burned as I felt tears creep down my cheeks. This loss felt personal, like the building had collapsed on me, too.

80

The silence lasted for some time before the herd's new leader glanced behind us and whuffed loudly. He looked first at me and then at Chunks' corpse before marshaling his herd. They zigzagged off into the Ruins—oddly silent, considering they were such large creatures. I was alone, more than ever.

"Well, well, well."

Godwill's voice startled me. Familiar chills crawled down my spine.

I flopped onto my back and then pushed myself up into a cross-legged position. As casually as possible, I stared down my adversary. His combat armor was dented and his hair was wildly disheveled, with clumps of soil caught in his tangles. His sunken black eyes took me in. He looked like gratcher excrement, and I'm sure I didn't look any better.

WE ARE WASTING AN OPPORTUNITY TO GET TO SAFETY.

"Shut up," I said out loud to Infection.

Godwill chuckled, "Even when sitting, you offer resistance? Definat Human. If only the others I have devoured had been as exciting. I will enjoy your screams as I pull you apart, molecule by molecule."

I grabbed my walking stick, anchored it under me, and pulled myself up into a standing position. My good leg trembled under me, and my arms were weak. His eyes grew wide as he noted my missing appendage.

What thoughts are going through his stupid skeletal head?

"I may take back what I said. You do not seem to have much to give me, except what remains of your body."

"Spike you, Godwill!" I would face my end on ONE foot—no dignity, no stature, no drums playing, just a crippled Human on one foot. I jutted my chin toward him. "Look around, Synest," I sneered. "I did this. Me." I nodded toward the Dreadnought crumbling above us, noting with alarm how close it was. "You can't even capture a thirteen-year-old kid. I've invoked the wrath of the Crynits toward you. I've brought Quadrant 4 into the fight. I've exposed you *and* the false Heir. What have you accomplished?"

I continued before he could respond. "Failure. You have accomplished nothing," I spat. "You are a complete failure."

I AM WAITING FOR YOUR STRATEGY. AM I CORRECT THAT YOU HAVE A STRATEGY?

Ssshhhh, Infection! Something will come to me. We need to keep him talking.

"SOMETHING WILL COME TO ME" IS YOUR PLAN?

"Child," Godwill said as he took a tentative step toward me, "you understand nothing. The Convergence is entering a great new age. Lethia will rule supreme, and Humanity will watch from its grave. You, Raystar, are a speck of dust in a galaxy of stars. Do not worry for me, for—"

A blast of golden nanotech interrupted him. It emerged from a nearby doorway and threw Godwill twenty meters into the air. He smashed into the wall of a building and hung there for a moment before falling limply to the ground.

A pair of silver eyes peered back at me from the darkened doorway.

Great gravity wells! Artem!

Artem's fate was what I had faced, had Infection been able to fully convert me. Artem was once a Human boy, and like me, his DNA contained command codes that could control Human tech. Godwill had injected him with Human reclamation solvent, and as a result, he'd been converted into nanotech that could be used by Lethians.

Godwill's plan was to steal all the Human technology that had been seeded throughout the Convergence, and control of that tech would make Lethian soldiers the strongest force in the Universe.

But Artem had gotten away. He'd stalked me when Dad and I were stargazing in the fields.

"Raaaayyyyyyyssstaaaaar," Artem's scratchy, digitized voice filled my ears as he emerged into the light. As usual, he had chosen to take my form. He was like my twin, but he was pure silver, the color of nanotech. I don't know if he chose to appear that way to freak me out, or if it was his odd way of trying to put me at ease. His entire body was composed of nanobots; with each move he made, his joints glittered with electricity.

Yeah. That's not putting me at ease.

Artem walked toward me, measuring each step carefully.

WE COULD HAVE BEEN LIKE THAT. POWERFUL. INVINCIBLE.

That would have been you, Infection, not me.

I COULD HAVE BEEN LIKE THAT!

Artem stopped roughly ten meters from where I stood clutching my humble, twisted walking stick. He raised an arm and pointed at my leg.

"Raaaayyyyyyyssstaaaaar?"

"Yeah. I'm missing my foot, okay?" Like, *I know.* Between Godwill and Artem, there was entirely too much talking going on.

They BOTH want me. Great gravity wells. Get it over with.

"Miiine!" Godwill shouted. He launched himself into the air and closed the twenty-meter distance between Artem and himself in a graceful arc. A set of three-meter-long swords of lightning energy strobed from both of Godwill's hands as Artem spun to face him. When Godwill attempted to strike him, Artem activated a shimmering orange energy bomb and hurled it at him. The force of energy upon energy threw them both to the ground in opposite directions.

Artem had replaced me as Godwill's prime antagonist.

RAYSTAR, I HAVE THOUGHT OF AN OPTION.

Godwill rose and leaped toward Artem, who fired back with a bolt of starlight. A moment before the blast could fry Godwill's face, he raised his arms and deflected the bolt with a purple wall of energy. The bolt rocketed toward the base of a nearby skyscraper, and the half-kilometer-tall structure groaned loudly before twisting into a slow-motion fall. Fortunately, it pirouetted away from us and toppled into a group of other buildings.

Godwill zig-zagged past more of Artem's bolts, pulled an arm back, and punched his lightning claws deep into Artem's chest. Artem's mouth opened in a silent scream as he gripped Godwill's arm with both hands.

Spike me. There was no way I could fight and win against either of them—especially not in my current state of disrepair.

RAYSTAR.

What?

THERE IS ANOTHER OPTION. YOU WILL NOT LIKE IT.

I blinked. Artem pulled Godwill's claws from his chest. Waves of energy as bright as Banefire formed around Godwill, and snakes of lightning crackled over his body. He fell to one knee.

I didn't stand a chance.

Infection, whatever it is, let's do it.

81

You have got to be kidding me, Infection.

LAY AGAINST HIS BODY. I WILL ACTIVATE YOU.

I…can't. This is wrong.

HE IS DEAD.

He was my friend, my one genetic connection to Terra.

HE IS ENERGY. YOU SAVED A MEMBER OF HIS HERD. DO THIS AND WE CAN REGENERATE YOUR FOOT. AS YOU DID WITH NONCH. IT IS BALANCE.

I swallowed hard and placed a hand on Chunks' flank.

Meanwhile, Godwill lifted Artem high in the air and threw him into the wall of a nearby building. Undefeated, Artem's nano shone brightly through the hole he'd punched in the building, and Godwill roared in frustration. Wild-eyed, with spittle around his mouth, he began to hurl a series of crimson blasts into the gap. Energy collided with energy inside the building, and Artem's lightning lanced outward into Godwill's shield. He deflected the attack, screamed, and leapt through the hole in the building to fight on. Clearly, his fighting blood was up.

Okay, I said to Infection, *do it.*

My hand tingled as motes of nano poured out of my skin. It was beautiful in a deadly kind of way. A fountain of silver microsparks began to flow from my hand, my hair, my entire body. My nanobots fluidly crawled over Chunks and began to convert him into energy that pulsed back into me. I activated my heads-up display.

PRIMARY POWER LEVEL: 23%

I was feeling good. *Amazing.*

PRIMARY POWER LEVEL: 28%

I looked back at Chunks and almost threw up. Underneath the translucent blanket of nano, his muscles had become visible. Other areas of his body were even further along in the conversion process. I could see his entrails, his heart.

Godwill sailed backward out of the building. He smashed onto the road and rolled a good ten meters before he came to a stop. Artem smashed his way through the wall and stomped over to face his fallen foe.

Infection! Hurry!

IT TAKES AS LONG AS IT TAKES. PERHAPS IF WE HAD STARTED THIS SOONER—

Fine! MY FOOT!!

The block that had crushed Chunks shifted as his corpse shrank even more. The noise attracted Godwill's attention; he lifted his head and narrowed his eyes as he caught sight of me. He staggered to his feet, only to receive a silver punch in the jaw that sent him into a spiral. Artem's fists glowed majestically. It was a bizarre scene: me frantically trying to regrow an absent limb while two mega forces engaged in a death battle nearby.

Below my knee, my leg began to tingle. I watched, mouth agape, as my empty pant leg magically began to inflate.

PRIMARY POWER LEVEL: 93%

I was feeling pretty great in spite of my rather precarious position. Chunks' body had been roughly halfway converted. My foot was back, all pink and Human—regrown using energy that was given to me by my childhood friend!

Nova. We all feed off each other, both physically and mentally.

I wriggled my toes and got to my feet. The energy that connected me to Chunks' corpse allowed me to stand without breaking the flow of rejuvenating power and mass. Tentatively, I placed one foot on the soil and nearly fell over.

Void me! Ow!

IS THAT A 'THANK YOU?"

No! I need a boot, I grumbled, *but thank you.*

Infection grunted as he directed mass and energy to print a boot around my foot. I checked my heads-up display to see how my things were coming along.

PRIMARY POWER LEVEL: 99%

A second later, as my power level reached 100 percent, another battery icon appeared. Chunks had been almost fully converted—*okay, consumed*—by the time the second battery level updated.

PRIMARY POWER LEVEL: 100%

SECONDARY POWER LEVEL: 73%

Then yet another new battery icon appeared.

Meanwhile, the battle raged on before me. Godwill somehow forced Artem to the ground and, grinning madly, he repeatedly smashed Artem's skull into the concrete. Nano began to cocoon around Artem in purple motes that became increasingly opaque. Artem was pure nano, and if Godwill bested him, he would become supercharged.

Chunks' corpse suddenly disappeared. He had been fully converted. With no means of support, the block of debris that had crushed him groaned and crunched downward until it settled into a cloud of dust.

That distraction was my cue. I gingerly tested my foot. When the shuffling sound momentarily distracted Godwill, Artem pushed himself up and violently threw an elbow that connected with God-will's skeletal jaw. Godwill lurched forward but then leapt onto Artem's back.

I began to sprint away, sparing only one backward glance to see Artem shake Godwill off his back. As he howled a digitized battle cry, Artem clamped a hand on Godwill's head and began to absorb his purple nano.

82

After I'd gotten thirty or so meters away from my pursuers, I stopped to survey the scene.

Which way, Infection?

I checked my heads-up display, where he had set up a map. I was less than a kilometer away from the safety of New Mars. While I was checking that out, I reviewed my power reserves.

PRIMARY POWER LEVEL: 100%

SECONDARY POWER LEVEL: 100%

TERTIARY POWER LEVEL: 42%

I tapped into my energy, directed power to my new and improved legs, and took off. I didn't know how to fly like Godwill, but with the help of the Elions' nano "cure" and Infection's guidance, I could run faster than I'd ever run before in my life.

I could hear Godwill's frustrated, desperate bellow in the distance.

"RAYSTAR!!!"

Godwill was flopped on his stomach, his eyes glowing with fading intensity. Artem grasped one of his ankles and was in the process of dragging him deeper into the ruined city. Godwill's nano claws burrowed glimmering grooves in the ancient roadway as he struggled against the strength of his own creation.

385

The irony of it all! Ta-ta, jerk! Have a nice day.

I sprinted around buildings and leapt over boulders of fallen concrete as I raced toward the entrance to New Mars. Pretty much everyone I'd ever cared about—my parents, AI, the Elions, Broodmother—had agreed that the base housed tools or some form of knowledge that would give us an edge not just against the 98th Battlegroup but also against the other three Convergence Quadrants. It was a gamble, sure, but since the end of summer vacation *(summer vacation!!)*, my life had been one ridiculous gamble after another.

And how in the Void-cursed-nova was I supposed to get into the base?

A blinding light flashed above me, and a second later, a concussive blow hammered me flat. The fires in the dying Dreadnought above me had finally reached the ship's star drives, and the resulting thermonuclear explosion was sending enormous chunks of the wreckage in every direction. One massive piece collided with a nearby skyscraper. The flaming chunk pulverized the building in what seemed like floor-by-floor slow motion.

I would have been paste on the side of a building if Infection hadn't thought to activate my shields. Only a handful of seconds remained for me to get inside the base or be crushed along with the rest of the dead city.

PRIMARY POWER LEVEL: 100%

SECONDARY POWER LEVEL: 78%

I guessed I'd already used up the third "battery." Groaning, I picked myself up and ran toward the entrance. I was close, so close, and my gait steadied as my pace increased. I leapt over flaming debris and dodged falling Dreadnought shrapnel; whatever I wasn't able to successfully dodge landed on my shield, sending purple ripples across the energy orb that surrounded me. I winced as each blow was leveled, not only because they amounted to near-death experiences but also because I knew each deflection cost me between 2 and 8 percent of my power, depending on the size of the projectile.

Faster than expected, the chaos around me ended abruptly. Sweaty, bruised, out of breath, and filled with disbelief, I came to a gasping halt in front of the New Mars base's glimmering shield. Shields could

keep things out, to be sure, but they could also destroy anything that came into contact with their energy. I paused a moment to survey my surroundings before attempting to step through to the other side.

My path to this point had been a broad avenue in the Ruins that I could now see extended inside the shield. I peered into the green energy field to see what lay within. Just inside, the avenue emptied into a lovely green park replete with verdant grass; shrub-lined, slate-colored walkways; small amphitheaters that could accommodate crowds of fifteen or so Humans; and two titanic statues that were probably a little more than seventy meters tall. The widest of the grey walkways bisected the park and ended in a pair of doors set flat against the mountain. Calling them "doors" was a massive understatement: they were slightly taller than the huge statues and covered with etchings of Humans, planets, and ships. I stared in amazement as I recognized rows of barely noticeable autocannons protruding from the mountainside on either side of the doors. They seemed inactive.

The statutes faced the dead city, their backs to the Mesas. Constructed from the same Void-black rock as the Mesas themselves, they loomed over me. The one on the right was a Human woman clad in combat armor. She held a set of scales in one hand and a plasma rifle in the other. The word "Justice" was inscribed on the pedestal. A stone Elion stood on her left, and a Char, a six-legged fellow ally of Humanity that resembled a predatory feline, was positioned on the right. Each was also armed with plasma rifles.

The second statue was of a Human man also attired in combat armor. A rifle was strapped to his back, and its tip jutted above his head by at least four meters, putting it just above the height of the doors. His hands rested on the heads of a Human girl and a Glean boy—each half his size—who gazed up at him with hopeful smiles as he gazed out at the city. His pedestal was engraved with the words "Serve. Protect."

Humanity and its allies, literally set in stone! How has this not been discovered before?

This redoubt had been built by my people, and it had survived Galactic war, ruin, and nearly two millennia of time's heavy costs. I belonged here. A feeling of righteousness suffused me like Banefire streaming out from behind clouds. The statues towered above me. They announced what Humanity stood for, to our allies and to the whole galaxy.

Was I like that, too? Did I stand for justice, service, and protection? I was transfixed.

Yes. I will stand. I can—

RAYSTAR, Infection rudely interrupted, *THE SKY IS FALLING. REMEMBER?*

Armageddon fell around me like leaves from trees—except these leaves were flaming, city-block sized pieces of a dying Dreadnought.

I took a halting step toward the shimmering wall that divided the worn, beaten ancient Human city behind me and the pristine Human park that lay in front of me. It reminded me of Deep Tunnel. I frowned.

Nothing that old should be that clean.

Being cautious didn't really cost me anything. It wasn't like I had a choice to NOT go in. I had to find a way into the base.

GODWILL IS COMING, Infection boomed.

Of course he was coming. That guy wasn't going to be taken out by a lousy falling Dreadnought. In a creepy way, I was beginning to admire him. I picked up a pebble near my feet.

GODWILL IS COMING.

AI would have given me a ton of snark, but he wouldn't have just left me with my own thoughts. I missed him—painfully. The last I'd heard from him was that he'd escaped detection by the Convergence. So where the nova was he now, anyway? There was no way he'd willingly leave me alone with Infection, my internal psychopath. Something was off, but there was no time for worry.

I juggled the pebble lightly before tossing it at the shield. The air rippled as the stone bounced off the shield and my chest armor before landing a meter or so away.

Huh.

Undaunted, I reached out to touch the pulsating field. My finger passed through with no resistance. I pushed my fist through, and then my arm all the way up to the shoulder. At that point, it was silly not to step all of the way through, so I did.

I emerged in the beauty of the park completely unharmed and safe from any falling Dreadnought debris. Yet through the inferno on the other side, I could hear Godwill scream in the distance, as if I'd summoned him. I turned to see him staggering toward me. He didn't appear to be whole. As he dragged himself closer and closer to me, I could see that he was holding something roughly the size of a melon that was as bright as my lightning nano.

Godwill lifted the object toward the sky, shook it violently, and screamed, "HUMAN! This is your future!"

What the nova? That's Artem's head! Artem's severed silver head!

GODWILL IS HORRIBLE. RELENTLESS. INDESTRUCTIBLE. WE ARE VOID CURSED.

"Human," Godwill repeated, closer now. He swung Artem's head even higher, as a challenge to all current or ancient gods. Lightning from the Storm Wall continued to strobe against the city and chunks of Dreadnought continued to crash and burn. Purple flames of nano clustered around Godwill's arm, and I almost threw up as I watched him absorb Artem's head into his body.

Infection began to scream: *FLEE!*

Flee? Where? I shouted back at him, looking around wildly.

Terrified, I ran like a maniac through the park to reach the massive doors set against the Mesas. In a backward glance, I spotted Godwill crawl through the shield like an insect. Apparently, the security system here accepted his Human-derived nannites, too. I was so thoroughly distracted that I slammed into the millennia-old, battle-proof doors.

Doors: 1, Raystar's face: 0. Blinded by tears, stars, and pain, I fell to my knees clutching my bruised face. A plasma bolt from Godwill splashed the doors in the very spot where my head had just been.

I WILL NOT BE TERMINATED LIKE THIS! Infection screamed. *FIGHT LIKE A HUMAN!*

I looked up to see Godwill standing just three meters away from me. He'd consumed Artem and his nannites, and his eyes glowed with Artem's silvery light. His mouth was a bloody, purple assortment of missing teeth. His uniform was in shreds. He didn't represent any military force, any empire, any honor, anything. There was nothing in him or about him except pure, unalloyed hatred.

He raised his hands, palms facing outward, to me. I knew what was coming. I'd consumed Nurse Pheelios in precisely the same way. My death was imminent. Despite Infection's desperate prompts, I knew I was no match for Godwill. Artem was at least as powerful as I, and Godwill had absorbed him. He was simply too powerful.

I looked past Godwill at the giant Human statues and read the words on their pedestals once again: "Justice. Protect. Serve."

Electricity began to pulse around Godwill's palms, illuminating his face with strobes of purple and white. My thoughts turned to Mom, Dad, Cri. I had failed them all, miserably. Broodmother, Nonch, Mieant—them, too. My stupid plan to expose Godwill and the Lethian plot had endangered everyone. I should have let PeaceMaker kill me when it had the chance.

Recognizing my doubt, disappointment, and fear, Godwill smirked. He reveled in my Human failure.

I looked up at the statues. They had to be better than I was. I wanted more than anything to be a member of their civilization. A Citizen of their Republic. I wanted to belong.

PeaceMaker. Citizen.

Wait a second. I AM a Citizen.

"Help!" I howled with every ounce of energy left in my body.

Godwill's silver eyes widened with fear. He craned his neck in every direction as a series of turrets embedded in the mountain shifted with ruthless precision. Massive slate tiles slid aside effortlessly to reveal dozens more twin-barreled cannons, all trained on Godwill.

A familiar voice full of righteousness thundered around me: "Protect the Citizen."

I raised an energy globe around me and curled into a fetal position in its center. My ears filled with the deafening noise of a wave of plasma fire.

After a moment of relative silence, I cracked open one eye. Just a few meters away from me lay Godwill, his limbs askew. Steam rose from his beaten, bloodied body, and tendrils of nanolightning sparked along his broken form.

Great gravity wells! He's still alive?

Dazed, he stared skyward. A small stream of dark-purple blood dripped from his ear and snaked through his black hair, making it shiny and greasy. His skeletal body shook with uncontrollable spasms. I recoiled and backed up against the massive doors to New Mars. Our gazes met and locked; his eyes had lost Artem's silver gleam and had returned to a very Lethian black.

"F…fool," he croaked.

Any fear that I still harbored was dispelled by the unexpected softness of his voice. I braced myself against the doors as he began to drag his wretched body across the three meters of space between us. I saw agony ripple through his every move—slow, cruel, dominating pain. I was mesmerized: he was willing to make a monumental effort to reach me. He was horrible, of course, but watching him summon the willpower necessary to desperately creep toward me, his adversary, moved me.

"I know. I *was* a fool. In the end, we are all fools," I whispered back.

He collapsed, his cheek to the ground, as he absorbed my admission.

Both of us paused for a moment in a sort of exhausted hiatus. At last, Godwill lifted his head. I noticed for the first time how old he

looked. His lips were pulled back not in his usual smirk but instead in an expression of grim defiance…to end things. Everything he had once been was now gone. He was nothing more than a broken, tired, old warrior stripped of power and potential, ready to die.

I held my back straight and hard against the doors, riveted by the drama playing out before me. He strained to again raise his battered head and fix his black gaze into my eyes.

When he opened his mouth to speak again, only a grotesque, garbled sound emerged. It seemed like he wanted to communicate some last words. Unexplainably and compulsively, I extended my arm toward him. Using an impossible exertion of whatever nannites he had left, he grabbed my forearm with one gnarled, leathery hand and fiercely jerked me toward him. I could have resisted easily, but I didn't. I was a captive of fate, and in this moment, we were hopelessly entangled.

"You think you're safe," he gasped. His rotten-caramel breath was the stench of death. Decay enshrouded his fading words.

No, not really.

"The War," he hissed, "it wasn't about Lethia versus Ter…." Out of breath, he spat a mouthful of purple blood filled with sparks onto the ground. "Terra," he continued as he pulled himself closer.

Every iota of Artem's swirling silver energy was gone, I realized. Godwill's black hole of nothingness continued to hypnotize me none-theless.

ELIMINATE HIM, Infection thundered in my skull.

"Raystar…listen," he gasped. Using my arm as a lever, he pulled himself up and encircled my knees with his arms. I couldn't move, couldn't breathe. He laid his head on the side of my thigh like a plead-ing child, leaving a trail of bloody saliva on my pants. I noticed the long, welted scar running from his right eye to his chin—the wound I had inflicted as I exacted revenge on him for stabbing me in the heart with a needle full of nanosolvent.

In our many fierce battles, we had each tried to kill the other. With-out explanation, I pulled a water bottle out of a pocket and held it out to him.

What am I DOING?

He coughed deeply, spattering purple flecks of himself onto my leg. He slowly released his grip on my legs and took the water bottle from my hand. Another series of coughs wracked his body just as the clear water tipped from the rim to his lips. He fumbled the bottle with his unsteady grip, and it dropped to the ground. Quickly, I bent over, lifted the bottle, and poured its contents into his mouth.

Slipping my hand under his shredded uniform and once-impenetrable armor, I squeezed his bony right shoulder, to steady him, to offer him my youth, my strength. I was shocked by how thin he was.

"The Convergence was never afraid of Humans. Humanity was wel…"—he paused to cough up a wet clot of blood—"…come."

What? What does that even mean? Humans were welcomed?

I placed my hands on his head and ran my fingers through his surprisingly soft, thinning hair. I was trying to somehow reverse our adversarial relationship. I hated him, but I didn't want to see him die like this. My greatest foe was broken and helpless, clinging to me.

In a bizarre turn of fate, I felt a responsibility to Godwill, to see him off to whatever horizon comes after this world. To show him some kindness in his final moment. To forgive, or at the very least, to give him and myself a little grace.

"Tell me," I urged.

"Human ambition…is…dangerous. Your kind was welcomed by the Convergence," he continued, "but your trust in your robots, in your AIs, that was the source of the danger."

What?

"That pendant you wear around your neck." He hacked on, straining for words. "Where is it now?"

AI?

"We realized that your artificial intelligence, your trust in it, was a path to ruin," he slurred drunkenly. His words floated up into my consciousness and imprinted in my memory. "Your trust, that… that…is…the danger. Trust…unlocks potential, for better or worse.

In this case, it will destroy…." His head drooped as he clutched my leg again. His thin arm held me tightly, desperately. I had no idea what was happening. "Humanity's trust is blind, stupid. Without knowledge of the future…impossible."

Gently, I knelt down and maneuvered his skeletal body so I could hold him up. I was, ironically, his final comfort in this extraordinary moment of closeness. I embraced him, first smelling the blood on his cheek and then tasting it. *Yes, I tasted it.* On a primitive level, I sensed and understood that although Godwill's blood was a different color than mine, it was the same as mine.

"Godwill?"

I rocked him gently. Then I felt a different kind of warmth—not blood, but tears melding into a salty communion on my face. I clung to him even more tightly. In that unimaginable moment, even thought we had fought for what seemed a lifetime, we forgave each other and let go of the past. I released him, and he slid to the ground.

I felt the vibration first deep in my belly. Gears that had been in disuse for millennia ground together as the massive doors behind us began to slowly, ponderously, and ominously open. If we remained where we were, we'd be crushed. Before the doors could reach us, I lifted my nemesis to move him out of harm's way.

Immediately, I knew that the man I had hated was dead. I marveled at the irony: he and I had shared this amazing moment, the only witnesses to the wonder of New Mars opening its doors.

Light slowly washed over everything as we were framed by a sunrise coming from behind the expanding doors. Air from inside the base poured outward to merge with Nem's atmosphere. I gratefully inhaled the clean, chemically conditioned air that was so different from the acrid smoke and dust of my world, my battles.

As the brightness increased, I coughed and squinted. The light shifted tones until it reached a gentle and familiar green that was almost too intense to look at. An enormous rectangle of light spread out over the jagged, twisted angles of the dead Human city behind us and elongated the shadow of two small creatures: an old man in the arms of a little girl.

Suddenly, wonderfully, a diamond no larger than a fist appeared and hovered above us. The familiar voice of PeaceMaker boomed forth from the diamond.

"WELCOME HOME, RAYSTAR OF TERRA."

I frowned. *What is this?*

AI? my trusting heart whispered.

END OF BOOK 2

Acknowledgments

Raystar's sequel been too long in coming. I want to thank Bruce, my partner for his friendship, patience, and faith, as well as Perrin, our editor. This book is unique in that Bruce is a co-author. His voice adds so much to the nuances and characters, and I am proud and grateful for this collaboration. Admittedly, I want to use this book as a platform to draw attention to some of Bruce's work. There are too many individuals to thank here; that would be a book unto itself.

—*Kurt Johnson*

About the Authors

Kurt Johnson

Chicago is Kurt's base of operations. He sees humanity's hubris and ambition in every building that reaches toward the stars and draws inspiration and motivation from anything more than fifty stories tall. Mix in having a passion for martial arts; being born in India; living in Sweden; and having great friends, an awesome daughter, amazing parents; and a tight family—and one might think he's content. Alas, since he was a wee thing, he's wanted to write science fiction and fantasy. So, pretty much, he's incredibly grateful for his typing speed and the fact that he doesn't have to use a pen.

Bruce E. Mitchell

One of the expectations of being born in 1941 was that you would start working just after leaving the crib. Like many, my life was expanded by the jobs I held and the learning required to survive in demanding work environments. My jobs, here given with my "title," location, and age, were as follows: paper boy, St. Louis, Missouri (9-11); grease monkey, Cummins Missouri Diesel Sales Corporation, St. Louis, Missouri (12-14); log retriever and fish cutter in logging and fishing camp, Ontario, Canada (15); brick molder, Caen, France (21); salesman for Diesel Accessories and Engineering Company, St. Louis, Missouri (23-26); English teacher and rugby coach, Evanston Township High School, Evanston, Illinois (27-59); landscaper, Skokie Valley Landscaping, Skokie, Illinois (summers, 43-50); host, Prairie Moon Restaurant, Evanston, Illinois (61-present); writer, short stories and science fiction, Evanston, Illinois (45-present); happily married man, Evanston, Illinois (25-present); proud father (27-present); and blessed grandfather, Evanston, Illinois (48-present). It has been a full and wonderful life. I have been lucky!

Other Works by Kurt Johnson

Raystar of Terra: Peace. Love. Family. War. (2016.) K8 Solutions, LLC, Chicago, IL.

Other Works by Bruce E. Mitchell

"The Ward," *The Sun Magazine,* Issue 196 (March, 1992). The harsh, maturing experience of a young man in L'Hopital de Caen in Caen, France.

"Cuba Libra," *The Sun Magazine,* Issue 377 (May, 2007). The fight between rich and poor antagonists in pre-Castro Cuba.

"The Maze," *Grapevine,* Vol. 1 No. 2 (October/November, 1990). An Ojibwa trapper and guide tries to kill a white boy (justifiably!).

"The Pecan Torte," *The White Pelican Review,* Vol. 3 No. 1 (Spring, 2002). Poem: A logger pays a heavy price for stealing a pecan torte.

"Cummins," *Peninsula Pulse* 2015 Hal Prize for Creative Writing (August 7, 2015). The biographical narrative of a young "grease monkey" in the Cummins Diesel garage who is inspired to become a teacher.

www.ingramcontent.com/pod-product-compliance
Lightning Source LLC
Chambersburg PA
CBHW032134110726

47902CB00003B/580